WILD HEART
of the
STORM

WILD HEART

of the

STORM

ERICA SEBREE

SQUIRRELED AWAY PUBLISHING
AUSTIN, TEXAS

First Edition: October 2022

Book Cover design by Seventhstar

ISBN 979-8-9866118-1-5 (paperback)
ISBN 979-8-9866118-0-8 (ebook)

Squirreled Away Publishing
Austin, Texas

To Deborah.

Thank you for believing I could actually do this.

Contents

TAMSLO MOUNTAINS
Altan
VALDIS ISLANDS
Periwen
CLAVLIN RIDGE
Briganport
WINSLOW
Debarrow
Tremaene
HEILYN DESERT
FOREST OF EOIN
SEA OF MUIRÍN
SOUTHERN PLAINS
BELFAY
ISLORAN
Rhoswen Harbor
Meallán
WESTERN FLATS
DONELLIS

Chapter One

FFION WOKE, BLINKING tears from her eyes. Her vision cleared, but the world beyond the small window in her loft was blurry with rain.

As the remnants of the dream faded, lingering at the edges of her mind, the rain let up. She tried to focus on the watery morning light as it seeped through the gray clouds, but it was no use. The memories returned.

Hot tears streamed down her flushed cheeks and the rain started anew, pelting the window with tiny, insistent drops.

It was the same dream that had recurred time and again since that fateful night—the night her parents had died.

...Captain Sullivan informing her that there'd been a terrible accident... Cadwyn attempting to comfort her...fearing that Tremaene was no longer safe, that Ffion must leave her home...

She closed her eyes, still hearing the captain's voice in her mind.

You'll be protected in Periwen.

Ffion glanced out the window as if she could see across the strange land, past the provincial villages and vast forests, all the way to the port towns lining the coast. A land that was said to be unreachable. Yet there she was.

There she'd *been*. For nine long years.

Safe. Protected from some unknown threat.

Trapped was more like.

She inhaled deeply, her despair giving way to anger.

Outside, the rain stopped. She watched as a few errant drops slid unhurriedly down the thick glass pane. Then, wiping the last of her tears, she crawled out of bed.

Rays of sun flickered through the maples. Their greenness was slipping beneath a wash of fiery hues more and more each day. Ffion adjusted her grip on the handles of her cart. It was a long trek to town, but she didn't mind the distance. She preferred it that way. After nearly three years of roaming the foreign continent, she'd happened upon the abandoned orchard of barren trees, drawn to the promise they offered. A new home. And most importantly, the small plot of land had been situated far enough from town that no villagers would happen past. A place where only the trees would know her secrets.

The dusty road was muddy from the rain. Ffion felt the hems of her skirts dragging through it. She groaned, knowing the dress wouldn't make it through another wear without a wash. At least she didn't need to spend her life wearing them.

A hare darted out from the woods, forcing Ffion to halt. Her breath caught when she spotted a hint of gray and white fur just beyond the tree line. She couldn't make out the whole of it, but her eyes widened as a tail flicked into view.

A wolf? She'd never seen one so close to town. She rose up on her toes, trying to follow its path through the thick underbrush. But it was gone. Disappointment settled heavily in her chest as she returned her attention to the road. What a sight it would have been—to see such a great beast up close.

As she neared the outskirts of Debarrow, she was greeted only by the sound of rainwater dripping from eaves. Windows were flung open, but the town hadn't truly begun to stir. Residents were still in their homes, stoking fires and tending to their morning chores. Hawthorn's had only just opened its doors, she knew, but the shop usually remained empty until midmorning.

At the town square, a wagon loaded down by towering crates sped past—the horse's leather boots squelching as they sunk into thick patches of mud. Ffion averted her face, though the driver paid her no mind.

Passing the bakery, the door pushed open and Ffion dropped her gaze again. But the woman with baskets smelling of freshly baked bread quickly strode past, intent on the tavern across the way.

Despite having lived in Debarrow for nearly six years, Ffion was only acquainted with one person—Carrick Hawthorn—and only because he'd agreed to sell her apples. Though she had more gold than she'd ever need, she rather enjoyed the long hours spent with her hands in the dirt, bees buzzing about her ears. And having goods to sell made it easier to blend in.

Carrick's doors were still closed, so Ffion settled her cart out front, letting herself in. Assuming Carrick was helping unload the delivery wagon she'd seen, Ffion made quick use of the empty store, gathering items with an efficiency that came from purchasing the same provisions every week.

She scanned the new spices hanging above the grain bins, but chose only a paper packet of dried cloves. The floorboards creaked, signaling Carrick's arrival. She turned to find the young shop owner watching her from behind the counter. His sleeves were rolled up to his elbows, his forearms resting against the polished wood. He tilted his head to the side inquiringly.

"Miss Ainsley, what a pleasure."

"Hello, Carrick." She nodded, setting her supplies on the counter.

Carrick straightened and began tallying the items. "I wasn't expecting you until the end of the week." He glanced up. The light in his eyes told her that he was delighted to see her sooner than he'd anticipated.

Ffion inclined her head toward her cart out front.

"Ah. And here I thought you'd come to see me."

"Carrick," she reprimanded gently, shaking her head.

"One can hope." He winked at her, then grabbed the canvas sacks and followed her out.

Ffion propped open the double doors as Carrick unloaded apples into shallow bins beneath the window.

"I love this time of year." Another smile slid into place—though truth be told, she rarely saw Carrick without one.

This time of year, she mused. Even after nine years on the continent, she was still adjusting to the cycles that brought about bitter cold temperatures, then warmer ones that miraculously summoned new life from the ground.

Without any intervention at all.

Seasons, they were merrily called, as if awaiting the return of warmth every year made the hardships of a frozen landscape more manageable. Though Ffion would admit that the anticipation of the first ripe apple made it taste all the better.

"I'm always amazed by your luck," Carrick remarked as he arranged the last of the apples. "From what I've heard, the other farmers and fruit growers moved north decades ago. That was the reason my great-uncle opened up shop here—he saw Debarrow's dwindling food production not as a reason to leave, but as an opportunity for the commerce he'd heard so much about along the coast." Carrick dusted off his hands, meeting her eyes with another smile.

"That was quite perceptive of him," Ffion agreed quickly, eager to be on her way. But Carrick had set her supplies behind him. Intentionally, she was sure. "Well...I must be going. It was nice to see you again."

"It certainly was," Carrick hummed, leaning a hip against the stand.

"Until next time, then." She made to move past him, to reach for her bags.

"And when will that be?" He ducked down to catch her eye. "Perhaps tomorrow night. What do you say—a pint at Mallory's?"

Ffion straightened. A grin threatened, but she pursed her lips together. Best not to give him any encouragement. "Asking me on a date, are you?" *Again.* As he did every visit. By that, one might think he wasn't the catch of the town—that every woman, young and old, thought him handsome and wickedly charming.

"I am." He tilted his head to the side, a lock of dark blond hair falling across his forehead.

Ffion offered a polite half smile. "No, thank you." It was the answer she always gave, though it seemed to do little in discouraging him.

"Hmm..." Something gleamed in his eyes. "I'll just have to try again next time, won't I?"

Oh, she knew he would. Ffion shook her head at him, though she couldn't help but smile. She wasn't sure why he bothered at all. For as long as she'd known him, her answer had always been the same. Ffion couldn't risk getting close to anyone. Their business relationship was as far as she was willing to go.

A man hollered from the back of the shop. "Seems the delivery man requires my attention." Carrick pushed away from the stand. "Will you wait a moment?"

He was gone before she could reply.

Ffion watched him through the window as he made his way out the back door, then quickly retrieved her bags. She needed to be going. The town was waking up.

A lone apple was hiding in the corner of her cart. She snatched it up and spun around to place it with the others.

Then stumbled to a stop.

Before her stood a man nearly a foot taller. Ffion stared up at him. *The town metalsmith,* her mind provided helpfully, even as every muscle in her body refused to function. But what was his name? Her eyes searched his imposing form, as if the words might somehow appear stitched onto his clothing.

As little as Ffion ventured into town, she'd seen the man around once or twice. He lived at the opposite end, so their paths rarely crossed. But on the few occasions when Ffion had seen the metalsmith from afar, she'd noticed how townspeople gave him a wide berth.

Standing so close to him, she understood why.

Slowly, she lifted her eyes to his.

Dark. Harsh. *Knowing.*

She blinked once. Twice. But couldn't seem to look away.

The man peered down at her, then canted his head a fraction of an inch, as if he found her amusing. Then his eyes narrowed—only slightly, but enough that Ffion suddenly felt exposed. Like he could see through her facade to everything hidden beneath.

"Miss Ainsley, it occurred to me that—" Carrick interrupted, coming to a stop just through the open doors. His hand rested on one of the handles as he looked between her and the metalsmith. He offered a nod to the other man, stepping closer to Ffion.

The metalsmith held her eyes a moment longer before breaking his intense gaze and slipping past Carrick into the shop.

Ffion stared after him. There was something about that man. Something...unsettling. It wasn't his size. Ffion would wager that the bulk beneath his shirt was solid muscle, but that didn't frighten her. In fact, his physique reminded her of Captain Sullivan.

She thwarted the memory his name summoned, grinding her back teeth with the effort. She couldn't bear to think of places or people she'd never see again.

No, it wasn't the man's formidable build. It was the way he'd looked at her. And that he hadn't spoken a word to her, not even a greeting.

Though she hadn't either, Ffion conceded.

It's nothing. She closed her eyes for a moment, trying to ignore her trepidation. There was little chance she'd run into him again anyway.

Carrick was saying something beside her.

"I'm sorry. What?"

He chuckled, grinning down at her. "I was just asking if you planned to attend the festival this year."

"The festival?" Ffion could hear the sounds of horses and carts, of people conversing, and knew she needed to leave.

"The harvest festival."

"Right. That's right. I...Well, I'm not sure yet. Perhaps," Ffion offered, only because she hoped it would bring an end to their conversation.

"Perhaps." Carrick nodded like he knew she had no intention of showing her face at such a rollicking event.

"Carrick, I really should..." Ffion glanced over her shoulder at the sound of two women nearing the shop.

"I almost forgot! Let me fetch your..." He held up a finger to stay her as he dashed back inside.

Ffion didn't wait. She hastily pivoted her cart, avoiding the approaching customers, then hurried away.

Chapter Two

BY THE TIME the morning light spilled through her kitchen window, Ffion was already arranging canisters of flour, sugar, and spices beside a mountain of apples. With the abundant harvest she'd had in the weeks past, she needed to catch up on pastries. Bruised or misshapen apples didn't sell, so she'd found a delicious use for them.

Setting a copper bowl in front of her, Ffion began peeling and slicing. Her father would've loved the apple pastries. He loved anything sweet. Though she wondered what he'd think of the strange fruit—honey sweet, yet crisp and tart.

Ffion's mind drifted to the last time she'd seen her parents—the morning she and Cadwyn had left on their trip to Donellis. It hadn't seemed odd at the time—her parents sending her away. But at only fifteen, it had been the first time she'd been apart from them.

If only she'd stayed.

Although...if she had, she might have been in the carriage with them.

Guilt clawed at her insides. She reached for another apple, cutting away the skin carefully with her knife, but the memories kept coming.

She wiped her hands, yanked off her apron, and went out back.

Ffion rolled up her sleeves, her muscles loosening with each step down the garden path. She knelt and began turning the soil beneath the overgrown raspberry bushes. The fuzzy stalks seemed to sway with her touch as she brushed them aside. Soon, she was lost in the feel of dirt beneath her fingers, humming contentedly.

Hours seemed to pass before the sound of gravel crunching snagged her attention. She lifted her head warily. When she saw Carrick approaching the gate, a mixture of irritation and alarm flooded her veins.

What is he doing here?

Ffion never had visitors, and for good reason. Visitors asked questions.

She clambered to her feet, noticing only then that she was more than a little covered in dirt. She brushed her palms against her pant legs. Her *rolled-up* pant legs. The heat of embarrassment rose along her throat as she recalled the rest of her unseemly appearance—her shirt had slipped over her left shoulder, hair pinned back carelessly, and no footwear. She curled her toes into the soft dirt, daring a peek at the back steps, where her shoes lay discarded.

Perhaps Carrick would take one look at her, then turn on his heel and flee back to the civility of town.

She could hope.

"Carrick," she managed.

"Ffion." He nodded, already donning a smile.

Ffion, she noted. Not *Miss Ainsley*.

"I'm sorry to stop by unannounced. I hope I'm not intruding."

"Of course not," she lied.

He said nothing for a moment, his eyes holding hers. Finally, it occurred to Ffion that he was waiting to be invited in. She looked down at the gate that separated them, then slowly pulled it open, forcing a smile as he stepped through.

Carrick took in the garden, turning in place. "You ran off so quickly yesterday, I didn't have a chance to pay you for the apples." He faced her again, offering a silver coin. Sunlight bounced off the smooth surface. She stared at it a moment, remembering the morning she'd spent hammering out Tremaene's crown from every piece of the gold Cadwyn had hidden in her cloak.

She reached out, then plucked it quickly from Carrick's hand, noticing how dirty her own were. *Although*, she considered, perhaps he'd leave sooner if she didn't hide the dark crescents under her nails.

"Thank you." She slipped the coin into her shirt pocket—their transaction completed. But Carrick didn't seem the least bit interested in leaving.

His unhurried gaze continued to survey every detail of her land.

"This is quite a world you've created here."

"Oh, I don't know about that." Ffion looked longingly down at her hand trowel, half buried in freshly turned soil.

Doesn't he have somewhere to be? A shop to run?

"Don't be so modest." He focused another of his brilliant smiles on her. "This land, this garden...it's completely remarkable. I understand now why I've never seen you in town for a midday meal. Have you always grown your own food?"

"Mostly." Ffion clasped her hands behind her back to hide her clenched fists. "I worked on the Dogherty Farm for a few months before I came to Debarrow. I learned a lot from them." She shrugged, uncomfortable with any topic relating to her past. Their encounters at Hawthorn's had never gone beyond the happenings around town or the weather. But the quicker she answered, the sooner he'd leave.

"Ah, yes. The Doghertys drop off a delivery every month. Lovely family." His smile widened. Ffion cocked her head to the side, wondering if he smiled even when there was no one to bestow it upon.

"Since I'm here," Carrick said as he took a step, closing the distance between them, "I thought I might persuade you to accompany me into town for a bite to eat."

"I'm afraid I already ate." Ffion pressed her hand to her stomach, praying to the gods it wouldn't grumble with hunger.

"Ah. Then tomorrow? We could ride out east, toward the lake just past Edriya. Have a picnic."

"I haven't a horse."

"That's no trouble, mine seats two."

Ffion opened her mouth to decline, but Carrick took another step—humor glinting in his eyes.

"Or better yet, let's hop on a coach and head to the coast. I hear there's a man there who juggles turnips."

A laugh escaped Ffion's lips. "Turnips? I was expecting you to say something dangerous...like daggers."

"Daggers?" He furrowed his brow. "Those have been juggled to death. Now, turnip juggling"—Ffion grinned and shook her head—"that's something to see."

"I'm sure it is," Ffion conceded. "And yet..."

"You're a difficult woman to entice. But I swear it, Ffion," he said, his voice caressing her name, "I'll think of something."

A crack of thunder shook the house. Ffion jolted upright in bed—drenched in cold sweat and gasping for breath, her hands gripping the sheets. Her nightdress was stuck to her chest and stomach.

Her breathing steadied as her awareness slowly found its way back to the darkened loft. *Only a dream,* she told herself as rain tapped the windowpane, slowing in time with her heartbeat until it eventually let up.

She'd dreamt of the morning she'd woken on a fishing boat in Rhoswen Harbor, along Periwen's southern shore. Only she hadn't realized where she was at the time. Hadn't even been sure how she'd ended up on a boat—her body aching and shivering beneath heavy layers of sodden clothes and Cadwyn's midnight blue cloak.

Ffion could still feel the swell of confusion in her mind when a stout man with a weathered face and a floppy-brimmed hat resting above gray eyebrows had clambered up from below deck and helped her ashore.

The man had found Ffion sprawled across a floating panel of wood. Her boat hadn't fared well in a storm, he'd said.

Not once had the memory of her passage across the sea surfaced in her mind. The only detail that mattered was that she'd arrived alone. Without Cadwyn. Her dear friend hadn't survived the journey.

Ffion had been unable to speak that morning, baffled not only by the man's unusual appearance, but by the look of the buildings edging the harbor. The structures had seemed so fragile, temporary—built not of stone, but with panels of wood washed in white, with sloping crimson roofs.

It wasn't until the man had found an innkeeper to take her in that Ffion had understood where she was. Alone in a back room, pulling on dry clothes the woman had scrounged up, Ffion had caught a glimpse of herself in a small mirror hanging beside the door. She'd gaped at her reflection for several minutes, lips parted, trying to make sense of the young woman staring back.

Realization had been slow to sink in, but as she'd pulled the snarled mess of her hair aside and trailed a finger across her cheek, then up over the rounded shell of her ear, she couldn't deny the truth of the situation.

She was in Periwen.

Alone.

Across the sea.

With no way of returning home.

The storm had been quite destructive. Ffion pulled her damp hair back as she stepped outside, plaiting it before it could dry into an unruly mess. She'd severed the long mass of tangles shortly after her traumatic arrival in Periwen, knowing she'd never be able to tame it on her own.

After spending the morning collecting fallen twigs and righting fragile plants in her garden, she turned her attention to the large branch hanging precariously close to her fence. She propped her tallest ladder against the massive trunk, then tied a rope around the end of the branch to angle it away from the fence. Saw in hand, she climbed the ladder, mindful of the aging rungs. When she reached the splintered juncture, she rested her hand on the trunk just above the break and began sawing through the connecting strips.

Her muscles burned after only a few minutes, though she made quick work sawing through the soft wood flesh. But she couldn't reach far enough to finish the cut.

Leaning over, she balanced on one foot. Peering down at her dangling leg, Ffion tightened her grip, realizing she was nearly fifteen feet off the ground. Although she'd spent much of her childhood climbing trees, there was usually a branch or toehold beneath her feet. She reached over carefully and resumed her sawing with smooth, measured strokes.

Ffion's breath shuddered, her muscles protesting. But the branch, heavy and swaying, held strong. Its final shreds seemed impossible to sever. Leaning farther, Ffion gained another inch of leverage. Dry wood groaned, then fractured.

"Shit." The word escaped her lips as the rung beneath her snapped.

The saw fell, her hands grasping at nothing. She twisted, trying to right herself before hitting the ground. All she managed to do was squeeze her eyes shut, dreading the impending impact.

She collided with something soft and leafy.

Ffion's eyes shot open. She was cradled safely in the arms of a massive branch. She hadn't crashed.

But relief was fleeting as her mind began reeling with myriad conjectures as the branch lowered her steadily to the ground.

Ffion rolled off and stumbled back, watching as the bough lifted and pulled back behind the wide trunk to resume its previously stoic height.

She gaped at the tree—its broken limb still hanging above her.

But the previously animated tree stood still.

"It can't be," she breathed. "Not here."

Magic didn't exist in Periwen.

Chapter Three

FFION STOOD STARING at the tree for what seemed like hours. It refused to move. Not even a lick of wind ruffled its leaves.

Another memory flashed in her mind—the day she'd fallen from one of the tall sycamores that circled the great lawn back home. Ffion had only been seven years or so, and thankfully her mother had been near. She could still feel the cushion of air her mother had summoned, pillowing beneath her as it lowered her gently to the grass.

Ffion angled her head, eying the branch that had reached out to catch her.

It can't be magic, she vowed with a shake of her head. It simply couldn't. She hadn't felt anything when she'd fallen. Hadn't directed the tree with any sort of innate power. Though she'd never felt magic working through her before—never would in Periwen—certainly one *felt* that sort of thing. The fog of glamour she'd crossed on the Sea of Muirín had prevented her magic from manifesting. At least, that's what she'd reasoned. Magic awakened in her kind by the age of twenty, at the latest. And Ffion was already into her twenty-fourth year.

She glanced down at her hands and rubbed them together, but all she felt was the familiar sensation of warmth.

"It just isn't possible." She told the tree firmly.

But what other explanation is there? The question slipped through her mind, unbidden. Ffion swallowed past the tightness in her throat, then finally turned her back to the tree.

She hastened through the garden, tripping up the steps to her back door. Slamming it shut behind her, she pressed her back against the solid wood, then slid to the floor.

Ffion's hands ached. She looked down at her white-knuckled grip on the corners of her basket, then set it down, flexing her hands. Her gaze wandered to the maples beside the lane. They stood tall, unmoving. A single rust-colored leaf floated down to the ground. But there wasn't a whisper of wind to carry it one way or another.

If only she could convince herself that the wind had swayed the branch into her path the day before.

Ffion retrieved her basket of pastries, settling it against her hip. Even wrapped in parchment, she could still smell the spiced apples baked between layers of golden crust. She breathed in deeply, letting the scent calm her frayed nerves as she strode toward town.

She stumbled mid-step as the throngs of villagers came into focus. Shifting the basket on her hip, she shielded her eyes and looked up at the noonday sun. Ffion only ventured into town during the early morning hours, when the town was still rising and the roads were quiet and empty.

I've pastries to deliver, she affirmed, then cast a final glance back down the curved road, toward her small cottage and the giant tree that had defied logic. But the trees were long out of sight. She forced her chin up, and tried to welcome the distraction ahead.

People flowed past one another, weaving around handcarts. Delivery women had sacks slung over their shoulders, men hefted barrels and crates. A young boy darted so close he kicked the toes of Ffion's boot. He didn't seem to notice. Ffion shook out her skirts, but her eyes were fixed on the sight of the small child. Six more followed. Running home for lunch, she guessed.

Ffion watched them a moment longer as people brushed by. It didn't matter how long she'd been on the continent, seeing so many children in one place remained a curious sight. It reminded her how short life could be, how quickly generations came and went in Periwen. It seemed to instill urgency, purpose.

"Mortality," she murmured.

Her mind snagged on the word. She tried to shove it aside, but the thought conjured another possibility she refused to consider.

Ffion tightened her hands on the basket as the weightless sensation of falling returned to her. Branches cradling her body. Catching her. Protecting her.

What would it mean if magic existed there, in Periwen?

No, she scolded herself, unwilling to dwell on the possibility. Magic didn't exist in that world. It simply...wasn't possible.

But the tree...

Ffion ducked into Hawthorn's, nearly knocking into a couple as they left. She mumbled an apology and wandered the aisles aimlessly. She wasn't in need of anything, but her mind was too scattered for her to speak with Carrick.

Vaguely, she heard his voice at the front, and that of an elderly man. The shop was otherwise empty. *Strange,* Ffion considered, trailing her fingers along the ribbons that dangled tauntingly from their spools.

"I was just about to close up," Carrick called over.

Ffion spun around. "Oh..." She gave another cursory glance around the shop. Indeed empty.

"Just for an hour or so," Carrick assured as she approached. "It's not like you to stop by in the middle of the day." He raised his eyebrows, though Ffion knew he could well surmise the reason for her visit given the basket of pastries she'd brought.

"I only wanted to drop these by." She carefully stacked the small parcels on the counter.

"I'm delighted to see you again..." Carrick began, but his voice faded into the background as Ffion focused on the task before her.

When she aligned the last pastry, Carrick lowered his head to catch her eye, saying her name in a way that indicated he'd called it more than once.

Her head snapped up and Carrick straightened. He seemed to be waiting for an answer. But to what?

"I...Yes. Of course," she replied with a nod that felt far too forced.

Carrick's smile spread until tiny creases formed at the corners of his eyes—bright with something that gave Ffion pause.

What had she agreed to?

"Wonderful," he proclaimed, rounding the counter. Ffion watched, bewildered, as he took the basket from her hands. "It'll be safe here." He winked.

"Safe?" she repeated.

"I'll lock up while we're out." He cocked his head to the side, looking at her like she was utterly adorable.

Dumbfounded was more like. *Out?* He'd said *out?* As in...

"Shall we?" He kicked the stop to the side, then held the door open for her.

Ffion blinked as her mind struggled to find an excuse, but Carrick was already ushering her out the door and across the crowded square.

Her heart felt lodged in her throat as they entered the tavern. Conversation hushed throughout the darkened room as the door swung shut behind her. Carrick gestured toward the closest bench. He didn't seem to notice the rapt attention they received, but Ffion could feel everyone's eyes on her. She sat rigidly on the hard seat, even as lively commotion started up again.

Carrick shot two fingers into the air and, in a matter of minutes, a woman slid a bowl of barley soup in front of each of them, then produced two rolls from her apron pocket.

"Anything else?" she asked, glancing between them.

"That'll be all. Thank you, Mallory."

She nodded sharply and left. Ffion stared down at her bowl, wondering if she could avoid speaking if she kept her mouth full. Thankfully, Carrick seemed well aware of her trepidation, keeping the conversation off her. He regaled her with news about town, his family in the east, and how he'd come to own his great-uncle's shop. Ffion nodded in between spoonfuls, relaxing slightly as the warm soup filled her belly.

After they finished, Ffion forced herself to match Carrick's leisurely pace as he took the long way back to his shop. The children she'd seen earlier had emerged from their homes, heading back to school, no doubt. A few snuck away to steal wish coins from the shallow pool in the center. *A fountain*, the townspeople called it. Ffion had seen plenty of fountains in her youth—majestic marble structures that shot water high into the air—and *a fountain* it was not. The stacked stones held no more than a foot of water, filled by a single rusted pump. But she couldn't help but smile at the delight it seemed to provide the children.

She'd never had time to appreciate the spirit of the small town. It must have been a midday break that had everyone strolling about. Couples held hands, women laughed together, people young and old seemed to find common ground in the heart of the village.

Ffion exhaled some of the tension she'd been holding. Perhaps she could live a bigger life than she'd previously allowed. Beyond her apple trees, beyond the garden fence that penned in her small world. What had she been afraid of all those years? That someone would learn her true identity, discover what she was capable of? What was the harm in living a full life, immersing herself in the place she'd chosen to call home? At that moment, she could hardly remember why she hadn't.

Ffion looked around, no longer worried about showing her face. A smile tugged at her lips, but slipped away just as quickly when a man hollered for attention at the edge of the square. Carrick pulled Ffion forward as a crowd gathered around the man. She pressed up onto her toes for a better look.

The man carried a bow, with a quiver slung over his back. But it was the lifeless gray wolf he dragged behind him that was causing the uproar.

Ffion edged closer, her throat tightening as the man yanked the animal another foot before dropping its hind legs. She stared down at the magnificent creature, lying prone in the dirt.

Raising his voice for all to hear, the hunter warned the people of Debarrow that he'd seen the monstrous wolf stalking the border of the village for days, and had killed it to protect the townspeople.

Ffion's heart ached as she eyed the innocent creature—a senseless death at the hand of a fearful man.

She'd glimpsed a wolf days before. Was it the same?

Her ribs clenched at the thought, and she inched closer.

The crowd pressed against her, wanting to see the beast for themselves. She heard the stifled gasps and whispered remarks as the hunter continued to profess his prowess as savior of the land. Ffion ignored his prepared speech, disgusted, as she took another step.

Carrick touched her elbow and positioned himself between her and the lifeless body of the massive wolf. But with another slide of her boot, Ffion found herself close enough to touch it.

A hum started in her ears, drowning out the hunter's voice as he droned on about his kill—stalking a semicircle around the wolf as he stirred the collective terror of the crowd.

Her head felt fuzzy, fevered. Pain radiated down her shoulders. *Not pain.* A strange sensation she couldn't name, something she hadn't felt before. It coursed through her veins, slithering down her arms beneath her skin, causing her fingers to tingle and itch. She flexed her hands, but the sensation wouldn't abate.

Shifting her stance to ease the discomfort, she noticed the arrow jutting out of the wolf's side directly above his shoulder.

Where it had pierced his heart.

Ffion rolled her shoulders. Perhaps what she was feeling was a sympathetic reaction to the pain the unfortunate animal had felt when he'd been so cruelly cut down.

Her eyes traveled along his prone form. The girth of its barrel chest was as wide as a tree trunk, and it looked to weigh nearly one hundred pounds.

Ffion fought her need to touch the wolf, to grant him a small amount of peace. Even as every nerve in her body urged her to reach for him.

As the humming between her ears rose to a near deafening level, she sucked in a strained breath and gave in, reaching her hand forward. Her fingers grazed his soft pelt.

The air rushed from her lungs, nearly toppling her as relief swept through her body.

The animal stirred.

Ffion yanked her hand back, holding it tight to her side as the ground seemed to shift beneath her. She swayed, her vision darkening at the edges as shrieks and cries went up around her.

But by the time knives were drawn and the hunter's arrow nocked, the giant beast had rolled swiftly to his feet. A flash of white and gray fur vaulted past, disappearing into the woods.

A strong arm came around Ffion, tugging her back. She stumbled into Carrick's chest, feeling as if every ounce of energy had drained from her body.

With effort, she lifted her head. Across the square stood a man, untouched by the chaos as onlookers fled or readied more weapons.

The metalsmith. Watching her. His eyes boring into her.

Ffion struggled to look away as Carrick wrapped an arm around her shoulders and ushered her toward his shop. She trembled, glancing back to where the wolf had vanished into the woods.

Though it wasn't the wolf Ffion feared.

He'd most certainly been dead before she'd touched him.

Chapter Four

THE CRUNCH OF dirt and Ffion's pounding heart muffled the frenzied uproar that still reached her down the road.

But she was alone, as she needed to be. Even as her thoughts kept repeating.

It wasn't me. It couldn't have been me.

After the wolf fled, Carrick had led her quickly toward the safety of his shop, misinterpreting the trembling of her hands as the same fear the townspeople held—that the wild beast could have easily turned on them instead of bolting back into the woods.

But the only thing Ffion feared was herself.

Her breaths quickened as her home came into view in the distance. She tugged her skirts higher, lengthening her strides.

Visions flitted through her mind. Her hand reaching out. The wolf reanimating.

She shoved them aside, tightening the grip on her skirts as she remembered the sensations that had streaked down her arms, into her fingertips. Would it happen again? Would something else trigger her power?

Ffion's breath grew shallow, her mind spinning with inquiries no one could answer. Because she was alone in Periwen.

"Good afternoon." A deep male voice startled her.

Ffion pressed a hand to her stomach, her heart rioting faster. She'd been ruminating so intently that she hadn't noticed the man's approach. And that voice...

She stifled a shiver, angling her down-turned face slightly to take in his heavily muscled, leather-clad legs, and the black-stained creases on his broad hands that hung loosely at his sides.

The metalsmith.

His eyes stared down at her intently—the same eyes that had watched her from across the square. Up close, she could make out their true color. Not the deep shade of roasted cocoa, but darker, with glinting amber near the irises.

She dipped her chin without uttering a word or breaking her pace.

"Miss Ffion Ainsley, I don't believe I've had the pleasure." He matched her strides with slow, long ones of his own.

How did he know her name? She'd never spoken a word to the man.

She didn't respond, trying instead to discern the reason for the unusual encounter. The metalsmith's workshop was at the other end of town. There was no feasible reason for him to be heading in the opposite direction. Her small property was the only destination at the end of the lane.

Unless...he was there to see her. The thought crept up her spine, raising the fine hairs on the back of her neck.

Ffion felt the heat of his body as he kept pace beside her. *Close. Too close.* Even out in the open, she felt trapped beside him.

"The name's Tearlach," he offered.

"I know your name," she lied. And didn't he have a surname? Perhaps he felt entitled to informality, even with a woman he'd only just met.

He veered closer as they continued down the road. The sharp metal scent that surrounded him singed her nose. Though it was blended with a familiar, wild note—something earthy and bracing. Something not of that world. She tried to place it, if only to distract herself from the voice in her head that warned her to stay away from him.

"That was quite the spectacle, wouldn't you say? I've never seen anything like it."

Was he truly making polite conversation? He didn't seem the type to enjoy exchanges that lasted more than a few words.

"You've never seen a wolf?" she mocked, hoping her irritated tone would convey her lack of interest.

"I could have sworn it was dead."

She turned to see his dark eyes contemplating her.

"And the next moment, it was as though its heart had never been pierced by an arrow."

Ffion forced her attention back to the road.

"It was almost like…" He inhaled slowly, as if considering his thoughts—though Ffion would bet he knew exactly what he was about to say. "Like *something* had ensorcelled the animal, giving it new life."

Ensorcelled? Did he mean magic? She resisted the urge to glance over at him, sensing his gaze upon her. It felt as though he was towering over her.

She needed to get home. Or cut back toward town so she wouldn't be alone with him.

Ffion gritted her teeth against the uneasiness he evoked and replied, "I might believe something like that were possible, sir, if you weren't referring to the stuff of folklore and storybooks."

He pressed on as if she'd said nothing. "Never heard of a human having that kind of power though. *Magic.*" He spoke the last word with careful enunciation.

Ffion swallowed, trying to calm her nerves as every muscle in her body screamed for her to run. Trying her hardest to sound uninterested, she told him, "Magic doesn't exist," then hurried on ahead.

For a split second, she thought he might not follow, but he met her stride a moment later. He turned and walked in front of her when she wouldn't stop, then cocked his head to the side and arched one of his dark eyebrows. "Oh, it certainly does, *Ffion*." He said her name like he wanted to devour it. "Just not in these lands."

Without another word, he strode away, disappearing into the woods.

A gust of wind whipped the hem of Ffion's dress. She reached her door just as lightning fractured the sky. She looked back once more—still disconcerted that the metalsmith had been able to sneak up on her—then slid her silver key into the lock.

Her secluded home had always been her refuge, a safe haven. But in that moment, the nearest residence down the road seemed uncomfortably far away.

After lighting the candles in her small sitting room, she went to bolt the back door—its heavy thud relieving a bit of her worry. She checked the front door again, then stared up at the dark loft, pondering the window tucked between the eaves. It had never latched properly, but Ffion decided it was unlikely anyone would climb the exterior of her home. *Unlikely.*

She banished the image from her mind, blaming the metalsmith for unraveling the last of her nerves.

She released her clenched hands and moved about with purpose, setting her kettle to boil, and stacking a new log atop the blackened ones in the hearth. The felled branch from the last storm smoked a bit before catching, but once Ffion slipped into a nightdress and returned with her nettle tea, the fire was warm and crackling.

She cradled the cup in her hands, letting the warmth seep into her skin as she watched the flames flicker along the charred wood, hoping that if she stared long enough she might forget the troublesome truths lurking at the back of her mind.

"I should eat something," she reasoned, knowing she'd feel better, that things would seem less dire if she could only manage to get something in her belly. But food sounded less than appealing. Even the thought of it made her stomach churn—a feeling all too similar to the sensations she'd felt right before...

Before her touch had brought a dead wolf back to life.

Ffion gripped her cup, smoothing her thumbs against the glaze. She refused to think of the pulsing sensations that had slithered beneath her skin as she'd reached out for the prone animal.

Magic.

She could no longer deny it.

She might have been far from the land where magic was intrinsic, and even though she was well into her twenty-fourth year—four years past the age when magic revealed itself in her kind—it had undoubtedly begun to manifest in her blood.

Ffion closed her eyes. *The tree. The wolf.* The incidents didn't seem connected. Earth magic, she guessed, though she couldn't recall ever hearing about the ability to renew life.

All she knew was that she needed to keep her power hidden. Couldn't let it slip again.

But how could she hide something that she hadn't a clue how to control? Ffion was completely alone in the human realm, without anyone to guide her through the bewildering and often severe transition of coming into one's magic.

She glanced out the rain-doused windows, wanting to pray to the gods for help—though they'd never answered her pleas before. Staring through the blurry pane at the grayness beyond, her heart skipped a beat.

"No," she breathed, as a more daunting realization hit. Lightning flashed, illuminating the trees against the darkening sky. Shimmering light coated the branches and leaves, lingering for a moment before fading away.

If she had magic—delayed or not, it had started to awaken—then she was inescapably locked into her immortality. From that day forward, she wouldn't age. The fragile mortality of her early life—the short life she'd gratefully welcomed since arriving in Periwen—was gone.

It wasn't fair. She clenched her jaw as anger swelled. Lightning struck closer, the trailing thunder shaking the ground.

Ffion had crossed the sea—breached the fog of glamour that divided her homeland from the mortal realm. Her appearance had shifted. She *looked* human. And when her twentieth year had come and gone without a trickle of power, she'd believed that crossing the barrier had not only blocked the ability for her magic to manifest, but had lifted the gods-blessed gift of a long life as well.

Only at that moment it seemed more like a curse than a gift.

If Ffion was forced to remain in the mortal realm, forever separated from her home and her people, a very real part of her had believed she could avoid the fate of her kind. She didn't want a life that would stretch on for centuries. She wanted to remain mortal, to grow old, to pass the years as the people of Periwen did. Instead, she'd be forced to watch generations of families live and die as she remained frozen in her youth.

Which meant...she couldn't remain in Debarrow.

Her heart sunk. Outside, the winds stilled as the wildness of the storm weakened. The rain persisted, its heaviness hanging over the land.

How long could she stay? She never partook in activities around town—barely encountered anyone during her weekly trips to Hawthorn's.

Carrick. Ffion cursed her foolishness. After so many years of avoiding any unnecessary interactions, she'd gone and agreed to a date. "A *date,*" she muttered.

She knew better. Since the morning she'd woken on the fishing boat in the harbor, from the moment she'd beheld her glamoured reflection in the mirror, Ffion had known she could never reveal her true identity.

She sipped her tea, not caring that it had gone cold and bitter. Her thoughts strayed to her orchard, her garden. She didn't want to leave. She liked her secluded plot of land. Liked growing things. It was something she was good at, something she'd chosen. Something other than the role she'd been born into.

For the first time in nine years, Ffion felt like she belonged somewhere.

Perhaps she *could* stay a bit longer. It would take another six years, maybe seven, before her eternally youthful appearance began to draw suspicion. Then she'd move on, start a new life in a new town.

Until then, she'd avoid everyone save for Carrick. Even with him she'd need to be careful to keep their interactions impersonal.

An image of the metalsmith forced its way to the front of her mind. *Tearlach.*

She remembered his intimidating presence on the road—could still feel him beside her. Her eyes darted around the room as she shook the prickling sensation from her body.

What else did she know of him? Before that day, they hadn't spoken to one another. Even at the shop, he hadn't said a word to her. "Why today?" she wondered aloud. Had he seen her touch the wolf? He'd been all the way across the square, beyond the crowd.

Ffion pressed her lips together. It was possible he hadn't seen anything out of the ordinary. *Possible.* And yet, she couldn't deny the inescapable shift in the air each time he was near.

If she wished to remain in Debarrow—and she did—it was time to learn more about the mysterious metalsmith.

Chapter Five

FFION VENTURED INTO the woods beyond her property, feeling determined. She wouldn't be scared off, or forced to leave before she was ready.

The harvest festival had begun that morning, offering the perfect cover. She'd hike one of her foraging paths to the other end of town and sneak a peek through one of Tearlach's shop windows.

High-pitched notes from a flute trickled through the commotion in town, reminding Ffion of her home in Tremaene and the Festival of Tahra. The decadent foods and elaborate decorations. Feasts and parties that lasted until dawn as her people honored the goddess of land and fertility.

Ffion imagined the sunset-colored gown she'd worn during her fifteenth year. The silk had been dyed a perfect gradient of buttery yellow, pink, and orange through the fitted waist, with the hem dipped in a red so deep it looked like the color of crushed berries. She glanced down at her worn cotton dress. "Hmm," she mused. Far from fashionable, yet quite a bit more comfortable. She pulled her skirts close to avoid some low-hanging branches, then halted mid-step.

The branches curved away, forming a clear path.

Ffion stared with a mixture of fear and awe at the forest's response to her presence.

It took several moments before she dared another step, continuing cautiously through the newly formed passageway, while doing her best to ignore the unnatural sway of branches.

As soon as Tearlach's property was visible through the tree line, Ffion hurried toward the workshop, pressing her back against the rough slats as she listened. There were no windows or doors along the back wall. When she heard nothing coming from inside, she crept around the corner and peered in the only window. Finding the dusty pane covered on the opposite side by a dark cloth, she moved toward the front of the shop.

One of the large doors was slightly ajar.

This was not the plan, she reminded herself. But there was no indication that Tearlach was in his workshop or anywhere on his property, so Ffion quickly slipped inside.

Her heart rioted in her chest as she took in the space. A massive forge occupied an entire wall—a few embers still glowing in its depths. But the rest of the workspace seemed rather small, much smaller than it'd appeared from the outside. Noticing a door along the back wall, she picked her way through the room and pushed it open.

Her eyes widened as she scanned the large, secret room—for it certainly wasn't meant to be seen. Swords lined every wall. She beheld each one, counting as she went, until her gaze landed on what seemed like a wooden replica of a man tucked into the far corner. It was splintered and covered in deep grooves, as if each sword had been tested on it. Why would anyone require such an apparatus? There was no military presence in the Winslow province, and the only fort she knew of was at the southern edge of the continent, in the Heilyn Desert. Had Tearlach spent time there? She'd assumed he'd always lived in Debarrow. Or perhaps he simply...enjoyed sword fighting...as a hobby.

She didn't want to think about the alternative.

Ffion hovered at the threshold of what could only be described as a training room, afraid to take another step. But the sword nearest caught her eye. It wasn't shiny or new like the others. It looked as though it had seen battles. The hilt was carved with whorls and inlaid bronze. It was beautiful. And strangely familiar. She couldn't recall seeing something so refined in the mortal realm.

Aware that she'd lingered too long, Ffion stepped away and slowly pulled the door shut. Thankfully, the workshop was still empty. She hastened through the maze of tools and implements, looking for anything else out of the ordinary. A long table was covered with rows of blades—knives, daggers, some were serrated or curved, each terrifyingly deadly. Her hand hovered over them, and she felt a strange twinge of discomfort, warning her not to touch.

She needed to leave, but hesitated a moment longer, curious. The metal seemed cold and...*wrong*, as if it would burn her skin if she risked touching it.

Ffion pulled her hand away, curling it at her side. *Now. I need to go now.*

She turned from the table and collided with the metalsmith's unyielding body.

Chapter Six

FFION LOOKED UP and met Tearlach's gaze, and for a moment saw her own eyes reflected in his. Both dark with hidden secrets.

She stumbled back, putting the table between them. How had she not heard him approach? *Again.*

He stared down at her as Ffion's mind tripped over possible reasons to give for her intrusion. But his deep voice broke the silence first.

"Didn't your parents teach you that it's not polite to enter without permission?"

The mention of her parents washed away her panic. A cold emptiness took its place, giving her a strange sense of courage. She met his tone with equal indignation. "Didn't your parents teach you not to startle people?"

He narrowed his gaze.

"I'm in need of some daggers." She raised her chin an inch, hating how easily the lie came.

He cocked his head to the side. "Really? And what does someone like you," he asked, looking her up and down, "need with a dagger?"

Ffion suppressed a shiver at his intense scrutiny. Then, with all the bravado she could muster, asserted, "So I can defend myself when someone sneaks up on me." She lifted a brow the way she'd seen him do and could have sworn the corner of Tearlach's lips curved up. The hint of amusement was there and gone in a second, and did little to alleviate the trepidation she felt being in such close proximity to him. Even with the table between them she felt the tight confines of the workshop, as if the walls were pressing them closer together.

She edged slowly around the table—bringing her nearer to the open door. *And to him.*

His eyes stayed fixed on her as she struggled to steady the beat of her heart and still her trembling hands.

"This one looks promising." Ffion picked up a small blade by its hilt. Careful not to touch the metal with her fingers, she made a show of inspecting the piece before placing it back down. Daring another look at Tearlach, she told him, "I'll think about it," and made to leave.

Her steps were painfully slow. She didn't want to appear like she was running away—which was exactly what she wanted to do.

Just as she reached the open door, Tearlach spoke in a chillingly calm voice. "You wouldn't want to be caught unaware and unarmed."

A threat? Her heart sped up, but she kept moving, kept her eyes trained on the gravel path that would lead her into town.

She didn't dare look back, though her ears were perked up at attention the entire walk. But all she could hear was the rollicking celebration ahead.

Ffion surveyed the crowded town square as she approached, grateful that she'd had the forethought to wear a dress. Carts and wagons lined the perimeter, filled with soft woven blankets and thick sweaters, squashes and pumpkins, and colorful flowers she'd never before seen in Periwen.

Debarrow, and the land surrounding the small village, was not known for its fertile soil. And taking in the array of food and wares, it seemed vendors had traveled from places far beyond the Winslow province.

Ffion did her best to blend in, winding through the packed square. She decided to stay for a short while, just long enough to confirm that

Tearlach hadn't followed. She only prayed that the road home would
be deserted.

Oddly enough, she felt safe amid the crush of people. The realization,
while unexpected, was reassuring. She feigned interest in a set of nested
baskets when a familiar voice drifted over her shoulder.

She turned and smiled at Carrick. A genuine smile. She was happy
to see her one and only acquaintance—someone who'd never once
intimidated her with a disquieting glare.

"I didn't expect to see you here."

"I...I told you I might attend." Even the memory of the lie felt bitter on
her tongue. But Carrick's eyes lit with amusement—it seemed he hadn't
believed her anyway. Thankfully, he didn't seem inclined to question her
presence. Ffion couldn't very well tell him that she sought refuge from a
certain metalsmith with dark eyes that seemed to penetrate her mind.

"Come." Carrick offered his arm. "Let me show you around." He
leaned in close and added, "As this *is* your first time."

Ffion twined her arm through his and let him lead. They admired
the work of skilled artisans and sampled fares. She caught a few
interested stares from the locals, but Carrick seemed to want Ffion all to
himself. That suited her fine as she wasn't eager to add to her short list
of acquaintances.

As the day went on, memories of Tearlach and his workshop kept
returning. How was it that he seemed to *know* her? Had Tearlach inquired
about her? She glanced over at Carrick as he haggled over the price of a
paper cone filled with roasted nuts.

"Carrick?" she asked as he passed over a coin, then offered the warm
hazelnuts to her.

"Hmm?" He rose a brow and tossed a handful into his mouth.

"What do you know about the metalsmith?"

Carrick's eyes narrowed as he swallowed. "Tearlach?" His voice was
edged with a protective note.

"Yes," Ffion hedged.

"Did something happen?"

"No, no," she assured him. "It's just, the latch on my back door is broken, and I thought he might be able to fashion a new spindle for it." Again, the lie came easily, but it was believable enough.

Carrick looked relieved at her innocuous request, which only stoked Ffion's suspicions. Perhaps it wasn't her untrusting nature that caused her to fear that Tearlach somehow knew her secrets.

"I assume he's able," Carrick told her. "Though to be honest, I'm not so sure he'd be willing. I've only visited his shop once. The previous smith, Declan, used to supply knives and other tools, along with shoeing the occasional horse. When Tearlach arrived, I went to inquire about his expertise. From what I saw in his workshop he was quite skilled at his craft, but he wasn't interested in supplying anything to the shop. In fact, I don't think he's sold a single thing to anyone in all the years he's been here. I've no idea why he even came to our village. Why take over the smithy if not to earn a wage?"

Ffion stared at Carrick for a long moment, his words churning through her mind. "That does seem odd," she agreed, nodding once. "You mentioned a...previous smith..."

"Declan. He just up and left without warning. Tearlach purchased the property shortly after."

"When?" Ffion fought to keep the panic from her voice, afraid she already knew the answer.

Carrick looked off into the distance. "Actually, it was around the time you came to Debarrow. Or maybe a few weeks later."

"I see." Ffion gripped her skirts so tight she worried they might tear. *The same time?* That couldn't be mere coincidence.

"Here." Carrick pulled her along. "You must try this fruit. They're sweet and chewy, a true delight. *Dates*, I believe they're called."

Ffion remained by his side, all the while scanning the crowd for a man with dark hair who stood nearly a foot taller than the rest.

Chapter Seven

FFION'S FEET WERE *wet from the dew-covered grass, but she didn't feel a chill. Several moments passed as her eyes adjusted to the darkness. She turned slowly, taking in the silhouettes of trees that skirted the glade where she stood. She didn't remember leaving her bed, and couldn't make out a path to indicate which direction she'd come from. Vacant darkness hovered above. Not a single star hung in the moonless sky.*

Ffion glanced down at her nightclothes. Why hadn't she thought to grab a cloak or shoes? She tried to recall the moment she'd left her bed, but remembered nothing.

She took a step, the mist clinging to her, moving with her every step. She couldn't see more than a few paces in any direction.

Then the fog started to ease back, forming a path. And something took shape.

Ffion tilted her head, trying to make out the figure.

A wolf.

He sat at attention twenty paces ahead, waiting.

Instead of being afraid of his proximity, she felt safe, like a blanket of warmth had encircled her. She watched for a moment, unsure of the wolf's intentions. Finally, he rose, turned slowly, then stalked into the fog.

Ffion didn't hesitate before following him. She quickened her pace trying to keep up, but the wolf pulled farther and farther away. Soon she was alone. The mist closed in around her until nothing was visible beyond her own body, not even the soft grass beneath her toes. She continued forward tentatively, and when the fog receded, the forest was gone.

A house stood in the distance, with smoke tendrils slipping from the chimney into the darkening sky.

Ffion focused on the sight, and realized she was looking down on the small cottage, her feet no longer touching the ground. And it wasn't just any home—it was her *home in Debarrow.*

With only a thought, she found herself drawing closer, able to see a young woman through the warm glow of the kitchen window.

Ffion couldn't believe what she was seeing.

It was her. *She was watching herself.*

Ffion looked on as the woman paced back and forth, stopping now and then to make notes on a sheet of paper. Ffion tore her eyes from the sight to search the rest of her property. The twin moons cast long shadows through her garden and the orchard beyond.

One of the shadows crept closer.

An alarming howl pierced the silence.

Ffion spotted a wolf standing in her garden, howling again.

Inside, her apparition opened the back door and stepped unawares into the open. One of the shadowy figures moved closer.

Too close.

Ffion screamed for the woman to stop. But there was nothing she could do as the scene played out before her eyes. The assailant grabbed the woman and put a knife to her throat.

"No!" Ffion's cry echoed as the mist began pooling at her feet. She tried to push through it, needing to save the woman—save herself. But the fog swirled and closed in on her.

"No, no, no! Let me go back!" she yelled into the nothingness.

———————

A crack of thunder jolted her awake. She was panting, twisting in her sheets. Feeling the firmness of the bed, her eyes sprang open.

Just a dream. It was just a dream, she told herself over and over.

After wiping the sweat from her brow, she carefully sat up and glanced across the bedroom loft. Having forgotten to close the curtain the night before, she could see storm clouds parting for one of the glowing moons. Stars winked into the sky as the clouds dissolved into inky darkness.

It was just a dream.

Ffion stared blankly at the rafters above until the last vestiges of the bruise-colored sky gave way to the comforting rays of morning. With an exhausted groan, she rose from the refuge of her bed and dressed for the day.

At the back door, she gazed out at her land for several long minutes before daring to open it.

Even knowing full well that her paranoia was getting the best of her, Ffion stalked toward the orchard, prepared to check every sliver of her property and the woods beyond.

After walking the rows of trees, circling the pond, and patrolling the wooded trails, she pushed tools and baskets aside in her shed, and inspected every corner and closet in her home. It didn't matter that she couldn't find evidence of any intruders, she couldn't seem to dispel the sense of foreboding the dream had imparted.

Noticing the bedroom window that had never shut properly, Ffion decided it was time to repair it. No longer trusting the tallest ladder with its broken rung, she chose the shorter one. It barely reached the second story, forcing Ffion to stretch up onto her toes in order to reach the hinge at the top of the window. At least it would be a simple fix. The bottom slat of the frame had been warped from years of rain.

She sanded the wood until it was level, then repainted it. It fit snugly when she returned it to the sill, but her precarious footing made her overly cautious.

When she felt for another screw in her pocket, the ladder trembled.

She dropped her tool, her hands flying to the window frame. She gripped it tight as panic chilled her veins.

The ladder stood firm, but the memory of falling from the tree returned in full force. Her stomach churned, so she didn't dare close her eyes. Instead, Ffion stared at her reflection in the wavy glass, taking slow breaths until the queasiness abated.

When she felt steady enough to return her hands to the ladder, she lowered a foot to the rung below, then glanced over her shoulder.

Her eyes locked with the dark ones of the metalsmith.

Tearlach stood on the ground below, his broad hands gripping the ladder. Trapping her.

Chapter Eight

FALLING FELT INFINITELY more appealing. Wind lashed against Ffion's face, but the shiver crawling down her spine had nothing to do with the sudden chill in the air.

Tearing her eyes from his, she quickly scanned the area, praying to the gods that they weren't completely alone.

They were.

Only the charcoal clouds assembling along the horizon were there to bear witness.

Tearlach's deep voice drew her back. "You shouldn't be doing that yourself." His eyes narrowed and he tilted his head slightly to the side. "It's dangerous."

Not as dangerous as you, she thought.

"What if you should fall? Who would catch you?"

Ffion stayed silent. She *had* fallen—the memory still fresh in her mind. There seemed a faint hint of knowing in the man's eyes. Had he beheld that incident as well?

"A fall would certainly leave you injured."

Ffion held back a shudder. Perhaps it was just the heavy resonance of his voice, but everything Tearlach said sounded like a subtle threat.

"Though I'm sure you'd heal rather quickly."

She blinked at his choice words.

The wind picked up as storm clouds rolled closer. Rain was surely coming. And Ffion was trapped on a ladder. For a moment she considered squeezing through the small window.

No. She wouldn't give him the satisfaction of seeing how he unnerved her.

"I can assure you, sir, that I know what I'm doing and am perfectly safe." Though safe from him, she wasn't sure. Ffion was drawn once more to his dark eyes and the unspoken things lurking within their depths. So familiar, so like hers.

She held his gaze, challenging him. Had he truly come there simply to taunt her? Perhaps he was repaying the favor of her earlier intrusion. Maybe it was all a game to him—to see how much he could unsettle her.

When she couldn't stand the knowing look in his eyes a moment longer, she averted her gaze. The ladder shook and Ffion gripped the poles, sucking in a breath. She peeked beneath her arm, and was stunned to find that Tearlach had released his hold and was backing away.

"Finally," she whispered as the first cool drops of rain pricked her bare arms.

"Be careful, Esme," Tearlach cautioned with a preternatural stillness in his voice.

Ffion shot him a look, her eyes growing wide. But he'd already turned away, striding down the road.

She continued to gape at his retreating form. *Esme?* Certainly, she'd heard him wrong.

Tearlach looked back once more, his stare potent and heavy with meaning, then gave a single nod as if to say, *You heard me right.*

Ffion couldn't move, her hands felt as though they'd melded to the poles of the ladder. The metalsmith knew who she was.

Despite the unceasing, frigid rain that soaked Ffion's clothes and blurred her vision, she stayed atop the ladder, staring down the vacant road. Her mind swam with implications she dared not give voice to.

Never heard of a human having that kind of power. He knew she possessed magic.

I'm sure you'd heal rather quickly. He knew of the healing ability intrinsic to her kind.

Then, he'd called her *Esme.*

Every time she thought about that name—the name she hadn't once spoken in the mortal realm, the name she'd left behind with everything else—the past from which she'd tried so hard to escape, to forget, drew ever closer.

If Tearlach knew her true identity, then he couldn't be from Periwen either. And if he wasn't from Periwen, then he, too, wasn't mortal.

Tearlach was from Tremaene. He must have somehow crossed the fog of glamour as she had, concealing his telling features and air of eternal youth. Tearlach was Fae. Like her.

Which meant Ffion's whereabouts were no longer secret. And she was no longer safe.

Ffion stayed long after the rain stopped, unwilling to set foot on the sodden ground below. As if she could somehow avoid reality if she stayed on the ladder.

When she eventually climbed down and made her way inside, the sun was sinking low in the sky. Water dripped from her soaked hair, leaving clear reflecting pools as she stepped into the kitchen. She looked away, not wanting to see the disguise staring back at her.

After forcing herself to dry off and change out of her wet clothes, she stood near the front window with a cup of tea, watching the hazy sunlight flicker through the trees. She couldn't bring herself to look out at her garden or her apple trees—didn't want to think about the life she'd built, the one she'd have to leave. So she stared at the mud puddles on the road and the rust-colored leaves of the maples across the way, hanging heavy and limp from the rain. But even the calming nature of the steeped chamomile flowers in her cup did little to lighten the hollowness she felt in her chest.

She would abandon her home. *Again.*

She'd need to tell Carrick—she owed him that much for his kindness over the years. Her finger traced a droplet as it trickled down the opposite side of the windowpane.

Carrick had mentioned visiting his sister's family one town over, but Ffion couldn't recall when he was set to return. She could write him a letter. It would be easier, though it felt cowardly.

No, she decided. She'd wait until he returned—tell him in person that she was leaving Debarrow. Though what she would tell him, she wasn't sure. Perhaps that she was going south, invent a distant relation who'd fallen ill or a friend who'd written in need of assistance? It needed to be convincing enough to make her immediate departure seem reasonable.

She'd think on that later.

The colorful leaves darkened to muted gray as the sky fell into twilight. Ffion built a fire, then shuffled into the kitchen and rummaged through her cupboards. She found an old stack of loose papers and began making a list of items she'd need to bring with her.

It didn't make sense to take her cart—it would draw too much attention, and she wasn't keen on leaving any tracks. She could move faster without it anyway. Her Fae heritage granted her a swiftness unmatched by mortals. That advantage alone provided her with a slight sense of security for the journey ahead.

She pointedly ignored the insistent voice reminding her that Tearlach was no mere mortal.

Ffion crossed out a few items on her list. *Only what I can carry,* she reminded herself. She didn't need much to start over anyway. The gold Cadwyn had secured in the lining of her cloak would see her well provided for. Stealing a glance at the warped floorboard that concealed her coin, she climbed the stairs to dress for bed. She gathered a few of her best-made shirts and pants, and a canvas pack. Then, kneeling beside the bed, she hefted the top three cushioned layers and reached her hand in to pull out a silver dagger. The blade was secured safely in a black sheath, embossed with golden leaves and vines. Ffion had shoved the weapon under her bed years ago, hoping never to need it. But her secrets were no longer her own, and thinking of Tearlach's startling presence, she vowed never to be caught off guard again.

Ffion tossed her bag of clothes over the edge of the loft, then pounded down the stairs with more force than she'd felt all afternoon. She scrawled another item at the bottom of her list, then paused mid-word, suddenly aware of the silence that had descended upon the land. Not one screech from the roosting grackles could be heard. Flocking in droves to her apple trees—a near-deafening noise every evening—the birds had gone quiet.

She lifted her head and listened intently. A wolf's howl tore through the silence. Too close to be coming from the woods.

Dropping her pencil, Ffion approached the back door with its small, square window. But the sky was dark, and she couldn't make out a thing beyond her own reflection. She reached for the knob, hesitated, then jerked her hand back as the wolf howled again.

Even in the darkness, she knew exactly where the wolf was. In her dream, the wolf had stood defensively in the center of her garden—his bay a warning of the shadows that prowled closer, moving in from the trees, nearing the back door.

How many were there? She remembered seeing at least five, though there could have been more.

"No, no, no," she breathed, backing away. She dropped to the floor. The fire lit her home from within, leaving her blind to everything that was happening outside.

But they could see her.

Ffion crawled along the floor, staying below the height of the window ledges. Her shoulder struck the leg of a chair. She squeezed her eyes shut as pain radiated down her arm. It was quickly forgotten when the wolf growled another warning. She could hear gravel grinding beneath his massive paws in what sounded like an imminent attack.

There was a nearly silent gasp just before she heard the snap of its powerful jaw. Ffion shuddered, imagining bones splintering, blood gushing as limbs were torn away.

She fumbled for her shoes tucked beneath the stairs, pulling them on hastily. The wolf was buying her time—time that had almost expired.

Without allowing even a second to consider what might be waiting outside, Ffion grabbed Cadwyn's cloak, unlocked the front door with shaky hands, then bolted down the road.

She sprinted toward the tree line across the road, throwing the midnight blue cloak over her shoulders to conceal the bright white of her nightdress.

Faster, faster, she prodded, thinking again of the dream. Could she change the horrible fate she'd witnessed?

Her eyes adjusted to the night. She could make out every obstacle as she raced through the brittle grass and brush. A gust of wind whipped her cloak about her legs. Ffion pulled it tight and spared a glance over her shoulder. The sky lit with a flash of lightning and she saw one of the intruders following, closing in on her.

Impossible.

If her pursuer was able to keep pace with her, then they weren't human, but Fae.

Shit.

A chase that should have had Ffion safely from danger in mere moments was all of the sudden considerably more dangerous. She needed to change course if she had any chance of outrunning the assailant.

Ahead, she could see the lanterns outside Mallory's tavern. Townspeople milled about. She left the protection of the trees, keeping close to the rear of the buildings. Blending into the shadows no longer seemed her safest course. She hoped the lights and witnesses would deter her assailant, but she couldn't simply burst into the crowd gathered outside Mallory's.

There was a narrow alleyway two doors down and Ffion raced toward it, offering up a quick prayer to the gods that she was not about to endanger any of the townspeople. Sparing a final glance to her pursuer, she slipped around the corner.

Someone grabbed her, shoving her up against the wall.

A powerful forearm pinned her across the chest as another hand covered her mouth, fingers digging into her cheek.

Ffion tried to draw breath, tried to scream. Thunder rolled in the distance and the alley grew impossibly darker as storm clouds shrouded the moons. She stared up at her attacker's face. Even in the darkness, there was no mistaking who the man was.

Tearlach.

His hold didn't let up, but neither did he move to wound her or drag her away. When he slowly lowered the hand that gripped her mouth, Ffion sucked in a tight breath. Tearlach held her gaze with an intensity that warned her not to make a sound.

She couldn't even if she'd wanted to. Her lips refused to form words.

What would he do with her? What was his plan?

With their eyes locked, he removed his crushing arm from her chest. Ffion inhaled deeply, still not daring to speak. She didn't even feel the rain pelting her skin until it gathered on her lashes, blurring her vision.

Tearlach put his back to the wall beside her and Ffion caught the glint of a blade as he pulled it smoothly from his belt.

Her heart leapt into her throat. Trying to will movement back into her legs, she slid one foot toward the pooling lamplight at the other end of the alleyway, never taking her eyes off the man next to her.

Footsteps approached from the direction she'd come, and before Ffion could fully grasp what was happening, Tearlach had seized the attacker's wrist, twisted the woman against his chest, and slit her throat in one fluid motion.

Ffion stared unblinking at the sight. Her body began to tremble. She could smell the coppery tang of blood as it poured from the woman's fatal wound, which had left her head at an unnatural angle. Ffion couldn't understand how drawing a small blade across a throat could nearly sever a head. Yet it had.

Tearlach pulled the lifeless body against the wall, out of sight from passersby. The sounds of the tavern hummed in the distance, a world away from where she stood.

Ffion peered at the crumpled body. "What..." she rasped. "Why?"

"She would have killed you." Tearlach's voice cut through the thickness of death that crowded the alley.

Ffion met his gaze. His eyes seemed darker in the shadows. "But how did you know? Why did you"—she could barely fathom the words—"*save* me?"

Tearlach wiped the blood from his blade, flipped it in his hand, and slid it back into his belt without taking his eyes from her.

He leaned closer, lowering his head to hers as he spoke in a low, clear voice—one that only she could hear, as if the slain body at their feet might otherwise learn their secrets. "Did you not think I would save the only heir of Tremaene?"

Chapter Nine

SHE'D NEVER SEEN a dead body. Somehow, Ffion expected it to look colder, almost gray. But the soft lamplight revealed the woman's still-pink complexion, as though the blood still flowed beneath her skin.

Tearlach lifted the limp form with almost no effort and stalked toward the woods. Ffion watched from the shelter of the building, unable to piece together what was going on.

Downed branches and dried leaves covered the forest floor, camouflaging the woman's body after Tearlach carefully placed it beside a fallen tree.

"You killed her," Ffion choked out when Tearlach returned.

Unfazed, he responded, "Yes, and I'll kill more if necessary. I guarantee she will not be the last."

"Who are you?"

"We need to leave this place." Ignoring her inquiry, he inclined his head, indicating that she follow him.

Ffion didn't move, didn't follow. She looked at the darkened area of packed earth near her feet. The scarlet-colored stain was hidden by night, soaking into the dirt as the rain continued, but there was no denying it was blood. Someone wanted Ffion dead and Tearlach had killed that someone. Though she'd seen it with her own eyes, the truth left her feeling disoriented.

"It's not safe here," Tearlach growled, striding back over to her. "You need to come with me."

Ffion retreated a step, her back hitting the wall behind her.

"Or do I need to carry you?" Tearlach arched a brow.

"No!" she cried. "I can't...I...Why did you..." She couldn't seem to form a coherent thought, but she was certain she didn't trust Tearlach and had no intention of following him anywhere.

"Now is not the time to explain. When we're safely away from the threat of assassins, you may ask all the questions you wish," Tearlach promised—though the look in his eyes seemed to amend the last part. "I'd rather keep the body count low."

Knowing she was on borrowed time, Ffion pushed away from the wall and followed. She wasn't ready to leave the protection of the man who'd saved her life.

The realization of that surprised her. He was the very person she'd planned to run from hours earlier. But in that moment, being near him seemed safer than being alone, or going back to where the attackers were surely looking for her.

They skirted the woods, staying far enough from the lights of the town. Ffion trailed a few steps behind. Tearlach continued to glance over his shoulder either from annoyance at her slower pace or because he suspected she might change her mind and run off.

Ffion tried to organize the horde of questions in her mind. So engrossed in confusion, she wasn't paying attention to where they were headed, and by the time she took in her surroundings, she was standing in a familiar gravel yard.

Tearlach slipped through the open door of his workshop, returning moments later with two large canvas bags. He carried a sword at his side, and though the metal only reflected the dim light of the distant streetlamps, Ffion could tell it was the worn, battle-scarred blade she'd seen in the secret back room.

She stood watching, unable to speak as he slid his sword through the leather strap at his back and pulled a saddle off the wall of the stable.

"It's time to leave." Tearlach finally looked at her, breaking the silence.

Leave? He couldn't mean...

Oh, no. He didn't plan to run from or wait out the attackers. He meant for them to leave Debarrow. For good.

Ffion cursed herself. Why hadn't she considered that Tearlach's plan might be more severe and permanent than anything she would have come up with herself? He wasn't from the mortal realm; he hadn't built a life there. He had no reason to stay.

It was finally clear why he'd kept to himself, why no one knew much about him. The man before her didn't care about the people of Debarrow. Tearlach, *the metalsmith*, wasn't real. His life was a disguise.

"I'm not leaving with you." Had he truly thought she would? "Just because you know who I am doesn't mean I'm required to trust you. I'm not going anywhere. This is my home."

"This is not your home," Tearlach countered. "And don't try to pretend that it is. Unfortunately for you, Princess, you don't get a say in this."

She hated the way he mockingly used that title, that he knew who she was. But she needed answers. So until she could figure out her next step, Ffion would attempt to stall the man who could easily pick her up with one arm and haul her off without a second thought.

"Who are they?" She gestured toward town and her abandoned home. "And how did they find me?"

"I would assume there's a sensor among them."

"Sensor?"

He exhaled, clearly irritated with her persistent need to understand what was going on. After scanning the area once more, he met her relentless stare. "We each have a magical signature from the time our magic awakens." He raised his brow, but she only furrowed hers. Tearlach took a breath and continued, "Those with the gift of sensing can detect that signature. More powerful sensors can even discern specific individuals based on that alone. Like yours." He strode toward the stable and opened one of the gates.

A magical signature? Ffion had never heard of such a thing.

Tearlach led a towering horse into the yard. She followed, set to demand that he explain further. Her building frustration toward the man was vying for more emotional and mental space than the threat of those seeking to kill her.

"How—"

"You were safe, hidden, before your magic began to manifest." He threw a saddle over the horse. "Now that it has awakened, I've been glamouring your signature. But even my power has limitations. When you use your magic, even unintentionally"—he glared down at her—"it breaks through the glamour and sends out a brief signal."

Not only did she possess a magical signature—something she hadn't been aware of moments earlier—but it could also be glamoured? And even though she couldn't feel it, there were Fae who could *sense* the invisible trait?

Tearlach seemed to read her thoughts. "I assume your parents were waiting to initiate you into the specifics of magic until *your* particular talents began to manifest."

Ffion blinked, trying to reconcile the deluge of new information. She opened her mouth, then closed it. There was so much she didn't know, so many questions to ask. Her mind stumbled across the closest one. "That means the fog…"

"Only glamoured your physical appearance, yes."

So despite the glamour, she could still be identified?

"I suspect your little *encounter*"—he narrowed his eyes—"with the wolf alerted someone to your presence in this land—someone who'd been waiting for the day when your beacon would finally go out into the world."

Ffion stared at Tearlach as he continued to ready his horse. She shook her head, as if it might dislodge some of her confusion. "Could a *sensor*"—her understanding of that particular ability was still a bit fuzzy—"pick up my signature from across the sea?"

From the look he gave her, it seemed he'd been considering the same. "Not likely."

Ffion swallowed, her throat suddenly dry. How long had they been scouring the mortal realm in search of her, waiting for the day when she could no longer hide?

"I assumed most had given up finding you when your twentieth year came and went without so much as a flicker of power. But your magic finally manifested, albeit late." Moving around the giant horse, he secured the packs to each side. "You have an unusual ability, as I'm sure you know." He cut her a glance.

She nodded, had suspected as much. Magic wasn't often used in Tremaene. Aside from daily conveniences of summoning or heating water, and lighting lamps, it was rarely needed. But she was quickly realizing how little she actually knew about the most vital trait her people possessed. Even with Cadwyn, who'd been fourteen years older, Ffion had only ever witnessed her air magic a handful of times.

"It was an accident," she defended. "With the wolf." One that had thoroughly frightened her.

"I know, and I'd hoped you'd be able to keep from slipping up again. But as an added precaution, I took steps to deter you from using it—lessening the chances of someone picking up your signal."

Ffion scowled at him. "By scaring me?"

"That was the plan, yes. Did it work?" His look told her he knew it had.

Looking away, she admitted in a quiet voice, "Yes." She hated him.

"It didn't matter." Tearlach shrugged his wide shoulders. "That short burst of magic was enough to get someone's attention. And now, Princess, it's time to go."

Ffion didn't know when the rain had stopped, but the wind suddenly picked up, swirling wet leaves through the yard. She brushed a damp curl from her forehead and looked around. The horse was saddled and ready. Her questions hadn't slowed his progress at all.

Ffion lifted her chin and met his intensely dark eyes. "Who are you, Tearlach?"

"Enough with the questions."

"Tell me." She clenched her jaw and dug her heels into the wet gravel. The wind lashed the heavy fabric of Cadwyn's cloak, sending a chill up her bare legs, making her aware that only a thin cotton nightdress covered her beneath. She tugged it closed, her fingers brushing against the object tucked inside her pocket.

Ffion could have sworn she saw a smirk on Tearlach's face, which only fueled her irritation.

He stepped toward her. "The longer we delay, the closer they get."

"Then you'd better talk fast."

He reached for her, but Ffion twisted away and pulled the dagger from its sheath, angling it up at Tearlach's chest.

He grinned. "What do you plan to do with that?"

Truth be told, she didn't know. Cadwyn had worn the dagger at her hip every day, but Ffion had never once seen her wield the weapon—wasn't even sure Cadwyn knew how. That wasn't true. Of course Cadwyn knew. A lady-in-waiting was always prepared to protect her charge.

Ffion held her hand steady. "I'll use it if I have to."

"No, you won't."

"You don't know what I'm capable of," Ffion threatened. She wasn't sure herself, but if she found herself trapped again, she'd fight back.

Tearlach's rich laugh encircled her, sending a shiver across her skin. "Sweetheart, you don't know what *I* am capable of."

Ffion stared at him, holding back a tremble that would surely betray her. She lifted the dagger another inch, closer to the center of his chest, waiting for him to speak, to answer the question he continued to evade.

"Fine. I'll tell you what's necessary. Then we leave." His words were clipped.

"Depends on what you tell me." Ffion put a step between them, her eyes never leaving his. She watched as his breath quickened and the muscle in his jaw went taut. She could almost see his frustration roiling beneath the surface.

He seized the dagger from her hand in a flash of movement.

Stumbling back, Ffion's breath caught in her throat, fearing he might turn the blade on her, that she'd finally pushed him too far. But Tearlach flipped the dagger and slid it into his belt beside the other.

He assessed her a moment longer before speaking. "Sully came to find me one day."

Sully? Captain Sullivan? Tearlach knew the captain of the royal guard? Hope bloomed in Ffion's chest at the mention of him.

"He informed me of his suspicions about the accident that had claimed the king and queen, and told me you were hidden away in the mortal realm. The captain needed someone to protect you and asked that I take a Lifeblood Oath."

A Lifeblood Oath? Perhaps it was similar to swearing one's life to a person or family—much like the royal guard pledged to crown and kingdom.

"What was the oath?" Ffion questioned when Tearlach seemed satisfied with his cryptic answer.

"It's a binding oath of protection that joins two people in life and death."

"Two people. You and I?"

He nodded.

She was bound to Tearlach? In life *and death*? Did that mean it could never be broken? Her heart sped up.

"It allowed me to track you here. I've kept watch over you since the day I arrived on the continent. And because your magic has since manifested, I've also concealed your signature."

When, exactly, had Tearlach arrived in Periwen? Six years in Debarrow, that much she knew. But had he been in the mortal realm before that? Ignoring her mind's insistent inquiries, she returned to the oath. "How was this *connection*," Ffion said, gesturing between them, unsure of what to call it, "created? I've never heard of such a thing."

"I hadn't either until that day."

She waited for him to continue, to explain how it had been done without her presence, but he seemed to think he'd offered enough. *Think, Ffion, think.* There was little time to consider her options. She needed to make a choice, if there was even one to make. Running had always been her first instinct, but she didn't stand a chance against well-trained Fae. So leaving on her own was no longer a viable option. Could she stay in Debarrow...somehow? She'd need to hide or leave for a short time until the assassins gave up and moved on. But she had to assume that whoever wanted her dead would send others to finish the job. More would surely seek her. Tearlach had said as much, and in that particular instance she happened to agree.

Staying would also put the townspeople in danger of something they knew nothing about. Ffion couldn't risk that.

"You can't leave on your own." Tearlach interrupted her thoughts. "Though you might have magic, it's untrained and untested. You wouldn't last more than a day against the Fae who are currently hunting you. And I'm sure you realize by now that staying here would only put each and every one of these humans at risk." He stared at her a moment. "These people have little to no defense against Fae."

The truth of the matter sunk in. She looked again at the bags he'd strapped to the horse and realized the contents of which had been packed before Tearlach had retrieved them from his shop. He hadn't been inside long enough to do anything more than collect them.

"Did you know they were coming for me?"

"I knew the enemy would eventually find you, yes." He held her gaze. "I've been prepared to leave at any moment since the day I arrived."

She still didn't know who the enemy was, but Tearlach seemed as much in the dark as she was on that point. Had she ever truly been safe in the mortal realm, or had she foolishly imagined it all those years?

"Okay," she conceded.

And with that single word, Ffion put her life in Tearlach's hands.

Chapter Ten

THEY BOTH TURNED as a cacophony rose from the town center. Shouts and screams were intertwined with the snarling of wolves. Their protection was likely misinterpreted as a threat, and Ffion hoped the hunters wouldn't have time to draw weapons on the creatures that had saved her life and were likely saving theirs as well.

Knowing they didn't have long, she eyed the two horses left in the stable. "Why can't I have my own horse?"

"It's safer this way, Princess." Tearlach mounted his steed. The look he gave her told her that it—or anything for that matter—was not up for negotiation.

She matched his glare.

Fine, she thought, clenching her teeth. But she refused his outstretched hand, unwilling to concede everything. Only the horse was far too tall, its flank nearly at her shoulder. She failed in her attempts to slip her foot into the stirrup. Where had Tearlach even procured such a towering animal?

It was clear Tearlach's irritation was winning the battle it had waged against his restraint. He let out a low growl, grabbed her arm, and pulled Ffion up in one swift movement.

She let out a small yelp as her behind met suddenly with the hard saddle. Her breath returned, but she tensed as Tearlach's forearm came around her waist. She was more than slightly uncomfortable with the instant propinquity between them, and tried to focus instead on her legs, squeezing them tightly around the width of the animal beneath her, trying to balance herself.

As the horse led them into the woods, Ffion twisted, hoping to steal one last glance at the place she'd chosen to call home, but Tearlach's massive chest and shoulders blocked her entire line of sight.

They crept slowly through the woods and Ffion was amazed at how little sound the giant beast made. Through the dwindling fog from the retreating storm, Ffion could barely make out the trail ahead. Tearlach didn't take it, nudging the horse farther west and avoiding the path completely.

Wise, she admitted silently. He was obviously better suited to the task of assessing surroundings and planning the most strategic course. She wondered what his profession had been back in Tremaene.

Once the clamor from town faded, Tearlach pushed the horse to a quicker pace, and soon they were racing through the forest. Trees flew by, and Ffion felt certainly she'd fall or be taken out by a low-hanging branch. She had nothing to grab hold of, except the arm that was wrapped around her. Reluctantly, she slid her hand over Tearlach's and held on.

———————

Golden light filtered through the canopy. Ffion struggled to keep her sleepy eyes open as she peered through the misty forest. They hadn't stopped all night. The sound of chirping crickets had melded into the calls of robins and mourning doves. Squirrels gave chase along branches, and bravely jumped from tree to tree. The sharp whistle of a chickadee drew her focus as she inhaled the beauty and peacefulness of it all, allowing the dewy scent of morning to awaken her senses.

Her nightdress clung to her skin, and the memories of the previous night flooded her mind. She squeezed her eyes shut, wanting to forget. She desperately needed something else to focus on.

"When are we going to stop?" Her voice was barely above a whisper. They hadn't spoken since leaving Debarrow.

"When it's safe," Tearlach replied in an equally hushed tone.

She was thankful he couldn't see her eye roll. What an answer.

Well, if he didn't stop soon, she might wet herself. Perhaps that would get his attention.

As though he could sense her discomfort, Tearlach pulled the horse to a stop. He dismounted and helped her down. Ffion allowed him to— either from weariness or at the sight of the great distance she'd tumble if she couldn't swing her tired leg just right.

"There." Tearlach pointed to a small outcropping thirty paces away. "Don't be long."

She resisted rolling her eyes again and silenced the choice words echoing in her head.

When she returned, Tearlach was waiting with his arms crossed over his chest, as if her small task had taken an eternity. She considered explaining that it was not as easy for women as it was for men, but decided not to fight that battle.

They resumed their hurried escape through the day. The deeper they ventured into the woods, the more Ffion relaxed. The sun had banished the darkness of night, her stomach was as good as full from the bread Tearlach had offered, and the eddies of her mind had slowed to a weak current. Animals kept close watch, making her grin each time a bird or small furry creature took interest as they traveled past. It comforted her to know she wasn't alone.

Ffion furrowed her brow, realizing how absurd that thought was. There was a man sitting right behind her. His thighs were pressed up against hers. She was anything but alone. It had become second nature for her to assume she was. But Ffion suspected she wouldn't be alone again for quite some time.

Tearlach didn't seem to notice the curiously observant wildlife. Or if he did, he didn't say. Ffion joked to herself that he was far too pompous to appreciate the beauty and life surrounding them.

Tearlach allowed a few pauses in the horse's run, granting the animal short breaks while he listened for anything unnatural hidden amid the sounds of the forest. He tended to veer the horse in a slightly different direction each time they resumed their canter.

Exhaustion fell harshly upon Ffion as the sun sunk lower in the sky. Her head continued to dip forward as she fought to keep her eyes open, wondering how much longer it would be until they were safe?

———————

It was early evening when they stopped for the night. Buttery yellow light flooded the forest floor as night phlox began to open, tickling her nose with a sweet mixture of vanilla, almond, and honey.

Ffion stayed near the horse as she was told. She might have argued had fatigue not consumed every muscle in her body. The sleek bluish-gray coat of the horse was soft against her hand. She reached up to stroke its neck, noticing the white spot on her forehead and the silvery streak contrasting her obsidian mane.

She heard Tearlach approach, no longer sneaking up on her as he once did—almost as if he was intentionally making his presence known so as not to startle her.

"What's her name?" she asked without turning.

"Whose name?"

"Your horse."

"The horse doesn't have a name. Don't fool yourself, Princess, anything can be taken from you. Never get attached."

Ffion exhaled her annoyance. It was sure to be a long night. She occupied her mind with possible names. The horse certainly deserved one after living with such an unpleasant man for so long. *Eimhir*, she decided, whispering it to the horse. It was perfect. The name meant "quick," which was fitting for the swiftness and stealth the magnificent animal possessed. She had, after all, managed to outrun Fae that were inhumanly fast.

When Ffion stepped away from the horse, she noticed a streak of rust-colored blood along the hem of her nightdress.

"I need a place to wash my things."

Tearlach moved around Eimhir to one of the saddlebags, ignoring her request. But when he returned to her side, he carried a stack of clothing in his arms.

"Here." He handed Ffion the garments, topping them with a pair of boots the color of brown sugar.

She stared at them for a long moment, trying to understand. They must have been someone else's—though she'd never seen Tearlach with anyone. Then again, she hadn't seen much of him at all until a few days prior.

"These are for me?"

"Who else would they be for?" Ffion scowled at him. He amended, "Yes, they're for you. And they should all fit."

They looked it, though she wouldn't be sure until she put them on. But how?

Her inquiring gaze provoked another response.

"I've been watching you for nine years."

A shudder went through her. If anyone else had uttered those words, she'd have gone running in the other direction. But Tearlach's voice did more than send shivers down her spine, it rendered her legs useless. He had a way of stripping her bare, making her feel as though she'd never had freedom or privacy, that her attempted solitude and safety had been nothing more than illusion, something easily shattered by the man who stood before her.

It also confirmed what she'd suspected—Tearlach had been in Periwen as long as she had, close enough to watch her when she'd explored the port towns along the western coast during her first year, searching for a way to return home.

Never in all her time in the mortal realm had she felt more alone than she had in those early weeks and months—before she'd joined the

Doghertys on their farm, before finding the orchard in Debarrow. Ffion had been completely alone in a strange land and Tearlach had been close enough to *watch* her? Without ever approaching or saying a word? He'd *allowed* her to be alone.

As much as she hated him for tearing her away from her home in Debarrow, she decided that she hated him more for keeping his distance. For keeping her isolated.

She hated him more for staying away.

It took a few deep breaths before she could meet his eyes again. "What's your real name?"

"My name is Tearlach. I've no enemies to hide from."

Fine. At least it was an answer. Though she could have done without the accusation that *she'd* done something to deserve enemies.

"And what were you before all this? Were you a metalsmith in Tremaene?" She imagined the beautifully crafted blades in his workshop—intricate designs covering the hilts, etched whorls flowing along the sharp silver.

"No. I trained warriors in the Tamslo Mountains."

Well, that explained his tact. And his arrogance. She knew little of the Tamslo Mountains or the territory north of it, just that a stronghold for the Tremaene army was located in the central valley. She'd seen it on an illustrated map that had once hung in her father's office. Altan, she recalled. That was the name of the fort.

Apparently Tearlach wasn't willing to offer more than that simple fact because he set about clearing a small area for a fire.

"I still need to wash up," Ffion reminded him.

He must have wanted the same thing. He grabbed a clean shirt from his pack and stalked past her.

"Come on."

Tearlach led them through thick brush. She couldn't see past the branches and the towering man ahead of her. When he finally stepped aside and held the last branch out of her way, Ffion's eyes fell on the shimmering waters of a crystal clear stream.

The spring was nestled in a gully, hidden by mossy rocks. Water trickled down larger rocks, then swirled through a wider section. River rocks lined the shore, allowing easy access.

Tearlach moved toward the bank, pulling his shirt off.

Ffion sucked in a breath as she watched the muscles across his back flex. She caught herself and shook the image from her mind, looking away quickly. Her cheeks flushed. Hopefully he hadn't noticed her stare.

She found a comfortable place to sit, pulled off her shoes, and began rubbing her feet. They weren't aching in the slightest—she'd been off them most of the day—but she kept her eyes downcast, stalling. She wouldn't look up and would certainly not undress while Tearlach was around.

A faint rumble came from the direction of the pool, sounding very much like a laugh. It took all of Ffion's willpower to keep from snapping her head up to scold him. She growled and clenched her teeth—quiet enough that he wouldn't hear—then focused more intently on the arches of her feet.

Was he finished with trying to frighten her? Had he moved on to making her uncomfortable? At least it distracted her from the threat that continued to stalk her.

She heard Tearlach emerge from the water. He came to stand in front of her, and she was grateful to see that he wore boots. Assured he was clothed, she slowly took him in—snug black pants, a smooth leather panel covering his torso, dove-gray shirt beneath, sleeves rolled to his elbows.

She watched as he ran a hand through his wet raven hair, slicking it back. It curled slightly at the back of his neck. If she wasn't set on hating the man, she might have found him attractive. She couldn't deny that his honed warrior body was a force she'd never seen the likes of before. If her mother and father had suggested she wed a man from Altan, her refusal would have been far less convincing.

"The light is fading." Tearlach's deep voice fractured her traitorous thoughts. "I won't be gone long. I suggest you wash up quickly."

She understood. If it was privacy she wanted, her time was limited.

"Do not leave this area until I return," he warned. "And never," he held her gaze, making sure she fully comprehended that his command was not to be taken lightly, "go off on your own. Understand?"

Ffion huffed out a breath and started toward the shore. Tearlach grabbed her chin and turned her to face him. The look in his eyes could have summoned a storm capable of destroying everything in its path.

"Understand?"

"Yes," she snarled.

He loosened his grip, looked her over once more, then stalked away.

Ffion made her way quickly to the water's edge, peeling her nightdress off as she went, not wanting to waste a minute to herself. Her once crisp, white clothing was soaked in sweat, stained with someone else's blood, and dirty from the dust she'd kicked up during her earlier escape.

Kneeling down near the water, she cupped her hands and drank for a good long minute. The water was frigid, but she waded in slowly, quickly acclimating as each part of her body sunk below the surface. The river rocks were smooth against her feet, and she was careful not to slip. Tiny fish darted around her legs, scattering with each step she took.

The middle of the stream was only waist-deep, so she lowered herself until the water reached her neck. She stayed submerged, the cold no longer affecting her. It felt more like a warm blanket, comforting, soothing her down to her bones. Ffion closed her eyes, moving her arms slowly through the current, then lifted her legs until she was floating. As her head tilted back, she opened her eyes to the canopy above, and the waning light of the evening sky. Not wanting to leave the smooth caress of the water, she swam toward the bank until the tops of her legs grazed the rocks.

She reached for her nightdress and pulled it into the water. Though the blood refused to wash away, it faded. She sat at the edge, her legs still in the water, and wrung out her clothing. As her skin dried, chills skittered across her naked body. Ffion cast a look to make sure she was still alone, then stood and carefully stepped onto the shore. She held the wet garment against her and scurried to the rock where she'd left her new clothes.

It didn't surprise her that Tearlach had planned for their escape and was ready to go at a moment's notice. It seemed he had a plan for everything, and likely several contingencies.

She slipped into the thick leggings—they fit snugly, buttoning up the side of her hip—then unfolded the olive green, tailored jacket, finding it long enough to reach her knees, with a slit down the back to accommodate their mode of travel. She held up what looked to be a heavy protective belt made of rigid, impenetrable material that could easily tie more than once around her midsection, then set it back on the rock.

Even the white linen shirt was made of tightly woven fibers and constructed better than any she'd procured in Periwen. *Where, exactly, did he get these clothes?* she thought as she pulled the tall boots up over her calves. They were made for warriors.

She grabbed the shirt off the rock when she heard the crunching of leaves behind her. Yanking it over her head quickly to cover her chest, she turned to find Tearlach approaching.

"I'm not done," she informed him.

"You look done to me."

Ffion scowled.

Tearlach jerked his head in the direction of their camp and walked away.

She gathered the rest of the clothing in her arms, then followed him begrudgingly.

He must have gone hunting in the time it had taken her to bathe; two dead rabbits were slung over his shoulder beside his quiver. Ffion watched as he set them on a flat rock near the pile of branches and twigs that would soon be a fire.

She couldn't tear her eyes away from the lifeless creatures.

"Don't touch them," Tearlach warned.

Pain pinched at the center of her chest, stemming from her back, between her shoulder blades. She could feel two distinct points— locations where each animal had been shot with an arrow. Ffion wondered how her magic worked, if there was a time limit on bringing something back to life.

Tearlach moved between her and the dead rabbits. He'd never let her near them.

Frustrated, Ffion gave up and searched the campsite, finding two bedrolls resting beside a fallen tree. Claiming one for herself, she unrolled it. The material felt as though it would keep even a torrential rain from seeping through.

After hanging her wet nightdress and still-damp cloak on a nearby branch, she picked up the wide belt and wrapped it around her waist, then tied the long bands together.

"Other way," Tearlach interjected.

Ffion gritted her teeth. Was he always watching her, even when occupied with another task? Presumably.

She twisted the belt so the widest part spanned her belly, then wrapped the ties around twice before securing them at the small of her back.

"What you did to the wolf, had it happened before?"

Though it was posed as a question, Ffion got the feeling Tearlach already knew the answer.

"No. That was the only time."

Tearlach grunted his satisfaction with her response, his eyes fixed on the growing sparks and smoking wood before him.

"I don't even know how I did it. I didn't know I *could* do it," Ffion admitted, hoping he might offer some insight.

Tearlach looked up. The silence between them stretched, and Ffion suddenly wasn't sure she wanted to venture into a conversation of any depth with him. Hastily, she pivoted to another topic. "I'm not eating a rabbit."

"Oh really? And what will the princess be having instead?"

Ffion could certainly do without the mocking tone; all it did was fuel her growing displeasure toward him. She responded by marching off into the woods to find something to eat.

Tearlach's growl reverberated off the trees a second before he was at her side, whipping her around to face him with no amount of gentleness.

"What part of this don't you understand? Those people want you dead and will continue to hunt you until they succeed." His eyes were wide, his jaw set.

Swallowing roughly, Ffion raised her chin. "How do I know *you* don't want me dead?"

His hands gripping her shoulders didn't loosen. He moved closer, staring down at her, using his size to intimidate her.

It was working.

"If I'd wanted you dead, you would be. And my life would be infinitely easier."

He released her and walked away.

The man was supposed to protect her; instead, he made her feel like she was an obligation.

Ffion didn't intend to wander far, knowing as well as Tearlach that threats drew closer the longer they stayed. She continually glanced over her shoulder as she searched, spotting a cluster of raspberry bushes. Ffion gathered two handfuls, then pulled a few wild carrots on her way back. She even managed to find a patch of mushrooms and some pecans scattered at the base of a tree.

The makeshift basket she'd made with the hem of her shirt below her belt was full by the time she returned. Tearlach glared at her through the flames as she brushed off a flat stone and arranged her trove atop it. She didn't return his look. He could stare all he wanted, they both knew full well that he'd known exactly where she was the entire time.

Ffion popped a raspberry into her mouth, then picked up another and held it out for him. A challenge. She even contemplated fluttering her lashes with the proffered fruit.

He didn't accept, just narrowed his eyes as he scanned the items she'd gathered. "You're almost as useful as a truffle-sniffing pig."

Her false smile faded. He definitely enjoyed infuriating her. *Fine. Let him.* She wasn't about to give up the animosity she harbored for him anyway.

After eating in silence—exceedingly aware that Tearlach observed her every move—Ffion moved onto her bedroll and asked where they were headed.

"Briganport."

Ffion thought for a moment. She'd heard of it, but had never made it that far when she'd traversed the western coast. Perhaps he needed to stop for supplies. She couldn't imagine they were far enough to safely stay for any length of time. Maybe they would head farther north after Briganport; there were bound to be many small towns between the northern coast and the Forest of Eoin's periphery.

Then she wondered—having not allowed herself to think on it before—why they hadn't gone south from Debarrow? There would have been far more options. The continent stretched on for weeks in that direction. She dropped the thought, knowing Tearlach must have had a reason, and as long as their escape would end at some point, she was fine with any town they'd eventually settle in.

Tearlach rose from his spot across the fire. When he pulled her dagger from his belt, every muscle in Ffion's body seized.

Then he flipped it in his hand and handed it to her, hilt first. "Keep this on you at all times."

She stared up at him before taking the blade, then set it carefully beside her on the ground.

But Tearlach didn't retreat. He stood there and raised his eyebrows as if to say, *On you, not near you.*

Ffion looked at the dagger, thinking for a moment what she could do with her own weapon, then picked it up and slid it through a small strap on her belt.

"Don't get any ideas, Princess." He walked away. Then, without turning, added, "Now, go to sleep," as if it were a command.

Overwhelming exhaustion struck Ffion. She could no longer keep her head up, her eyelids becoming heavy. She hadn't felt tired moments before. Some kind of magic? She managed to lie down on her mat before collapsing, unable to fight what her body demanded. She gave in to a yawn that relaxed her entirely. And when she glanced over to where Tearlach had resumed his spot near the fire, he watched as her eyes fluttered shut.

What have you done to me? she desperately wanted to shout, but deep, consuming sleep swept away her protesting thoughts.

Chapter Eleven

FFION FOUND HERSELF *beneath a midnight sky, circled by shadowy trees. She turned slowly, taking in the surroundings of the hauntingly familiar dream.*

A flicker of movement caught her eye. She turned as a gray owl draped itself on a low-hanging bough and folded its massive wings. Not a wolf that night, it seemed.

The feathered animal seemed to consider her for a moment.

Ffion waited, knowing she might not like what she'd be shown, but determined to heed whatever warning was given.

The owl dropped from the branch, swooping close to the ground as it stretched its wings to catch the air. Ffion followed the bird of night into the mist.

As the fog took her once again, she prepared herself for what was to come. Assassins...or worse?

But instead of a scene from the mortal realm, a vision from her past life rippled before her. The palace came into view as she floated toward the dimly lit chamber on the second floor. Gossamer curtains were drawn across the arched glass doors for the night.

Though it had been years since Ffion had walked the halls of her former home, she could still remember every detail. Simple gilding edged the white crown molding of the vaulted ceiling in her bedchamber. Sconces lined the walls, glowing softly against the lavender walls. Deep ebony floors were polished to a shine, offering a sort of comfort and warmth the marble throughout the rest of the palace couldn't provide.

A thick rug occupied the center of the room, edging the white stone hearth. Ffion could almost feel the soft pile between her toes as she gazed upon the scene from her vantage point. As she took in the room, she realized it wasn't precisely as she remembered. Her bed, with its spiraling posts, was untouched. Beside it sat a bassinet. Ffion willed herself forward until she hovered above a sleeping baby. The child's arms were draped above her head. So vulnerable.

Her attention strayed to the secret door at the far corner. Her mother stepped into the room with a man by her side—Captain Sullivan.

Ffion's eyes widened. Tears threatened as she gazed upon her mother. She was wrapped in a thick ivory robe, clasped by a silver and green brooch of intertwining leaves. Gold vines woven into the soft fabric shimmered in the light, and a hint of her mother's satin nightdress peeked through the open front. Her velvet slippers made no sound as she crept toward the bassinet.

It seemed peculiar that the captain was not in his typical royal guard regalia. He must have been off duty, for he wore only a tunic and fitted pants— though his worn leather sword belt was still fastened at his hips. Ever prepared to protect his queen.

Her mother lifted the baby, careful not to wake her, then laid her gently on the bed. Ffion shifted her position, angling to see the small pouch her mother produced from her robe. Inside was a gold chain with a small clear crystal that she coiled on the counterpane beside the child.

Ffion's confusion was mirrored by Captain Sullivan's expression. They watched intently as the queen unbuttoned the top of the child's sleeping clothes, pressed her thumb and forefinger together at the baby's chest, then pulled a strand of shimmering light away without touching or breaking the skin.

Ffion's hand went to her own chest, wondering what her mother had taken from her.

The queen held the necklace and let the glowing thread pool inside the hollow crystal. When the light faded, it looked as bloodred as a ruby. Her mother covered *her hands over the vessel and closed her eyes. Ffion drew closer, but couldn't distinguish the words of the spell her mother recited.*

When the queen opened her eyes again, she turned to the captain and handed over the necklace. He stared at the pendant for a long moment, as if he'd never seen anything like it. Ffion certainly hadn't.

"This crystal holds her lifeblood, Sully," the queen murmured as she closed her hand over his. "Now listen carefully. If you ever fear her life may be in danger, break the crystal and mix her lifeblood with that of her chosen protector's, then spill their joined blood into the flames of sandalwood, sage, and mugwort. Their souls will be united through this sacred Lifeblood Oath. They will be fated to protect one another—if one is alive, the other cannot die. But there is a limit to its range, so they must remain close at all times," she cautioned. "I trust you to choose her protector wisely, Sully."

Captain Sullivan nodded and lowered the chain around his neck. "But, My Queen, it seems too great a risk, keeping them near one another. If there were ever a threat to her life—even if her protector were the most powerful warrior who ever lived..." He paused, shaking his head. "My Queen, what would happen if both their lives were taken at once?" He waited for a response, but her mother gave none, only raising her eyes to meet his questioning gaze.

It was answer enough.

―――――――――――

Tearlach had the horse packed by the time Ffion opened her eyes the following morning. It seemed they'd be leaving before the sun had fully risen. Ffion pulled her shirt and jacket back into place before standing, then retrieved her nightdress from the branch where she'd left it to dry and wrapped it in her bedroll. Throwing her cloak over her shoulders, she walked to where Tearlach waited—arms crossed beside Eimhir.

"You could have woken me sooner," she accused at the sight of his clear impatience. He didn't say a word, just took the bedroll from her and secured the horse's pack.

The misty air not only welcomed morning calls from sparrows and bluebirds, it also summoned swarms of hungry biting bugs. Remembering the mint she'd come across the night before, she reached into her cloak, then rubbed the fuzzy green leaves along the exposed skin of her neck and chest.

Tearlach slapped his arm and grumbled something beneath his breath. Ffion considered letting him stay miserable, but thought it best not to anger her protector. She found another bunch in her pocket and offered it to him.

"Here. It'll keep them away."

Tearlach's expression looked like he was trying to reason whether the gesture was genuine kindness or a trick. He finally accepted the leaves and turned away, rubbing them up his arms and across the corded muscles of his neck. Then he mounted his horse without even uttering a thank-you. Reluctantly, Ffion took his outstretched hand.

After riding in silence for some time, Tearlach remarked, "The animals certainly seem interested in you."

The fauna had taken an interest in her again, and it seemed Tearlach wasn't as blind to their behavior as he'd been the day before.

"Are they? I hadn't noticed."

"Yes, you have noticed."

Damn him. Why did it always seem like he could read her thoughts?

"Perhaps it's because I don't hunt them."

Tearlach was quiet for a few breaths. Had she truly placated him with that response? Then she wondered if he suspected she was controlling the animals? She didn't feel anything—not a flicker of the sensations she'd felt before bringing the wolf back to life. Then again...she hadn't felt anything strange when the tree branch caught her from the fall. Ffion didn't *think* she'd commanded it. Could magic operate independent from a magic wielder? There was so much she still didn't understand.

"I'm not using my magic, if that's what you're worried about."

"I know."

He knew? How? Could he feel her magic? Was it somehow entwined with the connection that bound them to one another? She suppressed a shiver.

She desperately needed to glean more information from the less-than-loquacious man at her back. If his explanation aligned with her dream, then perhaps she could begin to trust him.

"Maybe they just fancy me," she hedged.

"Something like that."

Ffion wondered why Captain Sullivan had chosen him out of everyone in Tremaene. Why hadn't he just accepted the Oath himself, or selected a member of the royal guard—someone she at least knew?

"Tell me more about the Lifeblood Oath."

"What of it?"

Ffion gave an inward growl. Did he have to make it so difficult? "Why did Captain Sullivan choose you?"

"How would I know? I'm not privy to the workings of his mind."

Couldn't he at least speculate? Surely Tearlach had been given a reason. Ffion couldn't imagine Tearlach swearing a binding pledge and leaving everything behind without some sort of persuasion.

"Okay..." She moved on. "Then how did you swear the Oath? What was involved?"

"My blood was mixed with yours and spilled over a fire." He described the ritual as if it were such a common thing to do.

"My blood?" She feigned surprise. "How did the captain obtain *my* blood?"

"He wore a ruby around his neck. The crystal contained it. How he procured your blood, I do not know."

"A crystal?" Her voice rose as if she were hearing it for the first time.

"That's right."

At least his account sounded accurate.

"How did it feel? Once the ritual was completed?" she questioned cautiously, assuming Tearlach wasn't the type to tell anyone how he felt. Ever.

He tensed behind her and Ffion could tell he was holding his breath.

When he exhaled, he remained silent for a moment before replying, "It felt like a cord was being tightened, pulling me toward something."

She gave him a moment before she ventured her next question. "And that's how you were able to find me?"

"Yes."

"Do you still feel it, this cord between us?"

"Not when I'm near you."

She could tell there was more he wasn't telling her, but decided not to press him any further.

Salty air and the overwhelming smell of fish struck Ffion before she could see or hear the water as they came upon Briganport.

Tearlach reached back into one of the saddlebags, leaving Ffion without support for a moment. She leaned forward to keep from falling back into him. When he returned to his upright position, he brought an arm around to offer an apple.

She snatched the fruit from his hand and held it in front of her. "One of my apples?" Instead of a response, she heard a crunch as Tearlach bit into his.

Ffion turned it over in her hand, memorizing the eddying chartreuse across the vermilion surface of its skin. Holding it to her nose, she inhaled deeply, realizing it was the last of her fruit she'd ever taste. The last *apple* she'd ever taste.

The town came into view. It reminded Ffion of Rhoswen Harbor, where she'd originally come ashore. But Briganport had more sturdy-looking buildings with slate roofs and stone chimneys. Weathered paint chipped from the fronts of buildings along the main road, their heavy shutters thrown open to the sea air.

Tearlach pulled Eimhir to a stop outside a long building. The once cobalt exterior had faded to a soft cornflower blue. A wooden sign hung above the door with the word *Inn* carved into it.

As Tearlach tied the reins to the rail outside, he informed Ffion that she was to get a room inside and wait for him to return.

"Where are you going?" She tried to hide the eagerness in her voice—wouldn't want him to think she delighted in being rid of him.

"There are things I must see to."

Not an answer, as usual. Ffion turned on her heel and marched up to the front door, looking over her shoulder before she went inside. Tearlach was waiting for her, making sure she did as she was told. Muttering a few words under her breath, she stepped into the small foyer. There was a long desk at the other side of the narrow room, with a hallway stretching toward the back, ending at the beginning of a curving staircase. Ffion crept slowly through the quiet space. A large sitting room opened to the left, and the double doors opposite likely led to a tavern. The hearth was lit, giving the room a warm, inviting feel. Midday light poured into the room through wide windows that offered a charming view of the harbor.

The doors to the tavern swung open and a tall woman with silvery hair pulled back into a chignon moved behind the desk with a swiftness Ffion wouldn't have expected from a mortal woman of her age.

"How can I help you, miss?" Her pleasantly melodious voice filled the room.

"I need a room, please."

"Just you?"

"Yes, that's right." Tearlach could get his own room whenever he returned from wherever he was, doing whatever it was he was doing. She reached for the purse she'd managed to grab before fleeing her home. Not wanting to reveal just how heavy with gold it was, she felt around for a smaller coin and withdrew a single silver, sliding it across the counter.

After taking the money with her long, thin fingers, the woman pulled a ledger and pen from a drawer and began writing.

"Your name?"

Her name? Was it safe to give her name…either of her names?

The woman looked up from the book and tilted her head to the side, narrowing her eyes.

Ffion pulled out two gold coins—enough to rent all the rooms in the inn for an entire month. The woman's eyes widened for a second before she swiped them up and shut the ledger. Gold was gold, and the innkeeper didn't seem to mind the hammered faces that had once bore Tremaene's emblem.

"Right this way, miss."

Ffion was led up the stairs and down the hallway, back toward the front of the building. The innkeeper stopped at the last door, unlocking it with an ornate key dangling from an emerald green tassel. The woman held it out for Ffion.

"Thank you."

"Of course, miss." The woman nodded and left her alone.

Inside the room that dwarfed her tiny home in Debarrow, she removed her cloak and jacket, throwing them across the chest at the foot of the bed, then moved to the front window. She unlatched it, and the call of gulls instantly filled the room. The bed sat in the corner, but was angled out toward the center of the room. Ffion leaned against the edge, where she could see the waves as they frothed upon reaching the rocky shore. Boats wobbled back and forth, bumping into the long piers that held them.

While gazing at the peaceful scene, she spotted Tearlach conversing with a man at the dock. He had a bushy gray beard and wore a faded red hat, and was gesturing toward something farther down the shore.

Ffion might have tried to discern what was being discussed, but Tearlach seemed fully engaged in negotiations and she wasn't about to waste the opportunity.

She pulled on her jacket, grabbed the key, and headed back toward the woods.

Ffion wandered through the trees, relaxing more and more with each step, savoring the feeling of being alone again—even if she could only afford to do so for a brief time.

Her outstretched hands grazed rough bark as she wound her way through the maze of trees.

Her ears perked up. She wasn't alone.

She clenched her jaw, realizing that Tearlach must have followed her. Was she not allowed a few moments to herself? Ffion whirled around, ready to confront him.

Her heart stopped the moment she saw Carrick standing before her.

Chapter Twelve

"CARRICK," SHE WHISPERED, unsure if he was actually there, standing in front of her.

"Ffion." Her name was a caress on his lips, like he was dying of thirst and she the only thing that could quench it.

He lunged forward, wrapping her in a fierce embrace as Ffion struggled to make sense of his presence. What was he doing there? Had he followed her all the way from Debarrow?

He'd expect an explanation, but what could she possibly say? Her thoughts circled back to the excuse she'd fabricated the night she'd fled, when she thought she could leave Debarrow on her own terms.

Tearlach had taken her north instead of south as she'd planned, but perhaps the pretense of an ill relative or a friend who desperately needed her assistance would still suffice.

Had Carrick seen her with Tearlach? How would she account for the fact that she was traveling with a man she barely knew—a man who Carrick, and most people of Debarrow, seemed tentative of?

Carrick leaned back, holding Ffion at arm's length. She watched as his gaze raked over her, searching every inch. He looked haggard, she noticed, as if he'd not slept in days. Even without any indication that she'd been hurt, he pinned her with a penetrating stare and asked, "Are you all right? What has he done to you?"

He knew about Tearlach, then—clearly believed that the metalsmith abducted her. That Ffion had played no part in it—an innocent victim. Innocent she certainly was not. It might not have been her choice to leave with Tearlach, but it was because of her that assassins had invaded the town. *She'd* put the townspeople at risk.

Ffion had no idea what to say to Carrick, and the pressing reminder that Tearlach wasn't far and would soon track her down set her pulse pounding at her temples. "Carrick." She decided to stall. "H-how did you find me?"

A look of betrayal flashed in his eyes. His look made her realize that he'd expected her to blindly take his hand and run off with him. After considering her for a moment he stepped back, letting his hands slide away from her.

He explained that he'd been riding back into Debarrow on the northern road when he'd heard an uproar. "It sounded as though a pack of wolves had descended on the village. So I quickened my pace, needing to be sure you were safe." Carrick fisted his hands at his side. Ffion knew he wanted to reach for her again. "But as I raced toward the commotion, I passed Tearlach's property and caught a glimpse of him leading his horse into the forest with a woman seated in front of him. I recognized the cloak." He assessed her clothing then—pants, boots, and a jacket, none of which were hers. "I knew it was you, even in the dark. I watched him steal you away."

Rage flared anew in his eyes. He took her in once again, assuring himself that he'd found her, that she was real.

"At first, I thought it was best to follow quietly, thinking I might get you alone. But when he sped up, I lost you. I kept the same heading, knowing he'd need to stop eventually." He scanned their surroundings. "Then early this morning, when I stopped for water, I found a small pair of canvas shoes near a riverbank." *Her shoes.* She'd forgotten them. "There were remnants of a fire nearby. I knew you were close, and Briganport is the only town this direction."

He hesitated a moment, then pulled her into another crushing hug. "Where is he now, Ffion? How did you escape? Are you sure he hasn't followed you?" His words came out in a rush.

"Carrick—"

"Ffion, we don't have much time."

She could tell he was seconds from pulling her away. Did all men think the best option was to haul a woman over their shoulder and carry her to safety?

"Are you hurt? You must be tired. Do you have the energy to walk?" He released her only to put his arm around her shoulder, guiding her farther from town.

"Of course I can walk." She pushed away from him. He seemed surprised by her abruptness. He'd come to rescue her, after all. A pang of guilt furled in her stomach, inching its way toward her chest.

"We must hurry. He'll soon find you missing and set out to recapture you."

He most certainly would, though not in the way Carrick imagined.

And Tearlach wasn't the only one searching for her.

"It's not what you think. He's trying to protect me." Her explanation sounded weak even to her ears.

Carrick's lips parted. He studied her face for a long while, clearly bewildered by the statement. She only hoped he believed it.

"Protect you? By kidnapping you? You have no idea what his intentions are," Carrick accused. "I was right not to trust him," he muttered to himself.

"He was protecting me," she repeated with a bit more conviction. "Protecting me from...the attacks."

"You think the wolves were after you?" He chuckled, visibly relaxing. "Ffion, he probably used the wolf attacks as a distraction to take you away."

When his teasing laugh didn't defuse the situation as he'd surely intended, his smile faded.

Ffion lifted her chin, pulling a cold, impassive veil over her features.

"Ffion, if that's truly what you're worried about, I'll protect you."

"But you can't." She stared at him for a moment and decided she could convey a portion of the truth. "You don't know who I am, Carrick. Or where I came from, and why I needed to run away."

"Run away? You chose this?" Carrick shook his head, dismissing the notion, then closed the distance between them. "Then tell me," he urged. "Tell me everything and we'll figure this out. Together."

"I...can't do that." She averted her eyes. "And it's not safe for you to be here."

He surveyed the area again, likely assuming Tearlach was the implied threat. The only threat.

He was inches from her, his face deadly serious as he asked, "Ffion, what happened between the two of you? Did he threaten you? What did he say to make you abandon your life?" His eyes searched hers for the truth.

"Debarrow isn't the first life I've left behind," she told him.

"You never told me—" He waved away the revelation. "Even so, you don't have to leave this life behind." He clasped his hands around hers.

If only it were possible to stay. To live the life she wanted. But the past had caught up with her. She feared it always would.

Carrick waited for a response—so intent on having her, keeping her.

"I know that's what you want, Ffion. Let me take you home." A hint of a smile curved the corners of his lips. Such a familiar sight.

But Ffion put up a hand to stop him. "Carrick, I'm not like you. I have...magic." She held her breath.

He lifted a brow. "Magic? Like in fairy tales?"

She bit her lip.

"Magic doesn't exist, Ffion. Come, you've been through quite an ordeal, you're not thinking clearly. Let's go home and we'll figure everything out." He reached for her arm, ready to take her away.

"No!" she cried, surprising herself with the punctuated command.

Carrick took a step back and raised his hands as though she were a frightened animal.

Ffion cast a quick look around them, knowing Tearlach had probably found her gone and would soon appear.

"The people who were attacked by the wolves—not the townspeople, but the others... Carrick, they're not from here. They were searching for me. The wolves bought me time to escape, and Tearlach saved me when I couldn't outrun them. It's no longer safe for me in Debarrow, and it's not safe for you to be near me." Ffion took a breath, softening her tone. "It's not safe for you to *know* me."

She studied his face, hoping for an inkling of understanding. But the kindness and compassion she expected weren't there. Instead, she saw only rage and jealousy—emotions she'd never seen in Carrick's eyes.

"Really?" His reply dripped with contempt. "Those are the lies you're going with? At least tell me the truth."

Ffion blinked, her lips parting. What more did he want?

"If you'd rather be with that brute of a man than me..." The muscles in his jaw bulged when Ffion didn't deny his assumption.

Her chest felt like it was being cleaved open, but she knew it was for the best to let him believe the lie. She knew he'd never accept the truth. He couldn't understand it. And it would only infuriate him further if she tried to explain that she wasn't human, but glamoured to look so, that she was the only surviving heir to the immortal realm across the sea, and was being hunted by the same people who'd no doubt killed her parents—the king and queen of a kingdom mortals didn't even know existed.

No. The lie would keep him safe. And if she could bear to say one more lie—the one thing that would guarantee he'd walk away and never look back—she might keep him from danger. Even if it meant he'd hate her forever.

Meeting Carrick's accusing gaze, she said, "I could never love you, Carrick." She swallowed past the lump in her throat and delivered the final blow. "It's always been him."

She watched a myriad of emotions fight for control—anger, distrust, longing…defeat.

Carrick's gaze raked over her once more. Ffion averted her eyes, unable to endure his disapproval.

She heard him turn to leave and raised her head, watching as he stalked away, moving swiftly toward his horse. He didn't spare a final glance as he took off into the woods, leaving her alone.

Ffion's heart sunk as she collapsed on the forest floor. Tears threatened as she drew her knees in and cradled her head in her hands.

A branch snapped.

Tearlach had finally come to reprimand her. Ffion used what little strength she had left and struggled to her feet. She welcomed the distraction of anger.

Only it wasn't Tearlach.

A figure crept slowly—methodically—through the trees. Searching. He wore black leather, with fine, iridescent chainmail. The woman who'd pursued Ffion back in Debarrow had worn the same, with silver cuffs up her forearms, and curved blades strapped to her thighs.

But Tearlach had sworn that her magical signature was glamoured, untraceable. How had they found her so quickly?

Carrick.

He'd unknowingly led them right to her.

Chapter Thirteen

FFION COUNTED FOUR of them before dropping back to the ground. How many had she seen in Debarrow? Clearly some had escaped the wolves' lethal jaws. Or perhaps more had joined. There could have been dozens scouring the mortal realm in search of her.

She pressed her hands to the ground, gripping the vines curled beneath dried leaves, listening for sounds of a quickened pursuit. But the assassins' hunt remained slow and steady—thorough.

Her sage green jacket offered a bit of camouflage, and a few low branches blocked her from view. She crawled quietly over to a cluster of large rocks. Perhaps she'd discover a hidden cave beneath the lichen-covered refuge. She'd gladly crawl inside if it meant she'd be safely tucked away from the encroaching danger. The boulders were no taller than her waist, yet safer than standing out in the open. And she knew firsthand that outrunning them wasn't an option.

Ffion put her back to the large rock and curled her knees to her chest. She was still far too visible. If anyone got within ten paces, they'd see her. Maybe she *should* run. If she headed back to Briganport, toward the inn or the docks, there was a chance they wouldn't follow. Certainly exposing themselves to mortals wasn't something they'd willingly do. Although Ffion suspected they were desperate after their failed attempt in Debarrow. She couldn't safely speculate what they were or were not willing to do in order to capture her.

Or kill me.

She stifled a whimper. Where was Tearlach?

Shit. Her dagger was sitting on top of her cloak back at the inn. The only weapon she had and she'd failed to keep it on her. It wasn't much use in her hands, but could've given her a chance should anyone get too close.

If she survived, she'd surely receive a lecture about not keeping the dagger with her.

Ffion couldn't see anything from her position, though it sounded as if they were heading farther away.

Rising to a crouched position, she peeked over the top of the rocks.

Then dropped to the ground so quickly she was certain they'd heard.

They weren't moving farther away. They were closing in on her.

Even if she ran, they'd catch her before she could get anywhere remotely safe or defensible. She pressed her back against the rock and closed her eyes, curling her hands into fists as she silently waited.

Boots crushed dead leaves. Drawing nearer. The whack of a sword against a branch made her heart stutter—imagining it might be used on her.

Squeezing her eyes shut tighter, she gave a quick prayer to the gods that she might be spared. Why hadn't they gifted her with fire magic, or something more useful in a fight?

Leaves rustled inches from her.

Her eyes shot open.

But it wasn't an approaching assassin. She watched in wonder as the forest began moving around her.

The brambles beside her began to grow wider, taller. Their branches—once sparse—sprouted new blades that unfurled and expanded into deep emerald leaves. The dead leaves carpeting the forest floor shifted as creeping vines slithered from their resting place to find her legs. Ffion didn't dare move as they climbed her limbs, wrapping around her midsection and shoulders, then down her arms.

When the vines and leaves covered every inch of her, she released her breath, easing into the flora's embrace.

She was hidden. Completely and entirely hidden.

When the sound of footfalls came close again, Ffion knew they'd never find her. The forest was protecting her, just as the wolves had.

She remained there long after her pursuers retreated. Not only to make certain they'd truly moved on, but because she felt safe, hidden from the world. Secretly tucked away where no one could find her.

She wasn't sure how much time had passed when she finally assessed the protective suit of greenery that encased her. Eventually she'd need to free herself. If she wiggled about a little, perhaps she could—

Ffion froze as she felt, rather than heard, something nearing her. The air seemed to resonate—vibrating and flowing, searching and prodding.

She tried to peer through the layers of vines and leaves, even as she knew her efforts were futile.

Something tugged at her. Something inside her. It wasn't uncomfortable, just...strange, unfamiliar. A heaviness settled in her chest, feeling similar to anger. Or perhaps it was...panic?

The wolf? Had the wolf somehow found her? Had he come to warn her again?

It's a little late for that, she thought.

The vibration intensified and the pulling sensation became more urgent.

The vines were ripped away in an instant.

Ffion screamed.

She sighed when Tearlach came into view.

He towered over Ffion, a furious scowl on his face. And was that...a hint of relief in his eyes? It was gone before she could be sure.

"You were not to leave." His voice was steady, yet so taut with rage that she knew he'd snap if she so much as breathed wrong.

Tearlach inhaled deeply, like he was prepared to deliver a diatribe, but his eyes widened and he yielded a step as the branches surrounding Ffion parted and the vines receded along the ground.

Taking advantage of the momentary diversion, she pushed herself up and ducked past Tearlach.

It took only a second before Ffion felt him at her side again.

"What did I tell you? I can't glamour your signature when you use magic. Do you realize how stupid that was?"

She whirled around and glared up at him, jabbing her finger in the center of his chest. "I did *not* use my magic."

"Then what was that?"

"I don't know." Ffion met his angry stare, refusing to be the first to back down.

He considered her a moment, then grabbed her wrist and yanked her toward the main road.

"I can't protect you when you wander off like that."

Ffion shook off his grip. "I was fine the entire time." *Sort of.*

"Really? Is that why you were cowering like a little girl in the bushes? And don't bother lying to me, although I'll admit you've gotten rather good at it."

Ffion stormed ahead. It took two of her strides to equal one of his, but the vain attempt at outpacing him was satisfying, even if only for a second.

He met her an instant later, grabbing her by the shoulder and turning her to face him. "Look. I'm in charge here, Princess."

Ffion hated that name, but in that moment, it sparked something inside her. She was ready for a fight. Needed one. After lying to Carrick, breaking his heart, hiding from people who wished her dead, then being lectured to, she wanted to fight back. Anger was tangible, something she could grab hold of.

A fight with Tearlach would likely never be fair, but at least she knew he wouldn't leave when it was through. No matter what she said or did. That realization gave her a perplexing sort of comfort.

His large, calloused hands were still wrapped around her small shoulders. He leaned closer, holding her gaze. "I left my life behind to protect a girl who couldn't fight for herself, so you'll do as I say."

If she'd had her dagger, she would've pulled it on him. "*You* left your life behind?" She sucked in a breath, ready to explode.

But her rage slipped through her fingers before she could grasp it fully.

What about her? She'd left people behind, *all* of her people. She'd desperately wanted to stay in Tremaene, had argued relentlessly against leaving. But Ffion had woken up in a world she didn't recognize. She'd been given no choice. Even if Tremaene were ever safe enough for her to return, she wouldn't go back. She had nothing to return to. She no longer had a home, not in Tremaene. Not in Debarrow.

Tears rolled down her cheeks. She didn't wipe them away.

Tearlach loosened his grip, then removed his hands carefully.

She didn't try to hide what she felt. She couldn't. There was nothing left inside with which to paint a stony look on her face.

Their gazes held—neither saying a word—and Ffion wondered if he knew just how close to her heart he'd cut with those words.

She looked down, but made no move to step away.

No one would ever grasp what it was like to live her life, not fully. For nine years it had been a constant battle between the memories of Esme's past and the life she'd tried to lead as Ffion. It was a struggle every morning when she woke in a strange land, with no family and no place to call home.

Eventually, she looked up at Tearlach again, and it seemed as though he understood just how fragile she was, and that one more triggering remark might shatter her completely.

When she turned and walked on, Tearlach left her to herself for a few minutes before joining her, matching her weary strides.

"Did you know Carrick was following us?"

"Yes." His voice was softer than before.

"Why didn't you tell me?"

"He wasn't a threat." She glanced up at him, but Tearlach simply shrugged his shoulders. "And I thought you could handle him yourself, should he get you alone."

For that, Ffion was grateful. She didn't want to think what would've erupted between the two men otherwise.

"What did you tell him?"

"Another lie, since I'm so good with those." She arched a brow, attempting levity, but the truth of the words stung.

"One that will keep him away for good?"

"Yes." She swallowed, not wanting to think of how badly she'd hurt Carrick.

"Good."

They fell into silence until Tearlach mentioned, "I took care of them, by the way."

"The assassins?"

"Yes."

"I didn't hear anything." She glanced over at him. He stared back, but didn't respond. She understood—he was very good at what he did. A shudder went through her as she thought about what he might be capable of.

"How did you find me?"

Ffion saw the muscle in his jaw tense before he spoke. "I mentioned how I'm able to track you."

"Right, the Lifeblood Oath." She nodded, knowing there was more to it. If he could track her, why hadn't he come to find her as soon as he'd felt her leaving the inn?

"We're leaving Periwen in the morning."

Ffion nearly stumbled. "Where are we going?" Her voice was barely more than a whisper. She hoped he wouldn't say the word she dreaded.

"You know where."

"Tremaene?" she breathed, looking up at him, praying to the gods that that wasn't what he intended.

Tearlach said nothing, just kept walking.

"I don't understand." She shook her head. "If you killed the Fae that were after us, why do we need to leave?" Maybe she could convince him to let her stay.

"More will find us. You were never meant to remain here forever. And it's time to return home."

Home? She didn't have a home.

"But we can't. It's not possible. I've tried. We'll get turned around. Mortals aren't meant to find our lands," she said frantically.

"Then it's a good thing we aren't mortals."

Ffion scowled. "And just how do you plan to accomplish such a feat?"

"It won't be a problem. I've done it before." Tearlach looked down at her. "And so have you."

True. She'd made it across the sea, but had assumed it was an anomaly—that she'd happened upon a breach in the barrier that separated the mortal and immortal realms. There'd be no way for them to find that spot again.

And even if it could be done, she wasn't leaving. There was no way she'd return to Tremaene. Not ever.

"I'm not going back," she told him, coming to a stop.

"Yes, you are." He grabbed her by the elbow. "This is not up for discussion."

There was the warrior again. It seemed he hadn't vanished for long.

She refused to move. If she gave an inch, how much more would he take?

But his resolute stare didn't waver either, and Ffion's body betrayed her. Her breathing turned ragged and her knees started to shake. She was too close to breaking again.

Tearlach shifted his gaze, looking her up and down, then released her. He yielded a step to give her space, clearly realizing how his merciless tactics affected her.

Ffion turned and hurried toward the inn, not stopping when the woman at the desk inquired about a meal.

She was well aware that Tearlach followed as she climbed the stairs and made her way to her room. She couldn't fight the tremble in her hand as she held the key, and only managed to unlock the door on her third try.

Without acknowledging him, she slammed the door behind her.

The tall bed gave slightly when she climbed atop it. But she was too restless to sit, so she walked over to the window and placed her hands against the cool glass.

She stared, transfixed, at the waves lapping along the shore. The rhythm soothed her nerves, though the sight of the sea—and where it would lead—should have evoked worry instead.

Ffion didn't turn from her spot at the window when the door finally opened, then softly clicked shut.

Chapter Fourteen

"WHY CAN'T YOU go back?" Tearlach asked, the slats of the bed groaning as he sat down.

Silence stretched between them, before Ffion finally admitted, "I don't know how I got here. I was staying in Donellis with my lady-in-waiting, Cadwyn. We were there to take lessons from the masters in the artist quarter." She stared at her reflection in the glass, imagining Cadwyn standing beside her—her long crimson braid hanging over her shoulder. Ffion shook the impression from her mind and continued. "Captain Sullivan visited one night. He told me what had happened and that it wasn't safe for me in Tremaene, that I needed to leave. I protested—that much I remember—but next I knew, I was on a fisherman's boat, soaking wet and alone. I wasn't sure where I was, thinking I might have been somewhere along the southern coast, south of Donellis. Until I saw myself in a mirror. That's when I realized just how far from home I actually was. I waited in that little town for weeks, assuming the captain would come to retrieve me—like he'd promised." She stole a glance at Tearlach, who watched with an impassive expression as he listened. "When he didn't, I assumed something had gone wrong, so I tried to return on my own. I spent the better part of a year traveling up the coast, stopping at every port town and harbor—any place with a boat I could rent or borrow. I'd row out for hours, just to get turned around. Every time the shore dipped from view, it would appear again shortly after. I don't know how it happened. It must have been the fog keeping me from crossing back over to the immortal realm. But I kept trying, hoping I'd find a weak spot in the barrier. I refused to believe that I was trapped in this foreign place forever.

"I never gave my true name, never told anyone who I was. The mortals had two names, not just the one. Their second names didn't sound like any I'd ever heard. I came to find out that they were surnames, to identify their families. Strange, seeing as this land is so small. I can't imagine there would be any confusion. Ainsley and Ffion were characters in one of my favorite books..." She trailed off, thinking of the girls' adventures. In one of the stories, they'd found a secret book containing magical spells that had been lost to time, hidden at the base of an ancient tree.

When she was young, her mother would read Ainsley and Ffion's stories to her each night.

"I was never supposed to be a queen." Ffion's voice was small. "My parents were never supposed to die." She clenched her teeth, trying to keep the tears from coming again. "When I accepted that no one was coming for me—that I would never escape this place—I let go of Esme and everything she was. I let go of Tremaene. I gave up on my people, Tearlach." She turned to him. "I left them and then I just *gave up*. I should have tried harder. I should have kept fighting. I could have found a way to return, I'm sure of it. I quit too soon, too easily. How can I ever face them again? After all this time? They deserve better than me. They deserve someone who would never forsake them. They deserve someone who would have fought for them." She swallowed past the sharp, stabbing pain in her throat. "I'm not that person."

There it was. She'd finally said it. After a long exhale, she awaited Tearlach's reply.

When he spoke, his voice was calm, almost soothing. "Do not blame yourself."

She opened her mouth to refute his statement, but Tearlach held up a hand. "You were the only surviving heir to the Fae kingdom and were far too precious to remain in such a dangerous situation when the enemy had not yet been identified. Sully knew his place was in Meallán, with the royal guard. He needed to use his position as captain to uncover the truth about your parents' deaths. He wanted to accompany you, to see you here safely, to protect you. Believe me, I saw it in his eyes the day he arrived in Altan. I could see how much it pained him to let you go, not knowing when or if he'd ever see you again. But he understood that remaining in Tremaene offered the best opportunity to discover and infiltrate the enemy...until you were strong enough to return."

Strong enough?

"Magic." Tearlach answered her unspoken question. "Were you to have stayed in Tremaene before your magic awakened, you would have been far too vulnerable against whatever force overthrew the ruling power. He couldn't risk it."

"He couldn't risk losing the crown," Ffion corrected.

"You're not just a crown and you know that's not why he got you out."

She knew. Captain Sullivan had always been more than a guard. He'd cared for her as if he were her father.

"If Sully couldn't get word to me here in Periwen, I vowed to return with you once your magic came in. I'd hoped we would've had time to train your particular abilities, but circumstances haven't allowed for that. After you restored life to the wolf, I sensed a shift in the air, as if we were no longer the only Fae on the continent."

"Why didn't you approach me sooner? Why did you let me believe I was alone?"

"Sully knew he might not be able to retrieve you as promised, and he didn't want you to spend years waiting. He didn't tell you of his plans because he wanted you to have a life, to be free from the worry and responsibility for as long as you could—to have a normal, uncomplicated existence. I swore that I would keep you here and remain at a distance for as long as I was able."

She'd had a life, one she very much liked. But she couldn't help wondering if it would have been easier to know what was coming. Would she have purchased the orchard and coaxed the barren trees back to life, or would she have spent her time wandering the countryside, keeping to herself, never staying long enough to get acquainted with anyone? Were the last few years of peace worth the pain of leaving it all behind?

Ffion closed her eyes and forced out a breath. She could easily fall into a bottomless well of guilt and possibilities if she wasn't careful. And she wasn't sure she had the strength to climb back out after the day she'd had.

Recalling the word Tearlach had used, she looked questioningly at him. "*Keep* me here?"

For the first time since she'd met him, Ffion saw the faintest expression of culpability on his face. "It wasn't the fog that redirected your course all those times. When you made it far enough out to sea, when I was sure you'd nearly exhausted yourself and wouldn't have the strength to row out again...it was me who brought you back."

She gaped at him. *He* was the reason she was trapped in Periwen? She could have returned to Tremaene at any time?

The anger she wanted to feel at his interference barely sparked before it died out.

He kept me here.

It wasn't her fault. She hadn't given up on her people.

Ffion's face must have conveyed her understanding, for Tearlach said the words she needed to hear, though never thought she would. "Your people have been waiting for you, Esme."

That name had never felt so peerless as it did in that moment. She watched the unwavering look in his eyes and repeated the words over in her mind. They were waiting for her, they had *always* been waiting for her. They'd never given up hope that she would return. They'd known all along that she was alive and would come home when she was strong enough.

Perhaps she finally was.

Looking down, she inhaled deeply, the first truly steady breath she'd taken since fleeing Debarrow. *It's time*, she told herself.

"We leave at dawn, then?"

He dipped his head once in reply.

————————

Tearlach left after offering more bread and an apple from his pack, which Ffion declined. Food was less than appealing.

He explained with no small amount of annoyance that his errands had been cut short earlier and that he still needed a few things for their journey. Ffion promised to stay in the room—he made her swear it. She had no desire to venture out on her own again anyway and planned to make sufficient use of her time alone.

When the claw-foot porcelain tub in the adjoining washroom was filled with hot water and opaque from the oils and salts she'd found next to the sink, Ffion dipped her toe in. Savoring the feeling of the heat on her skin, she lowered herself slowly into the water. Unsure of when she'd have such a luxury again, she relished every second that passed while she was immersed up to her chin in the steamy bathwater.

Time slipped away as her sore muscles soaked. When her fingers were wrinkled, she stepped out of the tepid water and dried, reaching for her nightdress. She hesitated, thinking better of it. There was a chance Tearlach might come back to her room that evening.

Even after the restorative bath, Ffion was still bone-tired. Clad in only a shirt, she climbed onto the bed to pull her pants on, falling back against the mountain of throws and pillows to button them.

She promised herself she'd rest her eyes for only a moment, then awoke sometime later to a knock.

Tearlach wouldn't knock.

She hopped off the bed, padded over to the door, then placed an ear to it.

"Miss?" A cheery voice rang out, nearly startling Ffion out of her skin. *The innkeeper.*

"Yes?" she replied hesitantly. She didn't think the woman intended to do her harm, but wasn't about to open the door without an explanation for the visit.

"I was just bringing you dinner, miss. I thought you might want to take it up here instead of downstairs," she called through the door.

Ffion wondered if dinner was included with her stay or if it had something to do with the gold coins she'd given the woman.

Without much more consideration, she opened the door. The smell of food quickly flooded her senses. She wasn't aware until that moment how very hungry she was.

After Ffion took the heavy tray and thanked her, the woman nodded and stole a quick glance around the room before disappearing down the hall.

Noting the two covered plates and cups of burgundy liquid, she realized the innkeeper had assumed Tearlach was staying in the room with her.

"Not a chance," Ffion muttered.

She took a long pull from one of the cups as soon as she positioned the tray at the small dining table. The wine instantly warmed her blood. Beneath one of the covers, she found a golden brown corn cake with layers of thinly sliced patty pan squash, topped with a poached egg. A pile of sautéed spinach with toasted pine nuts sat beside a slab of roast chicken topped with oregano sprigs and some kind of creamy cheese that looked decadent. She took a swipe of the cheese with her pinky finger, too intrigued not to try it. Two small crescent-shaped pastries were set aside on a white linen napkin. They certainly had far more culinary variations than Debarrow offered.

Easing a fork under one of the corn cakes, she slid it onto her plate, then moved the chicken to the other.

Tearlach returned just as Ffion popped the last bite of her own pastry into her mouth. It was filled with raspberries and a hint of lemon, and tasted completely divine. Or perhaps it only seemed that way once she'd finished off her wine.

He quickly swept the room with a scrutinizing eye, which landed on the tray of food in front to her.

"What happened to 'I promise I'll stay in the room?'"

"Calm down. The innkeeper brought it up."

"Fine. But in the future, don't open the door for anyone but me." He shucked the pack off his shoulder, then dropped his belt and sword to the ground. She pondered how the good people of Briganport had liked the unapproachable man walking about their quaint town with a sword across his back.

Ffion gaped when he continued to untie his leather chest plate, alarmed that he might strip down right in front of her. With a few long strides, Tearlach strode past her and into the washroom, shutting the door just after she caught a glimpse of his shirt coming off.

Shaking the image from her mind, she looked over at Tearlach's belongings—discarded near the door and strewn across the foot of the bed. The innkeeper had brought up two entrées for them...Had he conveyed to her that they...Did he plan to *share* her room?

Why had she even considered that she might have privacy? After what had happened that day, he certainly wouldn't let her out of his sight.

A few minutes later, the water turned off and Tearlach returned to the main room—his wet hair dripping over his shirt. Thank the gods he was dressed and not in a towel.

Ffion followed him with her eyes as he took the seat opposite her and began eating. She was set to ask him about their sleeping arrangements— maybe suggest he sleep in the bathtub since she'd paid for the room—but was momentarily distracted by the confused look on his face.

"What did you eat?" He stared at his plate, full of chicken and little else.

She averted her gaze. "I might have eaten your corn cake and poached egg."

"You *might* have?" He arched one of his dark eyebrows.

"I did."

"Mm-hmm." He nudged the second pastry toward her, then began eating.

Ffion didn't hesitate to down it in two bites as she moved over to the bed. The sun was already hidden beyond the forest, casting a pink glow across the sea. She watched until the last fiery orange cloud melted into the cobalt night sky.

At first the bed had seemed rather spacious, but after looking uneasily between it and Tearlach, it seemed infinitely too small.

Tearlach took the tray and empty dishes, placing them outside the door. *Smart*, Ffion thought. Less likely to be disturbed by a curious innkeeper.

After locking the door, he stalked over to where Ffion sat on the edge of the bed. If he'd noticed her look of concern, he didn't seem to care. Without saying a word, he leaned over her. Her breath hitched at his sudden closeness and she moved instinctively away, pushing herself into the center of the bed. But Tearlach only smirked and reached past her to grab one of the pillows. Her veins flooded with relief—and something else she wasn't ready to identify—as he stepped away, pulling a blanket off the footrail.

Once he tossed them to the floor, Ffion was satisfied enough that she pulled herself up and slid her feet under the covers. Though it wasn't late, she could barely keep her eyes open. Turning toward the wall, she dropped her head on the too-fluffy pillow and squirmed around until she found a comfortable position.

The only thing that kept her from drifting off was the sound of Tearlach pacing the perimeter of the room, latching each window and checking the sturdiness of their frames. She turned to face him when she heard a heavy scuffing sound. He was moving a chest of drawers to block the door.

Slightly alarmed that he'd take such precautions when they'd slept out in the open the night prior, she asked, "Are we going to be safe here?"

"My magic will keep this room protected."

"How?"

"I have air magic."

Oh. "Like my mother?"

"From the stories I've heard, yes." Tearlach shoved the heavy piece of furniture into place.

"But I thought your magic involved glamouring." Although air magic would explain how he'd been able to turn her back when she'd rowed out to sea.

"It does." He stood back, assessing the position of the chest. "I was gifted with more than one magical ability."

"And how will your air magic protect us while we sleep?"

"It allows me to shield myself...this room...you."

"I see" was all she could manage. Could her mother shield herself, protect herself in that way? If she'd had that ability, why hadn't she kept a shield around herself at all times? She could have prevented...

Ffion decided not to follow that thought.

"As long as you're within my range," Tearlach added, his words edged with warning, "I can shield you."

"I get it. Is that all, then? Any other talents you haven't told me about?"

He met her inquisitive gaze with a cunning look she hadn't seen on him since before she'd discovered who he truly was, then went about the room snuffing out the lamps and sconces.

"What? What aren't you telling me?" she pressed.

He exhaled audibly when he reached the other side of the bed. "When one uses magic, I can draw it in and absorb the energy myself."

Ffion furrowed her brow, trying to make sense of what that entailed. She'd never heard of such a thing, though her lack of knowledge was quickly becoming the norm when it came to magic...and her fate.

"When you *absorb* it..." She wondered how absorbing one's magic would feel. "Can you command it or use it as your own?"

"Not in the way you're thinking. I can either dissipate the energy, thereby terminating that person's magic in that particular instance..." He walked over to his improvised bed on the floor.

"Or?"

"Or I can...*redirect* it," he explained, looking back at her, "back at the originator."

Ffion sucked in a breath. There was only one scenario when something like that would be useful—battle. She shuddered to think what turning one's power and strength against its bearer might do. She hoped never to see that aspect of his magic.

Settling back into the consuming layers of crisp linens, pillows, and feathery soft blankets, she stared up at the ceiling in the nearly dark room. "Seems you have quite a bit of power at your disposal, don't you?"

He didn't respond, so she glanced over at him—stretched out on the floor, arms propped behind his head. Tearlach met her questioning look with one that asked if she really wanted to know the answer.

Rolling back over, she mocked, "Then why bother blocking the door?"

He growled.

Chapter Fifteen

FFION WOKE SUDDENLY, covering her ears at the horrible sound of the heavy chest being moved across the floor back to its original location. Muttering to herself about him waking everyone at the inn, she rolled over to look out the window. She couldn't see past the reflection of a single lamp burning on the table in the corner. It was still night.

Tearlach was dressed and ready to leave when she sat up. How did he manage to wake ahead of the sun?

"I'll be downstairs, don't be long" was all he said before leaving her alone.

Despite her desire to aggravate him after rousing her from sleep in the most obnoxious way, she dressed quickly, pausing only briefly when she held Cadwyn's dagger. How much had Cadwyn known about Ffion's fate, about Captain Sullivan's plans? Had she been equally in the dark? Maybe Cadwyn had somehow survived and Ffion could one day return the blade and cloak. If she believed that possible, she might have enough strength for the journey ahead.

Downstairs, Tearlach leaned against the archway near the front door. His arms were crossed, making his muscled forearms seem all the more powerful.

A middle-aged man with pale eyes that offset his dark skin was perched on a stool behind the counter. He greeted her warmly. "Morning, miss."

"Good morning." She couldn't help but return his smile. His mouth was framed by wrinkles from a life of happiness.

"Have a pleasant journey."

"Thank you." She wondered what explanation Tearlach had given the man for their early morning departure.

They walked out and into the purple haze of fading night. A warm glimmer hovered above the still waters of the sleeping sea. It called to Ffion, as if it wasn't just the day that began in the west with the rising sun, but the entire world.

Few people were up and about. Some hauled carts up the main road, others unloaded crates along the larger docks. Fishermen arranged nets and coiled ropes, readying to set out on the open water.

"Where's Eimhir," she inquired as they neared the northernmost docks.

"Who?"

"Your horse. Where is she?"

"You named the horse?"

"*Your* horse. And yes."

Tearlach grumbled and Ffion found it amusing that she could manage to nettle him before the sun was even up.

"I took her to the stables last night. She'll be cared for."

Ffion looked up at him, surprised, and was about to tell him such when a man with a wiry gray beard, low-brimmed hat, and thick woolen sweater approached—the same man she'd seen Tearlach with the day before.

"Magnificent day to be on the water, I'd say! Not a cloud in the sky. And this must be your lovely wife." The man smiled to her as much as he could without dropping the wooden pipe clenched between his teeth.

Wife?

"Indeed it is. Yes, this is my wife." Tearlach put an arm around her shoulder, drawing her close. Every muscle in Ffion's body stiffened, becoming acutely aware of each point of contact between them.

The old man glanced at Ffion. "Are you sure you wouldn't like something smaller? Perhaps a boat that needs but one person to row it?"

"The one we discussed will suit us fine. She doesn't like it when I do all the work anyway." Then Tearlach winked at her. *Winked.*

Unamused by the charade, Ffion gritted her teeth and plastered a smile on her face.

They were led out a narrow jetty. The edge of town was quiet. It seemed the fishing boats and larger cargo transports kept to the southern end, where piers were wider and sturdier.

The boats along their dock were different, made for leisure. Most were humble fishing boats made for the shallows, painted with bright colors and lettering. A few had small enclosures, but the majority were simple rowboats.

As mentioned, the one they stopped beside was quite large for the two of them, with a mast in the center. Dark, varnished wood made the vessel seem graceful and refined against the aged, graying planks of the dock. Black lacquered seams ran along the edges, rising at each end where they met in elegant scrolls. The hull was far deeper than it'd first appeared, allowing ample space beneath the benches for storage. Three deep seats at the front and rear were set back from the center mast, enough so that one could sprawl out comfortably along the bottom of the boat.

It was hardly Ffion's first time out on the sea. The dark water didn't frighten her—so long as she didn't venture beneath the vast surface. And it wasn't the close quarters she'd be sharing that bothered her. But something had her stomach twisting in knots.

Ffion watched the boat rock gently as Tearlach tossed their packs into the hull. She hesitated. Taking that last step off the pier? There was finality to it. Knowing that Periwen would never be her home again.

The boat continued to sway in time with her thumping heart—faster and faster. She sucked in a breath when Tearlach broke the rhythm by stepping into the bow, jarring her from her thoughts.

A strong hand reached out for hers and she stepped away from the last thing that connected her to the mortal world. The man untied the back line and Tearlach moved to the front to shove away from the dock. She found a seat before losing her balance. A morning swim in frigid water wasn't a ritual she intended to take up.

Watching the old man as he waved them off, she finally found her breath. Ffion offered a strained smile to the last human she'd ever see. And she'd never even learned his name.

Her heartrending smile faltered when it occurred to her that he'd never get his boat back.

Tearlach responded before she could ask. "Don't worry, he'll be many silvers richer when he checks his pockets tonight." He angled the boat toward the shore, taking them farther north—away from Briganport and away from watchful eyes. After a few powerful strokes, Tearlach nodded to the other set of oars that jutted out at either side.

"What?"

"Row."

Looking to the mast with its waiting sail in the center, she wondered why he was even bothering. "What about your magic?" The moment she said it, she realized that a sensor might pick it up. She groaned inwardly. Rowing the entire expanse of the Sea of Muirín was not a welcome task.

"My magic isn't an issue. I'm able to keep my own power hidden… unless I choose not to."

Ffion furrowed her brow. What did that mean?

"But I won't until we're away from the harbor. That man believes we're out for a bit of sightseeing along the forested coast. If he sees us sailing out into the sea, a dozen boats will attempt to rescue us from the turbulent waters."

She glanced up at the mast again—it was built for the shallows. Only with Tearlach's air magic could a boat of that size traverse the sea.

"Time to show me what you're made of, Princess."

Ffion looked down her nose at him as best she could, being at least a foot shorter. He knew exactly what she was made of—had seen her row out nearly a hundred times. Before he'd turned her around.

She faced forward and gripped the handles. How did he manage to fully enrage her with so few words? Temper roiled beneath her skin as she funneled her fury into the oars.

"Don't call me that," she said through clenched teeth.

"Call you what?"

Oh, he knew. "*Princess.*"

"It's what you are, or were. I suppose *Queen* would be more appropriate."

"My name is Ffion," she enunciated each word, refusing to turn, unwilling to let him see how much he infuriated her.

"No. It isn't."

She didn't respond.

"How about Your Majesty, or milady? Heir of Tremaene? Your Highness, Royal—"

"Stop!" she cried before he could go on.

He waited.

"Esme, then. You may call me Esme."

Oh, he knew *exactly* what he was doing.

"Esme." His deep, smooth voice curled around the name. It was a challenge and a command, one that reminded her of who she was—the girl she'd buried away so many years earlier, below rocks and rubble and memories—and the woman she'd need to become.

It wasn't as though she hadn't thought about what would happen when they returned to Tremaene. But what she'd assumed would take months or even years to uncover was brought to the surface with a single word—her name—spoken by the only person who knew who she really was.

Every muscle in her body relaxed as she allowed the facade she'd kept in place for years to crumble to dust. It was freeing. The feeling made her queasy. A sudden rush that was overwhelming and dizzying...and she was sitting on a boat that was rocking her in circles.

Several deep breaths stilled the sudden swell of energy coursing through her veins unencumbered, easing it into a steady flow.

The sun finally greeted the day, piercing the morning mist and drenching the water and land in golden honey–colored light.

The brightness hovered in her periphery. But she didn't turn. The sun rose from across the sea, heralding the morning of a day she wasn't ready to meet.

Facing the light meant accepting that she'd left Periwen, that she'd left Ffion Ainsley behind. If she turned, she would be Esme. She wasn't ready to face the light. *Not yet.*

The darkness had kept her hidden for nearly a decade. A light so brilliant as the sunrise shining upon her cheek could easily shatter her into a million pieces if she wasn't careful. And there was no time to fit herself back together.

She took another long breath, holding it at the top of her chest, holding herself together, then let it roll down to her belly. She still couldn't look.

Scanning the tree-lined shore, she blinked the dampness from her eyes and searched for a point to focus on, a place to channel the anxious heat that pulsed inside her.

Esme. She was still Esme. And after so many years, the girl inside her was ready to burn all the darkness away.

The Forest of Eoin was bathed in bright fiery light from the rising sun. Below the illuminated kaleidoscope of autumn trees, she could make out the silvery white and gray fur of twenty or so wolves gathering along the border. They watched as Tearlach finally pulled them away from the shore. Out to sea.

A tear rolled down her cheek. She wiped it away and sat up straighter. Heartening herself, she inclined her head slightly. The wolves were saying goodbye; she was saying thank you.

If only she could have left differently. What would become of her orchard, her apples, her home? What would Carrick tell the people of Debarrow?

She glanced at the wolves on the shore as the stretch of water between them lengthened. They'd seen through the darkness to her wild beating heart. They'd always known who she was.

With each pull of the oars, she moved away from their protection. Unsure of what was to come, she offered up a quick prayer to Muirín—god of sea and water, and namesake to the unending sea that surrounded them—asking for safe passage.

Sparing a glance over her shoulder at Tearlach—silhouetted by the radiant light of the sun—she wondered if he too had noticed the wolves.

He had. His eyes locked onto hers with a penetrating, questioning gaze.

Esme turned back, raised her chin, and continued rowing toward the light.

Chapter Sixteen

AN ACHE SPREAD across the backs of her upper arms. Esme was used to manual labor, but it had been some time since she'd felt such a ceaseless demand on her muscles. Still, it felt good to be doing something that yielded results.

The sound of the canvas sail unfurling pulled her from the hypnotic state of rowing. As Tearlach's magic took over, her arms slackened at her sides, no longer needed. The sail filled with a steady current of air and took them quickly into deeper waters.

Her eyes fixed on the thin line of land as they drifted farther out, no longer able to make out the treetops as their colors bled into the sea.

Hours passed as she sat watching the horizon where Periwen had once been.

Water filled every corner.

There was nothing but water.

When the sun was overhead, its rays ricocheted off the glossy surface of the sea. Esme reached over the side, feeling the icy water thread through her fingers. Suddenly, her mouth felt parched.

The boat shifted and she turned to see a canteen of water held out for her. Esme took the container and nodded a thanks to Tearlach. He stepped back over the benches like they were nothing more than twigs blocking his path, then pulled out a few parchment-wrapped parcels from one of his bags. After ripping off a hunk of the dried meat for himself, he held up a small muslin pouch for her.

Curious, she navigated the hurdles between them and took the bag, finding it filled with dates. Surprised at the provisions Tearlach had gathered for their journey, she decided to take the seat across from him.

"Thank you."

He said nothing—a man who might have been more content with solitude than her.

But the silence started to press in. She ate her food quietly, thinking of something to say. By the time her pile of pecans was gone and the last piece of unleavened bread with cured tomatoes and peppers consumed, she wasn't any closer to a conversation topic.

Reclaiming her original bench, Esme stretched out and closed her eyes. Imagining she was alone should have made the quiet easier. It didn't.

She stole glances at Tearlach, turning away each time she thought her question would yield a dismissive riposte.

Finally, he asked in an agitated voice, "What?"

"Nothing."

"Then stop staring at me," he growled.

Esme took a breath, forcing aside the anger he evoked. When she met his eyes again, he raised an eyebrow, challenging her to speak. "What will we do when we reach Tremaene?"

As he held her gaze, Tearlach seemed to weigh something in his mind. Propping up on her elbows, Esme waited intently for the difficult answer to her seemingly uncomplicated question.

"I don't know," he finally admitted.

"You don't know?" she repeated with more than a hint of accusation.

Tearlach's chest rose and fell slowly. "I have no idea what we're returning to. I haven't had contact with anyone from Tremaene since I left. For all I know, war might have broken out. Everything could be gone."

Esme's breath hitched at the impassiveness of his tone, as if the words had little significance. Tearlach was a man who knew everything—or so she'd thought. He had every situation coordinated, every deviation planned for. Yet he'd failed to mention that he had no idea as to the state of their kingdom. They might be returning to death and ruins and he'd somehow forgotten to bring it up until he had her trapped on a boat with nothing but water surrounding them for days.

The shock in her eyes was not missed as Tearlach quickly amended his earlier assessment. "I'm sure all is fine. We'll find Sully as soon as we can."

He was placating her, but Esme was grateful for it as her optimism teetered on edge. Surely it was possible that they were returning to a world where everything had been worked out peacefully while they'd been away. Perhaps there'd never been a threat to her or the crown in the first place.

"Maybe it really was just an accident," she offered, "with my parents."

"Maybe."

It was a frail conjecture, but one Esme decided to hold on to. She sat up and faced Tearlach, needing a more substantial foundation if she was to believe it. "If there was never any real threat to the crown, who would have ascended the throne in my absence?"

"Didn't you pay attention in your history lessons, Princess?" he mocked.

She scowled.

"Esme," he rectified with a slight bow of his head. "A treaty was formed at the end of the Dark War between the ruling family and the high-priestesses."

Dark War?

"By relinquishing some of his power to the Order, your father restored peace to the kingdom while keeping the lands fertile and waterways flowing."

Her brow knit together in confusion.

"It also stated that if no member of the royal family remained, the highest-ranking high-priestess would rule Tremaene."

The sisters of the Order hadn't crossed her mind in years. Detached from the immortal realm, she'd had few reminders of their power.

In Periwen, the world seemed to balance itself without magic. But seasonal hardships were avoided in Tremaene with the especially powerful Fae. Each sister possessed a considerable magical ability, gifted by the gods. Some kept the lands fertile, others perpetuated the water in lakes, rivers, and streams. A few channeled the weather, bringing rain to dry soil or gusty winds to scatter seeds and spread pollen. No one element worked independent of the others. Every gift was required to maintain balance.

"So it's possible one of the sisters took over?" she hoped.

"It's possible." *But not likely*, was what he didn't say.

It was reassurance enough—that a benevolent caretaker of the land might be leading her people. But that single, optimistic thought was quickly eclipsed by something else Tearlach had mentioned. "What Dark War?"

A shadow crossed his eyes. "No one speaks of it anymore."

Apparently not if she'd never heard of it.

Thick silence hung between them as she waited for him to go on.

Finally, he spoke in a low, haunted voice. "Dark magic was used. Very few were left in the end."

Dark magic? It actually existed? The look in Tearlach's eyes told her that whoever had wielded that terrifying power had done unspeakable things. Perhaps that was why it had been written out of Tremaene's history.

"When did it end?"

"Well over a century ago."

"Did my father fight in it?" He'd reigned during that time, but she couldn't picture him as a warrior.

"Yes."

"And you?"

"Yes." The word was clipped.

"How old are you?" she dared to ask.

"Much older than you."

It was her turn to raise an eyebrow in query.

"Two hundred and sixteen years," he admitted.

Esme suddenly felt very, very young. She'd experienced so little in her brief twenty-four years. She stared at Tearlach for a moment, wondering how different he might've been before seeing war.

The image troubled her in a way she couldn't explain, so she redirected the conversation. "How is it you know so much about this treaty when I know nothing of it?"

"The lord of Isloran is my father. I'm his eldest son."

Esme sat up a bit straighter. Tearlach was son to the lord that held Tremaene's coastal province? Not just a warrior then.

"Your father is Lord Torin?"

"He is."

"Then why did you stay in Altan after the war?" Fighting in a war that required the involvement of the entire kingdom, she could understand— it seemed her father had been a part of it after all. But if Tearlach was heir to the Isloran holdings, surely his time in the aftermath of war would have been better spent at home, with his people.

He didn't answer.

"Why didn't you return home if—"

He cut her off. "I was promised in marriage to a young woman from a wealthy family when I wasn't much older than you."

Esme grew silent, barely breathing. If she moved an inch or even swallowed, it might've broken the spell—one where Tearlach revealed details of his past.

After a long pause while gazing out at the sea, he continued. "I was attending business in one of the smaller coastal villages—the front lines hadn't yet reached us. I returned home months later to find that she'd fallen in love with another. She confessed everything, said she didn't know what love really was before meeting her true mate. But she was prepared to uphold our arrangement anyway. I couldn't let her bind her life to mine if her heart was with someone else."

For a man with such intensely guarded thoughts, he revealed far more than expected. Esme watched his profile—his eyes never leaving the water. Then it struck her. "You loved her." It wasn't a question.

Tearlach's gaze didn't waver, didn't betray an ounce of emotion. "We called off the contract between our houses. But in doing so, she dishonored her family."

Dishonored *her* family? Having heard stories of Lord Torin's inexorable rule over his territory, Esme was certain there had been consequences for Tearlach as well.

"I helped her leave the province before any harm came to her or her mate."

Esme's eyes widened. She couldn't fathom helping someone who'd wronged her in such a way, let alone the other person who'd played a part in the betrayal.

"My father stripped me of my birthright as successor, naming my younger brother instead."

"And you joined the warriors in the north," Esme surmised.

He turned to her and inclined his head slightly.

"So you never married? In all those years?" She toed the question carefully, ready to jump back in an instant.

"Marriage shackles you, takes away your freedom. Cora would have given everything up for honor." There was a hint of sorrow in his voice for the woman he'd once loved, but Esme couldn't sense a drop of jealousy or bitterness in his tone.

"Honor supplies the shackles," she countered, "not the custom of marriage. Honor isn't a privilege or a mark of respect when it's used to please someone else's objectives. The word merely serves to force an obligation upon another." She'd spent many nights pondering the value of the word that'd been thrown around fallaciously since her youth.

He seemed to consider her argument, though he didn't respond.

"My parents were considering alliances for me as well." Esme looked down, not wanting to see Tearlach's face. "Can I tell you something terrible?" Her voice was soft, unsure.

When she glanced up through her lashes, he was watching her intently.

"When the captain came to see me in Donellis to deliver the news, somewhere in all my despair I felt a small kernel of relief that I'd avoided the fate of being bound to another in a political marriage." She looked away. "I thought of myself, my own selfish desires before I considered what would become of my people, my land, everything I was now responsible for." Her breathing was short and shallow after uttering a truth she'd kept inside for nearly a decade.

After a long stretch, Tearlach's deep, steady voice cut through the sound of water lapping at the side of the boat. "We are complex creatures, Esme." She glanced up at the sound of her name on his lips. "The crown is only one piece of who you are."

She sighed. "It doesn't feel that way." Lying back on the bench, she closed her eyes, feeling sapped of all energy.

But respite was not to be found.

"What about the shop owner?" Tearlach asked.

Esme slitted one eye and glanced over at him. "Carrick?"

"Yes. Mr. Hawthorn."

"What about him?"

"Did you love him?"

Esme narrowed her eyes, wondering why he was interested in a life that would no longer happen. Tearlach cocked his head to the side patiently. She couldn't stand when he did that—looked at her like he had nothing but patience, like he would wait forever for her to speak first. It infuriated her. Not that he did it, but that she couldn't help but concede.

"He was the only friend I had in that world." *And it didn't have to be that way,* she added silently.

The muscles in Tearlach's jaw tightened before Esme turned away and closed her eyes. Eventually, the soft afternoon light and gentle sway of the boat lulled her to sleep.

————————

She awoke to stillness. As though the sea had calmed to a smooth, unbroken surface.

Esme climbed over the seats and grabbed hold of the mast, eying the approaching fog. It stretched across the water from north to south, and soared upward until it disappeared into the pale blue sky. Iridescent ripples and shimmering lights played tricks on her eyes. Something powerful dwelled inside the fog, moving and shifting, skewing the view from one moment to the next. At first she saw through to the water beyond, then she was staring at her own reflection.

Having been asleep during her previous voyage across the Sea of Muirín, she hadn't witnessed the fog, and wondered how it would feel to cross through the ever-changing barrier of glamour.

Looking over to where Tearlach sat, she noticed his hand gripping the edge of the boat. His gaze was fixed on the water in the other direction— refusing to look at the dense, permeable wall hanging above the water.

Oh, no.

Esme took the spot next to him just as they breached the barrier. It draped itself around her, forcing the blood to course through her veins with such intensity that she felt alive and awake and sick all at once. Magic surged through her and whirled in the space around her. With a deep inhale, she felt light, then instantly weighed down by the force of it.

She could see nothing beyond her own body, much like the opaque fog in her premonitory dreams. A tingle of sensation ran along every inch of her, as if warm liquid was filling her up and settling just beneath her skin.

Trying to acclimate to the transformation, she took a slow breath and held it, only to cough it out as though she'd been kicked in the back when the fog shoved them out the other side.

The water churned, rocking the boat violently, before settling to a steady oscillation.

Nausea threatened as the agitation continued inside her. Her magic grew stronger. She could feel it taking up space within, searching for room. And making her sick.

She dropped her head between her knees and took slow, controlled breaths—in through her nose, out through her mouth, over and over.

Though it seemed she was handling it better than Tearlach—hearing him vomit over the side of the boat.

She allowed herself a small giggle that the fierce warrior felt just as much as she did, then thought better of laughing as even the slightest contraction of her muscles sent waves of pain humming through her.

When they were both breathing steadily again, she looked at Tearlach and opened her mouth slightly in awe.

"What?"

She snapped her mouth shut, tripped over a few words in her mind. "Nothing...never mind."

Though his voice sounded raw, he still managed to poke at her. "Have you forgotten what your kind look like?"

Esme didn't respond, simply shook her head as she studied his eyes a moment longer, then retreated to the other end of the boat.

It wasn't the point of his ears or the gold shimmer of his flawlessly youthful skin in the waning light. She'd only ever known him as human—had assumed some of his features had been dampened by the glamour to make him appear mortal and unremarkable.

Fae had varying shades of blue eyes, or sometimes a rare green like Cadwyn's. But Tearlach's eyes hadn't changed. They were *his* eyes, not the glamour's. His eyes were still deep in their darkness, flecked with sparkling amber.

She'd never met another of her kind with eyes as dark as hers.

Chapter Seventeen

ESME FOUND HERSELF *in a clearing, ensconced by mist.*

She knew the place. It was etched in her memory with glaring detail.

Hanging her head, she wondered if she'd be led toward a past event or a future one. When she glanced up, the wolf stood before her, six paces ahead. They were close enough that Esme could see the steam of his breath mixing with the fog.

Light shone on them, though there was no source, no moons above. His pale green eyes glowed, rimmed in black. He was beautiful, captivating, but she preferred the owl. The owl enlightened with information from a past she'd not been privy to. The owl instilled wisdom.

The wolf warned of danger.

They regarded each other for a moment, and when he seemed satisfied that she was ready and willing to follow, he turned and led her into the haze.

When the fog receded, revealing a dense forest of foreign trees—their branches so high she couldn't see where they began—Esme inhaled its alluring scent. The fresh, wild smell reminded her of something, though she had trouble placing it.

A woman stumbled into view, retreating from an unseen threat.

The panic in her eyes, in her tense body, was all too familiar. Esme stared down in fright, watching herself in the forest below, waiting for the story to unfold.

As if searching for an escape, the woman frantically turned in place, then shook her head adamantly. Whoever pursued was beyond the ring of massive trees and Esme's limited field of vision.

A commotion roared in the distance. It sounded like fighting, of metal clashing against metal. The woman was clearly frightened, looking for an opportunity to flee, yet hesitant to leave.

Where was she? Who was stalking her? And why wasn't she running if her life was in danger?

Finally, she chose a path and made to run. But it was too late. Another figure lunged into the scene. The woman ducked as a thick branch swept out and struck the attacker, taking him momentarily off his feet. He recovered quickly from the fall. The silver cuffs that adorned his muscular forearms glinted in the dappled forest light as he vaulted to his feet.

Backed against a tree, the woman feinted right, then slipped under her attacker's arm as he tried to snatch her. When he reached for her again, a giant root tangled up his boot, holding him in place. But he threw out an arm and yanked her leg out from under her before she could take off running.

She screamed.

Esme gasped.

The man jerked her back, dragging her along the forest floor. She twisted to free herself from his grip, clawing at the ground, struggling for her life.

Grabbing a fistful of her hair, the man yanked her to her feet in one swift motion.

Esme trembled as she watched him place a silver blade gently against the woman's neck as he whispered something in her ear.

With a burst of flame, his magic burned through the twisted roots to free his leg. He seized her around the waist, pulling her up as she grappled to make purchase with the ground. She fought. If he was going to kill her, she wouldn't make it easy.

But no, he wasn't planning to kill her, Esme realized. He would have done it the instant he'd had the blade to her throat.

Still she fought, kicking her feet out, trying to turn in her attacker's grip as he dragged her away. Her hand shot out, one final, hollow attempt to reach for help before they vanished into the fog.

The scene faded and Esme shook with fear, her hands clenched, nails biting into her skin.

It would come to pass. She knew that with certainty.

She needed to see it again. It'd all happened so quickly. Turning in place, she searched for another angle through the dense fog, another clue, anything that would help. Who was the man? How long did she have before he'd find her?

Dropping her arms at her sides, she raged into the mist, shouting her anger until it rippled beneath her skin, flowing out of her, dark and unforgiving, melding with the pure white fog.

A low rumble came from behind.

A growl? No, a voice.

Her name? Maybe she wasn't alone in the dream after all. She heard it again. Someone was shouting her name.

A jolt shot through her body, nearly knocking her off her feet.

The voice became louder and the dense fog swirled around her as everything went dark.

"Esme. Wake up!" Tearlach's hands gripped her shoulders. How long had he been calling her name? "A storm's about to hit. I need you in the hull, near the center," he commanded as he pulled her off the bench.

Wind was howling in the distance. The dream lingered in her mind, but her fury dulled as she clambered on shaky legs.

Grateful for Tearlach's steady hold, she stole a glance at the impending storm. But the fervent clouds that blanketed the sky in inky darkness dissolved into nothingness, blending with a flush of rose and purple predawn light.

Tearlach snatched his hands away, as though he might catch fire from touching her.

Esme looked up at him, surprised by his sudden reaction. He stared down at his hands, holding them out between them. After a moment, he lifted his eyes.

She wondered what he was considering as he glared at her for several long moments. Had she hurt him in some way?

Tearlach's eyes raked over her, as if he were trying to make sense of something. "Did you summon it?" His voice was both questioning and accusing.

"Summon what?" What was she being blamed for? She'd been asleep moments earlier, swept up in a dream that she'd ruminate over until it came to pass.

"The storm." Tearlach jerked his chin to where the tempest had been building its strength. "Did you create it?"

The morning sky was clear, not even a wisp of a cloud remained. Strange it had subsided so abruptly, but then she'd seen thunderclouds proliferate and scatter quickly before.

"No." Her voice rose in defense. Then, as though the clouds in her mind too began to clear, she wondered if it was possible. "I don't think so," she amended, growing unsure.

Tearlach shook his head, as if he'd misinterpreted the occurrence. "I didn't feel your magic. You weren't directing it." His tone sounded like he was trying to convince himself more than her. Though the admission that he could feel her magic was more than unsettling to Esme. Yet another aspect of their bond he'd withheld.

"If you didn't *feel* my magic, then how could I have summoned it?"

"I'm not sure."

Esme was learning that it was never a good omen when Tearlach was unsure.

"Has it ever happened before, summoning a storm?" he asked.

"If I could summon a storm, wouldn't I know it?"

He watched her, but didn't respond.

"No, I can't create storms," she defended. But as the silence stretched between them, she softened her voice. "Well, maybe. It's possible."

Thinking back over her time in Periwen, sifting through memories like pebbles on a rocky lakeshore, she considered the correlation. Analyzing one's connection to the weather was a perplexing concept. Although...as she thought on it, every instance that had once appeared coincidence no longer seemed quite so random or capricious.

The rain, her mind provided.

Rain was needed frequently to quench the dry soil—soil no farmer had worked in decades before she'd arrived in Debarrow, because the finicky weather and infertile land refused to yield fruit. Why, then, had it been so easy for her?

Esme had never given thought to a possible relationship, but the seemingly indiscriminate nature of the rain suddenly seemed suspiciously kismet.

Did I invite the rain? She'd never felt magic under her skin until the day she'd touched the wolf. And if her magic had awakened earlier than she'd thought, her presence would have lured the assassins years before they'd actually located her.

But if it wasn't *her* magic summoning rain, what was at work?

When her inundated gaze rose to Tearlach's, she realized he'd been waiting for her, as though he'd pieced it together far more quickly.

"The rain. I think I brought rain to my land when I needed it... somehow." Esme squeezed her eyes shut as the memories flooded her mind and lined up in perfect order. "And storms." She looked up. "Storms seem to follow my dreams. I don't know how...it was before... I don't know," she finished weakly, thinking of the numerous times she'd woken to the wreckage of violent storms after restless, fitful nights with inescapable renditions of her life, waking to a bed that looked as though she'd gone to battle against it. Downed trees, flooded ponds, and damaged property were all too commonplace when she suffered the tempestuous nightmares.

But not only dreams. Where storms arose from fear or anger, unceasing rains seemed to mirror her sadness or despair.

Realizing the correlation, she looked pointedly at Tearlach. He'd successfully evoked a few thunderstorms from her—torrential downpours that wouldn't let up, raging winds, blinding lightning.

Not just dreams, then.

"What kind of dreams?" He didn't seem disturbed by Esme summoning magic without her awareness, and without Tearlach sensing it.

"Not the pleasant kind. Most are memories I don't want to relive, but others..." She trailed off, thinking of how to explain the other type of recurrent dream that'd begun just before they'd left Debarrow. Could she even call them dreams?

Tearlach waited.

"Is there a way I could learn to control the weather?" she redirected, certain that if she told him about the other *dreams*, he'd likely think her crazy.

Tearlach answered without hesitation, as if he'd been waiting for her to make the leap. "If we can isolate the link."

"And how would I go about doing that?" She hadn't even grasped the magic she knew she possessed—the kind that gave life—and she was beginning to question how to control rain and storms too?

"Find the trigger."

The trigger? Troublesome emotions. If those were the links, she was in no hurry to explore her sway over the weather. As long as she possibly could, she'd avoid it, as well as Tearlach's interrogation.

"Can't your air magic protect us from storms?"

The corner of his lips quirked up as she skirted the subject again. "I can shield us from the gales and rain, even the lightning, but the storm's effect on the sea is beyond my control. And these waters can produce waves massive enough to capsize a boat three times the size of ours."

Esme recalled what the fisherman in Rhoswen Harbor had said, that he'd found her drifting out at sea on the remnants of a boat. She was lucky to have made it to Periwen at all.

Cadwyn hadn't been so fortunate.

Esme cleared her throat. "How does it feel when you access your magic?"

"I don't feel it, I command it. I think it."

"Really?" She blinked. It was that easy for him?

"Learn to control your thoughts, Esme, and you'll be able to control your magic. Mastery will come when you have merely to think a command for it to follow. Do not imagine your power as separate. You and your magic are one and the same. Accept that and using it will become second nature, as effortless as breathing."

She'd only felt her magic once and it hadn't been expected. Could it really be as simple as a thought?

No, she realized. Magic was anything but simple. Controlling her thoughts would take excessive discipline and training. There were far too many racing through her mind as it was, and to focus on one seemed near impossible. Perhaps there were other ways to access magic.

"What did you feel the day with the wolf?" Tearlach prompted.

She looked out at the sea, then reluctantly closed her eyes, putting herself back in the town center, watching as the wolf was dragged into view. Her fingers wiggled as the sensation returned. "It felt like vines were growing through me, up from my feet. The feeling traveled under my skin, spreading throughout my body until I could feel it hovering at my fingertips. Even thinking about it now, I can sense the vines just below the surface." She opened her eyes. "It started when I first saw the wolf, before I was close enough to touch him. The magic crawled through me then. I didn't think about what I was doing. I had no intention, not even an idea of what I was capable of. I just...felt its pain, its death. My heart went out to him and I needed to grant him peace."

Apparently she'd identified another trigger—death.

"But the tree—" She stopped herself, hadn't mentioned that particular incident to him.

"The tree that rescued you from the fall?"

He knew. But how? Had he been watching her *that* closely? When she'd thought herself completely alone, so far from the village?

He truly hadn't given her even a smidgen of privacy, had he?

And his expression didn't show the faintest trace of culpability or remorse for his spying.

Esme resigned herself. It was no use starting a fight in the middle of the sea. If he said something to enrage her even more—which she knew from experience was likely—where would she go? Or worse, what if his charming personality triggered a strong enough reaction to summon another dangerous storm?

She gritted her teeth. "Yes, *that* tree. I didn't feel anything when it happened, no sensations, no tingling. It just reached out...and caught me."

There was a perplexing look on Tearlach's face. He didn't appear unbelieving, just that he didn't quite understand her unique power. Esme wondered if he'd relinquished his claim that there was but one way to command magic.

After a moment, he asked, "And the other dreams?"

Shit. He remembered.

After so many days with him, she knew the game he played—that he wouldn't let up and that she'd eventually give in. Not bothering to delay the inevitable, she took a deep breath and answered. "Some of my dreams aren't from my past."

He arched a brow. "Where are they from?" She could hear the amusement in his voice and didn't blame him. Of course dreams didn't need to be from the past, some were thoughts or memories or observations, re-forming into new, untold stories in one's mind. Not all dreams were real, not all dreams had meaning.

Hers did, every one of them.

"The future." Though she was tempted to mention the other dream to prove her point, it seemed safer to keep it to herself. The insight heralded by the owl had assisted her when she'd needed to know if she could trust Tearlach. She wasn't ready to reveal that power, especially if the owl might again bestow valuable guidance.

The slightest hint of lightheartedness on Tearlach's face vanished. He went deadly still.

"Were you dreaming before I woke you?"

"Yes."

"Of the future?"

"Yes."

"Tell me what you saw."

She gave as much detail as she could recall, which was quite a lot. It was still fresh in her mind. Just by retelling it, her hands were slick with sweat.

Tearlach listened intently without saying a word until she finished. "Maybe it took pieces of your memory from the attack in Debarrow. Your mind might have simply rearranged the circumstances."

"No, it's not like that." She shook her head. "It was real, it *will* happen. The other dream felt the same, the vision revealed itself in the same manner. And I didn't recognize the forest. The trees were different, taller, grander, with rust-colored bark. It wasn't a forest in Periwen, and they weren't the trees near the palace in Meallán. Though it's been some time, I still know those trees."

"The other event played out exactly as your dream foretold?"

"It started to, yes."

"You were able to change the outcome?"

"I was."

Tearlach understood. Provided a warning, she'd made a different choice, a choice that had saved her from peril. When the next event presented itself, she hoped to again be granted enough time to react divergently.

"And you think this dream will come to pass?"

"I'm certain of it." Though she only had one experience to base her theory on, the truth of it resonated in her bones.

"When?"

"Soon." She winced. It was the best she could offer.

"Explain the forest again."

She did, closing her eyes and replaying the scene in terrifying detail once more. Esme described the deep green tufts of lily turf that dotted the thick carpet of pine needles, and the trees she'd never touched with her own hands. Doing her best, she explained the soft bark that looked like she could peel it off, and how the trees themselves towered over her. She posited that it would take the arms of a grown man to circle the girth of even the youngest tree in that forest.

"They sound like the redwoods in the Tamslo Mountains."

"I've never been to the north." She never would've seen the redwoods.

And the north was where they were headed. Tearlach's hard gaze told her he was thinking the same. Silence descended on them until all Esme could hear was the rush of water as it fled smoothly past the boat.

Hours were lost fumbling through tangled emotions and thoughts as Esme tried to make sense of everything she'd learned. When the light shifted to evening, they approached a small rocky island. Others came into view as they drifted nearer.

They were barren, desolate. Rough, rugged shores surrounded the dusty gray inlands. Each crash of a wave against the cratered surface seemed to wash a bit of the dead rock into the sea. And the fiery light of the sinking sun looked as though it might burn the already brittle land.

Desert islands? So close to Tremaene?

"The Valdis Islands." Tearlach's voice was soft as they approached the archipelago.

"I thought the Valdis Islands were—"

"They were once lush, thriving."

"What happened?" She knew the islands were home to a vast array of creatures, dense with plants and rare trees.

Tearlach didn't answer, just looked over at Esme, speaking volumes with his eyes. Something had happened while they'd been away.

But what could rip the life so completely from the once rich lands? And what did that indicate about the mainland they were returning to? Esme's breathing quickened.

Tearlach could surely see the fear in her eyes. He looked away, scanning the islands that spread into the distance. Without turning, he said, "Get some sleep, tomorrow will be a long day."

Tomorrow. When they'd reach Tremaene's shores. When Esme would know what had become of her kingdom.

Chapter Eighteen

ESME WOKE IN the night, thankful she hadn't been roused from sleep by another nightmare. A soft eddying glimmer skimmed the sky above, swirling in and out, expanding and unfurling across the sky. She'd forgotten how beautiful the Loinnir Lights were.

Hovering in the atmosphere, the lights mirrored the preternatural magic of the immortal realm. The ethereal aura hummed with a soft glow of refracted light from the single moon in the night sky—Mios, the pale-yellow orb, was the larger and swifter of the two moons.

She searched the sky for Neve. Though smaller, she was just as brilliant and bright. Esme wasn't surprised not to find her; Neve didn't appear as often. She admired how she unapologetically took her time.

Her chest expanded as she watched the enchanting luminescence swim above her. She'd been in the dark too long, spending nine years in the mortal realm with only the moons to light the delicately star-flecked sky.

Esme hadn't realized how much she'd missed the light.

Memories rose in her mind—gazing up at the night sky as a child, watching lavender darken to deep plum, emerald green ribbons lining the edges of the magical whorls. The Loinnir Lights were stronger and more vibrant above areas with highly concentrated magic. Out on the sea, with only the two of them, the lights were dull, with barely a viridescent whisper in the pale, translucent clouds.

"They've faded."

Esme startled at Tearlach's voice, nearly rolling off the bench before steadying herself. "What?" she asked, not completely cognizant of what he'd said.

"The Loinnir Lights, I've not seen them so weak before."

So it wasn't because they were still a good distance from the mainland. "What does that mean?"

"I'm not sure, but I suspect it's not a good sign."

Yet another indication that something had transpired in their absence. She prayed to the gods that there was still a home for them to return to.

———————

Waking again at dawn, Esme rose and scanned the water around them. Squinting against the direct light, she could see a sliver of land where the sun hovered between night and day.

She glanced at Tearlach, who looked like he'd been awake for a while. His jaw was set with tension as he scanned the horizon. His hair was in disarray, as if he'd been running his hands through it. He was worried, and Esme realized she'd never seen him that way. She wondered if he'd slept at all the night before.

"How long until we reach the shore?" she asked carefully.

He turned at her question, as though he hadn't realized she'd been awake, then looked back to where Tremaene peeked through the surface of the water. In a deep voice, he grumbled, "Soon."

They sat in silence as the landmass grew wider and taller in the distance. The sound of the waves racing alongside the boat began to grate her nerves. She'd had enough of the water, and would be glad to step foot on solid ground again.

"We'll need to start training your magic once we've secured a safe location."

He wanted to discuss training when so many unknowns rested between them and a secure future?

Then she understood—he needed a distraction from what was ahead.

"Is that safe? Using magic?" It stood to reason that if sensors had been sent to Periwen in search of her, they'd be in Tremaene as well. More of them, no doubt.

"It would be far less safe to leave your unpredictable magic untrained."

True, it wasn't likely she'd be able to control volatile emotions when they knew nothing of the state of their homeland. Threats could be lurking just beyond the shore. She needed to learn to manage her triggers—and quickly.

The land rose from the water faster than she'd anticipated, and soon the northern coast filled the horizon and most of the sky above.

She gaped at the fortifying expanse of the Tamslo Mountains. A solid rock wall reached into the crystal blue sky, higher than she could have imagined. Paintings and illustrations had done little to prepare her for the enormity of the range.

Its flat summit stretched as far as she could see, fringed with faint green grass. The exposed coastal face had a smattering of moss tucked into cracks and fissures. Tawny stone melded into a charcoal gray at the base—where it mingled with pebbles along the shore. Although *shore* wasn't what she'd call the narrow strip of land. It was barely deep enough to bring a rowboat ashore.

"I thought they were mountains."

"They are."

"It looks like one giant cliff to me."

"Is there a question?"

"I don't see how we can go ashore here." And there was no way they'd be able to traverse it once they ran the boat aground.

Tearlach didn't respond. He was busy scanning the crest and the narrow shoreline below. When he paused, she followed his gaze north to find three figures standing along the cliff's edge.

Esme instantly turned to Tearlach, afraid. But he visibly relaxed with a long exhale, closing his eyes. "Looks like we'll have some help," he said reverently.

"You know them?" she asked.

"I do."

"Who are they?"

"Family."

So they wouldn't be greeted by assassins. Esme couldn't have been more relieved than if she'd known them herself. They must have been his friends, since it was unlikely Tearlach's father or brother were even aware that he'd left Tremaene nine years earlier.

"How did they find us?"

"I released a short burst of magic when we left Periwen."

"Wasn't that dangerous? Anyone could have picked up your signal."

"It was necessary."

Esme clenched her teeth. "You could have told me."

He glanced at her as they neared the coast—uneven rocks scraping along the bottom of the hull. "When you need to know something, I'll tell you."

Her eyes widened with fury, but she didn't say anything. Her patience was running thin from his methods. What was she in for once they landed in his territory?

After bringing the boat up the slender shore as far as they could, Esme looked around for a place where they might reach the pinnacle and his waiting companions. Perhaps there was a crevice or valley he knew of.

They started north. Rocks shifted under Esme's feet, forming tide pools in her wake as she continued looking for any indication as to how they'd reach the top of the cliff. She couldn't find one.

After fifty paces, Tearlach stopped and looked up. Her gaze followed.

"Are they going to help? What kind of magic can get us up there?"

A rope dropped in front of them.

"The kind where you climb, *Your Highness.*"

Her eyes rounded as she surveyed the hundred-plus feet of vertical, jagged wall before her. Climbing a tree was one thing, but a rope up the side of a cliff was entirely another.

"But..." she stammered.

"You, yourself, said it was dangerous to use magic." He smirked.

She stole another glance down the shore, but the wall ran as far as she could see.

"After you, *My Queen.*" He swept into a deep bow and lowered his head. If she had fangs, she would have flashed them.

When he stood with a smug look on his face, Esme crossed her arms over her chest and said adamantly, "I'm not going first."

"Yes, you are. And you know that's not negotiable." He grabbed the rope and handed it to her. End of discussion.

She knew he wouldn't risk leaving her alone. Aside from his oath to protect her, he was probably worried she'd run. Taking the rope with a little more haste than she'd intended, Esme pulled herself off the ground and wrapped her legs around it, trying to find a comfortable grip.

"Don't wrap your legs, use the wall."

Without acknowledging him, she repositioned herself. When her feet slipped, she could practically feel the grin on Tearlach's face.

Determined, she hoisted herself up a few feet. It got easier the farther she climbed. Once she was ten feet off the ground, the rope went taut as Tearlach pulled himself up below her.

She was very aware of what was in his line of sight and tried to think of something else—anything else.

"Pick up the pace, Princess."

She shot him a venomous look, but kept climbing.

After another twenty feet... "A ladybug could outclimb you."

She didn't respond, just rolled her eyes.

Several more feet and... "You know, you could have commanded me to carry you, being that I'm your loyal subject."

"Are you *trying* to make me angry?" She glared down at him, only to see that familiar smirk on his face.

"Anything to get you to the top before the sun goes down."

Huffing a breath, she conceded that any distraction was welcome if it kept her from thinking about the long drop. Trees, even tall ones, were nothing compared to mountains.

They proceeded in silence until the top was within reach.

"If I dangle a pastry above you, like the one you stole off my plate at the inn, would that get you to move your—"

Her nostrils flared as she jerked her chin toward him. "You *gave* me that pastry," she shouted, then muttered a particularly vulgar word under her breath. But Tearlach merely arched a brow and inclined his head past her.

Esme looked up to find that she had an audience.

Embarrassment flooded her cheeks. She focused all of her attention on her hands gripping the rope, on her feet planted against the rock. But there was nowhere to go. She'd reached the top.

Glancing hesitantly at the company that awaited her, her eyes fell first on the woman in the group who wore a thoroughly unwelcoming and unimpressed expression on her perfect face. Her stance made it appear as though she'd been waiting for days.

It hadn't taken Esme *that* long to climb up.

The man beside her looked slightly surprised, with raised eyebrows—which she greatly preferred to the near hostile look radiating off the woman. Then there was the last man, who seemed utterly amused. He was strikingly handsome and had a smile—

Never had she felt her body go liquid and heavy at the sight of a mere smile. And yet his...

Esme's inelegant first impression was completely forgotten with that smile. She took his large, strong hand and he easily hoisted her up onto steady ground, his eyes never leaving hers.

Chapter Nineteen

KILLIAN. HIS NAME was Killian. The tall, well-built man with dark blond, tousled hair that fell nearly to his shoulders, and piercing cerulean eyes kissed Esme's hand and flashed her another smile before she remembered they weren't alone on the edge of a cliff. Killian chuckled when she nearly tripped over her own feet to step away from him.

The other man approached her and nodded. "Armel."

Esme inclined her head in return. Though Armel's shoulders weren't as broad as Killian's or Tearlach's, his tall frame and lean muscles gave the impression that his strength rested in agility. And where Killian's hair was messy and free, Armel's dark hair was short, tucked back behind the points of his ears.

The two men wore dark gray coats that swept to their knees. The smooth material looked heavy and protective, but seemed to contour perfectly around their muscular arms. Much like the chest plate Tearlach wore, theirs were made of something he likely wasn't able to find in the mortal realm. The gauntlets on their forearms and their tall boots were made of a similar material and looked as though they could withstand the edge of a sword. Both were armed to the teeth with curved, etched blades and daggers. Swords were strapped to their backs with hilts that matched the one Tearlach carried.

They were warriors. And very clearly Fae. Aside from Tearlach, she hadn't been around any of her kind in nine years. It was both comforting and overwhelming.

Esme had a million questions for each of them, but hesitated, turning toward the woman in the group. Her coat was a deep shade of green with a burnt caramel–colored chest plate that dipped slightly in the center, making her harsh wardrobe seem feminine. She carried just as many weapons, including a bow and quiver across her back. Standing nearly as tall as the others, the woman's pale blue eyes and short brown hair that fell straight to her shoulders made her look chic and put together.

Ignoring Esme completely, the woman fixed her eyes on Tearlach as he pulled himself up over the ledge. When he rose to his full height, Esme felt infinitesimally small next to the four of them.

"Hazel." Tearlach nodded to the woman. "I see you got my message."

Her name was Hazel, then. Killian, Armel, Hazel—Esme committed the names to memory.

Without responding, the woman wrapped Tearlach in a fierce hug. A twinge of jealousy tightened Esme's chest as he returned the sentiment. He'd never come close to embracing Esme in such a way. Not once. Even in the moments when she'd clearly needed it.

"I sensed you a few days ago. We set off immediately." Hazel's eyes were affectionate as she pulled away, holding Tearlach at arm's length. Then her expression turned unsure. "But I may not have been the only one, so we shouldn't linger."

Tearlach dipped his chin in agreement. Despite their aid, they still weren't safe.

Stepping away from Hazel, Tearlach sighed deeply as he moved to the two men, embracing each in turn. There was something about witnessing such a show of emotion between grown men. It reminded Esme that beneath the brawn and imperturbable self-command, they were still vulnerable creatures who cared for one another.

As he released Killian, Esme caught the faint indication of a genuine smile on Tearlach's face. She'd seen his arrogant smirk, but never a wholehearted smile. It was gone before she could fully absorb it.

Tearlach gestured to the group, then looked at Esme. "Warriors of the Tremaene army," he introduced, "and my personal band."

"I'm very pleased to meet you all." And she was. Though Hazel wouldn't meet her eyes, she felt safe surrounded by Tearlach's companions.

"Actually, we go by the Northern Rebels now," Armel corrected.

"Rebels?" Tearlach asked, keeping the worry from his voice—though Esme saw in his eyes.

"A lot has changed since you left."

They considered each other for a tense moment, before Killian stepped to Esme's side. "Nice of you to bring such a beautiful woman back with you." He nudged her shoulder and flashed another captivating smile.

Esme blushed at the compliment. He certainly knew the effect he had on women.

Killian inclined his head. "And your name, sweetheart?"

Esme's eyebrows scrunched in confusion. Didn't they know? "I...uh...I'm Esme," she stated as though it should have been obvious.

Killian, Armel, and Hazel stiffened instantly, staring at her in disbelief.

Hazel lowered her eyes to a scrutinizing stare. There were certain names reserved for royal heirs, and it seemed the woman before her was coming to the realization that Esme could be none other than—

"Esme? Princess of Tremaene?"

"But you..." Killian began. "We believed—everyone in Tremaene believes—that you were killed shortly after your parents died." He winced.

Esme's lips parted. They thought she was dead?

Well, she considered, someone certainly didn't think so if assassins had come looking for her.

"Sully never told you?" Tearlach leaned back, casting a stunned look on each of them.

"Does it look like we knew?" Armel tilted his head at Tearlach.

"After Sully informed us about the royal family," Hazel offered, "and that he suspected it was not an accident, he told us he'd sent you on a mission to find and protect a hidden magic in an uncharted land that could potentially restore the kingdom. And that you might not return for several years."

A hidden magic in an uncharted land? Was that all Esme was to Tremaene? She struggled to keep her face impassive.

"Where have you been these last nine years?" Hazel asked. "I wasn't able to pick up your signal until a few days ago." Esme could see the anguish in the woman's eyes. Had she spent all those years wondering if Tearlach would ever return, if he was even alive?

"We were in the mortal realm."

They gaped at him.

"Past the fog?" Hazel asked with disbelief. "But how?"

Collecting himself the quickest, Killian sidled up to Tearlach and swept an arm over his shoulder, leading them down into the valley. "You have much to tell us, brother."

The others were so caught up in questioning their long-lost comrade that Esme was quickly left behind. Everyone was talking over one another, and she could only pick up a few threads of the conversation. At one point there was mixture of laughter and offended grumbles when Hazel mentioned she'd kept the men in line while Tearlach had been away. Eventually the discussion turned to the course they'd take back to Altan—which direction would be fastest, safest, where they'd make camp.

Trying to meet their long strides while taking in the expansive majesty of the Tamslo Mountains sprawled before her, the chatter faded from Esme's awareness.

As they approached the tree line, Esme slowed her hurried pace. She gazed up at the row of towering trees, trying to make out why they seemed so familiar to her. Perhaps it was the scent of the forest—a fresh, earthy embrace that awakened all of her senses.

The others had moved ahead, already within the shadows of the forest.

Esme caught up to the others just as Hazel cursed.

The sound of an arrow whizzing overhead had Esme dropping to the ground. She heard it strike a nearby tree, but she couldn't see anything beyond the wall of boots and armor surrounding her.

But that protection didn't last long. Tearlach barked an order and Armel, Hazel, and Killian took off without hesitation, ready to engage.

Tearlach hauled Esme up, only to drop her back on the ground at the base of a tree. "Stay down," he snarled before running toward a charging assailant who'd just drawn a blade.

Esme didn't question his order. She stayed low, crawling around to the other side of the trunk, hoping to remain unseen.

Against her hands, the bark felt soft and fibrous...as though she could peel it away in strips.

Fear coalesced in her mind as she darted a glance at the surrounding trees—her breath trapped in her lungs.

She'd seen them before.

The same trees from her dream.

Chapter Twenty

HER HEARTBEAT KICKED up to a wild beat. Holding her breath, Esme peered around the tree.

Killian was engaged with a man, pushing him back with each sword clash until he ducked low and jutted the blade up into the man's abdomen. Esme jerked her head away at the sight.

Closer to the tree line she spotted Hazel, standing motionless beside a wide trunk, unseen save for the point of the arrow she let loose a moment later. Esme didn't need to see the arrow meet its mark—the grunt that followed told her as much. Scanning the area again, she found Tearlach fighting two men at once. How many were there? They were surely outnumbered.

A branch snapped behind her.

No.

Esme spun around, putting her back against the tree. Remaining still, her eyes darted from one tree to another, searching for movement. But there was nothing.

Then a bit of silver twenty paces away flashed in the dappled light. Rolling to her hands and knees, Esme crawled carefully to the other side of the tree—placing her in full view of the many battles being waged. She lowered herself as much as she could, feeling far too exposed.

There was no one left to protect her. She caught Tearlach's eye as he took down the second man. Their eyes locked for a fraction of a second before he turned and engaged with another attacker.

Esme held her breath—her eyes wide with fear—then shoved the thoughts from her mind and started digging frantically through the thick carpet of pine needles for anything she could use as a weapon. Her dagger felt heavy at her side, but she didn't like the idea of being close enough to use it. A branch would be better, or a stick with a sharp point.

She would not be taken. *Not this time.*

If faced with the same man from her dream, she'd fight. Stealing a quick glance around the trunk, Esme looked for signs of his approach.

Nothing.

Was he still there or had he taken up a new position? Had he seen her?

As panic started to rise in her throat, a deep voice blasted into her mind.

Get up in the tree! Now!

The air rushed from her lungs. The voice was not her own.

Imminent danger lurked ever closer, but all Esme could think about in that moment was the voice in her head.

Later, she scolded herself. There were far more pressing matters.

Looking up at the towering tree, she considered the validity of the command. How had it not occurred to her? It was the easiest place to hide—the only place—and was far safer than attempting to fight. She had no skills, dagger or no. And trying to use the blade would likely result in getting herself killed faster.

She stood, eying the trunk. Climbing a tree wasn't the issue—Esme had been climbing since she was a child—but climbing *that* tree would be an issue. She knew from the feel of the bark that it would be difficult to grip. Where the trees she'd climbed were narrow enough to wrap her legs around or bumpy with knots and ridges for hand- and footholds, the tree before her was neither.

Movement caught her eye.

The attacker shot out from behind a tree ten paces away. Esme stifled a cry, slamming her back against the tree as he lunged for her.

A massive branch swung down, knocking the man to the ground.

Without hesitation, she turned and gripped the tree, knowing exactly how the rest would play out.

The man groaned beneath her and Esme knew he was righting himself. She didn't have long.

Clinging to the trunk with her knees, she scrambled to the first branch. It was by sheer act of will that got her there. She grabbed the limb and released the trunk, swinging her legs up toward the branch.

A hand fisted around her ankle.

Esme kicked blindly with her other foot, but the man ducked and caught it in his strong grip.

Her hands started to slip on the soft bark.

Help, she whimpered silently. There was no use saying it aloud, no one would be able to come to her aid.

She pulled her foot free from her boot and kicked the man's face. He cursed and yanked her other leg hard enough that she lost her grip with one hand. Esme reached to reclaim the branch, risking a glance down as she clutched it.

Two thick roots wound up the man's legs, tugging him back. Esme fought off his grip and clambered up the tree.

Once she reached a sturdier limb, she paused to steady her breath, peering hesitantly through the branches beneath her. The sight of her attacker slicing through the snaring roots was only visible for a second before the boughs moved, crossing over one another to hide her from view.

Pulling herself to a higher vantage point, she searched the forest for her companions.

Stay up there, she heard. It was the same voice, low and threatening, echoing through her mind. Esme swallowed the impulse to snap back, to refuse, but in truth she had no intention of coming down.

Through narrow lines of sight, Esme caught a glimpse of Tearlach as he bolted toward her. The massive tree shook slightly before the zing of a sword halted the tremor. Then all she could hear was a wet choking sound below. She winced, trying not to picture it.

A ball of fire exploded nearby. Flames licked the tops of the trees.

Magic. But whose? Surely that was dangerous. Not only would the use of magic further compromise their trail, but the burning treetops would absolutely draw attention.

A column of water twisted up through the trees, extinguishing the embers before the forest could ignite.

"Water magic," Esme breathed as smoke rose into the sky. She'd never seen water magic before. It was quite rare.

Another flame caught her attention—a streak of fire arched over the canopy. The flaming arrow caught its mark with a cry. Esme only hoped the arrow was one of Hazel's.

It took several long, tense minutes before the forest finally went quiet. And several more minutes until Tearlach's voice called up to her.

Esme sighed, sinking down on the branch.

"Where's Esme?" she heard Killian ask. There was clear concern in his voice, so she pulled herself back to her feet and started down.

Tearlach must have indicated her location, and that she was safe, because Hazel and Armel departed upon seeing her up above, heading back to where fighting had been heaviest. Before Esme reached the lower branches, she caught sight of them again—each dragging a body toward the cliff's edge, pushing them over to the shore below.

She looked away, trying to forget the image of life being discarded so easily. She couldn't let herself feel anything, not when her emotions could easily trigger magic she had no control over.

When she stepped down onto the lowest limb that would bear her weight, Tearlach—assured that she was in one piece—stalked off to help the others, leaving only Killian to wait for her.

Still ten feet from the forest floor, Esme inched off the branch and wrapped her legs around the tree. Going up had been much easier...or maybe it had been the fear of being captured. She grimaced at the thought of sliding down, at what it would do to her hands.

"I've got you," Killian promised from below.

She squeezed her eyes shut at the thought of letting go. Of falling. "Oh, that's not necessary, I can manage. I've done this before." *Well, sort of.* Never with a tree of that size. But she didn't need to be rescued, and she especially did not need to fall into Killian's arms. His strong, capable arms...

No. She definitely didn't need that.

Easing away from the safety of the limb, she lowered a few feet.

"You've got nothing to prove, sweetheart. Just let go."

Easier said than done.

"I swear, I'll catch you."

Esme grabbed hold of a thin branch with her right hand. It bowed, yet held her weight as she reached for it with the other.

Then cracked.

Shit. Esme flailed, grasping for contact. She managed to grab hold of another branch, but it tore easily from the trunk.

The air left her lungs. Her eyes squeezed shut.

Steady arms caught her, absorbing the impact. Esme inhaled deeply, regretting it the moment she smelled Killian. Biting back a whimper, she fluttered her eyes open.

Killian was much too close. Esme shied away. She couldn't handle the roguish look in his eyes while they were entangled.

She struggled to her feet. Her legs took too long to regain their balance, but Esme refused to reach back for Killian. She shot a look at the tree—the one that had assisted her escape from the enemy only to let her fall into Killian's arms. It seemed trees had a sense of humor.

"Not so bad, now was it?"

"Um, no. Thank you." She brushed the dirt from her pants, feeling her cheeks heat at his nearness.

Where was her boot? She needed to find it before Killian attempted to slip it on for her.

She looked up at the approaching footfalls. Hazel and Armel continued to scan the area, but Tearlach's gaze was fixed on her. Before she could break the stare, his eyes cut to Killian. How had the tension swelled so quickly after winning a battle? Shouldn't there have been a collective feeling of relief?

Esme ducked away, finding her discarded boot a few paces from the base of the tree. She poured all of her attention into pulling it back on.

"We need to head north, lead them away from Altan," Killian offered in a tone that seemed placating.

"I agree, we go the long way," Armel concurred.

Hazel strode off in that direction, leading before Tearlach could object. She kept close to the edge of the forest, though still inside the shelter of the trees.

Killian stayed back, walking close to Esme as the others were drawn into another discussion.

Expecting something flirtatious, Esme was surprised to find Killian nothing but attentive and understanding. He asked how she was doing, not letting her brush the question away with a simple "fine." He seemed genuinely concerned with how she was coping.

"Climbing the tree was a good idea."

Esme grimaced at the mention—at whose idea it was. "Sure. I ran and hid while the rest of you fought."

"Your life is worth more than any of ours, Esme. Especially mine." He grinned, the only indication of the coquettish man she'd seen earlier. "Leave it to us."

"How can I do that? I put everyone around me in danger just by setting foot in this land." She tried not to think of what her mere presence had inflicted on the innocent people of Debarrow. She hoped they'd been spared.

"You've done no such thing. If people are searching for you, it only means you're very important. Or they wouldn't want you so badly. All the more reason for you to trust us to protect you."

They walked in silence until Killian offered, "They may not have been looking for you anyway."

Esme knew that wasn't true, she'd seen what would've happened had she not made it up the tree. That man would have taken her. They wanted *her*, no one else.

"Scouts have been patrolling the north for years, killing rebels and rebel sympathizers—though we've not seen them this far into the mountains before. The Clavlin Ridge is not easily crossed and we quickly stop them before they make it too far into our territory."

Hazel beckoned Killian before he could elaborate. Picking up the pace, he urged Esme along as he gave Hazel directions to an outcropping where they might camp for the night.

Taking the opportunity to slip away, Esme moved over to Tearlach and grabbed his elbow. There was something she needed to know.

"Can I speak with you?" Her voice was quiet, though not quiet enough. Hazel shot her a glare over her shoulder. Esme couldn't blame her. She'd be just as unfriendly if a strange woman had shown up and pinned a target on *her* back.

"Go on ahead, we won't be far behind." Tearlach turned to Esme. "This had better be quick, we can't stay long in one place." He surveyed the area as he spoke.

"The attack...it was like the dream."

"I know."

"But it didn't play out exactly the same." She canted her head to the side, challenging him, seeing if he would reveal anything.

He simply raised his brow in question.

"It started the same, but then a voice told me to get in the tree. It kept me safe, kept me from being taken."

Tearlach's gaze was unyielding, but Esme caught a flicker in his eyes.

When it was clear he wouldn't admit anything, she said, "It was *your* voice."

Still nothing.

"Why was your voice in my head, Tearlach?" she demanded.

Glancing toward the others as they marched on, Tearlach stepped closer. "An unexpected side effect of the Lifeblood Oath."

"It allows you to communicate with me without speaking?"

"It would appear that way, wouldn't it?"

Esme clenched her jaw. Couldn't he just answer—

She sucked in a breath. "That means—That means *you* can hear *me*, doesn't it?"

Tearlach took far too long before replying a simple "Yes."

She gulped down a breath. "Since when?" Her anger mounted.

"The day you fell from the tree in Debarrow."

That long? Her eyes widened. He'd been listening to her thoughts that long?

Her chest filled with heat and fury. She ground her teeth, glaring at him. "Why didn't you tell me?" Her hands fisted at her sides and a clap of thunder sounded just off the shore.

Tearlach was on her in an instant, gripping her shoulders. She could feel the thrum of magic slip from her, flowing into his hands. The dizzying sensation lasted only a moment as he absorbed her energy.

"Not. Now." His voice was threateningly soft.

She tried to slow her breathing. As much as she wanted to rage at him, Esme forced her thoughts aside, turning to memories of her garden, her apple trees.

"I can't hear everything," he said quietly. "It's not that invasive. I believe…" He sighed. "It seems to only happen when you're in danger, in need of protection. And I assume you'll begin to feel the connection as I do now that your magic is becoming stronger."

Esme searched his eyes as the events in Debarrow came into clearer focus. That was how he'd known about the tree, how he'd found her that night in the alley. Tearlach hadn't witnessed any of it. He'd *heard* her call for help. That was the part of their connection he'd been keeping from her.

Another moment passed and slowly Tearlach lifted his hands away, seemingly satisfied that she wouldn't evoke another storm. Then he stalked back toward the others.

It wasn't attacks or unknown threats that would summon her magic; Tearlach was as much a trigger as an enemy.

She followed behind, glaring daggers at his back.

Chapter Twenty-One

WHEN ESME JOINED the group again, she welcomed Killian's attention. Armel seemed the quiet one, Hazel barely acknowledged her, and Tearlach...well, it would be fine if she didn't have to speak with Tearlach for a good long while.

"I'm from Talare, a small village in the north," Killian told her. Esme was appreciative that Killian hadn't turned any of the questions back on her. She wasn't ready to talk about her time in Debarrow.

"It's far beyond the mountains, in an area that's scarcely populated," he continued. "I wouldn't be surprised if you'd never heard of it."

"And your family?"

"I didn't know my father. And after my mother died, Hazel's family took me in."

Esme halted and turned to Killian, knowing all too well the pain and struggle of going on after such a thing. "Killian, I'm so sorry. Truly."

He nodded. "Thank you, but I really am fine."

"How old were you?"

"Just a boy, but I remember the time we had together." After pausing for a long moment, he went on. "She was a seamstress, had her own shop at the far end of town. One night, she went back for something and inadvertently caught two thieves ransacking their way through the darkened buildings. She got in the way."

Esme took his hand firmly until he looked over. "Were they brought to justice?" Killian shook his head, kissed the top of her hand, then pulled her on. They walked in silence for a while.

"Hazel and I were just kids when we started talking about becoming warriors, to fight in the war and protect those who couldn't defend themselves. It hadn't reached the mountains yet, but we'd grown up on tales of men that had gone off to fight for our people." As he recounted adventures of his youth, Killian's mood shifted back to what Esme was coming to understand as his usual lighthearted self.

"At sixteen, I decided I couldn't wait any longer and announced I was leaving for Altan. Hazel's parents argued that I was too young, but I refused to listen. Nothing could've stopped me. The day before I was set to leave, Hazel informed them that she would be joining me. They objected, of course, but the next day we set off."

Esme was impressed by Hazel's determination. "Did they finally accept her decision?"

"Nope. She hasn't heard a word from them since."

"How long ago was that?"

He looked at her and grinned, his eyes sparkling. "A very long time ago."

She averted her eyes, feeling uncomfortably young once again.

"And the others, how did you all become friends?"

"Most of the warriors had been fighting for years when we joined. War was new to both of us, so Tearlach and Armel trained us on the battlefield. It was harsh, but effective. No better way to learn than in the midst of a raging war. By the time it came to a close," he continued as his bright blue eyes took on a darker shade, "the four of us were all who remained of our faction in the north. We formed our own kind of family. Years later, Tearlach was named commander and appointed the rest of us to his personal band."

Commander? Tearlach was the commander? Yet another thing he'd failed to mention.

Killian went on to tell of his magic—that Hazel's had manifested as fire, as did Killian's a few years later. They learned their skill together on the battlefront, guided by Tearlach and Armel.

Esme began to wonder if Killian's relationship with Hazel was more than a childhood friendship, turned family. The look on her face must have conveyed as much.

"Hazel is my sister, she's always been that to me," Killian clarified, arching a brow knowingly.

Esme's cheeks flushed and she looked away. There was no reason to feel jealous. What a silly notion. She'd only just met him.

"And if Hazel's interested in anyone here," he added, inclining his head toward the others, "it isn't me."

Who, then? Armel, Tearlach?

Tearlach. Just thinking his name summoned the anger she'd neatly tucked away.

Glancing up ahead to where Tearlach stalked beside Armel and Hazel, Esme conjured up a few mocking comments...and maybe a less-than-savory insult. Directing her thoughts at him, she tested their inconvenient connection.

He didn't so much as look in her direction. Maybe he was right. Maybe it did only work when she was in danger.

When they stopped to make camp, Killian set off to check the perimeter. Unsure of her role or what skill she might offer, Esme stood off to the side, watching as the others worked together effortlessly. Each knew exactly which task they were best suited for, as though they'd been doing it their whole lives. Even after the years Tearlach had been absent, they still fit together seamlessly, as if no time had passed at all.

She wanted to help, even opened her mouth a few times to offer, but knew she'd only get in the way.

The grumble of her stomach reminded her how long it'd been since her last meal. She snuck off into the woods to find food, fairly certain that any offered by her new companions would be of the meat variety.

She foraged through the brush, humming softly to herself as the world faded into the background. When she rose from her crouched position, Tearlach's presence startled her into dropping every last item she'd gathered.

Esme scowled at him as he leaned casually against a nearby tree, his arms crossed over his chest. Though anyone who knew him could tell his stance was anything but relaxed.

She bent down to retrieve her scattered goods, wondering why she'd thought even for a moment that he'd let her go off alone.

Ignoring Tearlach, she set off toward camp.

Tearlach fell into step beside her, peering down at the outstretched hem of her shirt. "This is why you've risked us being seen? Some mushrooms and a few nuts?"

"Though I adore your company, I'm perfectly capable of finding my way back," she asserted.

He growled and shook his head.

Killian raised his eyebrows as she walked into camp and found a spot next to him. He smiled and told her quietly, "You're getting under his skin. Not many people can do that."

"Yeah, well, so is he."

As she cracked the nuts she'd foraged, she watched curiously as Hazel started a fire with what seemed like nothing more than a blink of an eye.

"You have fire magic, right? Like Killian?"

"Fire, yes. Like Killian, no." She didn't look up.

Armel clarified. "They were both given power from Aeveen, goddess of fire. Hazel's magic is very precise, cutting, where Killian's magic is a bit more..."

"Reckless," Hazel finished.

Killian replied in a swaggering voice. "The goddess knew I could handle more of it."

"Killian is no longer allowed to start campfires," Tearlach interjected, looking briefly at Esme.

"Your eyebrows grew back, old man."

Tearlach growled.

Esme suppressed a laugh, shocked that Killian was still alive after something like that.

Hazel and Killian continued discussing their magic—comparing stories, arguing whose was better, and how each defined the term "better." She even caught Armel laughing. Up until that point, he'd seemed the most serious of the group, aside from Tearlach. But even Tearlach appeared less stern after being reunited with them.

"Hazel is also a sensor," Tearlach informed her. Esme looked at her in amazement. Two magical gifts? She'd been wondering about it since Hazel had mentioned picking up Tearlach's signal off the coast.

"And you?" She turned to Armel.

"Water magic."

Ah. It had been his magic that quashed Killian's intrepid display of fire during the attack.

"What are you able to do with it?"

"Direct it, freeze it...fill lakes and streams." He shrugged his shoulders as if it were nothing special. Esme stared at him, then glanced around the circle, awestruck by the talent surrounding her.

"It's pretty rare, he has quite a gift." Hazel darted a glance at Armel.

Directing an element was one thing—something Esme hoped to master one day—but creating it...well, Hazel was right. Armel was quite gifted.

Clearly not comfortable with the attention, Armel quickly turned the attention to Esme. "And what about your magic?"

Four sets of eyes fell on her.

Though she'd been avoiding Tearlach, she conceded a look to him, unsure of what to say.

"It's still awakening," he answered for her, "but it appears she has a considerable sway on the weather."

"That could be rather useful," Armel remarked. "We haven't seen rain in ages."

Esme furrowed her brow at the comment. But before she could ask, Tearlach explained his plans for training her new ability once they arrived in Altan. She wasn't sure why it would be any safer to use her magic there, but understood that it was better to have her power under control than not. And her training wouldn't just be in magic, she'd learn fighting techniques from Armel, Hazel, and Killian as well.

Esme's *resurrecting* power wasn't mentioned. Tearlach must have had cause to keep the knowledge of her unusual talent between the two of them, she just couldn't reason what it was.

Chapter Twenty-Two

DESPITE A GLARE from Tearlach, Killian escorted Esme to a nearby stream the next morning. The sun-kissed sky glowed a soft orange, sending rays through the thick tree trunks. The rocky shore gave way to deeper water that flowed swiftly into a wide gully.

Esme twisted to look over her shoulder at Killian, who wore a mischievous grin. She gave him a pointed look that said she had no intention of removing any clothing until he left.

He held up his hands. "Can you blame me?" His smile grew as he turned to walk away.

Esme undressed and waded in. The chill of the water coaxed her to wash quickly, and in no time she was back at Killian's side. When they returned, she noticed a hawk lingering on a high branch of a redwood. He'd been there since dawn, watching from above.

Tearlach offered her a piece of bread and some dried fruit. She didn't need to see his eyes to know he was irritated. "Eat quickly, we're leaving soon."

Armel set a cup of water beside her on the log. She thanked him and took a sip. After swallowing the sweet nectar, she gulped down the rest. Never had water tasted so good. Staring at the empty cup in wonder, she looked again at Armel. Oh yes, the man truly had a gift with water. He offered her a slight smile, then flicked his hand toward the fire to douse it.

Out of the corner of her eye, Esme caught a flicker of golden feathers as the hawk leapt from its perch. It dropped toward the center of the small clearing. Esme eyed it warily in the few seconds it took to descend, worried she might not be awake and that the hawk was yet another messenger come to reveal a foreboding danger.

It swooped parallel to the ground and Esme gasped at the sudden flash of light and ruffling of feathers that preceded the animal's shift into its true Fae form.

The men cursed and lowered weapons Esme hadn't noticed them draw. Hazel reprimanded the man that stood before them as she slid an arrow back into her quiver. "It's really not wise to startle people who are trained to kill," she warned.

The man wore a brown tunic, with black, scaled gauntlets edged with silver brads. His long dark hair was secured with a strap at the base of his neck. Without his guard uniform, it took Esme a moment to realize who he was. But those kind, blue eyes...She could never forget those.

"Captain Sullivan," she breathed. "You're alive. You're here." Her voice began to rise as the realization fell fully upon her.

His mouth curved into a smile as he took her in as well. They stood unmoving for a moment, Esme mirroring his wholehearted joy with her own smile.

"Esme," he sighed, as though the weight of nine years had been lifted. He stepped forward and wrapped her in a hug.

When he pulled away, Esme stood stunned, unable to speak. He turned to address the others, informing them that when he'd returned to Altan they'd been gone, tracking down a signal from Tearlach. Another sensor had been able to pick up their group, but the signal had been lost before he could get an exact location.

"I assumed it was your glamour." He looked to Tearlach, who nodded in reply.

"Then how did you find us?" There was a sharp edge to Hazel's question.

"I circled above the mountains last night until I caught sight of your fire. I found no others patrolling the area. Do not worry." Hazel relaxed, and the captain added, "I didn't think it best to *startle* anyone last night." He gave her a smirk. "So I waited until morning."

"And what about her?" Hazel jerked her chin toward Esme.

"Ah, yes. That. I do apologize for keeping that information from all of you. It was safer for Esme, and everyone in Tremaene, to believe that she was no longer alive."

Hazel huffed, grabbed her pack, and disappeared into the woods.

"We should go." Armel glanced at Tearlach and Killian.

The men followed Hazel, giving Captain Sullivan and Esme enough distance so they could speak privately.

"Let me first say, Your Highness, that I'm sorry for failing to protect your parents. I should have been with them." The directness of his words struck her right in the center of her chest.

She looked up at him and saw the sorrow pooling in his eyes, as though he'd wanted—*needed*—to say those words to her every day since that fateful night. He carried as much of a burden for their deaths as Esme did for leaving her people. Taking his hand in both of hers, she held his gaze. "It wasn't your fault. Do not blame yourself."

They spent a time walking in silence before Sullivan confessed his reasoning for what he'd done—that while Esme had believed her trip to Donellis was to expand her awareness of the arts, it had been a purely preventative measure to keep her away from the capital city of Meallán... and it had been her mother's idea. The queen had feared something was coming, something that would threaten the crown.

Esme thought again of her premonitory dreams and wondered if her mother had been privy to such visions as well. But why had she never spoken of such things with her? Guilt twisted her stomach as she reflected on her carefree youth, when she'd thought nothing could touch her or her family. If she'd known, she could have done things differently.

Sullivan explained that upon receiving word of her parents' deaths, he'd taken his hawk form to meet Esme secretly. Trusting no one, he'd avoided every guard between Meallán and Donellis. After leaving her suite that night, he'd spotted a guard heading toward the villa who'd not been sent by him. As captain of the royal guard, orders were given by him, and him alone. And while Sullivan had captured the lone guard, the man refused to reveal who'd sent him. Using a memory spell to plant a few select impressions in the guard's mind, Sullivan had convinced the guard that he'd killed the Princess of Tremaene.

The captain again apologized to Esme for perpetuating the falsehood of her death, but assured her that it had been a necessary precaution. It wouldn't have been safe for anyone to know she was alive with the treason lurking within their kingdom. He swore he'd wanted to protect her in Periwen, but once it had become clear that her capture had been ordered, Sullivan knew he couldn't follow her across the sea. So until she was grown and could wield her own magic, he decided that no one could learn of her whereabouts or that she even lived.

Sullivan had stayed in Tremaene, away from her, to keep her safe.

But he hadn't sent Esme to a foreign land without protection. He'd heard tales of a legendary warrior who commanded the army in the north. And while Sullivan hadn't initially been aware of Tearlach's ability to glamour magical signatures, learning of it only solidified his decision to select him as Esme's protector.

"Esme." He took her hand, pulling her to a stop. "Please forgive me for not telling you more at the time, and for not coming to find you in the mortal realm. I wanted you to be free of this for as long as possible, to not worry every waking moment about what might come to pass. I wanted you to live."

He searched her eyes for forgiveness. Not just from her, but from her mother and father—those he'd spent the last nine years believing he'd failed.

"I forgive you, Captain Sullivan. I know you did what was required. And I did live," she promised with a faint smile.

Everything he'd done had been for her protection. He'd pledged his life to her family and the crown, and while he hadn't been able to watch over her in Periwen, he'd done everything in his power to protect the only heir of Tremaene.

He nodded, but looked as though he struggled to accept her forgiveness, having no doubt questioned his decisions endlessly over the years.

After a moment, they continued walking, though still a good distance from Tearlach and the others. Quietly, he began, "Your lady-in-waiting, she…"

Esme put up a hand to stop him. His words were spoken softly, but they struck hard nonetheless. She didn't need to hear the rest. That short phrase was confirmation enough of what she'd most feared and had long denied. Though the events of that night and the following days at sea were lost memories, she was certain Cadwyn had been with her, that they'd fled together. But her dear friend had not survived the journey.

She knew what the captain would say, he'd offer his condolences for the loss of yet another person she cared about.

Sullivan searched her face, then nodded his head at her unspoken request not to say anything further. But his expression was not what she'd expected. It didn't seem to be understanding that shone in his eyes, but confusion.

He circled back to his story of finding Tearlach, giving the same account about the Lifeblood Oath. And with that, a tightness Esme had harbored since Tearlach had first entered her life—the last tiny bit of disbelief—finally released its grip.

"Sullivan?"

"Yes?"

"Who's been ruling in my parents' place?" She was surprised nothing had been mentioned by him or the others. But then…she also hadn't inquired about it.

He seemed shocked. "Did no one tell you?"

"Tell me what?" Esme sensed she wouldn't like what was coming.

"Orianna rules Tremaene."

Esme tried to place the name. A high-priestess, and a young one at that. It was like Tearlach had said. Perhaps things weren't so bad.

"She took over after the accident? That's what the treaty dictates, does it not?"

"Yes and no. You're alive, so the stipulation that a high-priestess be given the throne does not apply. It never has. Esme," Sullivan spoke carefully to her, like she wasn't grasping something that was right in front of her. "You are the heir to the throne. The crown of Tremaene is rightfully yours."

"Yes, but," she said, taking a deep breath, "what if I choose not to rule?" She shied away from the stunned glances Tearlach, Killian, Hazel, and Armel turned on her, realizing they'd heard everything.

Turning to Sullivan, she attempted to convince him. "I've never been trained for the role. Maybe it's best if a speaker for the gods led the people of Tremaene instead of me."

Everyone froze. The tension was palpable as Esme risked a glance at the others. No one said a word, they only looked on in silence. She instantly felt like she'd betrayed not just them, but her entire kingdom. Again.

But surely they must have considered the same. She had no experience as a leader. She was only thinking of what was best for her people.

"My dear, Orianna poisoned and killed every priestess in the Order—disguising it as a strange illness—then orchestrated your parents' fatal accident in the ravine." He paused a moment, letting the atrocities sink in. "She did not humbly and selflessly accept the throne in the absence of any surviving member of the royal family, she stole it through force and deception. Through murder."

The ringing in her ears had risen to such a high decibel, she could barely hear Sullivan's last words. A tremble ran through her body and left her feeling so weak she felt as though she might collapse.

She could feel the presence of the others as they drew closer, then the weight of a steady hand on her shoulder. It all made sense—why no one had come looking for her, the reason Tearlach hadn't dared to bring her home until her magic had awakened, until she could defend herself. Because it still wasn't safe in Tremaene, not for her.

She opened and closed her mouth several times as the truth set in.

Sullivan voiced the words she couldn't. "Orianna has been waiting nine years for your magic to manifest so she could find you. She will stop at nothing until she finishes what she started."

Chapter Twenty-Three

STRENGTH SEEPED IN from Tearlach's touch. Esme glanced up at him. Did he know about Orianna, about what she'd done? Had the others informed him? Had he…kept it from her?

The look in his eyes said it all—he'd known. And hadn't told her.

She pursed her lips together and focused on the solid earth below her feet, trying to calm her pounding heart.

With a sigh, she met his gaze again. Tearlach did nothing without reason, she knew that. There was a flicker in his eyes—fury was roiling beneath his calm exterior. It wasn't just about her. Orianna hadn't only taken Esme's family and her birthright, she'd stolen Tremaene from its people. From Tearlach. From everyone.

Seeing her understanding, Tearlach dipped his chin a fraction of an inch, then lifted his hand away.

Silently, they resumed their trek north. Questions spun in her mind, each fighting for her attention and weaving a picture she could barely stand to see.

"Sullivan?" The captain took a step closer to her. "How does the high-priestess know I'm still alive?" The revulsion toward a woman she'd never met threatened to make Esme sick, but she inhaled slowly, curbing her temper. She needed to understand everything. And that wouldn't happen if she allowed anger to leak into her blood.

The captain paused a moment, but seemed to decide it was best to tell her everything. "After arranging for your protection," he said, nodding toward Tearlach, "I secretly returned to Meallán, seeking the guard who was sent to...capture you." He said *capture*, but they both knew capture wasn't what the man had been ordered to do. "The commotion of the king's and queen's deaths made it difficult to find answers. A high-priestess from the Arlais temple in Belfay had already been summoned by the council, and the royal guards were searching for you. I was able to meet in private with some of the city guards, who confirmed that the guard sent to kill you had informed Orianna of your death. His body was later found outside the city wall. I believe she saw through the false memory I planted and assumed you'd gone into hiding. But you were only fifteen, just a girl. Without magic, you weren't a threat to her. So long as you never returned."

And there she was, standing on Tremaene's soil. Had she started a war simply by setting foot in her kingdom?

"A few weeks later, Orianna announced publicly that you'd been killed. I wasn't there, but was told her performance was quite convincing. And with my absence aligning with yours, the high-priestess named me as the one who'd murdered you."

Esme sucked in a breath. Orianna was far more scheming than she'd first imagined. Although, blaming the captain made perfect sense—anyone close to the royal family could pose a risk to the woman's reign. And with the uncertainty of his whereabouts, pinning a treasonous murder on the captain of the royal guard would keep him away and thwart any who considered rising against the newly crowned queen.

Esme clenched and unclenched her fists until she quelled the tempest rising inside her. Tearlach took a step closer as they hiked up a particularly steep incline.

"What of the others at the palace?" She wasn't sure she really wanted to know, afraid she might learn that countless people who'd been part of her life were no longer alive. But she needed to know—had to know everything.

"Some of the staff were able to leave unnoticed, others stayed on. Orianna wasted no time replacing those in positions of power, though a few guards from your parents' reign remain to this day. Some are still able to slip us information. The others...well, I wouldn't necessarily count them as loyal to Orianna."

Esme breathed a sigh of relief that they'd been spared, and that some were still within the palace walls. Certainly that was a good thing. Wasn't it?

When they stopped for a midday meal, Esme sat quietly on her own. Sullivan had been a comforting, familiar presence, but she needed space. The indistinct chatter of her companions faded as she gazed up at the canopy and through the rows of thick tree trunks.

If Orianna was the only remaining high-priestess, how were the trees alive? How were the streams still flowing with water? The longer she pondered it, the more she realized that the forest wasn't exactly thriving. There was something missing...many things missing.

Perhaps she'd been in the mortal realm too long and had forgotten what the immortal wilderness was like. While the Tamslo Mountain range wasn't a place she'd ever visited, she could tell it wasn't what it had once been. Only ancient trees stood in the forest, with a few hardy plants dotting the soil.

Where were the flowers, the creeping vines, the ferns and fuzzy mosses, the purple and red lichen...the birds? She strained her ears, but couldn't hear even a faint chirp. How had she not noticed until that moment? There were no signs of life. No dragonflies or crickets, no bees buzzing. Where had they gone?

As if he'd heard her thoughts, Tearlach informed the captain that they'd passed the Valdis Islands before reaching the coast.

"What is left of them?" Sullivan begged.

"Only rock. They're completely barren."

He shook his head and sighed. "Without high-priestesses to summon raw magic, the land is suffering. Streams and shallow lakes have dried, rain never comes. Some residual magic remains in the ground near the temples, and the deeper rivers running through city centers have been diverted toward the surrounding farmlands, but few tracts of land are still tenable. As it were, many have been forced to settle in Meallán—the only place where raw magic is still brought to the surface. Animals have migrated north, but we see fewer and fewer creatures as the years pass. I'm not sure where they've gone. Perhaps they've found land that continues to thrive."

"But the redwoods, the stream we crossed…How is such a large swath of forest sustained by so little water?" Esme wondered.

Sullivan explained that Armel, along with two other water wielders in Altan, had managed to keep the lake in the central valley and many of the winding streams throughout the mountains filled.

Such a use of magic must have been a substantial and constant strain on their power. But that couldn't be the whole of it.

"I suspect others may be contributing," Sullivan suggested.

"What do you mean?"

"I've heard whispers that there are unordained priestesses in the far north, women who would have avoided the collapse of the Order. I believe they're keeping this area alive through whatever young power they have."

It was a glimmer of hope in an otherwise grim situation. Esme took a deep breath and stood. Armel, Hazel, and Killian had already continued on. Tearlach pushed off a nearby tree and the three of them followed.

"I'm afraid there's more." Sullivan spoke softly, as if he regretted having to tell her.

Esme's heartbeat sped up again, fear edging its way in, seeking space in her body. Tearlach dropped back and walked beside her, ready to siphon her magic if she couldn't contain it.

She nodded for the captain to continue.

"Though Orianna's reign started quickly, and even appeared legitimate, it didn't take long for the people of Tremaene to speak out against her. The land and waterways were suffering, yet she made no attempt to seek out successors for the Order, causing most neighboring territories to rise in opposition." Sullivan paused, his gaze dropping to his boots. "In response, the high-priestess...took to executing citizens—anyone who protested her, and even those who had not."

The woman had already killed every sister in the Order and the king and queen of Tremaene. Had she not done enough? Stealing a breath, Esme silently promised herself that their deaths—every innocent life taken—would not go unpunished.

"We have reason to believe," Sullivan went on, "that she falsifies disloyalty."

"You know for sure?" Tearlach posed.

The captain nodded. "We've learned that many of the Fae she's killed possessed very strong or unique magical abilities."

"She's eliminating anyone strong enough to pose a threat against her," Tearlach reasoned.

Which could only mean one thing, Esme realized. Orianna knew war was coming.

"Thankfully, the north remains relatively safe," Sullivan assured her. "Only I risk venturing past the Clavlin Ridge anymore."

Tremaene wasn't just unsafe for Esme, it was unsafe for everyone... and she didn't like the thought of Sullivan going anywhere near the palace, or that woman. Though she conceded that he was their only connection to the capital city. As a shapeshifter, he could easily travel unseen, secretly watching the enemy staking claim over the kingdom from the vantage point of his winged form. And enemy she was—not just to Esme, but to all of Tremaene.

Orianna needed to be stopped, and Esme would do whatever it took to make sure that happened.

Her thoughts returned to the attack the day before. She'd *hidden in a tree* instead of fighting. Hiding was no longer an option. She'd need to learn how to defend herself—before they reached Altan, if at all possible. Surely Killian would assist her.

Before she could hurry ahead to ask him, Esme caught the hushed tone of Sullivan's voice behind her. Sneaking a glance over her shoulder, she saw him put a hand on Tearlach's shoulder.

"Thank you for keeping her safe." The tremor in Sullivan's voice tightened something in Esme's chest. She knew how hard it'd been for him to send a stranger in his place, to watch over a girl he, himself, had sworn to protect. Sullivan had put her in someone else's hands, trusting that person with her life.

Though Tearlach's gaze was hard, it yielded the faintest amount of understanding as he inclined his head, accepting the captain's words.

Chapter Twenty-Four

THE CAPTAIN TOOK a seat beside her that evening, and while Esme loved him like a father, she worried he might inform her of yet another atrocity that Tremaene had suffered in her absence.

He took a long pull from a small copper mug, his eyes never leaving the flickering flames of the campfire. "Did your mother ever mention that we grew up together?"

Esme's worry vanished. She straightened, piqued with curiosity. "No, she never told me."

"I knew her long before she was crowned."

Sullivan had always been more than the captain of the royal guard; he was a family friend and one her mother had rarely called by his full name or title. *Sully,* she would call him. But Esme had never given it much thought, her parents never put on airs with the guards or the palace staff.

"We're both from the north, that you must know." He glanced at Esme and she nodded. "Fae offspring are rare and being that we were the only children in town—though I was a bit older—we banded together."

They were rare. She considered for a moment whether her parents had thought they might never have a child, and how fragile their royal bloodline was.

"Your mother fancied my shapeshifting abilities." He chuckled and his eyes grew unfocused. "Her favorite was when I tried to replicate a peacock. After seeing an illustration in a book, she'd fallen in love with their iridescent plumage. But I didn't get the back feathers quite right and ended up toppling over every time I tried to lift my train."

So the muster of squawking birds that occupied the palace grounds was her mother's doing, Esme mused.

"Sully, can you shift into any animal form?" He smiled and she knew it wasn't at the question, but at the name she'd chosen.

"If I've seen it, then yes."

"What about another Fae form or a human?"

"Not I, my dear. But I wouldn't think it impossible. The variations of our magic are vast."

They certainly were. She veered away from the topic of magic. "And how did you find your way to the palace?"

"I went off to Altan when I was about your age, though it pained me to leave my family and your mother. I was appointed to the royal guard shortly before the Dark War—" He stopped and glanced at Esme.

"I know about the war."

He nodded and the look in his eyes told her that it hadn't been his choice to keep the sordid history of their kingdom a secret from her.

"I fought alongside your father for many years, then your mother when she joined—"

"My mother fought in the war?" Esme exclaimed.

"She did."

Esme looked down, realizing how little she knew about her own mother. Come to think of it, she'd never even heard the story of how her parents had met, she'd merely assumed it had been a political arrangement.

"Is that how the two of them came to know one another?"

"It was. When our numbers were diminished, and her company merged with ours near the end, she found me. I made the introduction."

The future queen of Tremaene battled in a war against dark magic? Esme's mother was as much a warrior as her new companions were—and one skilled enough to gain the attention of the king of Tremaene. It was almost unfathomable. She wondered what role her magic had played in all of it. Esme couldn't picture her slender, gentle mother as a fighter.

"I...how did she..." Esme couldn't quite wrap her head around it. The image she had of her mother was transforming within her memories. Imposing, yet just as beautiful.

"She was an extraordinary woman, your mother." Sully gave a faint smile.

Then why had the truth been concealed? Why keep something so fundamentally paramount from her?

"I remained with the royal guard after the war. Then shortly before you were born, the previous captain died and your mother appointed me to the position." He looked off into the distance and Esme wondered what he was remembering.

The following day, Esme kept her distance from the others, shying away from conversations of plans and strategies. She was sufficiently overwhelmed as it was.

She watched Killian as he was pulled into yet another debate. Esme couldn't help but be captivated by his animated expressions and the way he always gave the others room to speak, never letting his temper show even when he disagreed. She began to wonder if he was even capable of anger or irritation. And best of all, he never brought up topics with Esme that made her curse the fact that she'd been born a princess with the future of an entire kingdom in her hands.

When they stopped midday, Killian took her aside and showed her how to throw a punch.

Well...he tried, at least. Esme was grateful for the wide redwood trunks that kept the view of her silly-looking attempts from the others.

After nearly throwing out her shoulder, she asked if she could try using his sword. He laughed at her. Actually laughed. She would've been furious had his laugh not been as intoxicating as his smile.

"I just want to get a feel for it. I've never held a sword before."

"Honey, you've got to master these weapons first." Killian raised both of her hands.

He had a point, though he said nothing about the dagger she carried at her hip. Perhaps he would show her how to use it. She might have threatened Tearlach with it the night they'd left Debarrow, but truthfully, she had no idea what to do with the blade.

When they joined the rest of the group, Esme got an icy glare from Tearlach. The man didn't seem pleased with her unapproved lesson from the other warrior.

The next day, Esme asked Killian about her dagger—how to use it and if it was the kind of blade one could throw.

She didn't miss the quick glance he stole at Tearlach.

"It would be best to wait until we reach Altan. But come along, I've got better things to show you." He jerked his chin in the direction of a small clearing twenty paces away.

If Tearlach didn't pick up her spiteful thoughts at his interference, the look she shot him certainly told him as much.

Once they were out of sight, Killian wasted no time showing her how to maneuver out of his grip. He demonstrated how to twist her arm to release a hand grabbing her wrist—even told her not to be above biting someone, that it might give her a brief moment of surprise so she could escape.

He finished by showing her how to free herself when captured from behind. Esme didn't mind that lesson at all, and was glad he couldn't see the blush on her face when he wrapped his arms around her. He insisted she stomp on the instep of his foot. She refused, even when he assured her that it wouldn't hurt him much.

But their breaks were always much too short, and while Esme loved spending her days and nights surrounded by towering trees, she was growing tired of the trek.

Each night, she'd sneak away when the others were occupied. Though the forest wasn't thriving, it still provided for her. She'd learned where to find nuts, mushrooms, and edible roots, making quick work of it. And each night, there'd be someone waiting to escort her back.

She was always watched, always followed. Never alone.

It took two more days, but they finally left the cover of the ancient trees and climbed what she was assured was the last ridge before they'd descend into the valley. Posts dotted the top of the mountain that curved off into the distance.

As they hiked up the rugged slope, Esme asked Sully, "Why didn't my mother create a lifeblood ruby for herself?" The question had been tugging at her mind since she'd had the dream of her mother pulling the silvery strand from Esme's chest as an infant.

"She did," Sully surprised her. "Though I didn't learn of it until I witnessed her create one for you. She told me that she'd been joined with the king near the end of the war."

If she'd had a binding connection with Esme's father, then why hadn't it kept them both safe? Could it fade over time, be broken?

"When your father was shot with an arrow, she saved him."

"My father almost died in the war?" Esme exclaimed, causing heads to turn in her direction.

More quietly, Sully replied, "Those joined through a Lifeblood Oath are connected in a way that each can save the other."

Yes, she understood that much. But it didn't make sense. If it kept them alive—"Then how did they..." She couldn't finish the question. Tearlach's earlier explanation filtered in—something about being bound in life *and death.*

"It is not enough if both are drained of their magic." Sully's eyes grew sorrowful. "Or if both are fatally wounded. One must be strong enough to keep the other from death."

That was how Orianna had managed to kill them—together.

Esme didn't respond, and Sully respected her need for silence as they approached the summit. She glanced over at Tearlach. The lifeline they shared was meant to protect her should she be in danger, though it clearly had limitations. Could it be broken? Being tied to Tearlach any longer than necessary was...less than desirable. And she especially didn't want him in her head for centuries.

Perhaps Sully knew a way. She'd ask later, when they were less likely to be overheard. Her eyes flicked to Tearlach—watching her.

A flourishing valley swept out before her as she crested the ridge. Dense foliage of jade and laurel green filled the valley, and all thoughts of life and death and war and irritating warrior protectors dropped away.

It would take a good half day to reach the valley floor. Esme couldn't make out much through the canopy—save for a few stone towers peeking through the thicket—but joy swelled within her at the sight of the thriving landscape.

That night, they made camp out in the open, atop the natural fortress created by the surrounding ridges. Sully explained that during the Dark War, people in the north had moved to Altan for protection. The steep continental divide of the Clavlin Ridge, combined with the easily defensible valley, made it a perfect stronghold.

"Many remained after it ended and now live along the border, making room for the growing number of Northern Rebels."

"Northern Rebels?" Esme remembered hearing Armel refer to themselves as such, but hadn't thought anything of it at the time.

"When you left, I took over Tearlach's position as commander and built a force large enough to take on the queen's"—he stopped—"*Orianna's* army."

"You've been planning this for some time."

"We have."

"Then what have you been waiting for?" If he'd amassed enough warriors for an army, why not take action? Why let Orianna's tyranny continue?

"I've been waiting for you."

Esme looked over at Sully. "But what if I never returned? My magic didn't manifest at twenty years, when it should have. How did you know I'd come back?"

"I held out hope. Knowing the fog might alter your magic—likely the reason for your delayed awakening—I continued to wait, and have been fortunate in my efforts to hold off the impatient generals. I believed you were alive and that was enough." He paused, stealing a breath. "You are the rightful heir to the throne, Esme. The people of Tremaene need a queen to lead them, not an army of rebels."

Chapter Twenty-Five

ESME WOKE TO the sharp, lilting cry of a wren. A smile spread across her face as the call was returned by another.

The fresh mountain air filled her lungs as she rubbed the sleepiness from her eyes. It wasn't yet morning, but the soft heathery-purple sky told her it wasn't far off. She rolled to her side, content to watch the sun crest the western wall of the valley.

By the time a third wren joined the chorus, Esme's companions began to stir. Their decamping had been quick and efficient each morning, but the air that day was charged with even more immediacy. It wasn't a sense of urgency, but the exhilaration of homecoming. Hazel, Armel, Killian, and Sully had only been gone a short time, but Tearlach's return seemed to be felt by all. It was as if they couldn't reach Altan soon enough. There was no waiting for the sun to break the horizon, and no one bothered with a fire—which meant there'd be no tea.

"There'd better be tea in Altan," Esme muttered to herself as she hastily packed her things, her stomach growling.

Tearlach tossed her a corn biscuit when she pulled her pack up over her shoulder. Apparently breakfast would be had on the go.

Soon after they set off, light flooded the sky, pouring into the valley. Esme could make out scattered openings in the thick canopy near the stone towers in the center. And when the sun was high in the sky, she spotted water flowing down a deep cut in the northwestern cliff.

Their progress slowed as the slope steepened and the terrain became uneven. The others climbed down rugged stone walls and slipped through narrow passes at a pace Esme couldn't match. Each time they vaulted from one boulder to the next, she found alternate ways around. But though her pace was slow, someone was always there to offer a hand or lift her off a ledge when the drop was too far. And that someone was usually Killian.

As they neared the bottom of the basin, they were greeted by a wide gully with a quick-moving stream. It edged the perimeter, separating a forest of warm wood and foliage from the cool stones lining the base of the mountain.

Esme took Killian's arms as she hopped off a precarious overhang of toppled boulders. She spared one glance at the abrupt drop beside the already narrow path, then followed the others carefully, keeping one palm against the waterworn rock and her eyes fixed on the ground.

At last, she spotted a wooden suspension bridge up ahead and sighed with relief. She'd been praying to the gods that they wouldn't have to climb down to cross the swift-moving water.

Thick ropes were stretched across the bridge, secured by posts hewn from the mountain itself and a sturdy redwood at the opposite end. Esme climbed the stone steps, then ventured onto the planks, gripping the ropes tightly as she crossed.

The sound of chatter drew her attention to the trees. She searched the branches above, and her eyes widened as she saw a house set high in a tree. Though it looked like a child's playhouse, she quickly realized there was an entire village hidden in the canopy. Sully had mentioned how families had made their homes in the sturdy, ancient redwoods, but Esme hadn't truly believed it until that moment. Narrow structures—some two and three stories tall—hugged the trunks as high as twenty or thirty feet above the forest floor. The circular dwellings were lined with wooden shingles and connected by suspended bridges and platforms, crisscrossing between the thick columns of trees. Steps were set into a wide trunk, winding down to the ground from a platform where several people had gathered to watch them pass.

Esme hurried to catch the others, glancing up at the houses every few steps. Killian was waiting up ahead, but he was the only one. It seemed there'd be no break until they reached the fort.

The dense cover of trees eventually thinned as wide stone buildings came into view. Two towers rose up from the largest building, breaking through the canopy.

At the unfamiliar sight and the many people moving about up ahead, nervousness and unease set Esme's heart to racing. She moved closer to the shelter of her convoy, and Tearlach spared her a glance—his first since they'd crossed the bridge. She wondered what was running through his mind, what he felt. He was returning to his people, his family, after nine years.

He was home.

Esme's legs felt heavy at the thought. She let the others move ahead and swallowed past the lump in her throat. She could never really return home, not like Tearlach. Watching as he made his way down the main path, she realized how much she envied him.

She looked away, brushing a stray tear from her cheek. Then suddenly Killian was there, draping an arm around her shoulders, pulling her gently forward.

"Come along, sweetheart. They're going to love you," he assured with a coaxing smile.

Up ahead, she watched Tearlach stride into camp with such confidence. It was as if he'd been born a warrior, a leader. He walked into the camp as though he'd dreamed of doing so every day since for the past nine years.

As they reached a cluster of tents—one of many, Esme realized—near a stable that went on for more than a hundred feet, Killian slipped away to greet an approaching woman. Others quickly swarmed him—most of whom were females.

It was strange to feel so invisible after striving for exactly that during her time in Periwen. Glancing around nervously—as though a familiar face might suddenly appear—Esme comprehended just how many people lived and worked in the valley. There were thousands.

Veering closer to the stable, she noticed smaller structures and temporary dwellings squeezed between the giant redwoods. Taking up every available space.

Looking back at Killian and the gaggle of women that seemed quite accustomed with his coquettish nature, she caught his eye. He angled his head toward the main building, and Esme followed as he tore himself away from his many admirers.

Killian led her through the droves of people that flooded the center of the camp. She spotted Tearlach up ahead. He'd drawn a rather large crowd himself. His welcome seemed heavier, more reverent, as lines formed and people offered respectful handclasps and bowed heads. But he wasn't simply an esteemed leader being received by his people, Esme could sense trust and mutual friendship. Tearlach seemed genuinely happy to be there, surrounded by the family he'd chosen. It was a side of him Esme had seen little of.

Training areas were set up along the main path—a dirt-packed ring roped off for sword fighting, a wide yard lined with archery targets, a row of tree stumps for knife throwing.

The crowd near the main building grew as word spread that their former commander had returned after years of an unexplained absence. Though some wore protective coverings and armor similar to those of her travel companions, many were more casually dressed. Women wore leggings and tall boots, fitted shirts and shells made of a sculpted material that laced up the front. Most of the men donned linen shirts beneath tunics that ended mid-thigh. Gray, green, tan, and rich browns made the warriors of Altan blend with their surroundings—so unlike the polished palace guards she'd grown up with.

Women continued to welcome Killian home, though Esme couldn't understand why—he'd only been gone a matter of days. She watched with a hint of jealousy as he leaned in close to whisper to one such woman. But the look on the woman's face didn't give the impression that she'd received one of Killian's flirtatious comments. Instead, the woman pulled away and peered over his shoulder, meeting Esme's eyes for a moment.

It didn't take long before Esme noticed that faces were turning toward *her* and not Killian. Her trepidation mounted as murmurs spread through the crowd. She narrowed her eyes at Killian, who only gave her half a grin.

"Do they know who I am?" she demanded. Surely they didn't believe Sully had been responsible for her death, or they wouldn't have allowed him to become their commander. But if he'd kept secret that she was still alive, how did they know who was in their midst?

When they began to kneel, Killian whispered, "I may have let it slip that I've been off rescuing our long-lost princess."

Of course he had. Killian certainly enjoyed being the hero.

He winked at her and gave her arm a tug, urging her on. She focused her attention on Tearlach and Sully up ahead. They were conversing with a group of warriors, and by the look of their attire and stance, they were high ranking. Hazel and Armel stood off to the side, engrossed in their own conversation.

Esme hastened her steps, wanting to be through the crowd as quickly as possible. Memories of her royal life cascaded through her mind at an alarming rate—grand entrances, parades through the streets of Meallán, public outings to the theatre, parties at the homes of noble families. But those had all been for her parents—for the king and queen of Tremaene, not for her.

Yet nothing from her past could compare to what she felt as she gazed out across the crowd that encircled her, pouring out of tents and buildings, filling every open space in the vicinity.

They were kneeling...before *her.*

Esme's cheeks flushed, and she hurried to Killian's side, offering awkward nods to the few she dared to make eye contact with.

Once they reached the others in front of the heavy doors of the main building, she refused to turn around—infinitely aware of the hundreds of eyes fixated on her.

Sully halted his discussion with Tearlach and three other intimidating warriors who regarded her with incredulity and guarded astonishment at her arrival. "I'll clear out my quarters and have the room prepared for you." Sully gestured for a young man to come forward so he could give the order.

"She stays with me." Tearlach's voice was low and authoritative.

Though it was no surprise to her, the others looked taken aback, almost offended at the implied lack of security within their fort—and that Tearlach would be sharing a room with her.

Esme glimpsed a flare of jealousy in Killian's eyes, though he covered it well beneath his relaxed stance and carefree expression.

"As her sworn protector, her safety is my responsibility," Tearlach explained, though he didn't have to. He was no longer their commander, but she sensed he wouldn't be questioned.

No one, aside from Sully, seemed to know about Tearlach's role as her protector. But that seemed reasonable given that they'd only just learned Esme was even alive.

"She has a tendency to wander off," he added, breaking the growing tension—though Esme wished it hadn't been at her expense. She would have scowled at him had they not been surrounded by so many epic-looking warriors that still didn't know what to make of her presence.

"Set up two pallets in one of the guest quarters," he informed the young man Sully had summoned, who ran off, eager to assist the former commander.

Esme heard Killian's slight exhale at the implication that she wouldn't be sharing a bed with Tearlach.

As the crowd pressed in, eager for a closer look, Sully gestured for them to move inside. Esme risked one quick glance. Everyone had since risen to their feet, but the mass of gatherers parted as one person shoved their way to the front.

She saw a flash of red—the end of a long braid whipping in the air.

Esme sucked in a breath, unable to move, unable to fully believe her eyes.

The woman broke free from the throng of people. Esme willed her legs to move, to run toward her, but she couldn't convince them to move.

Then everything went silent—her hand shaking as she brought it to her lips, trying to hold back a cry.

Tears flooded Esme's vision a second before Cadwyn collided with her, crushing her in an indestructible embrace.

Home. Esme was finally home.

Chapter Twenty-Six

ESME MELTED INTO Cadwyn's arms.

It was impossible, but she didn't care. Her family, her childhood friend, her lady-in-waiting—she was alive. Cadwyn was alive.

Tears ran freely down her cheeks as Cadwyn released her, holding Esme's face between her hands.

She studied her like she couldn't quite believe that Esme was real either. When she brushed the tears from Esme's face, Esme finally let herself smile—though it only triggered Cadwyn's tears. They collapsed into another hug, holding each other so tightly that Esme could scarcely breathe. She didn't care. Her need for air paled in comparison to having Cadwyn back.

When at last they pulled apart, there was nothing more to do. So they laughed, their tears turning to uncontrollable giggles.

"I promised we'd be reunited, didn't I?" Cadwyn's voice was quiet enough that only Esme could hear the words.

She nodded ardently, remembering the last night she'd seen her dear friend.

Cadwyn looked past her, and Esme followed her gaze to see Tearlach, Sully, and Killian standing behind them. Even Armel and Hazel had come to see what the commotion was about.

Sully smiled at her, but confusion shone on the faces of the others. If Cadwyn had been in Altan for any length of time, it was clear she'd not revealed her relation to the Princess of Tremaene.

Tearlach offered a single nod. Though he'd never met her lady-in-waiting, he must have guessed that the woman she embraced so fiercely could be none other.

Esme stepped forward—her hand gripping Cadwyn's, unwilling to let go—ready to make introductions. But Tearlach held up a hand, suggesting instead that they move inside. They still had an audience, after all.

Once the heavy doors shut behind them, Hazel and Armel headed toward the large dining area—visible through the tall archway to the left. Killian followed, though not before offering Esme a contented smile.

"I'll stay with Cadwyn." Esme turned to face Tearlach.

He raised an eyebrow, his unspoken words saying something to the effect of, "Not a chance, Princess."

Esme straightened, standing as tall as she could, and held his gaze. Then waited for him to concede. Just once he was going to be the one to break first.

Tearlach glanced at Cadwyn. Taller than Esme by several inches, Cadwyn stood with a protective arm around her—just as determined, her emerald green eyes holding as much of a challenge as Esme's.

"Fine," he gritted out. Esme's brow shot up in surprise, but then he added, "Cadwyn can stay with us."

It was concession enough, and Esme wondered if it had caused him physical pain to offer such a compromise.

She looked up at Cadwyn, not about to force her friend to share a room with a man she herself could hardly stand. The woman raised her chin slightly, as though she could look down at Tearlach. She was tall, but no one matched Tearlach's height and girth.

After a strained moment, Cadwyn nodded her assent.

Through the main corridor and central courtyard, Esme followed Cadwyn, amazed at how expansive the building was. She'd seen so little of it from the outside. Cadwyn's room was located on the third floor and the two worked together to gather her things while three armed guards waited patiently in the hall. The room Tearlach had secured was on the first floor, facing the main yard and training grounds. Esme guessed that the first-floor location had something to do with the added escape option of the window. Was she really in that much danger inside a stone fort surrounded by trained warriors, in a camp that was warded by a towering mountain range, with guards stationed every one hundred feet along its uppermost ridge? Certainly she was safer in Altan than she'd been in the forest. Or even in the mortal realm.

When three pallets were brought in, the small room felt even more cramped. Cadwyn and Esme pushed two of the beds together at the far corner, then moved Tearlach's to the opposite side—as far away as possible.

Although Esme didn't intend to waste a moment with her friend, they were both famished, so Cadwyn left to procure food from the kitchen as Esme inquired about the location of the showers from the female guard, hoping they were private and close by.

The bathing pavilion was outside, and though she argued to be escorted there, Esme was politely informed that she was not permitted to leave the main building without Tearlach. Too tired to voice her aggravation, she settled for a simple change of clothes.

Cadwyn's extra tunic and pants had no chance of fitting, so Esme resorted to rolling the sleeves twice, and tying a belt around her waist to keep the bottom hem from tripping her. There was likely a seamstress or tailor in the camp. She'd see about acquiring new items in the morning... after she got her shower.

When the pair sat comfortably on their joined beds, propped up against a mountain of pillows that Cadwyn had lifted from a linen storeroom, they began recounting the last fateful night they'd seen one another. Esme needed to fill in the missing hours and days between falling asleep in her villa suite in Donellis and ending up across the sea in Periwen.

Her parents had just died, and Cadwyn was all she'd had left in the world. She was afraid, and rightfully so having never been on her own a day in her life. After hours of talking and crying and pleading with her friend that night, Esme had convinced Cadwyn to accompany her across the sea. And that was all she could remember before waking up on a boat along a foreign shore, soaking wet and alone.

"I wish I could have gone with you, but staying in Tremaene was the only way I could protect you. My magic would have compromised your safety." Cadwyn looked down at her hands. "And I knew you never would have left on your own. I'm sorry." She lifted her eyes, searching Esme's. "I'm sorry I let you believe we would be together. I'm sorry I sent you away, forcing you to make that journey on your own."

Esme took Cadwyn's hands. "Don't be sorry. Never apologize for keeping me safe. I know now how dangerous things would have been if I'd stayed. And you were right," she said, giving her a tight smile, "I never would have left without you."

Cadwyn returned the smile, though it didn't reach her eyes.

It was true, Esme had desperately wanted her friend with her in that strange and lonely place. And with Tearlach's ability to glamour magical signatures, it would have been possible to conceal Cadwyn's as well...if only Sully had known of that particular gift.

Then again, if Esme had simply accepted the captain's condition that she go alone, Cadwyn never would have been pushed to deceive her. She would have known that her friend was safe all along, living in Tremaene.

If only she'd listened.

Esme pressed her lips together, there wasn't space in her already full heart to think on possibilities that no longer mattered.

"How exactly did you *send* me away?"

"Sleep magic" was Cadwyn's quick response. "Once you drifted off that night, I used it to keep you in a deep slumber for several days."

Sleep magic? She'd never heard of such a thing—though she wasn't sure why that kept surprising her. Her thoughts drifted back to the first night she'd spent in the woods with Tearlach, to the strange, heavy feeling that had overcome her right before she'd fallen into a deep sleep.

Did he possess sleep magic as well? Another thing he'd failed to mention. Perhaps it was an extension of air magic—the element both Tearlach and Cadwyn controlled. When was he planning to tell her about that? Likely never, given that it gave him control over her without her having knowledge of it.

"Your Highness?"

Her eyes snapped back to Cadwyn. The look on her face must have been irate, because her friend suddenly seemed worried.

"It was the only way; I knew you wouldn't willingly leave without me. Please forgive me."

"No, no, it isn't that," she assured her. "I'm sure it was necessary. My mind wandered for a moment. I was thinking of something else." *Of someone else*—someone who still harbored secrets it seemed. "What happened after that?"

"I carried you to the docks."

Esme's eyebrows shot up. Her lady-in-waiting had carried her out of the room, out of the villa, through the hilly, narrow streets of Donellis, and down to the docks...in the middle of the night? Esme was about to ask how she'd accomplished such a feat, but instead simply gave Cadwyn a smile that told her how utterly impressed she was.

"What, did you just throw me over your shoulder?"

Cadwyn shrugged in response, which only made them break out in laughter.

"And the guards? How did you get past them?" There'd been several stationed outside their rooms that night, along with a dozen or so throughout the first floor and gardens that surrounded the opulent residence. There was no way they would have allowed the princess to leave her room and go out into the city with only her lady-in-waiting attending her.

"I didn't have a choice."

Esme's eyes widened. "What did you do?"

Cadwyn raised her palms in defense. "I just put them to sleep for a while."

"Well with what you've told me so far, you seem in rank with the rest of the warriors in this place." Esme smiled, wanting to know exactly how Cadwyn had come to live in Altan among the warriors.

Smirking at the comparison, Cadwyn continued. "It was dark at the docks, but I found a suitable boat—one that wasn't too large, coated in black varnish that wouldn't easily be noticed against the dark water. I wrapped you in my cloak that I'd lined with all the gold and silver we'd brought for our stay in Donellis. I hoisted the mainsail, offered up a prayer to the god of sea and water and directed the wind to send you straight to Periwen's shores."

It seemed so simple when Cadwyn explained it, though Esme knew it had been anything but. The torturous look in her friend's eyes told her that no part of the ordeal had been easy. She'd been forced to send her charge away—and deceitfully at that. She'd cast her out from her home, not knowing if the only heir of Tremaene would arrive safely in the mortal realm, or whether or not Esme would ever be able to return home.

The past nine years for them hadn't been so different, it seemed. The effects of which they might never recover from. So too with Sully. Even Armel, Hazel, and Killian. They'd all let go of people they knew they might never see again.

Cadwyn leaned over and brushed a tear from Esme's cheek.

"Wha—What happened when I left?"

After taking a deep breath, Cadwyn responded, "I couldn't risk going back to the villa, and I knew I shouldn't return to the palace. I thought about staying in Donellis in case Captain Sullivan came back, but I knew that when dawn broke and the guards came to, the city would be torn apart in search of you. And if Sullivan didn't trust the guards, I knew I shouldn't either. I decided that the mountains would be the most secure place, so I made my way north. The royal guards told me stories when

I was a girl about the continental divide that separated our kingdom and the camp in the central valley that was protected by the natural rock fortress. Besides, where better to hide than with trained warriors whose loyalty to the crown is legendary?" She winked. "I heard news as I traveled, of the chaos in the capital city. It only strengthened my resolve. Then whispers began circulating that you'd been killed. I knew they weren't true, but I grew suspicious of whoever was spreading such rumors. I prayed the warriors in the north were still loyal to the royal family and was relieved to find that they were. What I didn't expect was to find the captain here, leading them. Neither of us ever revealed that I'd come from the palace or had any connection to you. No one believed that absurd rumor that Sully had killed you. He told you, didn't he?" Esme nodded. "Even so, we never let it slip that you were still alive."

Esme leaned back, thinking about the discussion she'd had with Sully before they'd reached the valley, when she'd refused to let him mention Cadwyn. His expression hadn't seemed to convey condolences, Esme remembered. He'd been about to inform her that Cadwyn was waiting for her in Altan, that they'd be reunited.

If only she'd let him finish.

"Sully told me how he'd sent a protector to find and watch over you in Periwen, the former commander no less. Before today, I'd never met Tearlach. But if Sully was going to send anyone to keep you safe, it seems he chose well."

Esme let out an exasperated breath.

"Oh? Was life with him difficult? He seems such a...pleasant man." Cadwyn's eyes twinkled with amusement, having already been on the other side of an argument with Tearlach.

"What life? I only learned who he was when he took me away from the home I'd made there." Bitterness edged into Esme's voice, corroding the lightened mood she'd had since landing in Cadwyn's arms.

"You mean he wasn't there protecting you?" Cadwyn turned incredulous.

"He was," Esme sighed. "But I never knew. Cadwyn, I had no idea Sully intended for me to come back to Tremaene. I thought I'd been sent away and would never be able to return home. I thought I was trapped in the mortal realm forever. And Tearlach, he was just this cold, unsociable villager—a metalsmith I rarely crossed paths with. He didn't so much as look at me until...well, it's a long story." One that exhausted her simply by mentioning it.

Her friend nodded with understanding, knowing it would take time to process all that had happened.

Esme knew Cadwyn had many things to share as well. Nine years resulted in endless stories of people and adventures and life-changing decisions, experiences they'd both lived through without the other.

Later, after Esme convinced one of the guards to bring more food— reasoning that it was safer for him to go because Tearlach certainly wouldn't be happy if Esme had to sneak off on her own—they sat cross-legged on the floor, surrounded by food-laden trays, copper mugs of wine in hand, and continued to recount what had happened in the years they'd been apart.

Cadwyn had found her place among the warriors and had quickly been apprenticed to a healer. Esme couldn't think of a better calling for her former attendant, whose caring and protective nature had always kept her from harm's way as a child, and offered emotional support and camaraderie to Esme in her more formative years.

But Cadwyn hastened over her years in Altan, wanting to know more about Periwen. Esme painted an idyllic picture of her uncomplicated life in Debarrow, skipping over the years she'd spent trying to cross the sea and return home. Being able to tell someone about the life she'd built made her feel...proud. Esme, the princess of the immortal kingdom, who'd rarely ventured past the palace gates, had tended her own land in a faraway village.

They'd both changed so much, grown up so much.

When Esme explained, in animated detail, what had happened when the tree caught her, she hopped up from the floor to show Cadwyn how she'd been positioned on the ladder that day. Then she knelt down and braced her hands on Cadwyn's shoulders and told her of the day she'd brought a dead wolf back to life with her touch.

Cadwyn stared at Esme as she told the tale, completely awestruck. "I've never heard of such a thing."

"Nor had I. No one but Tearlach knows. I think he's worried about it, about what it might become once my power manifests fully. It was less than a month ago when it all happened. I still understand so little about it."

"Your secret is safe," Cadwyn assured her, taking Esme's hands in her own. "Is that why Tearlach brought you home, because your magic finally came in?"

"Not exactly." Esme went on to tell her about the assassins, and how Tearlach had reached her just in time, killing one of them right before her eyes.

Cadwyn's jaw dropped and she gaped at Esme. But before she could say anything, the door swung open and Tearlach appeared in the doorway. He hadn't knocked.

As he strode in, eying the empty cups and plates on the floor, Esme glanced over her shoulder at the narrow window. Night had fallen. How long had they been talking?

He dropped a heavy pack on the bed near the door and informed the two young women that it was time to sleep.

"I'm not tired, would you mind leaving us for—" Esme began.

"Sleep. Now." He turned his back to them. It was a command and one she realized he could back up if she tried to fight it.

Esme gritted her teeth, wondering how many times he'd used sleep magic on her without saying a word about it.

"That won't work on me," Cadwyn said sweetly, though Esme could sense the warning in her tone.

Tearlach turned and arched a brow. "I wondered how you managed to get her to Periwen. But while it may not affect you," he addressed Cadwyn before turning his unyielding stare on Esme, "it will still work on you, *Princess.*"

"Queen," Cadwyn corrected, her voice going deep and authoritative.

Tearlach considered the self-possessed woman for a moment and Esme wondered if he'd met his match in Cadwyn.

"Well, *Her Highness* needs to rest. She starts training tomorrow." His lupine grin told Esme it wouldn't be an experience she'd enjoy.

Cadwyn opened her mouth again, with what was sure to be another lesson in respect for their sovereign, but Esme held up a hand. "It's not worth fighting him."

Tearlach extinguished the lamps in the room with a swift swirling breeze as Esme quietly amended, "At least not about *this*."

A low growl came from across the room. She would certainly pay for that.

Training. Tomorrow.

She'd be ready for it, as long as she got a shower first.

Chapter Twenty–Seven

TEARLACH WAS GONE by the time the sun painted the sky a rosy pink. Esme slipped from the room, leaving Cadwyn to sleep. It seemed healers didn't start their days as early as warriors.

Two guards escorted her to the showers. She could hear water running at the far end, but it was relatively quiet. Wooden slats with narrow gaps lined the floor to allow for drainage. Dozens of shower stalls ran down both sides of the open-air pavilion. The glossy wood panels that separated each shower didn't reach the floor and only stood to offer a small amount of privacy. Though she wasn't tall enough to see over the tops, she imagined most could.

Her guards, both male, hung back several paces as she entered one of the stalls. A panel hung in the center, separating the shower from a small dressing space. Esme undressed and stepped under the copper showerhead, twisting the handle all the way to the left. A startled cry stole her breath as icy cold water hit her skin.

"Miss?" one of the guards questioned.

"I'm okay." She shivered. The water was cold, but it was better than nothing. They were made for efficiency, not luxury. She imagined being submerged in a hot bath as she scrubbed vigorously under the pelting water.

After wrapping herself in a towel, which barely kept the goose bumps from breaking out across her flesh, Esme stepped around the partition. Her eyes landed on the fresh clothes neatly stacked on the bench. Suspiciously, she lifted the garments, wondering who'd been mere feet from her as she'd stood bare skinned under the shower spray.

The clothes weren't just clean, they were new—and they fit perfectly. *Tearlach.*

Her guards revealed nothing when she left the stall and made her way toward the row of sinks at the far end. Her gaze instantly locked with her reflection in one of the hanging mirrors. It was the first time she'd seen herself since the human glamour had been lifted by the fog. She leaned over the wooden counter for a closer look.

The freckles on her cheeks had already vanished when her magic first manifested, but she pulled aside the neck of her shirt, finding unblemished skin on her shoulders as well. She drew her fingers along her cheekbones, mesmerized by the pale gold shimmer. Turning her head to the side, she could see the hint of an iridescent rainbow playing across her skin. She looked eternally youthful—always would—but there was something different, something she hadn't seen in years. Perhaps it was her flawless skin or the points of her ears. She ran a fingertip along the shell of her ear, shivering at the feel.

She looked...*Fae*, she realized, smiling.

It had been many long years of hiding who she was.

Glancing down, she sighed, wishing she could blame the glamour for her small stature. She hadn't been blessed with the trait that all other Fae females were given—tall, slender bodies. Glamour or not, tall was something she'd never be.

When Esme returned to her shared room, Cadwyn was waiting to braid her hair—which was already drying into wavy curls that wouldn't be conducive for whatever training Tearlach had planned. Esme hesitated for a moment before gratefully accepting the offer.

After Cadwyn had plaited both sides, intertwining them at the nape of her neck, Esme resecured her belt and remembered her dagger—Cadwyn's dagger. She scrounged through her pack, pulling out the midnight blue cloak as well. Holding the items out, she grinned as Cadwyn took in the sight of them. "Yours. Thank you."

Cadwyn took a tentative step, then reached out to run the thick fabric between her fingers. She lifted her eyes to Esme's. "Keep them. Besides," she said with a shrug, "I purchased a new cloak years ago."

"Then at least take the dagger."

Cadwyn looked past her. Esme turned to see Tearlach standing in the doorway. How did he do that? She hadn't even heard the door open.

Recalling his warning about keeping the dagger on her at all times, Esme defended, "Why do I need a weapon when I have your charming self to protect me?"

A muscle feathered in his jaw as he stared at her, unblinking.

Probably not the right thing to say, but she charged on. "And I'm surrounded by warriors who know how to wield weapons far better than I do."

Esme turned back to Cadwyn and forced the sheathed blade into her hand. She accepted it without another word.

Following Tearlach silently through the camp—out of the camp, she soon realized—she saw several leveled gardens scattered throughout, taking advantage of any available sunlight trickling through the canopy. And the waterfall she'd spotted the day before fed a wide lake. Beside the flowing water was a trail leading into the mountains, which Esme assumed was the only possible way for horses to get in and out of the valley. The entire length of the pass was patrolled, from basin to ridge.

"Why didn't you tell me you were a commander?" she asked Tearlach when the silence had gone on too long.

"That title has nothing to do with my ability to protect you. And I'm no longer their commander." There wasn't even a hint of resentment in his voice.

"Do the others know about the Lifeblood Oath?"

"No. And they don't need to." He cut her a sharp look. She didn't question it further.

After winding through a dense patch of forest, they came upon a steep bluff, its precipice reaching only half the height of the surrounding mountain range. A narrow passage led to a small, secluded clearing, protected by the circling rock wall. Redwoods crowded the edges, and the entire area spanned no more than sixty paces in each direction. But it would keep them out of sight.

They'd be practicing magic, then.

That was the only reason Esme could imagine for Tearlach taking her to such a private and naturally protected location. Although the protection was likely for those who dwelled in the valley, not for her. And without knowing exactly what she was capable of, it seemed the extent of her magic would be kept secret as well—even from Tearlach's closest companions.

He threw down a pack and looked at her. "Show me what you can do?"

"Excuse me?"

"Your magic, summon it."

"I don't know how to." She staggered back at his abruptness.

"Yes, you do. You've done it before."

"Is it really safe? With Orianna knowing I'm here?"

"No one will touch you here. Now quit stalling."

She blew out a breath. It was bound to be a challenging day.

"Start with the trees, the nature around you," he suggested. *Not the volatile magic that calls upon storms,* was what he didn't say. "Magic is a part of you. It doesn't need to be difficult. Think back to the events that helped you conjure it before."

Magic was as unique as the person wielding it. And with her gifts being so rare, she'd have to figure out how to access it on her own—while Tearlach watched.

Realizing he'd offer nothing more, Esme paced the circumference of the clearing. The sooner she could discover how to draw out her magic, the sooner their *training* would be over.

She slowed her steps and closed her eyes, hoping to command it with her thoughts—as Tearlach had suggested so matter-of-factly. Thinking back on each situation, Esme visualized the moments that preceded the protection she'd received from roots, tree branches, and vines. She imagined the assassins searching the forest for her outside Briganport. Clenching her fists and squeezing her eyes shut tighter, she painted the scene in her mind—every detail of them hunting her.

Her eyes shot open and she looked around, expecting to see some hint of her magic at work. Anything would have been a good sign—a branch reaching for her, roots rising from the ground.

But nothing had changed.

Tearlach hadn't moved from his position against the tree either. "Anytime, Princess."

She growled and closed her eyes again.

For hours, she continued her futile attempt to summon even the tiniest ounce of her power.

"Maybe if you'd *help* me," she gritted out as the tether on her patience began to fray. Just as she said it, a gust of wind knocked her to the ground. Esme scrambled to her feet and glared at Tearlach. "How is that going to help me?"

He held her gaze, though he didn't respond—at least not in words. The air shoved her off-balance again, but she fought against it. His magic was far stronger than her.

In less than a second, a gale force wind pinned her against the wide trunk of a redwood. She couldn't move.

Tearlach shoved off his tree and stalked slowly toward her. When he stood a mere foot away, he raised his chin slightly. The restraint of his magic lifted her from the ground and pressed her farther into the bark of the tree until she was eye level with him.

Her stunned gaze held his as her mind spun with curses she wanted to hurl at him. But before she could speak, the air gripped her tighter, squeezing her throat until she could barely breathe.

She tried to pull in a gulp of the crushing air that surrounded her. Would he really kill her if she couldn't figure out how to use her magic? After everything he'd done to save her?

Tearlach stood, unmoving—watching, waiting.

Esme gasped for air. He wouldn't kill her, would he?

Fight me, a voice inside commanded her.

She wanted to scream, to tell him to stop. She wanted to claw at the forceful magic that crushed her windpipe. But she couldn't move, couldn't breathe.

He was going to kill her.

Terror lanced her veins, sending burning hot blood coursing through her body, trying to keep her alive as blackness started to crowd her vision and a high-pitched ring sounded in her ears.

Then she heard the groaning of roots as they pierced through the ground below her. Traveling upward from the base of the tree, they circled the area around her legs, sparking as they came into contact with the air magic that held her in place. Vines unfurled from the branches above, dipping down to curl around her. Esme could hear the sizzle and smell the faint tinge of smoke as magic met with magic. Tearlach's invisible grip weakened, burning away when touched by her power.

She saw thin strands of smoke waft around her, and soon Esme was able to draw in a ragged breath. Tearlach remained impassive as his magic lost its hold on her. Finally, she dropped to the ground.

Esme closed her eyes, struggling to steady her frantic heart. After a protracted moment, the slithering sounds of recoiling vines replaced the pounding in her ears. She could feel the twisting roots recede into the ground beneath her hands.

"What was it like?" Tearlach's deep voice severed the quiet she sought.

She seethed, silently, but ultimately decided that as much as she wanted to, she didn't have the energy to rage at him—or try to kill him.

She thought back on the experience, on how it had felt. In the past, her magic had only shielded her. Never had it fought or battled its way to protect her. And never had it come up against another's magic.

Either her power was still growing or she'd failed to realize its potential before. Her magic seemed to transform and provide whatever she needed at the time.

Glaring at Tearlach, and ignoring the voice in her head that pointedly reminded her of his attack—and that he'd nearly suffocated her—Esme answered, "It felt different, like a...warm pool inside me. That's where it came from. I drew my magic up from the source inside me and let it flood my veins...let it spread through my body until I could feel it in my skin." She looked up at the tree she'd been forced against. All evidence of her magic gone.

It hadn't felt that way in Debarrow. When she'd touched the wolf in the town center, the magic had come from the land, as though she'd been channeling something that wasn't hers.

But when Tearlach's magic threatened, her magic had felt different, *very* different. For the first time, she'd been able to sense the center of the power inside her.

"Then harness that feeling."

"You said it was about controlling my thoughts," she bit out.

"I know what I said." Something flickered in his dark eyes. "It seems you're stubborn in all matters. Replicate that feeling until it becomes second nature. Now, do it again."

She braced herself for another attack, but Tearlach merely took up his previous position against the tree and crossed his powerful arms over his chest.

Another hour passed, and Esme was unable to conjure roots or vines. "Have you trained others that were new to their magic?"

"Yes. Many."

"Then why isn't this working? I'm trying to feel it, trying to think it, but nothing is happening." Esme was growing more frustrated by the second.

"Your particular variety of magic is unique. Though earth magic or controlling the weather are both rare, they do exist. Your *other* gift... well, I've never heard any account of a Fae having the ability to bring something back to life. And the way you initially triggered your power gave it a path. We're not starting from the beginning here. In a sense, we need to work backward—break down the triggers and redirect the power."

She sighed. "Then let's work on the weather," she suggested, anything to get her mind away from slithering vines and crawling roots.

"Tomorrow."

She turned away and closed her eyes, so close to releasing all her frustration on him. From the attack that had drained her energy and nearly killed her to the aggravation of being unable to summon anything else, she was done. Her feet hurt, the piercing pain between her brows refused to let up. And she was hungry.

Steadying herself, she faced Tearlach, and in her sweetest voice asked, "Don't you think we should head back? It's nearly midday. I'm quite famished."

He laughed, clearly seeing right through her facade. "You haven't earned your meal yet, Princess."

Esme sucked in a breath and exploded. "I've had it with you telling me what to do! What I'm *allowed* to do. So what if we have this binding connection? It doesn't give you the right to treat me like this! First you spend months thwarting my attempts to return, then after I build a peaceful life for myself, you drag me from my home and force me to leave everything behind. And you never, *ever* tell me what's really going on— what you have planned. It's always your call, never mine, never what I want, what I need...how could you...why didn't you..." She wanted to keep going, to blame him for everything, but feeling the prick of tears, she jerked her head away.

Swallowing the pain and anger she'd been denying, Esme stepped toward her discarded cloak, picked it up, and walked out of the clearing without meeting Tearlach's eyes.

He wasn't the enemy; he'd kept her safe. He'd rescued Esme when her past had finally caught up with her.

But that did little to quell the betrayal she felt.

Tearlach didn't respond to her barrage of accusations, didn't even force her to stay and continue training when she was certain he would.

As she emerged from the narrow gap in the rocks, Esme looked up to see rain-heavy clouds just before they faded into the clear blue sky. She could sense Tearlach as he approached, though he remained a step behind as they walked back to the fort.

———

Esme was pleasantly surprised when Killian found her outside the dining hall—just after she'd eaten enough to last her several days. Trying to summon magic drained her energy more than expected.

But she quickly realized that Killian's visit was not a chance encounter. He'd been sent by Tearlach. She almost collapsed on the floor of the great hall when he informed her that they were to start training with swords that very afternoon.

Her darling protector was certainly making his point. It seemed there'd be no rest until Tearlach was satisfied that she could defend herself.

As they headed back to the same clearing where she'd spent her morning wearing a tread in the layer of pine needles that covered the ground, Esme asked why she couldn't be taught with the others in the training grounds. It wasn't as though they'd be practicing her untested magic.

"Tearlach would prefer that the people of Altan not learn too much about you and your abilities." Killian looked down at her with an apologetic smile. "Or lack thereof."

Though she understood Tearlach's caution, Esme wondered if he had genuine suspicions about the people who lived in the valley.

"You're actually going to let me use a sword?" she asked as they climbed through the narrow pass.

"Of course. It wouldn't be very effective sword training if I didn't," he replied with a glimmer in his eyes.

"What happened to 'You've got to master these weapons first?'" She held up her hands, reminding Killian of his refusal to let her touch a sword before.

"It seems Tearlach deems you worthy of using weapons now."

"And Tearlach has the final say? In all matters?"

"When it comes to you, yes."

Esme rolled her eyes and turned away.

Killian grabbed her arm and turned her to face him. Towering over her, he held her gaze—every trace of his lighthearted nature gone. "He will always be our commander, Esme."

Though it was unexpected, his words didn't surprise her. If there was one thing she understood, it was loyalty. And the loyalty among Tearlach's band reminded her of the relationship between her parents and the members of the royal guard. Esme had been certain that more steadfast devotion couldn't possibly exist. But as she studied Killian's face and the unwavering look in his eyes, she considered that perhaps Killian, Armel, Hazel, and Tearlach were the exceptions.

She dipped her chin slightly in acknowledgment. A corner of Killian's mouth quirked up, breaking the tension between them.

He stepped away. "What's it like to be back?"

Esme took a breath, grateful for the change in subject. "There's something familiar here, something comforting. I'm not sure what. I can't quite place it. I've never been to Altan, but it somehow feels like home." She was almost ashamed to be telling him how untraveled she was. Esme should have taken more interest in her kingdom during her early years.

"We didn't know Cadwyn was your lady-in-waiting, but it was smart of her not to reveal it until you returned."

"I was...relieved to find that she was alive and well."

"Yes, I could see that." He smiled.

Esme looked down at the ground. "I didn't know what I would be returning to...who would still...be here."

He waited until her eyes once again met his. "I'm glad you have her back. I can see how important she is to you. It's good to have someone you can talk to." Though he spoke of Cadwyn, Killian might have been referring to himself.

He pulled one of his swords from a sheath at his hip and laid it on the ground nearby. Apparently she wouldn't be holding a sword after all.

The next hour passed slowly as Killian walked her through postures and footwork. She felt foolish when he insisted she practice over and over the proper way to pivot. When he finally seemed satisfied, he positioned her feet and handed her his sword, taking her hand to place it precisely on the hilt. Then he stalked around her, assessing her stance and grip. But he didn't instruct her on the way to use it, allowing her time to get acquainted with the weight of the blade.

Killian continued circling her. "Watch the eyes. A poor fighter will show you exactly where they plan to strike. Be aware of your surroundings and note any obstacles in your path."

Esme nodded without confidence as sword fighting quickly became more complicated than she'd anticipated. Couldn't she simply swing the blade around and hope it made contact with her enemy?

"Use your"—his eyes traveled up and down Esme's body, sending a shiver along her spine—"small stature to your advantage." He gave her a hint of a smile, but it quickly vanished as he went on with the lesson. "Stay low, cut low. You don't need to aim for the chest or the throat to take down your opponent. Go for the legs and slice deep. If it's deep enough, your attacker could bleed out before being able to heal."

Esme shuddered at the thought. With their natural healing ability, it would have to be a sizable gash. But then, she *was* learning to defend herself in what would be life-or-death situations. She needed to get over her hesitation to inflict pain on those who intended her harm.

"And if you can't get a second thrust after engaging, retreat immediately."

Retreat. She liked the sound of that. Surely she could master something her instincts were screaming for her to do anyway.

When they finally finished for the day, she asked Killian to show her a bit of his fire magic. Though she'd caught a glimpse through the redwoods during the attack, she hadn't seen it up close.

No sooner had the request left her lips did a fireball shoot into the air.

Esme gasped at the intensity of Killian's power as the heat licked at her skin.

Armel emerged from the trees as if summoned by the display. "It seems I've arrived just in time. Before Killian burns the forest to the ground." He smiled at his friend.

Oh, no. Armel could only have been there for one reason. Would Hazel show up next?

Perhaps she could keep them talking until dinner and skip whatever Armel had planned for her. "I haven't seen much of your magic either." Esme gave her brightest smile. "Would you mind?"

Armel flicked a glance at Killian. Water followed, splashing his face. Esme couldn't help but laugh. And luckily Killian seemed used to it, wiping his brow and shaking his head with mock dismay. She wondered how often Armel's water was needed to stabilize Killian's reckless magic.

"You know you're making it rather difficult for me to impress Esme, *old man.*"

She turned to Armel. "Old man? Exactly how many years are you?"

"Many years more than you."

"That's a given." Esme could very well be the youngest in the entire camp. "Older than Tearlach?"

He nodded.

"Older than Sully?"

"Not quite."

She wanted to ask more, curious about Armel's life and why he became a warrior—the quiet man hadn't offered her more than a few words since they'd met.

"If you're quite finished," he said with a grin aimed at Killian—they'd clearly not been working with swords when Armel had arrived, "I'm told Esme requires a lesson in knife throwing."

"Then what, archery after dinner?" She couldn't keep the irritation from her voice. It had been a long day, and it was getting longer.

"Tomorrow," Armel corrected.

"Great." Her response failed to mask her dread at the prospect of working alone with Hazel.

Killian hooked the toe of his boot under his blade, and tossed it into the air, catching it easily. Taking a step closer, he lowered his head to whisper in Esme's ear. "I'll tell her to go easy on you." He gave her a wink, then—making a show for his friend—he bowed and kissed the top of her hand. "Until tomorrow, sweetheart."

Armel rolled his eyes.

"She's all yours," Killian called back as he left Esme and Armel alone in the clearing.

Chapter Twenty-Eight

"NOW FOR YOUR weather magic. Start with something small—a rain cloud."

Esme glanced up at the pale early morning sky, then back at Tearlach as he stalked across the clearing to take up the same position as the day before.

"I thought you said you could help me with it," she reminded.

"Did I? I said I knew of it."

"So you're not going to help me?" Esme propped her hands on her hips.

He grinned and raised a brow, but she held up a hand to stop whatever unpleasant tactic he had in mind.

"Don't."

Tearlach gave her a look that told her she'd better figure it out on her own—and quickly—if she wanted to avoid his intervention.

She removed her cloak and began pacing the same path, searching her mind for memories, triggers. Having only recently learned of her connection to storms, she tried to recall the kinds of dreams that had her waking to the aftermath of destructive winds and lashing rains.

But she wasn't about to wait for an attack to trigger one. She glanced at Tearlach. *Rain cloud,* she reminded herself, *I only have to summon a rain cloud.*

An hour passed with nothing to show for her efforts. Tearlach hadn't moved from his spot against the tree, showing little more than an impassive expression.

Esme blew out a breath and dropped to the ground—pacing clearly wasn't helping. Then she remembered, it wasn't only dreams of sadness or anger that summoned storms. She'd unknowingly invited rain to her land over the years.

Closing her eyes, she pulled herself away from the valley and pictured her garden as though it was sprawled out before her. The sound of the wind through the redwoods faded to the background as she imagined herself walking the rows of apple trees, squinting against the bright summer sun. She envisioned herself at the base of an apple tree, touching the dry, parched soil with her palms.

Esme funneled her awareness to the feel of the rain, letting it consume her—the moisture clinging to her warm skin, the smell of wet earth filling her nostrils...

And when the sound of steadily falling drops was all she could hear, Esme opened her eyes.

Fog hung in the air around her. Droplets were so near to forming, she could almost taste them.

Then it vanished, dissolving into wisps of vapor until the clearing held nothing more than redwoods and pine needles.

"Try again." Tearlach's voice drew her gaze. He was completely unimpressed.

Though Esme concentrated in the same manner for another hour, the fog only made its appearance once.

———————

Wielding a weapon was nothing like tilling soil or pulling a cart into town. But even with the effort she exerted each day, her knife throwing skills hadn't progressed in the slightest.

Armel had endless patience, offering quiet encouragement every time a blade sailed past one of the giant trees without grazing it. But as frustrating as the skill was, Esme found knife throwing to be a blissful pastime compared to her lessons with Hazel.

Archery was torturous. And Hazel's patience as a teacher...well, she had none.

During their first lesson, Hazel had instructed Esme in proper form and technique with the bow. *Just* the bow. Esme would have been insulted, except the simple task of pulling back the weight of the bow caused her arms to tremble almost instantly. It was to build up strength, Hazel had explained. At least the woman had offered gloves, or Esme's fingers would have been shredded and bloody by the end of that first afternoon. Nocking the arrow hadn't come until the following day, which only offered a new set of physical trials.

Hazel clearly harbored a special kind of loathing for Esme—one she couldn't see a way to remedy as it was based purely on Esme's parentage.

After their third lesson, her archery instructor passed her off with the two waiting guards. Esme sighed in relief, watching Hazel stalk toward the main building without a backward glance.

It was easy enough to persuade her escorts into taking the long way back. They passed the stables, then turned down the main path. Esme caught sight of a shock of red hair, and came to a stop beside the rope that marked the boundary of a wide training yard.

"Why didn't you tell me of this secret talent?" she called over to Cadwyn.

Her friend spun around, looking a bit sheepish before a composed veneer slid back into place over her features. "It's only a hobby. I assure you." Cadwyn handed over the rest of her daggers to the woman beside her, then ducked under the rope. "I picked it up a few years back." She shrugged. "With little else to do here, training and fighting are the only entertainments we have."

Esme cocked her head to the side before glancing pointedly at the cluster of blades embedded in the barkless stump—Cadwyn's target.

But Cadwyn kept her chin up and seemed not to notice Esme's insinuation.

It was certainly more than a hobby.

———————

Two more days of failed magic and frustratingly repetitive weapons training went by, and sword fighting seemed to be the sole thing Esme was even remotely good at—if only because it was easier to hit a target with a long swinging blade than by knife or arrow.

Moving on from positioning and theory, Killian began to let Esme practice with the weapon itself. He walked her through attacking and thrusting. Over and over and over.

Each time they circled one another, Esme's eyes would shift to the uneven ground, being careful of her foot placement. When Killian lunged, she'd pivot and attempt a counterattack. More than once, she'd lose her footing. And more than once, Killian reached her before she fell.

After she tripped for the second time that afternoon, he gave Esme a moment to catch her breath and steady herself. As she tipped back her canteen, leaning against a nearby tree, she noticed his lingering gaze.

"You must have had men lining up at your door in Periwen."

She coughed on a gulp of water, thinking of the one and only man who'd sought her attentions.

"One man in particular, then?"

Glancing over at him, Esme paused only a moment before pushing off the tree and moving to stand in the center of the clearing opposite him. When she raised her blade, Killian lifted an inquisitive eyebrow, then took up his position.

Esme attacked first, something she hadn't attempted before. But Killian effortlessly parried and riposted. His blue eyes were alight as he regarded her.

"That's a 'yes,'" he ventured.

She looked away.

He sighed, realizing it wasn't a topic she cared to discuss. "I'm sorry, Esme. You know, we've all let go of people. But Tearlach, Armel, Hazel, and I—we've made new lives here, made our own family."

A life...a family? Was she supposed to make yet another life for herself? Find another family? How many times would she have to do that? And if she let them in, if she became one of them, what would happen if she lost them too? Start over again?

Turning to him once more, Esme advanced without warning. Killian pivoted from her thrust. She didn't retreat like she was supposed to, carelessly attacking again. Killian ducked from her swing. Again she lunged for him. But that time, after he dodged the blade, he came up beside her and grabbed her wrist.

She couldn't meet his eyes.

He gently peeled her grip from the weapon. Once she dropped it, Esme flexed her fingers, fearing she wouldn't have been able to let go without his help.

Killian spoke quietly, calmly. "He was from a different world. It never would have worked." Esme looked up. Killian stood mere inches from her.

It wasn't that Carrick was mortal and she wasn't. Or rather, it wasn't only that.

Killian watched her intently as emotions warred for her attention. Would he look at her like that if he knew what she'd done? That she'd lied to Carrick—betrayed a man who'd cared so deeply for her he'd traveled day and night to reach, to rescue her.

Esme took a deep breath as Killian took a step closer.

"There will always be room in your heart for him," Killian tried to reassure her. Esme swallowed past the tightness in her throat. "You don't need to forget about him, and you shouldn't. But with time, I promise you," he said, his gaze intensifying, "the pain will take up less and less space inside you."

"I hope so." Esme's voice was small, weak from guilt. She wasn't sure when his hand found hers, but it was strong and warm and she didn't want him to let go.

"You can trust us, Esme. All of us...even Hazel. You'll see when she warms up to you." His serious expression yielded slightly. "We've all sworn to protect you with our lives."

"You...What?" Esme had assumed they were only loyal to Tearlach.

"He didn't ask it of us." Killian shook his head. "It seems Tearlach's time away made him forget what we were. What we still are. The four of us will always have each other's backs, no matter what. Whatever or whomever he vows fealty to, we all do—emphatically and without question."

Killian ran a hand through his golden hair, then stepped away, taking up a ready position.

Esme regarded him a moment longer, then raised her sword in response.

Chapter Twenty-Nine

"AGAIN," TEARLACH ORDERED from across the clearing.

Esme exhaled, dropping her arms to her sides. She was tired, and it wasn't even midday.

Inhaling a deep breath, she raised her hands and called upon the fluffy wisps that hovered atop the mountain crest, swirling them down into the valley until they merged into a larger, grayer cloud.

After running through that aspect of her ability several times, she was told to focus her efforts on rain once again. "*Without* your hands this time."

Esme rolled her eyes. It was easier to let her hands direct the magic. And no matter how silly it made her look, it seemed to be the only trick that consistently yielded results.

Rain, he'd demanded. Rain was harder. Though she'd begun to master cloud formations—transforming them from light and fluffy to dark, gray, and saturated—a light sprinkle was all she'd been able to coax from them. And it took copious amounts of energy to do even that. Storms persistently remained out of reach—no lightning, no thunder, just a few small clouds with the slightest bit of precipitation.

Tearlach stalked around her as she panted in the center of the clearing.

"I can't do it."

"You can and you will."

"Are you going to attack me again?" she hissed.

"If that's what it takes."

He drew closer, invading her space. She yielded a step, struggling to remain firm. "I'm not afraid of you."

He laughed. "Really?"

With another step, Esme's back hit a tree. She sucked in a breath, then clenched her fists, feeling the familiar tingle of magic running along her skin. Roots rose from the soil, coiling around Tearlach's legs.

"Not that," he growled, slicing clean through the thick roots with a knife.

Esme gaped at him as he then brought the point of the blade inches from her throat. Focusing everything she had on the roiling pool of magic inside her, she turned her head away from the knife tip a second before a branch swung out.

Tearlach ducked before it could strike him. When he rose, the look in his eyes was nothing short of furious. He braced his hands against the tree on either side of her head and leaned in, holding her gaze.

She stopped breathing, bracing herself for what was to come. But she didn't look away.

"Better." The vibration of his deep voice ran down her spine. He turned and walked away, calling back at her, "Rain. Now."

By the end of the session, she managed to summon rain, actual pouring-down rain. And it had everything to do with Tearlach. Though he didn't provoke her again, Esme found she had a wealth of past interactions that she could draw upon. Those from Periwen worked especially well at fueling a powerful reaction.

Though she'd figured out how to summon rain, she could only sustain it for a short time before it transformed into something far less formidable. And practicing all morning had left her cold and wet.

She stood and stared at Tearlach as her soaked clothes dripped onto her boots. Tearlach didn't seem to mind, but Esme was unable to suppress a shiver. It had been hours. Esme was hungry and tired, and her eyes pleaded with him to let her stop.

Tearlach jerked his chin toward the passage out of the secluded valley, and pushed off the tree. Esme stumbled forward.

A warm breeze quickly dried her clothes as they made their way through the labyrinth of trees that skirted the camp.

"Why haven't you taught me to use any weapons?"

Tearlach arched a brow down at her.

"I mean besides magic."

"Killian's better with a sword."

She highly doubted that. After all, Tearlach was the legendary warrior—the one Sully had chosen to protect her.

"Really, then why isn't Killian the commander here?" she goaded.

"He's good, perhaps the best fighter I know, but he's impulsive. And impulsivity in battle can be risky. Fighting is not always the wisest option."

"Says the warrior."

He took Esme by her shoulders, halting her. "There's no need to put yourself in the line of danger when escaping or hiding will suffice. *Both* are far safer and more effective strategies."

She furrowed her brow.

"It's true. Unless you have no option but to fight, don't engage. Do you understand?"

Esme nodded.

"Do not think it cowardly; hiding just might keep you alive."

He walked away, Esme trailing a step behind. *Interesting*, she thought. Tearlach had mocked her for doing exactly that in the woods near Briganport. *Cowering like a little girl*, he'd said.

Tearlach left her at the entrance of the dining hall in the care of two guards. After filling a plate with roasted root vegetables, a handful of walnuts, and a thick slice of sourdough bread with raspberry preserves, Esme returned to her room, passing the man and woman who were stationed outside her door that day.

Something caught her eye as she closed the door. She crossed over to her pallet, staring down at the object perched against her pillow—a dagger, with a note beside it.

She unfolded the thick paper and read the perfectly scrawled words.

You will keep this one.

Lifting the small weapon—lighter than she'd expected—she gripped the hilt. It fit perfectly in her hand. She ran a finger along the straight ridge in the center of the silver blade, then opened her hand to admire the handle itself. Made of rich, warm wood, with a natural pattern of golden wood grain running the length of it, the simplicity was stunningly beautiful.

When she turned it over in her palm, her breath hitched. Her eyes fixated on the elegantly engraved *E* near the base of the handle. She traced the curves of the letter. It couldn't have been something Tearlach had simply procured somewhere in camp. The dagger she held was made for her.

Esme turned at the sound of the door, meeting Tearlach's unreadable eyes. He glanced at the blade in her hand, then met her gaze again.

"I'll be occupied for the remainder of the day. If you plan to wander off, take an escort."

"But—" she began, confused.

"The rest of the day is yours."

She gaped at him, unsure of what to say. Her entire existence had come to revolve around her safety and his directives.

"I'll be here," she assured him, unable to think of anything she'd rather do than collapse on her bed and sleep until the following morning...or even the morning after that.

He nodded and left her alone.

Esme looked back down at the blade, before tucking it under her pillow and curling up beside it.

————————

Blackness surrounded her. It was cold, stinging her skin. Esme pulled her cloak tighter around her chest—a bloodred cloak she'd never seen before.

The palace loomed ahead as the darkness melted away. Gravel crunched beneath her feet when she took a tentative step along the wide, circular path.

It was night, but the Loinnir Lights cast a cool glow to the smoky haze that clung to the ground. Esme turned back to the city behind the palace gates, and gasped at the sight.

Meallán was on fire.

Smoke rose from every building as flames snaked through the streets.

The dream was not a memory.

Looking down at her clothes—clothes that weren't familiar—she prayed to the gods that it wasn't a premonition.

The dream hadn't started the same way as the others. And it felt different, very different. She'd not been led by wolf or owl. In those dreams she was an observer, removed from the scene, never making contact with the people or places that played out before her.

She ran to the gates, shoving them open, needing to see everything she could before she woke. Coughing from the smoke, she covered her mouth with the edge of her red cloak. Bodies lined the streets. She tried to find any survivors, but the city was quiet.

She was too late. No one was left.

What had caused such destruction? And how could she prevent it?

Making haste back to the palace, she stumbled through the charred gardens, past the fountain that had boiled to steam, finally reaching the open, high-arched doors.

A woman appeared at the top step, draped in white diaphanous robes that pooled at her feet. A silver crown was perched atop her long silvery waves. She looked pure and radiant.

Esme knew she was anything but.

She'd never met the high-priestess, but Esme was certain that the woman standing before her was Orianna.

Meeting the woman's calm gaze, she took the remaining steps to stand before her. Narrowly containing the wild and violent fury that thundered in her heart, Esme was set to demand what the woman had done to her city. But the sight of blood stole her focus. She glanced past the woman who'd slain her people to see a body sprawled on the floor of the entrance hall.

A woman lay faceup in a pool of her own blood, eyes still open in horror, mouth slightly agape as though she'd been screaming right up to the moment of her death.

Esme took a hesitant step forward, looking down at herself. Then screamed.

ERICA SEBREE

Chapter Thirty

A CLAP OF thunder jolted her from the nightmare. Esme took in the sight of her surroundings in a sweat-drenched panic. She was in her room in Altan—the sounds of calamitous winds tearing through the valley. Hail pounded against the window. She looked out just as a jagged bolt of violet light cut through the stormy yellow sky. A booming roll of thunder followed, shaking the foundation of the building.

Esme shuddered as the vibration ran through her bones.

The door crashed open, and Tearlach was practically on top of her before Esme could fully register what was happening. He seized her by the shoulders.

"Let go!" she managed, grabbing at his wrists in a feeble attempt to rip free from his hold. But Tearlach didn't budge—wouldn't even meet her eyes. His were firmly fixed on the scene outside the window.

A calming heaviness spread through her veins, and Esme quit fighting Tearlach's grip. Her body went slack beneath his protective hands. The storm outside abated. The skies cleared, and golden rays of sun pierced the treetops.

Esme held her breath as Tearlach's eyes found hers. He'd drained the magic from her, ceasing a devastating storm that might have ravaged the entire valley.

When he at last let her go, Esme slumped back against the wall.

Tearlach settled on the edge of the bed. "A dream?"

When Esme didn't respond, he turned toward her. All she could do was nod.

"And? What did you see?" He ran a hand through his raven hair. For a man who possessed such self-restraint, her magic seemed to easily unravel him. Or perhaps it was her.

"I...don't remember." She looked into the depths of his eyes, hoping it would keep him from sensing the lie.

Tearlach considered her a moment before looking away. He knew. But might grant her reprieve from having to relive it...at least for a moment.

Standing to leave, Tearlach hesitated. "Sully and the generals are meeting upstairs."

He didn't need to elaborate, Esme knew they were making plans to overthrow Orianna—a topic she was unwilling to face. But she'd been avoiding it long enough. The Northern Rebels had been preparing for years, and her sudden appearance had no doubt changed the equation.

"You know you're a part of the strategy."

"I know. Should I—"

"Only if you want to. But at some point, you'll need to be aware of what will happen."

Esme looked down at her hands, wishing there was some way to avoid what was to come. After a moment, she rose and followed Tearlach from the room.

As they crossed the main hall, Esme saw the aftermath of the storm through the open front doors. The ground was flooded, debris strewn about. Water flowed away from the center of the valley, ponding in low-lying areas, but ultimately seeking the river that ringed the perimeter. People hurried to right anything downed by the storm, others stood stunned, staring at the sky above.

How long had it been since they'd seen rain, no less a storm?

Feeling Tearlach beside her, she asked, "How did you know it was me?" Had her panicked thoughts alerted him?

Only a dream, she reminded herself as images of a burning city flickered in her mind.

"There are no high-priestesses left to summon the power of Tuireann and I know not of any other storm wielders in Altan." Tuireann, the god of sky. He was the one who'd *gifted* Esme with her destructive magic.

"If you hadn't stopped me..." She looked up at Tearlach.

"You might have washed away the entire camp?" He raised his brow. Though he seemed unworried by the prospect, Esme knew how easily he could shield his true concerns.

She turned away from the scene and let Tearlach lead her toward the back stairs, where a familiar voice called out. Killian reached them quickly, taking the stairs two at a time.

He leaned in to murmur in her ear. "Impressive."

Esme felt her cheeks heat, but she managed to meet his smiling eyes—he was clearly awed by her magic. "I'm not sure it counts if I was asleep," she evaded.

"Even more impressive." He winked at her as they reached the top floor, then pushed open the heavy doors of the war room.

And war room it was. Across the long table—where maps covered every available surface—Sully raised his head, meeting the stunned look in her eyes, then made his way over.

Esme took in the rest of the room. Hazel was seated to the right. Armel leaned against the wall behind her, patiently waiting for the group to reconvene. He caught her eye and inclined his head to her. So that was the reason she wasn't receiving lessons that afternoon.

Sully swept an arm over Esme's shoulders, turning her to meet Neala, one of the generals. The woman moved a small metal piece on one of the maps. Her long blond braid swished over her shoulder as she turned and nodded to Esme, offering her a wan smile before returning her attention to the table.

It was oddly comforting to see everyone in the room wearing casual attire—high-ranking officers and warriors alike. No one carried more than a dagger or short blade. No swords, no arrows. Still warriors, every one of them, but it would be through the strategies formulated in that very room that they'd win the coming war. And judging by the clutter of documents, inkwells, metal figurines, measuring instruments, and maps, it had been an arduous week for the lot of them.

Two more entered the room, talking boisterously between themselves. "Gittan," Sully addressed the woman in the plum-colored tunic as she sauntered to the far end of the table, then gestured to the man who'd entered with her, "Fulton." When both gave their attention, Sully put a protective hand on Esme's back. "I'd like to introduce Esme, Princess of Tremaene."

The double doors clicked shut behind her as Gittan made her way back over. The woman took both of Esme's hands in hers, looking into her eyes as if they'd known each other a lifetime. "Your Highness, so good to meet you."

"And you, as well."

When the general moved back around the table, Esme spared a glance at Fulton. It wasn't only that he wore black on black that made him seem enigmatic, his expression offered nothing. Esme wasn't sure what to expect from him. Everyone had greeted her differently. Some were happy to make her acquaintance, to find her alive after so many years. To others, it seemed her unexpected presence caused only a ruination of plans that had been in place for years.

Fulton nodded curtly and turned away. She placed him in the latter category.

Sully claimed his position at the head of the table, but no sooner had conversations started up did the arguing begin. A few remained quiet, listening, but the generals and Sully all talked over one another.

Esme stayed silent, though she inched closer to the table to get a better look, trying to grasp what was being planned for the take-back of their kingdom.

The sight of the maps and the many, many lines drawn across cities and provinces consumed Esme. Her mouth dropped open as she scanned the battle plans. *Perhaps it's not as bad as it looks*, she tried to reassure herself.

Somehow, she'd let herself believe that the six of them—Tearlach, Sully, Killian, Armel, Hazel, and herself—would steal into the palace late one night and depose the thieving high-priestess. She closed her eyes. How could she have been so naive? The woman had murdered her way to the top, and had continued to do so once she'd claimed the throne. Did Esme truly think she could stroll into the capital city and demand her crown?

"I'll say it again," Fulton's heated voice broke in. "The army needs to lead the attack from the north. It will take far too long from any other direction." The general slammed his fist down with unrestrained anger.

Tearlach leaned over, resting his palms on the table, keeping his voice level. "And I'll tell you again, General. Attacking from the north is ill advised. It's far too exposed. The longer route will keep our forces out of sight and give us a chance to set up a perimeter."

"He's right," Neala agreed. "Forming a perimeter should be our main concern. No one in or out of the city."

Tearlach shot her a glare. That wasn't exactly what he'd suggested.

"Keeping the citizens *safe* is our main concern," Sully corrected. "I'll get word to the guards, alerting them as to the night we plan to descend on the city. They'll keep the residents inside their homes and evacuate those closest to the palace."

"How many do you have in the palace guard?" Tearlach inquired of Sully.

"I have contact with about a dozen."

"Out of?"

"One hundred or so."

Those numbers didn't sound promising. Orianna had no doubt brought in guards who were loyal to her and had discharged those who weren't. At least Esme *hoped* they'd been released.

Tearlach focused on the large map before him that showed the layout of each floor of the palace and the surrounding grounds.

"What about the tunnels?" Neala asked.

Tearlach looked up. "Evacuating the city will draw too much attention. We can't risk it. Word will have reached Orianna by now that Esme is in Tremaene. Every inch of that city will be patrolled."

"Apologies, Princess, but we've had to reconsider our plans now that you've returned," Gittan explained.

"If we trap her in the palace, we may be able to get the citizens out of Meallán," Neala suggested.

"How many reside in the palace?" Tearlach asked.

Silence stretched as the generals and Sully shared tense looks. It clearly wasn't the first time such an idea had been brought up.

What will happen to them? Esme thought in horror. How many staff lived and worked in the palace? How many innocent lives would be forfeit? They didn't deserve Orianna's fate. Not one of them, no matter who they were loyal to.

"It may be our only chance to take her down," Fulton defended without addressing Tearlach's question.

"He's right," Gittan joined in. "Cahir can turn the palace to rubble. It's destructive, but effective."

"Who's Cahir?" Esme dared to ask.

"A soldier with earth magic," Fulton offered without looking at her.

"He can split the land in two, send shock waves through structures. I've heard stories from the war, and while I've only seen his work on a smaller scale, I wouldn't question his ability to bring down the palace," Gittan elucidated.

Earth magic could do such a thing? It sounded far more catastrophic than anything Esme possessed. Something that damaging would surely wipe out more than the palace. And even if it did, how could they be certain it would kill Orianna?

"And if she survives?" Tearlach scanned the table, making eye contact with everyone who clearly thought that razing the palace was a sound strategy.

Hazel, Armel, and Killian had remained quiet, following the conversation without offering advice. She wondered what their roles would be. They weren't generals, but they were part of Tearlach's band. Although...Tearlach was no longer the commander.

As she thought more about it, she realized that they might be the ones to get her safely into Meallán if Tearlach and Sully were occupied with the army.

No one answered Tearlach's question, but Gittan offered an alternative. "There's always the option of using fire in the storm drains beneath the city."

"Killian?" Fulton looked to him. "Would the other fire wielders be capable of something so large scale?"

"Some are quite powerful," he replied with none of the bravado Esme had come to expect from him. He seemed equally horrified by the proposal as she was.

"And if we pair it with air magic..." Fulton began.

"Yes, I was thinking just that. Who in the camp do we have?" Gittan looked to Sully.

Esme's brows furrowed at the seriousness with which the generals discussed such a widespread underground explosion that could wipe Meallán off the map.

She'd foolishly assumed it was just an outrageous idea to exhaust before they moved on to a more precise and less devastating one.

But the exchange continued, names were written down, lines were drawn across the map of Meallán. Soon the city was covered in deep red ink so thick it looked as though blood ran through the streets. It soon would if the proposed plan was carried out.

Esme shook her head unbelievingly at the words she heard, realizing that she wasn't about to witness a small takeover, but a full-scale war—one that the people of Meallán would pay for with their lives. It was more than she could withstand.

She knew killing Orianna was necessary, especially if they needed to thwart what had been foretold in her dream. The woman needed to be finished—permanently. Esme was even willing to do it herself if she felt she stood the smallest chance of defeating the infamous Fae.

But what the generals were proposing...it wasn't right.

"This cannot be the only option," Esme interjected, finding her voice.

Every pair of eyes fixed on her except Tearlach's. He held each of their gazes in turn as she found the strength to say what needed to be said.

Gittan was the first to respond. "This is the only way. You don't understand how powerful she is." To her credit, the woman addressed her with respect instead of condescension.

"Perhaps I don't, but I do know that we cannot allow innocent people to die. There has to be another way, one that doesn't result in starting a war over a single person. She must have some weakness." Esme looked to the others, searching their faces for understanding.

"She is more powerful than thirty men," Neala explained. "That's why we must bring an army."

Esme glanced at the others, but they all seemed to understand something she didn't. They'd been planning a war for years, any solution that would have resulted in fewer casualties had been considered and rejected long before she'd arrived.

But she refused to stand by as they destroyed her kingdom—her people. Too many had already died at Orianna's hand, and her tyrannical rule would not end with more.

"We cannot stop violence and destruction with more of the same. If we do that, we're no better than her," she pleaded.

"With all due respect, *Your Highness*," Fulton spat the title. "You know nothing of warfare or what it takes to bring down an enemy."

She could feel power thrumming off Tearlach at the perceived threat. Even Killian moved closer, glaring at the man who'd addressed her as though she were nothing more than a bug to be crushed.

Esme took a calming breath, but didn't return his clear disdain when she addressed Fulton. "What kind of world would we be creating if we—"

"You are a child! You have no say in this!"

Storm clouds gathered in her mind, magic tingling beneath her skin.

Easy, Tearlach's voice warned.

Esme inhaled deeply, forcing down the urge to let loose her magic, and met Fulton's rage-filled eyes.

"Then find yourself another queen."

Chapter Thirty-One

FULTON'S NOSTRILS FLARED, but Esme held his fiery gaze, knowing the power she held—the only power she held. Sully had made it clear that the people of Tremaene didn't need an army—and especially not a general—leading them. Fulton knew it too.

They needed her. By name alone, they needed her.

So with that sliver of superficial authority, Esme held her ground. Her demands *would* be met.

"General," Sully warned.

Fulton swept his hand across the table, knocking over a line of small metal pieces, then huffed back into his chair.

Esme's heart rate slowed and she spared a glance at Armel and Hazel, who'd both risen to stand beside her. The room was quiet as Sully stared down Neala, then Gittan, landing last on Fulton. The look in his eyes made it clear that no one should dare challenge Esme again.

Sully's expression softened to one of kindness and encouragement as he returned his attention to Esme, reminding her so much of her father in that moment.

Realizing everyone in the room was waiting for her, Esme cleared her throat and tried to think of something—a plan, the start of a plan...

anything. She'd never been the one people looked to. Never been the one to lead.

Orianna's magic, Tearlach's voice prompted.

Resisting the urge to look over at him, Esme straightened her shoulders and asked in a clear voice, "What do we know of Orianna's magic?"

Sully cast another look at everyone gathered around the table, then finally took his seat. The others followed suit, but Esme remained standing for a moment, shooting one last glance at Fulton, then perched herself on the edge of her chair.

Sully addressed Esme, explaining the reports he'd received. It seemed Orianna preferred using water to torture her subjects, and drowning was her execution style of choice. She also possessed a great prowess in air magic, using it to shield herself from both magical and physical attacks, leaving her practically untouchable. And if that didn't make the woman enough of a threat, there were whispers of other unusual talents used for manipulation. "Magic of the mind" was all Sully said. Of course nothing could be confirmed as that particularly terrifying weapon couldn't be seen, only felt by those subjected to it.

By the time Sully finished recounting the horrendous events he'd learned of over the years—or witnessed himself on occasion—Esme's stomach was churning.

While it was commonly known that priestesses each had a considerable wealth of magic—an indication that a young woman might one day join the Order—the diversity of Orianna's power was deeply unsettling.

Tearlach sat deadly still beside her, revealing nothing. And if Esme hadn't noticed the tightening grip on the arm of his chair, she might have believed he found the information unremarkable.

"Her magic doesn't sound like that of a high-priestess," Esme observed.

"It's quite anomalous for a high-priestess—or anyone, for that matter—to have such a range of magic, especially at so young an age,"

Sully agreed. Esme's clear confusion had him explaining further. "Magic can grow stronger or take a new form with extensive training, but only within the realm of one's original ability—simple water magic turning to ice, for example." He inclined his head toward Armel.

"You mentioned she was young…" How could Orianna have developed such multifariousness so quickly?

"She is. I would say she's no more than one hundred years or so."

"Then how is her magic so…superior?"

"Tell her what you suspect." Neala nodded to Sully.

All eyes turned to the commander.

He looked down for a moment before giving his attention to Esme. "There was once a powerful Fae who stole magic by taking lives. Not all of one's magic, but a fraction of it was transferred through the act of killing."

Hazel cursed at the same moment Tearlach quietly muttered, "Dark magic."

Esme spared him a glance, seeing the same haunted look he'd had on the boat when telling her of the Dark War.

"I didn't behold it myself during the war, but—"

"Then how do you know it's true?" Esme interrupted Sully, hoping it wasn't possible. Having such a wealth of magic could make a person invincible.

When he didn't respond, she pressed him. "Who, Sully? Who witnessed that kind of power?"

After a pause, he answered. "Your mother."

Esme's eyes grew wide. Her mother?

"She was…confronted with him during the war." Sully held her gaze and the rest of the world dropped away as an image formed in Esme's mind—her mother facing a towering, malevolent force.

After letting out a shaky breath, she posed the only question that needed to be asked. "And how…how was he finally defeated?"

Sully looked down at the table, before replying, "He wasn't."

Murmurs sounded beside her as Sully expounded. What had begun as an insurrection by those who believed the Order of high-priestesses should rule Tremaene, turned into what was later deemed the Dark War when an unnatural army of creatures invaded from the west, massacring all in their path. Everyone in the kingdom had joined together to defeat the dark magic wielders that bathed their land in blood. Their leader had only been stopped when his magic was drained enough to imprison him.

"And where is this *thing* now?" Tearlach demanded.

Apparently a few important details of Tremaene's past hadn't been kept only from Esme. She wondered what else had been concealed from her, from all of them.

"His tomb lies deep within the ground on a faraway island, east of the mortal lands."

"There are no islands east of Periwen," Esme argued. She'd memorized maps of Tremaene and the world beyond their shores at a young age. And she knew for certain that there were no islands past the mortal realm.

"It does not exist on any map. After he was entombed, a shield was created by very powerful magic to keep the place hidden. To this day, he remains in a state of eternal sleep, never to be disturbed."

"And you think Orianna has the same ability," Killian surmised.

Sully glanced at the generals. "We believe so."

The room fell silent.

"How?" Tearlach's tone hadn't lost its edge.

"The executions," Esme gathered.

Tearlach looked at her, a question written on his face.

"Sully told me—" She stopped and turned to the commander. "That's why she executes Fae who possess powerful or rare magic," she inferred. Sully dipped his head. "She's not eliminating people who threaten her reign, she's killing them to steal their magic." He nodded again.

In a low, calm voice that Esme knew was anything but, Tearlach asked, "How many has she killed?"

Sully looked to Tearlach. "She has amassed a great power, if that's what you're asking."

Tearlach tipped his head back to look up at the ceiling, then took in a long, deep breath. The movement was so unlike him. Except for a few instances, his reactions were usually controlled. He was struggling with something, Esme knew, watching him closely. Like he'd decided something he'd hoped to avoid.

His eyes eventually found her. "Then there's only one way."

Esme studied him as the room remained quiet. It was as if he was thinking of something only the two of them would have knowledge of. Something from their time in the mortal realm? From Debarrow?

Tearlach's workshop.

Finally, it made sense. Why the blades had seemed strange. *Wrong.*

"Iron," she breathed, staring at Tearlach.

He didn't look away, confirming what she feared.

Chapter Thirty-Two

"IRON?" GITTAN SCOFFED.

Iron was poison to Fae—it disrupted magic and healing abilities, making their kind as vulnerable as mortals. Small amounts were used by rulers past to imprison or incapacitate enemies. Dungeon walls had been made of the harsh metal before it was discovered that being merely in the presence of it could weaken magic and cause sickness.

As a weapon, iron was deadly. It could end an immortal's existence with only a draw of blood.

Gittan waited a moment, then narrowed her eyes when neither Tearlach nor Esme rescinded the idea. "All traces of it were mined and countervailed millennia ago, the rusted remnants and dust scattered at sea."

"And even if raw iron could be obtained, no one could wield such a weapon," Neala expounded with a sympathetic shake of her head as though she felt pity for Esme believing such a thing.

Esme looked to Tearlach.

"Iron still exists in the mortal realm," he informed them.

Gittan and Neala paled at the words, even Fulton had the sense to sit up straighter at the statement.

"Tearlach ran a smithy in the small town where we lived."

"You didn't," Hazel began. "Tell me you didn't bring any back with you." She looked horrified at the thought of Tearlach putting himself at risk.

When he gave a single nod in reply, Hazel sucked in a breath and both Armel and Killian cursed. Neala pulled away from the table like Tearlach himself was made of the lethal material.

"How were you able to even touch it?" Hazel braced her hands on the table. Her eyes scanned Tearlach like she needed to convince herself that he was okay, that there were no residual effects from the contact.

"I'm fine," he assured her. "It drains my magic, but over the years, I've built up a strong tolerance."

"I still don't understand." Hazel shook her head, then furrowed her brow. "Your magical signature...it was weak when I picked up your signal weeks ago. I thought it was because you were so far away, but that wasn't it. You had iron with you; you brought it here. It makes your magic weaker"—she looked him over once more—"but doesn't nullify it completely. How?"

Every pair of eyes were fixed on Tearlach, and Esme realized that no ordinary Fae would've been able to withstand such prolonged exposure.

"What kind of weapon are we talking about here?" Sully leaned forward, resting his forearms on the table. "A sword, dagger, arrowheads?"

"A sword and several throwing knives." He turned to Hazel again. "It isn't as bad as it seems," he promised with a soothing tone. "They're wrapped in wool to minimize the interference with my magic—or anyone else's—and the hilts are made from elder wood. Its healing properties keep the iron from affecting me too much. At this point, its presence feels more like a dull pain than anything deadly."

"But it is deadly," Hazel reminded him. Esme's chest ached at the worry in her voice.

"Which is exactly why it will work against Orianna," Tearlach pointed out.

Hazel held his gaze a moment longer before turning her attention to Armel and Killian, her eyes pleading with them to say something, anything to convince Tearlach not to further risk his life.

"What if she can sense it…the iron?" Killian questioned. "She's taken magic from innumerable Fae. We don't know what all she's capable of."

"He's right. We don't know if you'll even be able to get close enough," Sully added.

"We'll have to weaken her shield first," Armel offered, even as Hazel's eyes shot icy daggers at him.

Tearlach nodded to his friend, but Esme could tell he was holding back. There was more to it, something Tearlach hadn't mentioned yet. The man who always had every detail accounted for was slowly guiding them down a predetermined path.

"And once her magic is depleted…" Killian prompted.

Tearlach glanced over at Esme. "As soon as her shield is down, the only thing I'll need is a distraction."

Killian cursed under his breath as he and everyone else at the table turned to Esme.

She would be that distraction—the bait.

———————————

Though Hazel remained firmly opposed to Tearlach's insistence to put his life in danger, plans continued. The meeting went into the night as Esme watched Tearlach fall back into place with his fellow warriors. It was as though he'd never been anything but their leader. Even Sully sat back and yielded the floor as Tearlach led deliberations with the generals.

By the time the first glow of orange colored the sky, a plan had been agreed upon. The army would leave Altan the following week, going west through the mountains toward the foothills, before turning south toward the central province of Belfay—the home of the capital city of Meallán. But they wouldn't breach the city walls. The troops would stay hidden from Meallán and Orianna, yet close enough to offer support if needed.

A small group of warriors would stay behind to protect the families who lived in the Altan. And once the army was in position, Esme, Tearlach, Sully, Armel, Hazel, and Killian would traverse the mountains directly to the south. Without the hindrance of horses, they'd use a hidden pass through the Clavlin Ridge, then secretly make their way to Meallán—to Orianna.

Up until that point it'd been easy enough for Esme to stay in the present moment, to not think about what was to come. It had been the only way to save herself from being debilitatingly overwhelmed every second of every day. But she could no longer avoid the future.

And there would be no more waiting, because timing was a crucial part of their plan.

The night before the Dawning of the Light—which honored Aeveen, goddess of fire—both of the moons would align in darkness. Without the refracted magic of the Loinnir Lights, it was the only truly dark night of the entire year. And on that night, all over Tremaene—in every city and every province—people would extinguish their lights at sundown.

It was the perfect opportunity to slip into the city unseen.

The following week passed too quickly. After a day of surprisingly light training, Esme joined the others gathered in the largest training yard.

The army was set to leave the following morning, but it seemed no one wanted to admit the true reason for the celebration—that it might be a farewell. There was a chance not all would return.

Esme refused to think about it, keeping a tight smile on her face as she reached the festivities. *They will return*, she told herself with each step. *Every one of them.*

Fighters and families came together, joining hands and dancing to the music of flutes, recorders, and harps. Banquet tables were piled with trays of roasted vegetables, sweets, rolls, and fruit. A feast set for heroes. And they were. No matter what happened, they would always be heroes to her.

After eating her fill, Esme found a bench set farther back, content to spend the evening there, watching the merriment. But Cadwyn spotted her almost immediately.

"Go back to your friends," Esme encouraged, knowing Cadwyn might not see them again for some time.

"I want to spend tonight with you." She offered Esme a cup of wine.

"No, I insist. They're leaving tomorrow. We'll still have time together." Cadwyn studied her hands and took a deep breath, which instantly unsettled Esme. "What?" she begged.

"I'm going with them, with the army. I'm leaving tomorrow as well."

"No" was all she could say.

Cadwyn knelt down and took Esme's hands. "I am. And I'm sorry I didn't tell you sooner. I knew you would object."

"Of course I would. There's no reason for you to go. You're not a warrior, Cadwyn. Please don't do this," Esme beseeched. "Don't leave me." Her voice was near breaking.

"I'm not a warrior, but I am a healer. I can be of service, and they might...need me."

Cadwyn was right. If something interfered with their plans and the army was forced to intervene, they'd need healers. But Esme needed her too.

Cadwyn assured her that she'd be nowhere near the fighting—if it came to that.

After a heavy silence, Esme took a sip of her wine. She realized there was no talking her out of it. It certainly hadn't worked in the past. Cadwyn would go. She'd serve Tremaene to the best of her ability. Always had and always would. To stay would mean that she wasn't the person Esme knew her to be. Cadwyn was a woman of strong convictions and unyielding loyalty. And for that, Esme loved her fiercely.

Hours passed, and with the wine warming her blood everything seemed to melt away. The music grew louder and faster and Esme found herself in the center of the crowd, dancing with Cadwyn, hands joined, spinning in circles. When the song ended, everyone cheered. She couldn't recall the last time she'd felt so happy, so free.

The musicians rose and bowed, taking a much-needed break. But even without music, the world continued to spin.

Eying a table of treats, Esme made her way over, taking each step as gracefully as she could—which was no easy task after three cups of wine. Once she spotted a vanilla scone with raspberry icing, her face broke into a giant smile. She popped the whole thing in her mouth and turned to find Killian's eyes on her. He looked at her the way she'd looked at the desserts laid out on the table.

Esme covered her mouth and swallowed quickly. Killian stepped closer and her heart beat faster. The ensemble started up again with a slower tune. The beautiful, swirling melody reminded her of a time when she'd been nothing more than a princess without a care in the world. For one night, she'd let herself enjoy that peace. Because Esme had no idea if she'd ever have it again.

Killian's crystal blue eyes glittered in the torchlight as he offered his hand.

They danced. And just before the second number came to a close, she gently rested her head against his chest. Killian pulled her closer, tucking her into his strong embrace. When it ended, he bowed his head and kissed her hand before Cadwyn stole her away.

"Well, *that* certainly looked cozy." Cadwyn pulled her toward a table of sparkling drinks and punch. Esme's face heated instantly.

"He's only...well, he's training me how to wield a sword," she replied, knowing full well how absurd her explanation sounded.

"Mm-hmm" was Cadwyn's only reply as she ladled some punch.

After dancing another three songs with Cadwyn, Esme broke off to procure more wine, finding that she'd never enjoyed the drink so much. More than half of the casks were empty, but when she found one that was still heavy with wine, a large hand gripped hers before she could turn the spigot.

"I think you've had enough." A quiet, deep voice wrapped around her—one that in her hazy state she couldn't quite place.

As she turned to see who'd thwarted her mission, her previously cheerful demeanor fell.

"I'll decide when I've had enough, thank you." She defiantly removed Tearlach's hand to fill her cup—to the brim, just to make her point.

Keeping her eyes locked with his, she held the mug to her lips and drained its intoxicating contents in only a few gulps.

He watched her without saying a word as she set the copper mug on a nearby table with a bit more force than she'd intended, then started back toward the celebration.

A few feet were all she managed before the world tilted beneath her and the ground looked much farther away than it should have been.

Reaching her hand back, Esme hoped to meet the edge of the table before she lost her balance. Instead, two strong arms swept her up. She curled into the warmth against her cheek as darkness took her.

———————

Regret slammed into Esme the moment she woke the next morning. It felt as though a vise had gotten hold of her head and was testing the limits of its torque. She moaned and held her face between her hands.

The room was bright from the sun that had likely risen hours before. She peered through the slits in her eyes to see Cadwyn dressed and packing the last of her things.

Then she remembered it was the day Cadwyn would leave.

Not wanting to waste another moment in bed—no matter how much her body protested—she got up. Noticing she wore the same clothes from the night before, Esme tried to recall exactly how she'd made it to bed. But thinking only caused the vise to tighten.

After breakfast and a good amount of strong tea, Esme started to feel a little less like death. She followed Cadwyn to where the army had gathered, catching sight of Sully and Tearlach with the generals at the head of the assembly.

But the leaders were no longer the main focus of attention. All eyes had found her.

Pangs of guilt spread through Esme's chest that she hadn't spent more time getting to know the many warriors that were going off to fight. For her.

For Tremaene, she reminded herself as Cadwyn pulled her into a final embrace.

"We'll be reunited soon. Very soon. I promise," Cadwyn vowed, just as she had nine years earlier.

———————

Tearlach went easy on her that day, for which she was infinitely grateful. She'd expected punishment for her foolish choices the night before. But she didn't need more punishment. And he seemed to know that. With the aftereffects of the wine still making their way through her body, and the emotional drain of Cadwyn's departure, there was nothing Tearlach could do to make her feel worse.

When they left the clearing at midday, Esme was starting to feel like herself again. But there was still a nagging question she'd been meaning to ask since the day in the war room—one she wasn't sure how to broach.

"Tearlach, the enemy who was trapped at the end of the war…" She struggled to find the words. "Who…was he?"

Esme wasn't sure he'd respond, noticing the muscle in his jaw tighten. When he'd briefly mentioned the Dark War during their journey across the sea, it was clear he didn't often speak of it. And for good reason. Esme didn't want to think what it would have been like to fight side by side with thousands of warriors to then walk away as one of only four who'd survived the final battle.

After the silence stretched between them, he replied, "Our faction in the north never crossed paths with him, just his underlings. The war ended, but we never learned how. We only knew that the enemy leader had been destroyed somewhere in the west. Rumors made their way across the kingdom, but nothing was ever confirmed."

"I see." Esme fidgeted with the ties of her belt, needing to know if that drop of fear she felt was warranted. "The magic Sully mentioned...about killing someone to steal their power..."

Tearlach stopped suddenly and stared down at her. Esme stumbled beside him.

"Ask it," he demanded.

Her mouth opened and shut several times before she managed, "If you can absorb magic, does that mean...Can you..."

"No," he told her adamantly before turning and stalking back to camp.

Esme could have sworn there was a flicker of hurt in his eyes.

Her chest constricted with guilt. How could she have even *thought* him capable of such a thing?

Chapter Thirty-Three

ESME FINISHED DINNER quickly before anyone could join her, then managed to sneak past the guards while Tearlach spoke with them. Really, what danger was she in anyway?

Wandering down an empty path, she found a circle of long, curved benches. *Alone,* she sighed, sinking onto the cool plank of wood and dropping her head back to enjoy the night sky.

Nebulous lights danced above through the small opening in the canopy. The echoing strands of lilac, aquamarine, and jade winked in and out, twisting and merging against the inky night sky. Oh, how she'd missed staring up at the Loinnir Lights.

The sound of a nearby bench creaking had Esme tensing. Perhaps venturing out without an escort hadn't been such a good idea—one that Tearlach wouldn't let her forget if he found out.

She turned her head to the side slowly—as if she could somehow avoid being seen if she didn't make sudden movements. Her body slackened when her eyes fell on Armel.

She sat up. Armel was seated at the far end of an adjacent bench, bathed in the soft luminescent green from the glowing sky. He wasn't the last person she expected to see, but also not the first. They'd spent the afternoon training and he'd barely spoken to her—a few pointers here and there, but nothing beyond the realm of technique.

"I met your mother once, before she was Queen." He glanced in her direction.

Esme moved closer. "Really?"

He looked up at the sky, as if seeing some far-off place. "The war had just begun and she was part of the faction stationed outside our small farming village in the Western Flats.

"A wildfire broke out early one morning. I was making my way home after tending the sheep, and I saw smoke rolling off the fields in waves. I started running, but the warriors camped along the western edge of the village were faster."

He paused for a moment, seemingly lost in the memory. Killian had told her Armel didn't have family aside from the three of them, and Esme had a sinking feeling she knew where the story would end. She rubbed the ache in her breastbone as she waited for him to continue.

"Our only source of water was a small creek, but it was more than a hundred paces away. Those on horseback hauled buckets as fast as they could. There was even a water wielder among the warriors. She saturated the soil before it could spread to the outermost fields." He glanced at Esme, before returning his sights to the sky above. "I was young, and my magic was still in its early stages, but I tried to help—even managed to fill a few troughs of water before my power was depleted.

"We couldn't stop it. The fire spread rapidly, setting bales of hay ablaze once it reached the village. And when the first home caught, others quickly went up in flames. I couldn't reach my mother." He shook his head. "Our home was at the farthest end, and the smoldering debris blocked my path. I turned back to try another way, but the smoke was so thick I couldn't see more than two steps in front of me. That was when I heard the thundering hoofbeats of a rider. It was your mother." He glanced at Esme again. "It took her only minutes to draw the air from the flames, saving what was left of our village. That kind of control and expansiveness...she had an extraordinary gift. Her magic was so powerful, so precise—she saved hundreds that day."

When Armel didn't continue, Esme asked carefully, "And your mother?"

"Our village was lucky. Only a few perished. But my mother…she was one of them."

When he looked over at her, Esme could see the lights from the sky reflected in his gentle blue eyes. Sadness lingered there, even after so many years. Esme swallowed, wishing there was something she could do to ease his grief.

She noticed the silhouettes of Hazel and Killian as they made their way over, so she moved closer to Armel, took his hand, and thanked him for telling his story. It had been a long day, and there was little else she felt she could offer.

"I think I'll head in."

Armel nodded. "Your mother was an extraordinary woman. I'm sorry you lost her."

"I'm sorry about your mother as well. But I'm glad you found a family here, with them." She inclined her head toward Killian and Hazel.

"You will too. We're not meant to be solitary creatures, Esme."

Esme found Tearlach and Hazel alone in the dining hall the following morning. But instead of joining them, she motioned for her guards to stay back—amazed when they obeyed her—then peeked through the gap where the massive door hinged.

Tearlach sat at a long table with stacks of supplies for their upcoming journey. He made notes in a small book as Hazel arranged blades into neat rows of sharpened metal.

"Another rapier or two and perhaps a half dozen more short blades?" Hazel questioned.

Tearlach glanced down the rows of weaponry. "That should be sufficient."

"And what would you like *her* to carry? How has her training been with the others?"

"There hasn't been much progress." Tearlach's voice didn't hold any malice, but Esme felt as though the words had stabbed her in the gut.

She'd gotten better. Considerably. Before arriving in Altan, she'd never held a weapon—aside from Cadwyn's dagger. But to a warrior, she supposed her minimal improvement didn't amount to much. And though Tearlach's approval was of little significance to her, Esme decided that in the few days they had left in the valley she'd do her best to advance her skills. Not for him, but for herself. She didn't want to rely on Tearlach or any of the others if danger found her.

"It matters little," Tearlach stated, "she won't be anywhere near a fight."

Esme wanted to march in there and demand why he was even bothering to train her. To keep her busy all day? His own form of entertainment?

As her anger started to seethe, she reaffirmed her decision to strengthen her fighting skills before they left—without his help.

"What about her magic? Has she gained control over it?"

"Some, but it'll take years for her to master it."

Esme inhaled a sharp breath and tried not to take the remark personally. She knew it took years to master one's abilities, decades even. And if anyone was to blame for her slow progress, it was Tearlach. If she'd been given an instructor who knew her particular trait and did more than trigger her magic with physical attacks, she might have been closer to having a handle on it.

"We don't have years, Tearlach. We have days. Will she be able to hold her own if it comes to that?"

There was a long silence and Esme wondered if they'd discovered her eavesdropping. She peered through the crack again, but neither looked in her direction.

"She will," he told Hazel, surprising Esme. Though she hated to admit it, a trickle of pride swelled in her chest.

Backing away quietly to give herself some distance, she marched back toward the hall as loud as her soft boots would sound on the floor.

"Good morning," she called in a voice that was more chipper than usual.

Hazel spared her a glance before returning her attention to the weapons.

Tearlach didn't say anything either, but his eyes followed Esme as she went to pour a cup of tea. When she peered over her shoulder, his eyes were still on her. They held a knowing look.

Her cheeks heated and she quickly turned away, cursing herself and their...*connection.* There was no way she could ever sneak up on Tearlach. He knew where she was at all times.

Esme hastily grabbed a few leftover scones and a handful of walnuts, then hurried out of the hall.

When Tearlach didn't come to retrieve her for their morning lesson, Esme decided to seek out Killian. She found him walking back to the main building from the shower pavilion, and instantly averted her eyes. When Killian reached her, Esme risked another look, doing her best to ignore that his wet hair was soaking the front of his shirt, revealing every line of his muscled chest and abdomen.

Her attentions clearly hadn't gone unnoticed as Killian's mouth hitched into a playful grin.

"Good—" Esme cleared her throat. "Good morning, Killian."

"Good morning, sweetheart. What can I do for you?" His voice sounded innocent enough, but there was a wicked gleam in his eyes. She fixed her gaze on the ground, as though the sparse patches of grass were far more interesting than anything she'd ever seen.

"I was hoping you could give me a few extra lessons." She peered up through her lashes. "I want to be able to defend myself better."

His flirtatious expression vanished, replaced by a sincere smile. "Of course. Give me a second to grab my things."

They spent the morning running through basic foot placements again, then added a few advanced techniques. After parrying and riposting dozens of times, Esme managed to catch the tip of her sword against Killian's throat before he could block her.

He brandished his blade before dropping it to the ground in defeat.

Esme stepped back and fisted her free hand at her hip. "You're letting me win," she accused.

"I would never." He retrieved his weapon, then put a hand to his chest in mock offense. "I'm hurt you would allege such a thing."

"I think you're capable of most anything when it comes to women."

He stepped closer, dipping his head to the side. A few locks of his golden hair fell across his face as he held her gaze. "But something like that won't work on you."

It wasn't a question, but his eyes were clearly asking something. Something he wasn't allowing himself to ask.

Esme tried to slow her breathing as tension sizzled between them. The way he looked at her and the smell of crackling fires and warm spices that always seemed to surround him overwhelmed her senses.

And they were standing much too close.

Ducking her head, she backed away from his intense gaze. "Let's go again," she insisted as though they were nothing more than sparring partners. "And don't let me win this time."

Once she found her starting stance, she risked a look at Killian. The side of his mouth quirked in amusement.

Esme gritted her teeth, scolding herself for being so easily distracted. He certainly knew the effect he had on her.

"As you wish." Killian's eyes stayed on her as he slowly bowed his head. Then advanced.

Chapter Thirty-Four

ESME'S SWORD SKILLS improved with Killian's instruction—though she couldn't say the same for archery or knife throwing. Killian continually won each match. He was no longer letting her win, but Esme made him work for his victories. And when she ended up on the ground from a misstep or failed counterattack—which happened quite often—Killian was there to offer a strong, sturdy hand up. Holding on a few seconds longer than was necessary.

And while her body took the brunt of her physical training, Esme's magic exhausted her mind, which was beginning to feel a bit like sludge.

Her storm magic grew stronger, though she had nowhere near enough control to summon her power with a mere thought. Her storm clouds were more compact than they'd been, allowing her to direct the course of winds and rain more accurately. Lightning was close; she could feel it. Tingles ran down the tips of her fingers when she funneled the full force of her power into a storm. But all she could manage were a few crackles and sparks of white light that quickly fizzled in the rain. It was hardly useful as a weapon.

Hail, on the other hand, proved to be quite effective.

That morning, she channeled her magic into a dense ball of ice midair, letting it drop from the sky to strike Tearlach square on the head.

Not a wise choice, she realized too late.

Her amusement was utterly crushed a moment later as Tearlach pulled the magic from the space around her, sending hundreds of tiny ice pellets back at her, battering her skin.

Esme swore never to do it again, throwing up her hands to block the barrage. The hail fell to the ground, ricocheting off her boots.

"I thought you needed to touch me to siphon my magic." Esme peeked between her fingers, scrunching her face in confusion.

"I never said that."

"Then why did you—"

"It's more efficient that way. And in the case of the storms you summon with your dreams—"

Nightmares, she amended silently.

"Nightmares," he corrected.

Esme's eyes flared. That was one thing she still needed to work on—how to keep *him* out of her head.

"They were building strength and threatening to spiral out of control before you even woke." Tearlach stalked closer. "In those instances, *Esme*—" He rarely called her by her name, and never in that tone. She struggled to take in a breath as he took another step into her space. "—touching you was necessary."

She focused all her energy into appearing impassive, to not betray her pounding heart.

"Now, let's move on to your other talents." He arched a brow and smiled in that predatory way that told her he was once again provoking her.

Esme held back the growl in her throat as Tearlach spread his hands wide, waiting for her to engage her earth magic. *With pleasure,* she thought.

With great effort she focused intently on the small reserve of magic she had left, drawing roots and vines toward her, wrapping them around

Tearlach. She threw everything she had at him. And Tearlach stood there, taking it, letting Esme's grip on him tighten.

As she reached the last drops of her magic, a strange euphoria swept through her.

She collapsed onto the ground.

When Esme came to, Tearlach was sitting at the base of his usual tree with his head back, eyes closed. How long had she been out?

"Next time"—he didn't open his eyes—"try not to use everything you have. Expending all your energy until you lose consciousness is not going to help you in a fight."

Esme clambered to her feet. "How long was I asleep?"

"Maybe an hour."

"Oh." She glanced up through the breaks in the redwood branches. It was almost midday. "Are we done then?"

"You're not getting off that easily." He grinned, then started toward her with a canteen of water and a pouch of dried fruit. "How are you feeling?"

Taking a deep breath, she scanned her body. "I feel...rested." She furrowed her brow.

"Good. Let's go again."

Esme sighed, then ran through the drill a few more times. Tearlach didn't let her go too far, warning her when he felt her magic shallowing out.

"I thought you said she had storm magic," Killian said by way of greeting.

"She has that too, but this," Tearlach explained as he gestured to the retreating vines and roots that had surrounded him moments before, "has been more challenging. And until we learned what she was capable of, it was safer to keep it a secret." He shared a look with Killian, and Esme wondered what unspoken words were being expressed. Killian simply nodded.

"She's starting to gain control." Tearlach circled Esme. She propped her hands on her hips and turned to face him, not particularly appreciative of the way Tearlach was appraising her. She noticed Killian's grin out of the corner of her eye. "And I want to see what your fire can do against her magic," Tearlach told Killian, backing away.

Killian's eyes glittered with anticipation as he stepped closer to Esme. "Let's see what you can do," he murmured, his voice rich with intrigue.

After Esme glanced at Tearlach—arms crossed over his chest, waiting, observing…judging—she closed the distance with Killian, then took a deep breath and shut her eyes. Feeling the roots move beneath the earth, where they lay dormant, still, awaiting her request, they sprang up from the ground, slithering toward Killian. Her eyes remained closed, but in her mind she could see the rough, woody roots entwining Killian's boots.

Hearing him inhale sharply, her eyes shot open, pausing the course of the growing flora. But as soon as she saw how enraptured he seemed by her power, she continued with a smile. Earthy roots became smooth, splitting into thin corkscrew vines, spiraling up his legs and wrapping around his midsection. Satisfied with the cage she'd coiled, Esme turned her attention to the tips of the newly formed vines until leaflets popped out along the ends of each stem. Raising her head, she met Killian's eyes and offered a playful grin as white, five-petalled flowers budded and bloomed with the alluring scent of honey and sweet citrus.

"Killian." Tearlach's warning tone reminded them that they weren't alone.

"Right," Killian replied as Esme bit her lower lip.

They shared a mischievous look, then Killian straightened, his gaze becoming serious and potent as he summoned his magic. Flames licked at the roots, attacking the thickest of them near the ground. Esme kept her hold on him, yielding only a step as she watched him work. Thin flickers of fire traveled up his legs, fighting Esme's magic. Smoke encircled the greenery, but when his fire failed to free him, Killian started twisting and wrestling with the vines. Esme tightened her hold, biting back a grin. Finally, he gave up struggling and sagged against his bindings, smiling unabashedly as he surrendered.

"Nicely done," he marveled, still within her grasp.

Esme's cheeks heated at the admiration in Killian's eyes. He could have held her there forever, with only that look. But she heard Tearlach's approach, and stumbled back, releasing her magic.

———————

The night before they were set to leave, the families that resided in the valley gathered to share a meal. Esme weaved through the trail of torchlights and delivered a tray of pastries to the serving table.

"Princess! Princess!"

Esme spun around, her heart already hammering in her chest. At the sight of a child running toward her, she knelt down before they could draw too much attention.

"You're the princess?"

"I...am. My name's Esme. What's yours?"

"My name is Erena," she proclaimed proudly, lifting her chin.

Esme's heart clenched. It was a name she hadn't heard in years— hadn't let herself think about it, even in the shelter of her mind. Because hearing that name was almost more than she could bear.

Her heart slowly regained its rhythm. She fought back tears as she repeated the name in a quiet voice. "Erena?"

"That's right! Mama says I'm named after the great queen of Tremaene."

"Yes." Esme swallowed hard. "Her name was Erena."

"I never got a chance to meet her, but I know she was beautiful." The girl spun around as if she embodied the very essence of the late queen. "Mama says you're going to be just like her and that we'll be able to return home soon."

Esme summoned the most collected look she could manage. "And where is home?"

"Well...this is my home." Little Erena gestured to the trees behind her. "But Mama and Papa are from Belfay. Do you know it?" Esme nodded. "Papa says there used to be all kinds of animals there, furry ones and feathered ones, even scaled ones with long tails." Her eyes grew impossibly wide. "I didn't believe him at first—we only have small brown birds here—but then Sully showed me some of the creatures. Do you know Sully? He's a shapeshifter!" The small, spirited girl finally took a breath, bouncing with energy.

As if on cue, a golden hawk swooped down into the small crowd, taking shape between Tearlach and Armel. Sully had left Altan two days earlier to confirm the location of the army.

"Yes, I know Sully. And shapeshifting is rather spectacular," Esme agreed. "What kind of magic do you hope to have when you grow up?"

The girl thought for a moment, putting a finger on her cheek as she contemplated. Esme could barely hold in a laugh as she beheld the ardent child.

"I want storm magic, like you!"

It seemed word had traveled that Esme had been responsible for the massive rainstorm that had nearly washed the camp away. "Storm magic, huh?" She would have guessed fire, imagining the lively woman the young girl would one day become.

Little Erena leaned in, hooking a finger in the air to invite her closer. Esme chuckled and turned an ear toward her.

"Mama told me that you're going to bring magic back to the land."

Her eyebrows rose. "Oh, really?"

Erena continued in a conspiratorial voice. "She says animals will return and flowers will bloom again. Did you know that there were once fields of flowers more colorful than the Loinnir Lights, and vines with pink-colored flowers that climb walls? Have you ever seen such a thing?" Her voice rose again.

Esme nodded as a memory took shape in her mind. The rosebushes that hedged the palace grounds...the water lilies that floated near the lakeshore...the night-blooming moonflowers that could be seen across the rolling hills...

But in the years she'd been gone, the high-priestesses had been killed, and Tremaene had become a desolate, barren land. Though Altan was thick with redwoods, it was mostly devoid of wildlife and plants that weren't cultivated for food. And as for the rest of the kingdom...she wasn't looking forward to seeing what was left of the lands south of the mountain range.

Sitting back on her heels, Esme cupped her hands to the dry soil at her feet and drew up a bright green shoot that budded into a flower with yellow petals that blushed toward a vibrant pink along the edges. She plucked the stem from the ground and placed it gently in Erena's palm. The young child was stunned into silence, watching the magic worked before her eyes.

When the girl's eyes met hers, she whispered, "I want flower magic too."

"Erena," a woman called.

Esme looked up to see a woman with long, honey-colored hair—the same color as Erena's.

The woman faltered as she caught sight of her. "Your Highness." She gripped the skirts of her dress and bowed her head. "I hope my daughter wasn't bothering you."

"Not at all." Esme smiled, looking down at little Erena once more. "It was a pleasure to meet you, Erena. I do hope we'll see each other again very soon."

———————————

Esme stared out the window beside her bed, unable to sleep. She didn't like the quiet, though she wasn't sure why. After being almost completely ensconced in solitude back in Periwen, one would think she'd be used to it. But without the sounds of footfalls in the hall, or laughing and conversation coming from the yard outside, she felt...lonely. And she wasn't about to ask the warrior sleeping by the door for a dose of sleep magic.

Not yet, anyway.

She simply needed a distraction from the journey ahead. And if sleep was lost to her, she might as well practice a bit of magic. She'd never tried it indoors, after all.

Waking Tearlach with a localized thunderstorm wasn't something she wanted to risk, so she opted for the earthier of her magics. It was becoming fairly easy to summon her power, directing it with only a little concentration, no longer straining her the way it had before.

In the span of a few breaths, vines began traveling up her. Esme wasn't sure where they were coming from, but she didn't care, delighting in the feel of them tickling her feet and legs. She sent runners along the bed and up the wall behind her. As they climbed higher, she angled her head to see the interwoven ivy cover the wall.

But there was only bare stone behind her.

Still, she could feel them—the vines, the leaves, the tiny clusters of flowers. They were connected to her, and she knew the vines were *there*. Only...not there.

Not *visible*.

Somehow, she'd managed to create invisible vines—vines she could feel, vines she could grow and direct. Vines that were just as powerful as the ones she'd trapped Killian with, that even fire magic couldn't destroy.

Vines that no one could see.

Well, that's certainly useful, she realized.

"Enough of that." Tearlach startled her from across the room.

"Enough of what?" she replied innocently, her voice pitching too high.

"Stop playing with your magic. We have a long journey tomorrow and I've no intention of carrying you."

How did he even—

"I know everything."

"Stay out of my head," Esme growled, flipping onto her side as Tearlach chuckled.

Chapter Thirty-Five

ESME PULLED OPEN the heavy doors only to collide with a thick layer of mist. Her heart instantly beat wildly at the sight of it.

It isn't a dream. She forced a slow breath.

Her nerves were already frayed. The morning hadn't been easy. She wasn't sure why she'd expected Tearlach to wait for her when he'd never done so before, but something about waking in that cold room without Cadwyn, without Tearlach, had made her panic.

She tugged at the hem of her emerald green coat. It was perfectly tailored, falling to mid-thigh. And with the thick protective pants that hugged her legs, the tall sturdy boots, and opalescent gray gauntlets that flexed with her every move, she nearly looked like a warrior. Running her fingers along the dagger and sword at her side, she tugged Cadwyn's cloak tighter across her front. The added layer wasn't necessary—and in a few minutes it would make her warmer than she cared to be—but Esme couldn't imagine leaving it behind.

She flattened her palm against the door and looked out at the camp. She narrowed her eyes, unable to see anything but the watery morning light that struggled to pierce the fog.

Something brushed her shoulder and Esme yelped, nearly jumping out of her boots.

"Killian," she breathed as he stepped around her, his expression turning flirtatious with that single word.

"Sorry for startling you. Though I can't say I mind when you say my name that way." He offered a smile—one that never failed to make Esme forget everything else around her. But when his tongue slid along his lower lip, and he dropped his gaze to her mouth, she couldn't even remember her name.

Killian chuckled, clearly aware of the reaction he'd caused, then draped an arm around her and tucked her into his side. The door shut with a resounding thud, causing her to jolt.

"Come on, jumpy, let's go save the kingdom."

Of course he was eager about the prospect. Esme on the other hand? Not so much.

The fog closed around them as they moved away from the cover of the building, swarming the empty space they left behind. Being unable to see more than one pace ahead was unsettling, even with Killian at her side. Her previous encounters with such dense fog had led to visions she wished not to see again.

Luckily, she hadn't been visited by the wolf or the owl for quite some time. As for the other strange dream—the one where she'd seen her own dead body splayed on the marble floor of the palace? She'd conveniently discounted it as nothing more than fears coalescing in her worried, exhausted mind. That was surely the reason she still hadn't mentioned it to Tearlach. Surely it was...

They joined the others. Tearlach, Armel, and Sully wore uniforms similar to Killian's—a blend of warm caramels, deep browns, coppers, and silvers. The flexible, metal armor that covered their arms and torsos looked like shiny fish scales. Hazel wore varying shades of green, but not the heavy, protective shoulder plates of her counterparts. The absence likely allowed for better access to her bow and quiver.

Esme listened silently as Tearlach and Sully recapitulated the specifics of their journey. Sully had learned from the city guards that Orianna's scouts were out in triple force after several had failed to return.

She knew exactly which scouts had never made it home—she'd cowered in a tree while her companions had killed them.

The surge in numbers indicated that Orianna knew for certain of Esme's return to Tremaene.

In Altan they were protected by the shelter of the mountains. But once they left the valley, Tearlach would glamour their entire group, keeping them invisible to other sensors. Hazel had vehemently objected on that point, because in addition to the iron weapons he carried— refusing to let anyone else shoulder the burden—glamouring more than himself and Esme would be a constant strain on his magic.

Hazel worried about him. It was clear to see. Esme knew too well that worrying after one's friend for so long became an ache that never truly eased.

But Tearlach's magic was essential if they were to cross the kingdom unnoticed.

When they finally left the camp, the others flanked her. Esme resisted the urge to roll her eyes. It wasn't the least bit necessary. But as they passed families descending from their homes in the trees, she wondered if they'd done it as a show to the people of Altan that their future queen was well protected.

Her eye caught the little girl, Erena, as she was hoisted up on her father's shoulders.

The journey ahead terrified her, and Esme had done superbly well at holding herself together until that point. But seeing the faces of the people she needed to defend from Orianna's tyranny—the people who'd been *her* responsibility since her parents had died—tears threatened to spill down her cheeks.

She fixed her gaze on the ground, unable to meet their hopeful looks.

A strong, reassuring hand rested briefly on her shoulder. She glanced over at Tearlach as his hand dropped away. He lifted his chin an inch, implying that she do the same.

Esme closed her eyes a moment, then held her head high as they left the valley.

Killian and Esme circled each other the following afternoon. Readying her attack, she stepped carefully, crossing left foot over right.

Her ankle hit a patch of uneven ground and she pitched forward. Two large hands grabbed her waist before she could hit the ground. Tearlach swung her back to her feet, then glared at Killian.

"Didn't you teach her to always be aware of her surroundings?" Tearlach demanded of him. Esme's face heated with embarrassment.

"Day one, Tearlach. She's just not used to the terrain."

"She needs to be. No two environments will be the same. Make sure she—"

"Stop talking about me like I'm not here," Esme bit out, throwing an irritated look over her shoulder as she retrieved her blade from the ground. Killian had the sense to look contrite when she took up a position across from him.

Killian said something to her—undoubtedly about the importance of being aware of one's surroundings—but she couldn't hear anything over the ringing in her ears. Why had Tearlach chosen that moment to show up? Not that she would have preferred falling...exactly.

She stole another glance over her shoulder, only to find that Tearlach wasn't the only one who'd taken an interest. *Wonderful. An audience.* Even more pressure not to make another mistake.

As they faced one another, Esme pleaded silently with Killian, begging him not to let her win. Somehow that seemed worse than tripping—even with the possibility of landing on her sword.

Esme scrunched her forehead and considered it might serve her better if she gave up her priority of saving face.

Their swords collided as they attacked, parried, and riposted through the narrow clearing of redwoods. Then Killian caught her blade, sliding his sword down the length of hers until they were locked together. He gripped her wrist at the same moment Esme grabbed his, blades crossed before them.

Killian towered over her, his eyes telling her to forget the people around them. She funneled all of her strength into her arms, using the ground beneath her as leverage against his powerfully muscled body.

It would have been so easy to use magic, to end the duel with a precisely angled whip of a tree branch or a few snaking vines. But she couldn't. She'd been warned not to. In Altan, she'd used it every day. She'd grown accustomed to it. And suddenly she was no longer allowed to engage with it.

It needed to be unleashed. Her magic swelled inside, the pressure building more and more with each passing hour, beckoning to be used, to be played with. She wanted to indulge the desire. Her skin tingled, her whole body humming with anticipation.

Don't you dare, a voice warned.

Esme nearly growled, catching herself at the last second since Killian was the person standing before her, and not Tearlach. But she let his unwelcome voice fuel her fight, shoving Killian away.

He yielded a step. Esme knew how much stronger he was, but she also knew he was putting up a good fight. Taking the opportunity, she advanced, attacking three times before he swung at her.

Esme ducked from the blade, but when she came up, ready to lunge, the tip of Killian's sword pressed against the skin above her collarbone. There was a whisper of a smile on his face as they locked eyes, both breathing more heavily than they had moments before.

She dropped her sword as applause filtered through. Apparently they'd put on a good show.

Instead of scouting the area with others, Tearlach settled in beside Esme that evening as she watched Hazel attempt a spark by striking two pieces of obsidian stone together. The task was clearly aggravating her. She sighed and looked up, locking eyes with Esme. Something flared in Hazel's stare and Esme wondered if the woman blamed her for the prohibition on their magic.

"Don't even think about it," Tearlach warned. Hazel growled softly, narrowing her eyes, but returned her attention to the stones.

"You'll get used to it."

Esme turned to Tearlach. "What? Hazel? I've had enough lessons with her to—"

"The constant thrum of your magic," he clarified.

Esme's lips parted. "I...I don't...It's not..." she tried. But it was useless to deny her thoughts. She'd been unable to think of anything but the mounting pressure of her suppressed magic. Her desire to summon vines and swirl them up around her legs just to feel an ounce of relief from the intensity that was almost too much to bear.

"Get used to it?" Her voice sounded desperate as she looked up at him.

Tearlach studied her a moment, but didn't say anything more.

Esme shifted away. If he wasn't going to offer useful advice—or any advice at all—she'd rather be alone with the uncomfortable sensations. Maybe she'd give counting her breaths another try.

Tearlach reached over and rested his hand on hers. Before Esme could pull away, the air was forced from her lungs as he drank the magic from her overflowing well.

He didn't take much, just enough to soften the edges, freeing her mind to focus on something other than the continuous rhythm of power pulsing inside her.

Her muscles went slack. She inhaled deeply, taking a long, languid breath.

By the time she turned to thank Tearlach, he was already striding past Hazel and into the trees.

———————

With her sleep untouched by premonitions, Esme grew more confident in the success of their journey. Killian remained at her side most days, keeping her company with stories of his childhood with Hazel, while Sully reminisced with her each night by the fire.

After several days of traversing the narrow valleys that dipped between peaks and ridges, they reached a mountain face taller than any she'd seen beyond the shore—one that stretched so far west to east that she couldn't see where it began or ended.

The Clavlin Ridge, Esme realized as she gazed up at the rock wall that seemed to crowd the sky. Thankfully, they wouldn't need to scale it. Not many knew of the Northern Pass—her knowledge of Tremaene's geography didn't go beyond maps, and the secret passage through the ridge couldn't be found on any. She'd only learned of it during the meeting with the generals.

In fact, none of her companions had been inside it, which made finding the hidden entrance a challenge. Tearlach halted the group at the foot of the steep rock, searching the mountainside before deciding they should continue west.

Killian, Hazel, and Armel went ahead to search for the concealed entrance, while Esme stayed behind with Tearlach and Sully. She tried not to feel as though she was being looked after by two giant nursemaids. To her delight, Sully launched into another tale of the childhood he'd shared with her mother. It seemed he enjoyed his renewed role as confidant and guardian rather than commander.

Killian called from atop a narrow ledge above the gully—one that contained only a dwindling trickle of water, a sight that was becoming more frequent the farther south they ventured.

Jagged boulders that looked as though they'd tumbled from the mountain crest gathered in teetering precariousness. Nothing about the monoliths looked intentional, offering a perfect disguise for the entryway into the mountain. Esme was impressed that Killian had managed to find such a well-concealed place.

Armel and Hazel ducked inside after him, and once it was deemed safe, Sully hoisted Esme up into Killian's waiting arms.

A flame pierced the darkness, bathing the passageway in honey-colored light. Hazel lit the other silver-handled torches, passing them back. Esme took hers, trailing her other hand along the curved wall to keep her balance down the steep decline.

Grooves ran horizontal to the ground, signs of a long-ago river that had formed the secret tunnel. Flickering torchlight played along the walls, highlighting layers of red porous stone and smooth rock the color of sand. The light dissipated high on the walls, stretching to reach the ever-rising peaks above.

The temperature dropped the deeper they traveled. Esme breathed in the smell of wet stone. Echoing footfalls surrounded them, spreading out and bouncing around the hollowness that yawned open. When the passage opened into a vast cavern, the light from their torches barely penetrated the darkness.

Esme took in the immense space that might have fit the entire palace within it. Stalactites clung to the high, vaulted ceiling, dripping down to meet their mirroring spikes rising from the floor. Water percolated through the wall at the far end, filling a massively deep pool that occupied half of the space.

Stepping carefully across the slick stone flats, she approached the pool. The light from her torch reflected against the turquoise surface. There was a rock shelf circling the pool, no more than a foot beneath the surface. But beyond that—

Esme slid her foot back, her eyes fixed on the drop-off past the ledge, where the light of her torch was swallowed by darkness. She tore her gaze away, searching the cavern for another tunnel, desperate to disprove her fear that the only way out was through the terrifying depths of the underground lake.

The others had dropped their packs near the edge of the water, stripping off armor and weapons.

"No," she breathed.

Hazel and Armel climbed the rocks near the wall where the water disappeared, surveying the dark pool like it was nothing more than an obstacle.

"What about here?" Hazel crouched, pointing down into the water near a small cascade of flat stones.

Tearlach moved to her side, waving his torch slowly back and forth to catch the light on formations far below the surface. Before they could agree, Armel dove in from the opposite side, cutting through the water until he melded with the darkness.

Sully came up beside her, but Esme couldn't look away from the place where Armel had disappeared.

"This, my dear," Sully explained with a sweep of his hand, "is the reason the Northern Pass remains hidden."

Esme couldn't respond. Her throat refused to work. It had gone dry in the humid cave air.

All she could do was stare at the bottomless, strangling, inky black water.

Chapter Thirty-Six

ESME'S FEAR SEEMED unfounded. She'd always been brave as a child—swimming in the lake day and night, weaving through lily pads while fish tickled her feet.

Even waking on the fisherman's boat in Periwen after surviving a wreck at sea hadn't stoked a fear of water.

But looking out at the water before her—deep and wide, with a terrifying drop into darkness—was another thing entirely. It was as if every muscle in her body had seized up, keeping her from going any closer. As if it knew that danger dwelled just beneath the surface.

The others were already wrapping their packs in thin, silky material meant to keep their supplies dry. Esme glanced at Armel, wondering how much of a risk it would be for him to use his magic to part the water. But even something so small as a short burst of power would alert Orianna's scouts to their whereabouts, and Armel directing the water of an entire lake would hardly be magic on a small scale.

There was no other way. They'd have to swim.

Heavy clothing, boots, weapons, and armor were stuffed into packs or bound together. A small bundle of dry wood was covered in the waterproof material as well. Esme reluctantly pulled her sword and dagger from her belt, adding them to the mountain of weapons, then removed her protective coverings, boots, cloak, and jacket.

She inched back toward the water's edge, determined to enter under her own volition, lest *someone* drag her in. The few remaining ripples lapped against the rock before Armel dove in again—a rope tied around his waist.

Esme counted the seconds it took for him to reappear. She hoped the swim wouldn't be too far, wasn't sure how long she could hold her breath. It was already coming in short bursts as she stood there watching.

When he emerged, hoisting himself up onto the ledge, he pushed his wet hair back, then told them, "It's about fifty feet straight under."

"Fifty?" Esme nearly choked on the words.

"Oh, that's nothing," Sully assured her, taking her tone as surprise instead of dread. "You'll be popping out the other side in no time."

"And how…how deep is it?" She tried her best to sound as though the thought of holding her breath and swimming through dark water without a light to guide her was no different than a delightful splash in a fountain.

"The rock cuts away about ten feet down." Armel gestured toward the wall where the lake seemed to end. Only it didn't.

Ten feet down, fifty feet through the darkness without a pocket of air, then another ten feet to the surface on the other side.

A lot of feet and a lot of water. Esme gripped her belt, needing something to hold on to.

Hazel and Killian tied up each bundle of gear as Tearlach addressed the group. "We go one at a time. Wait for the signal before following. Killian, you'll go first, followed by Sully, Hazel, Esme, and myself. Armel, you'll bring the rope through."

At least she wasn't going first or last. Armel's task to stay behind also meant he'd need to extinguish his torch before going into the water.

Killian swung a pack over his shoulder and secured two others to his belt. He tested the tautness of the rope—Esme watching him nervously, fearing the weight of their supplies would pull him down. But he was through the water, vanishing into the abyss in the span of a few seconds.

Sully followed as soon as a tug on the rope indicated Killian's arrival on the other side. Then Hazel. If Esme hadn't been impressed with the woman's skill before, she certainly was after watching her drag the massive bundle of weapons into the water with her.

Then it was Esme's turn.

Her legs felt heavy as she struggled to move forward. Armel had turned away, keeping an eye on the cave entrance until everyone was through.

"Do you want me to go with you?" Tearlach leaned in to offer.

Esme stared at the water, wondering what else was down there. After a protracted moment, she shoved her fears away. "No. I'll be fine." Her words held more conviction than she felt, but she was determined. There were far more perilous things ahead and proving to herself that she could conquer one obstacle on her own might convince her that she could do it again.

She climbed down the rocks until her bare feet touched the cool water.

Esme had only herself to worry about. Tearlach shouldered the three remaining packs of supplies and his iron weapons. Armel would bring their armor through.

Shivers spread along her skin as she inched toward the drop-off. She told herself it was from the cold water.

She lowered herself down, dangling her legs off the edge, all the while keeping her eyes fixed on the peaked ceiling. After allowing herself three deep breaths, she slipped in.

Managing to keep her head above water, she swam toward the wall. The sound of Tearlach entering the water behind her echoed through the cavern. Would he follow his own orders and wait until she was through? The thought forced a grin past the rigidly tense muscles in her jaw.

Her breathing was already labored, but she kept moving until her hand touched the stone wall, slipping along the slimy sheen. There was nothing to grab on to and no place to rest her already tired arms and legs. She couldn't wait long.

Glancing over her shoulder at Tearlach, she could tell he was about to give her the same warning—not to waste her energy treading water. She eyed the line of the rope once more, confirming that she was right above it.

Sucking in the biggest gulp of air she could withstand, Esme closed her eyes and plunged straight down. Once her hand gripped the rope, she pulled herself into the underwater passageway.

Fifty feet. Only fifty feet. The words cycled through her mind as she followed the rope. Her plan had been to keep her eyes shut. It was too dark to see anything anyway. Her body shuddered at the thought.

But her imagination might have been worse, conjuring images of—

She yanked herself forward and forced her eyes open. The water was so cold it felt like needles. And she still couldn't see a thing. There was no light, nothing to indicate how much farther she needed to swim.

At least the frigid water kept her focused on the physical discomfort.

Until something slipped past her foot.

Esme cupped a hand over her mouth to keep from sucking in water.

And dropped the rope.

No!

She spread her hands through the water frantically.

Where was the rope?

How much longer could she hold her breath?

She was trapped.

Terror flooded her veins.

Forward. She needed to move forward.

Which way was forward? There was no way to orient herself. She twisted, grasping handfuls of empty water, trying to find the rope.

Something churned the water beside her.

A whimper vibrated in her ears as she was propelled by the movement. Or pushed away...she wasn't sure. The force made her feel like she was tumbling even deeper.

Still, she managed to turn toward the disturbance. As frightened as she was, she knew better than to place her back to whatever lived down there. It was big, of that she was certain.

Her lungs burned. She didn't have much time. Even if the *thing* that dwelled in the darkness didn't devour her, her lungs might very well give out before she reached the other side.

Something snaked around her waist.

Esme screamed, the last of her air escaping from her lips.

She tried to pry it away—

Tearlach.

Esme instantly gave up her struggle, gripping his muscled arm, holding on as tight as she could. He moved quickly through the water with a swiftness she wouldn't have thought possible for such a sizable man.

In only a matter of seconds, she saw a faint glow fluttering in the distance, growing brighter as Tearlach propelled them forward.

Esme's lungs screamed to take a breath as they emerged from the tunnel. Tearlach pulled her hands from his arm and shoved her up toward the surface. Esme didn't hesitate, kicking her legs with everything she had left.

Her lungs spasmed, but she was so close—her arms reaching for the precious air above.

A hand broke through the water and cool air touched her face.

Esme gasped as Killian hauled her out of the water. She sagged into his embrace. He tried to steady her, then scooped her up instead, setting her limply on a wide, flat rock.

"She's just cold," Killian assured the others. "I'll warm her up." But the look he gave her told her he'd seen the panic in her eyes—that it wasn't just the cold making her shiver.

Water crashed onto the rock ledge of the pool as Tearlach rushed up, tossing packs to Sully and Hazel as if they weighed nothing, then pulled himself up and out in one fluid motion. As much as Esme wanted to throw her arms around him and thank him for once again saving her life, she couldn't meet his eyes.

"It's okay. You're okay," Killian whispered as he rubbed his hands vigorously up and down her arms. "Why didn't you say something? I would have gone with you." He looked anguished seeing her obvious distress.

Esme could only offer a slight shake of her head, even when Killian's brow furrowed with concern. He continued his ministrations until her body stopped trembling.

Chapter Thirty-Seven

KILLIAN TOOK HER canteen to refill it. With the rivers running dry, Esme was worried it would be their last chance to do so. She wrapped her cloak around her shoulders, choosing to leave her protective plates in her pack—her damp clothes felt heavy enough. No one seemed to mind as they replaced their own armor and weapons. Not even Tearlach spared her a glance. In fact, he hadn't looked at her once since they'd emerged from the lake—hadn't mentioned his underwater rescue to the others either.

She wondered what would have happened if he'd arrived a moment too late. Would their connection have kept her alive?

She wasn't inclined to find out what tugging on that lifeline would feel like.

Sully and Hazel took the lead up ahead. And with Killian and Armel at the back, Esme was stuck with Tearlach in the middle of the group. Killian's laughter ricocheted off the walls, floating up to meet them, but even that didn't coax a smile or remark from Tearlach.

Esme decided to embrace the silence between them. Her muscles were weary, and with the remnants of the underwater currents swaying in her mind, all she could manage was to watch her footfalls and hope to remain upright.

When the passageway opened into another vast cavern with antechambers and alcoves along the periphery, they stopped to make camp. Esme wasn't sure how anyone could discern the time of day inside the mountain, but didn't question it. She unfurled her bedroll and collapsed onto it.

Through the thin layer of bedding between her and the cave floor, Esme could hear a faint humming. She opened her eyes and lifted her head. The humming continued.

"Over here." Tearlach summoned her to one of the chambers that he'd deemed more secure—one that would fit the entire group. Esme begrudgingly dragged her mat across the cave, the mysterious murmur forgotten.

She lay down again. Even the smell of food couldn't keep her eyelids from falling closed. Darkness encircled her, closing in on her. Just like the water had, rolling past her, through her, rocking against her heartbeat.

All she'd had to do was keep hold of the rope. And she'd failed. If she couldn't manage something so simple, what would happen if she found herself face-to-face with Orianna? Would she fail then too?

The current continued to move through her. Like water, but unlike water. She felt her body sway with the motion, though she knew she was lying still on her mat.

Her awareness of her surroundings dropped away, melding with the humming she'd heard before. A vibration, she realized. Something that was calling to her. Like the steady breathing of an ancient beast, stirring below the mountain.

Magic.

Though not her own.

It was familiar—the sound in her ears, the hypnotic pulsing that ran along her skin—but it wasn't coming from within. It was almost as if she was sensing the boundless magic of the world itself.

Only it wasn't boundless. It wasn't resting gently beneath the surface. It felt imprisoned, confined somehow. The source where raw magic dwelled—magic that shaped every living thing in the immortal realm, created every plant and tree perfectly, every drop of water and gust of wind—was...*trapped.* The life force of their world was thrumming for release. Esme could feel it. As if it were pleading with *her* to set it free.

The thrumming intensified, mirroring her own heartbeat, responding to her query.

It was almost too much. She forced her eyes open.

But she was no longer in the same cave she'd drifted off in. She was alone, sitting on a rock in the center of a flowing, shimmering pool. The smell of spring grass, misting rain, and apple blossoms filled her senses as she inhaled deeply. Threads of light swirled through the sacred space. Esme reached out to touch one. It was like stretching into the night sky, her fingers dancing through the Loinnir Lights. *Magic.* She was surrounded by pure, raw magic.

At the peak of the cave she saw thick, bunching roots that looked as though they'd existed before the space had even been formed, before the world itself had been built. She could only imagine the size of the ancient tree that grew above.

The scrape of metal against the stone floor brought her back. Her eyes fluttered open.

A plate of food had been set beside her.

Was it only my imagination? she wondered hesitantly. Or had she seen a place that actually existed?

Finding herself standing in a familiar clearing, Esme knew for sure she was dreaming. She raised her chin, peering out across the fog, scanning the tree line, looking for her messenger.

The wolf appeared and Esme followed. When her surroundings transformed, she immediately committed the thicket of thorny bushes and barren trees to memory. Without leaves, it was hard to discern what had once grown from the dried, brittle branches, but they were clues nonetheless.

Her heart thundered in her chest. She inhaled slowly, willing herself to stay calm—to watch the premonition without reaction. Without emotion.

Below, she saw herself, dressed in the same traveling clothes she'd worn every day since leaving Altan. The other version of her seemed unhurried, her eyes drawn to something high above. Tearlach walked a few paces ahead and—if she was to guess by the short, dark hair—it was Armel at her back.

The fog shifted, revealing two large boulders beside a patch of dry undergrowth. Esme watched as, below, she ran her hand along the gray stone, tracing the line of a once green vine that clung to its side. Ahead, Tearlach held up his fist, halting them.

"Fall back!" she heard Sully shout from somewhere beyond.

Tearlach shoved her to the ground near the base of the boulder—a finger to his lips his only warning before he and Armel were gone, weapons drawn.

She tucked herself into the gap between the boulders as clanging metal sounded in the distance.

Hazel cried out. Esme surged forward into a low crouch, needing to see what was happening. She drew her sword quietly from its sheath as she crept away from the shelter of the rock.

Then stumbled to a stop.

A whimper escaped from her mouth as she dropped to her knees, her sword falling to the ground beside her as she clutched her hand to her chest.

———————

Esme jolted upright, her hand still pressed against her chest. She looked around the darkened cave. Mist hovered a few feet above the ground, clouding the flame from the single torch into a wide glowing orb. She blew out a breath and focused on where she was, telling herself that she was safe—that they were all safe. At last, the mist evaporated.

She peered out at the dark recesses of the cave, thankful that she'd woken when she had, before unknowingly summoning a storm so deep inside the mountain. Though another second or two might have given her valuable information. Instead, she'd seen only a glimpse of the unremarkable natural features—brittle branches tucked into a rocky outcrop. It wasn't much to go off of. All she knew was that the location was somewhere between the Clavlin Ridge—where they'd emerge from the cave—and the capital city of Meallán.

Lying back on her bedroll, she stared up at the ceiling, visualizing every detail of the dream. When Tearlach and Armel had left her side, she'd heard fighting in the distance. Then Hazel crying out. Even the memory of the woman's voice sent a shudder through Esme's body.

Had Hazel been hit? *Would* she be hit?

After that, Esme had seen herself crawling out from between the rocks, looking as though she was about to throw herself into the fray. Only she'd stopped short, her hand flying to her chest. Had she seen something? Had *she* been hit?

Esme's mind was churning with scenarios by the time the others roused. She ate the food she was given and packed her things abstractedly, knowing she needed to warn Tearlach.

If only she had more to tell him. The location. If someone had been injured...or worse.

She looked across the cavern, pulling her pack on, but Tearlach was striding away with Armel and Sully.

"Sleep well?"

Startled, Esme sucked in a breath, even as Killian's smooth voice slid over her. She blinked up at him.

His brow furrowed with concern as he stepped back, assessing her.

Esme tucked a loose curl behind her ear, realizing only then that she likely looked as though she'd had a far worse night than a sleepless one.

"Not quite," she admitted.

Killian lifted his chin, gazing down at her. "Cave floor too hard for you?"

Esme's mouth dropped open. She propped her hands on her hips, set to tell him that she wasn't some sort of spoiled girl, but Killian leaned in, crowding her space with his heat and the spicy scent of his soap.

"Didn't I tell you my bedroll is made of the finest cloth in all of Tremaene? Thick enough that you'll never feel the ground beneath it, yet so soft"—he dropped his voice—"that you won't need even a stitch of clothing."

Esme's cheeks felt like they were on fire as she struggled not to ask if he'd truly slept in the nude. "That sounds...comfortable."

"Oh, it is. And I'm willing to share."

She nearly choked. "I doubt there'd be room for two."

He leaned in, his breath whispering against the shell of her ear. "Only if we lie very, *very* close together." He winked, adjusted one of the straps of her pack, then nudged her forward.

Esme couldn't do anything but follow as every other thought eddied from her mind.

Chapter Thirty-Eight

THEY WALKED IN silence for what seemed like hours. The endless rock did little to hold Esme's interest, so her thoughts kept drifting back to Killian. He kept pace behind her, though he wasn't close enough for them to converse without the others hearing. But she was acutely aware of his proximity nonetheless, making it impossible for her to think on anything other than the words he'd spoken softly in her ear. When he'd implied that they share a bed.

The memory of his voice sent a shiver down her spine. Certainly he'd only intended to coax a smile from her, to bring a bit of levity to what would be a long, tiring day. Still, she couldn't help but imagine what would have happened if she'd turned toward him when he'd spoken those scandalous words, with his lips so close...his breath the only thing between them.

Her toes curled inside her boots. She shook her head and tried to focus on the unremarkable texture of the stone walls.

It wasn't until they reached the others at a junction where four additional tunnels branched off the main one that Esme decided she preferred the silence and monotony of her surroundings. Killian left at Tearlach's direction, surveying the leftmost passageway. Sully and Armel took the two in the center.

Then Tearlach took the one on the right.

Leaving Hazel behind to watch her.

Though she wasn't sure that was Hazel's understanding of the situation. The woman slid down to the ground, propped her folded arms on her raised knees, then let her head fall back against the wall with her eyes closed.

They'd been alone before. Many times. But during their training sessions, there'd been a defined objective, with set roles—Hazel as the instructor, Esme as her student.

Esme glanced over at her again. Hazel's profile was lit by the torch she held loosely in her hand. She was beautiful, striking. How had Esme never noticed before? Perhaps it was Hazel's unusually relaxed posture that caused her ferocity and impenetrable facade to momentarily slip away. Esme stared at her with a newfound appreciation for Hazel's feminine features. The sharpness of her eyebrows that perfectly framed her eyes—a pale blue when they were open and glaring at Esme's imperfect archery form. Her angled jaw drew attention to the natural red tint of her full lips.

She truly was stunning. *Even without smiling,* Esme added silently, grinning to herself.

"What?" Hazel demanded, her eyes opening narrowly.

"Oh. I was just…" What could she say? *Admiring your beauty?* There was no chance that would go over well. "Sully mentioned that you help in the kitchens…that you like baking," she recalled. A harmless enough topic.

Hazel stared at her for another second before looking away with clear disinterest.

"I used to make pastries with the apples from my orchard," Esme offered, if only to have something to do before the others returned. Silence didn't usually bother her, but the tension between her and Hazel was verging on hostile. "My kitchen was one of my favorite places. When I was busy with flour and sugar and fruit, everything else dropped away. I wasn't my past or the lies I'd told to keep myself safe. I was just…me." She glanced at Hazel, who seemed more interested in a vein of rust-colored stone high on the wall. "Did you ever feel that way? Like nothing else existed? As if there was nowhere else in the world you were supposed to be, but in that place, with your hands in the dough, flour covering your shirt?" Esme held her breath, hoping for a response.

"I helped in the kitchen," Hazel finally replied, her voice void of emotion, "because it was required of me. Obligations are rarely enjoyable." She turned and looked pointedly at Esme.

Obligation. Of course. She was nothing more than an obligation.

Hazel returned her attention to the tunnel entrances. But Esme wasn't going to give up so easily. If Hazel wouldn't admit her enjoyment for baking, then she'd find another subject—anything that would yield more than a cutting response.

"Killian told me you have a sister," she ventured, knowing it was a risk to bring up something personal.

"I don't have a sister," Hazel snapped without hesitation.

"Oh...perhaps I misheard."

"A sister," she enunciated the word, "would have responded to one of my letters. Just one. A sister would have made sure I survived the war that kept her and our family and our village safe from harm. A sister would have accepted the choice I made even if it differed from her own. A sister would have supported me no matter what."

Esme's lips parted, though she didn't dare respond. She'd struck something deep. She couldn't begin to imagine what that kind of rejection would feel like. Not having a family—that she understood. But having a family who refused to acknowledge their own daughter's or sister's existence...it somehow seemed worse.

Her gaze softened, hoping Hazel might glance over and see the compassion in her eyes. Hazel carried around as much pain as Esme did... as much as any of them did.

Would Hazel ever be able to forget the past? After so many years, what would it take for someone like her to let others in, to let herself be happy, to forgive?

Esme wasn't sure it was even possible. She certainly hadn't forgiven herself for leaving Tremaene. For running away when her kingdom was ravaged, her people tortured and killed.

"Those men..." Hazel broke through Esme's dispiriting thoughts, inclining her head toward the tunnels. "They're my family, more than any by blood have ever been."

Esme nodded, though Hazel still wouldn't look her direction. She understood the bond they shared; it was the same one she had with Cadwyn. She was like a sister to Esme. And Sully, with his protective disposition and even-tempered guidance, had always seemed more of a father figure than the captain of the royal guard.

"It's a good family," Esme told her. "You chose well."

She looked down the darkened tunnels, wondering if they might be her family one day too. Killian kept her spirits high, using his charismatic nature to make her smile and laugh, to keep her from succumbing to the fear and anxiety that threatened to swallow her. Armel had even opened up to her, and while she still didn't know much about him, she enjoyed his calming presence. And though her first non-archery conversation with Hazel had been strenuous, there was a glimmer of hope that they might one day do more than merely tolerate one another.

Then there was Tearlach. While she'd never admit it to him, she never felt safer than when he was near. She couldn't imagine embarking on such a monumental and dangerous journey without him at her side.

"They're the best family I could ever hope for." Hazel finally bestowed a glance toward Esme. "And I would do *anything* to keep them from harm."

Maybe there wasn't much hope for the two of them after all. Or perhaps, Esme considered, in her own rigid way Hazel was extending an invitation. She couldn't be sure. Likely the former, judging by the frigid look Hazel gave her. For a woman that could wield fire, she was exceptionally good at appearing the opposite of warm.

Luckily, Armel chose that moment to return, fracturing the tension that had mounted yet again. He gave Hazel a quick glance, lifting his brow as if to inquire as to whether she was okay.

He thought *Hazel* was the one to worry about?

"Anything?" Hazel asked.

"Nothing." He walked over to where Hazel sat, shrugging out of his weapons, then seemed to catch himself and their proximity. He settled for a spot equidistant between Esme and Hazel.

Esme pursed her lips and tried not to notice. Did the others know what was going on between them? Judging by the interactions she'd seen and the way they gave such high praise for one another, Esme guessed they'd had feelings for one another for a very long time. Because there was definitely something between them—spoken or not—because friends didn't look at each other that way.

When Killian returned, he regretfully informed them that his passageway eventually narrowed so much that he couldn't belly crawl his way through. Esme hoped that particular tunnel wouldn't be their only option.

Tearlach simply shook his head when he rejoined them, taking in the mirroring gestures from Armel and Killian. "Well, let's hope Sully finds us a way out." His cadence almost sounded humorous, but Esme could see the concern in his tightly set jaw.

Fortunately, Sully returned with promising news.

———————————

As best she could guess, it was late the following day before they reached the end of the tunnel. A thin line of light piercing the cavern wall was the only indication they'd reached the edge of the Clavlin Ridge.

But the pass they'd taken was secret for a reason. A colossal boulder stood between them and the world beyond. Even if they could risk using magic, Esme wasn't sure it would help with such a feat. She approached the blockade, looking up until she could see the top curve away. Her companions were already investigating the sides of the massive rock. Tunneling under wasn't an option, the stone floor was an unbroken slab that could very well stretch hundreds of feet into the earth below.

Two recesses flanked the boulder—one large enough to fit the giant rock, the other no wider than three feet. They'd have to roll it.

At least she wouldn't have to swim an underground lake. Anything was better than that.

Esme didn't even offer to help as the others took up positions at one end. She'd only be in the way. But even with the strength of five warriors, they only managed to shift the stone a few inches, revealing an opening too narrow for even her to fit through. Not only that, the boulder didn't stay in place once moved. The stone floor sloped up at each side, causing the massive barrier to crash back into place once it was released.

On their second attempt, Esme was able to shove two packs and two bundles of weapons through the small gap, stumbling back quickly as Tearlach, Sully, and Armel repositioned themselves to bear the weight so Hazel and Killian could slip through.

Then they waited.

Esme scarcely drew breath in the stillness that followed. Only when she heard the faint sequential rapping of the hilt of Killian's sword did the muscles in her shoulders relax.

Tearlach, Armel, and Sully struggled to roll the boulder aside again, allowing Hazel and Killian back in.

There was a small outcropping that would provide cover, the two of them explained. But beyond that, it was at least thirty paces to the shelter of a small, wooded area. Hazel assured Tearlach that she hadn't sensed anyone nearby, growing more defensive the third and fourth times he questioned her.

When the rock was once again heaved to the side, the remaining supplies, armor, and weapons were shoved through to Hazel and Killian. Sully followed, leaving only Armel and Tearlach to bear the weight of the boulder. Esme was amazed that only two of them could support it, but she didn't have time to think about it as Sully called her through.

Sunlight blinded her as she emerged. She blinked to adjust her eyes, then glanced back to see Tearlach holding the boulder completely on his own. The muscles in his arms and shoulders bulged and rippled as he shifted his position until he could clear it. He gave a short, guttural sound as he forced the heavy rock off his shoulder, letting it slam shut with thunderous reverberations.

They stood in silence for several tense moments—Tearlach's heavy breathing the only sound. Esme prayed to the gods no one had been close enough to hear the crash.

Sully took off to join Hazel and Killian, but Armel and Tearlach remained with her. Armel appeared to be recovered, pacing back and forth as if anxious for them to move out.

But Tearlach…He seemed exhausted from the exertion. It was understandable given the strength needed to shoulder the weight of the massive stone. Still, Esme couldn't recall ever seeing him so wearied. Even after fighting off the assassins when they'd reached Tremaene. And the amount of strength he'd needed to lift a boulder of that size…She looked over at him again. His breathing had returned to normal, but a sheen of sweat covered his chest and arms. When he'd taken up his position to lift the boulder the second time, his shirt sleeves had been rolled up to his elbows. By the third time, his shirt was gone, tucked into his belt. She averted her eyes before he caught her staring, taking in the full view of the Clavlin Ridge.

If she wasn't aware that the entrance to the Northern Pass was right in front of her, she wouldn't have been able to find it. Nothing about that particular spot along the sheer mountain wall indicated the vast tunnel system beyond. Once it had rolled violently back into place, the seams looked like nothing more than fissures, merging with other cracks and shallow crevices to camouflage the only movable stone.

Her gaze traveled up the ridge, set aglow by the afternoon light. It was so high it was almost impossible to see the summit. Even though she'd seen the beginnings of it from the mountainside, seeing the untraversable ridge that divided the mountains from the lowlands was something else entirely. No army could cross such a barrier. It truly was a stronghold—likely the only reason Orianna's domination hadn't reached the people in the north.

A single, barren tree clung to a narrow ledge twenty feet up. Its bare branches were twisted, its roots clutching the rock below, burrowing into the mountain.

Esme narrowed her eyes. There was something about that lone tree. She spun around, her eyes returning to the outcropping. Small barren trees, patches of thorny brambles tucked between the rocks, dead grass mixed in with small bits of stone, the remnants of a vine clinging to—

No. She'd forgotten about the dream. Hadn't warned Tearlach.

She prayed it wasn't too late.

"Tearlach," she said in an urgent whisper, hurrying over to where he leaned against one of the large rocks. She grabbed him when he didn't respond. He opened his eyes and glared at the hand gripping him, Esme's nails biting into the corded muscles of his forearm. "I've seen this place."

The fear in her eyes must have told him the rest. His own deep brown eyes darkened instantly. He shoved off the rock. Armel was beside him in less than a second, eyebrows raised in question, knives ready. Tearlach glanced down at Esme, his eyes boring into her. "An attack?" She nodded in reply. "How many?"

"I—I don't know."

"Fall back!" Sully shouted from a distance.

Tearlach shoved Esme to the ground, thrusting his finger toward a small space between the rocks, then took off running. Armel was already gone.

Esme crawled into the narrow crevice. It was too late. She'd failed. All she'd needed to do was warn them, to tell Tearlach about the dream, and she'd failed.

Hazel's agonizing cry echoed off the mountain wall.

Metal crooned as weapons struck—the clamor edging closer.

Her sword, Esme remembered. She could fight. No matter that Tearlach had wordlessly commanded her to stay put, she couldn't let herself cower. Not again.

Rising to a crouch, she unsheathed her blade, then crept out from behind the barren branches. The fighting quieted, and she hoped that the remaining voices belonged to her own.

Pressing her back against the rock, she inched closer to the edge of the outcropping. Tearlach and Hazel were approaching. Carrying something between them.

Not something. *Someone.*

They were carrying Killian. And he wasn't moving.

Esme dropped to her knees as her eyes fell on the arrow protruding from his chest.

Chapter Thirty-Nine

WEAPONS CLANGED TO the ground, forgotten, as Tearlach and Hazel gently lowered Killian. Armel and Sully knelt beside his lifeless body. Hazel curled a hand around the damaged armor, pressing down, then pulled the arrow free. She snarled at the thing, throwing it aside as though touching it had caused her pain.

It might have, Esme realized as she saw the metal tip of the arrow.

It was made of iron. *Shit.* Orianna's scouts possessed the poisonous metal as well.

Armel unclasped Killian's chest plate, letting Hazel pull it off carefully. Blood pooled on top of his shirt, more with every movement. Armel tore through the crimson-soaked fabric, exposing Killian's fatal wound.

Blood. There was so much blood.

Esme prayed it was a good sign—if he was bleeding, then blood continued to flow through his veins. Hazel balled up the shirt to staunch the endless flow as Esme crept forward on her knees.

But the closer she got, the more she could see. Her heart clenched beneath her ribs. "Is he…" she tried to ask, but couldn't form the word.

No one answered.

Hazel kept repeating his name over and over, as though trying to wake him from a deep slumber—her voice breaking. Armel seemed deeply focused, though his clenched jaw indicated the severe emotions they all felt.

Esme looked down at Killian again.

Killian...Killian was gone.

She rubbed at the ache in her chest. It was *her* fault. Not the arrow. Not the one who'd fired the shot. She could have prevented his death. But she'd failed to warn them.

When she looked over at Tearlach, their eyes locked. *Do something*, he ordered. *Bring him back.*

Her eyes widened at the command. She shook her head a fraction of an inch. She couldn't. Killian was a grown man, there was no way her power could—

Bring. Him. Back.

Esme's lips parted as she stared up at Tearlach. The voice in her head wasn't one of a commander, but of a man who'd just watched his brother die.

Please.

That single word, spoken by such an unbreakable man, contained enough desperation that tears gathered on her lashes.

Tearlach's face remained hard, unrevealing of the grief roiling just beneath the surface.

Esme watched his chest rise and fall quickly, then nodded once and crawled closer to Killian's body.

Tearlach came forward and placed a hand on Hazel's shoulder. He spoke her name softly, as if not to startle her. The woman's hands were shaking; she wouldn't remove them from Killian's chest. Tearlach glanced down at Esme, then pulled Hazel away.

"No!" Hazel screamed. "We don't have much time—" Tearlach circled her in his arms, turning her into his strong body. She wailed into his chest.

The sounds of her cries broke what was left of Esme's heart. Hazel thought it was over. They didn't know about the other facet of Esme's magic. And she wasn't about to tell them, not when she was fairly certain her untested healing power would do nothing for a grown man of Killian's size.

But she had to try. She'd use everything inside her if it meant bringing him back.

Sully remained by Killian's side as Armel stood and backed away—his face drawn.

Esme gave Tearlach one last beseeching look, then leaned over Killian's chest.

The bleeding had stopped. It had been a fatal shot. There wouldn't have been time for his natural healing ability to repair the damage. And with the iron-tipped arrow that had pierced his heart...

Dead. He's dead, her mind told her. But she ignored it and unclenched her hands, laying them over the wound.

She had no idea how to summon the magic she needed. With the wolf, it had been an accident. And in all the time she'd spent training with Tearlach, they'd never once explored that aspect of her power.

But she quickly discovered that she didn't need to do anything. Heat radiated from Killian's skin—so hot it felt like it might burn a hole through her palms. She could feel blood coursing through him as his flesh began seaming back together. The familiar feeling of invisible vines slithered beneath her pressed hands, stitching muscle and skin. Esme couldn't have pulled her hands away if she tried. It was like they were fused to him.

Within moments, the skin that had been ravaged by the wicked iron weapon felt smooth again. When she sensed the connection release, Esme carefully lifted her hands to reveal the newly closed wound—without a trace of a scar.

The others had joined her and Sully on the ground, but Esme didn't look away from Killian. He was healed. Healed, but...not alive. Not breathing.

No heartbeat.

A cold sweat broke over her skin as she realized there was nothing she could do to neutralize the iron that had poisoned his blood. His wound was closed, his heart mended, but it wasn't enough.

Killian was still gone.

Tearlach knelt down across from her. *Keep going*, he told her.

Wiping her bloodstained hands on her pants, she leaned forward again, cradling Killian's perfectly still face with her palms. Her eyes didn't leave his. She willed them to open, willed him to see her again.

"Killian," she whispered. If only he could hear her voice, maybe he'd return. "Killian, come back." Her quiet voice broke.

Then the air was forced from her lungs.

Killian's chest rose, filled with breath. With her breath.

She heard a collective gasp as Esme drew another breath, willing it into his body, filling him with her life force.

Her eyes strayed to his chest, watching for it to begin its own rhythm. When she turned back to his beautifully peaceful face, she leaned closer, until her breath touched his lips. "Killian?" Her voice was small, as though she might scare the life away.

His eyes opened, locking with hers instantly, piercing all the way through her.

She couldn't move. It felt like she was dying and waking at the same time.

"Esme," he breathed, bringing tears to her eyes. The way he looked at her...It was like she was the only thing that existed in his world.

And for a moment, only Killian existed for her. Their hearts beat together, as one.

It was as if her life-giving magic had wrapped around them both, mending his heart and fusing the broken pieces of hers.

Their breaths intertwined, and Killian reached for her. He winced in pain, but gripped her hand, holding on so tightly she was sure he'd never let go.

"Esme," he said again as a tear of his own rolled down his cheek to the blood-soaked ground.

She opened her mouth to speak—to tell him that he was okay, to assure him that it was real, that he was alive and that she was there with him—but the edges of her vision blurred and a heaviness settled over her.

She tried to blink away the sudden dizziness, but collapsed onto Killian's chest.

His desperate voice echoed through her mind as he cried out for her.

———————————

Esme was pulled under as Killian yelled for her, his voice frantic. But she couldn't reach him.

She could hear Tearlach telling them that she was merely asleep.

Only she wasn't asleep.

And yet...she wasn't awake either.

Her eyes refused to open. She felt hands lifting her, then laying her gently on the ground. Gravel pressed against her cheek. That, she could feel. Could hear the voices around her.

But her eyes refused to open.

Her throat worked as she tried to form words, but her tongue felt heavy in her mouth.

Her body seemed to have given out after she'd exhausted her magic, though her mind, her thoughts remained.

We need to move quickly, someone was saying. *More will come.*

Was that Tearlach? His voice sounded far away.

She heard Hazel, her voice nearly as frantic as Killian's. Only she wasn't concerned for Esme, she was apologizing for failing to sense the scouts, taking full blame for what had happened to Killian.

It wasn't your fault, Esme tried to tell her. It was she who'd failed to warn them, who could have thwarted the attack.

The others vehemently refused to accept Hazel's culpability, but it was Tearlach who finally dispelled her contrition, claiming that his glamour must have hindered her sensing ability.

Esme couldn't tell if he was certain or if he was just protecting Hazel. If it was true—if Hazel couldn't sense magic...

The thought slipped away and the texture of the dirt against her skin began to soften. Until she couldn't feel anything.

Until there was nothing.

———————————

Boots thundered against the ground. Esme's body jostled with each heel strike. She was being carried. A familiar scent spread through her lungs as she took in a breath.

A muffled voice sent a low rumble through her body, though she couldn't make out the words.

She tried to grab hold of something—the smell of the air, the feel of the strong, solid arms carrying her, the voices surrounding her...

But she was swept away again to the in-between.

———————————

It was the stillness that woke her next. When the constant moving had ceased, Esme could hear Tearlach's breath as his chest rose in time against her curled body. It came quickly and she was fairly certain it wasn't the result of running.

Things hadn't gone to plan. And Tearlach was angry. Esme tried to open her eyes, but still, they refused.

"Let me take her," Killian insisted.

Killian...alive, she remembered.

"You've been injured," Tearlach declined.

Injured? He'd been more than injured.

"Then let one of us help," Sully offered.

"She's my responsibility."

"She's *our* responsibility," Killian asserted.

Esme's weight shifted, and she could hear Tearlach take a swig from his canteen. *Water.* She wanted water. If only she could—

But they were moving again. And she was still in Tearlach's arms. The rhythm of his hurried pace lulled her back into unconsciousness.

Her eyes finally opened. She was tucked under a blanket, beneath silhouetted trees. The moons were mere slivers, drawing closer together. Nearly aligned.

Her arms felt heavy, but she lifted her hands to her face, trying to scrub away the fogginess of her mind. Memories crept in slowly. One of Killian lying on the ground—

She jolted upright.

Killian. Dead.

No, that wasn't everything. She shook her head.

Her hands had pressed against his chest. Her breath filling his lungs... her heart beating with his...bringing him back.

Her heart sped up, and her eyes skidded wildly over the sleeping bodies nearby. Was he still alive? Was he well?

The lights from the sky were dim, making it difficult to see much. She counted the figures. Only four...

"He's fine. He's asleep."

Esme's head jerked toward Hazel's voice. The woman was leaning against a tree, watching over the camp. The outstretched branches on either side looked like they stood sentry along with her.

"You've been out for more than a day."

That long? "Where are we?" Esme croaked.

"Belfay. Only a few days from Meallán."

Esme nodded and reclined back on her bedroll. She focused on the stars above and the milky lights swirling in and out. But her heart continued to beat rapidly. She needed to see Killian with her own eyes, though it seemed that would have to wait until morning.

"Esme." It was only the second time Hazel had spoken her name.

She glanced over at her. Hazel shifted to her other foot and a stream of pale moonlight spilled across her face, setting her blue eyes aglow.

"Thank you for bringing him back," Hazel told her, then shoved away from the tree to walk the perimeter.

Killian was seated beside her the next morning. Upon seeing her eyes open, he visibly relaxed.

"Hazel said you came to last night."

"I did." Esme's eyes fell to his chest. She wanted to reach out and touch him, to feel his heart beating. "Are you...are you all right?"

"Better than ever." A flirtatious grin spread across his face, only to slip away. "You shouldn't have done that." Killian shook his head, his brow furrowed in distress. "It's my job to protect you, Esme. And I...I thought you'd sacrificed yourself for me."

Seeing the pain in his eyes, she knew he was reliving the moment she'd collapsed onto his chest. She could still hear his voice as he'd cried out for her.

He'd thought she'd given up her life for his.

"Killian." She reached for him, needing to comfort him. "I'm fine. It didn't harm me."

"You've been unconscious for more than a day. We didn't know how long it would take for you to recover." His face matched his anguished tone.

Esme bit her bottom lip. It wasn't the first time she'd drained the well of her magic, but what she'd done for Killian had taken far more than expected.

"And didn't I tell you that your life is worth more than mine?" He attempted humor, but his smile didn't reach his eyes. "I'm important to some, Esme, but you are important to *many.*"

She pressed her lips together as tears threatened. Moisture gathered on her lashes, and Killian moved closer, swiping his thumb gently under her eye.

"You're important to me, Killian." She wiped the other tears away. "I couldn't lose you."

"Esme," he breathed. They were close enough that she could feel the heat coming off his body. "Don't ever scare me like that again." He focused on her so intently that his eyes looked like they could set the forest ablaze, and she wasn't sure if he wanted to scold her or kiss her.

Reaching out, she laid her palm against his chest, feeling his heart beating through the thick weave of his shirt. It sped up at her touch.

She lifted her eyes to his. "Then don't die on me again."

"Deal." He covered her hand with his, but couldn't seem to return her smile. He held her gaze a moment longer, then peered over his shoulder, seeming to remember that they weren't alone.

At least they'd been granted a moment of privacy while the others broke down camp.

Killian rose, helping Esme to her feet. But instead of stepping away to keep a semblance of propriety, he pulled Esme in and wrapped his arms around her. His hand moved down her back, pressing her closer to him, holding her tighter than any friend should. But Esme found she didn't care, sinking against him, letting him hold her for as long as he needed.

A throat cleared nearby and Killian slowly, reluctantly, set her away. He stared down at her, then leaned in once more, his lips brushing her ear as he spoke in a voice that made her shiver, "You have no idea how hard it is not to kiss you."

Esme sucked in a breath as his fingers trailed down her arm.

He stepped away with a grin and Esme dropped her eyes to the ground, knowing full well her cheeks flamed crimson. She was glad to see his levity return, though she could have done without the embarrassment painted so clearly on her face.

She busied herself with packing until Tearlach crouched down beside her. He took the mat from her hands.

"In the future…" he began. Esme's eyes strayed to the mat as he expertly rolled, then secured it to her pack. "Tell me when you have a dream like that."

She dipped her chin. "I know. I'm sorry." Her guilt returned swiftly. She kept her eyes downcast, fearing what she might see if she looked up at him. Disappointment, anger…some other judgment that would leave her feeling worse than she already did.

"Don't be sorry."

Her eyes lifted to his.

"What you did was…" Tearlach took a deep breath. "Thank you."

She stared at him, unblinking. He handed her the pack and walked off before she could say anything.

Armel and Sully each expressed their gratitude as they moved out, but the entire group fell into a heavy silence as the morning stretched on.

When Esme's thoughts quieted enough for her to notice the forest around her, she realized how the trees that had been nothing more than dark outlines the night before had changed little. In the light of day, every tree was bare, empty, gray. She tried to convince herself that it was simply winter, that the leaves would return the following spring. But winter didn't exist in Tremaene. Nor spring.

Life would not return. The forest was dead.

When they reached the southern edge of the forest, her eyes took in the vast expanse of the lowlands. They were in Belfay, close to Meallán, surely something would look familiar.

But the lush, rolling hills to the west, continuously blanketed with wildflowers of every color, sat cold and lifeless in the distance.

"What has she done?" she whispered, stopping to gape at the dry, brittle remains of thick grasses matted in clumps along the slopes.

"Esme?" Killian turned when she fell behind. But his eyes dropped to her feet. His usually bright smile shifted to something else.

She glanced down. Bright green shoots were growing over the toes of her boots. A patch of fuzzy moss and leaves spread out around her. And behind—she glanced back—a trail followed from the woods. Even the barren trees she'd mourned were sprouting needles and tiny leaves, the gray bark warming to hues of reds and browns.

"What's this?" Hazel demanded, her eyes hard as she glared down at the ground, then back up at Esme.

"Her magic," Killian answered, having witnessed her earth magic back in Altan.

Hazel advanced on her, coming to stand inches before her. "You're using magic?" she accused.

Tearlach grabbed Hazel's arm. "She's not," he assured, yet gave Esme a probing look nonetheless, like he didn't quite trust what he felt through their connection. Not when it was so at odds with the evidence at her feet. "She's not," he repeated, turning back to Hazel. "No one will sense it."

Hazel only stared at him, eyes narrowed. Tearlach's glamour truly was interrupting her sensing ability, then. Esme wondered if it felt the same as depleting one's magic, or if it felt like losing one of her other senses—sight or taste or smell.

"If she's not using her magic, then…?" Armel moved to Killian's side, his dark eyebrows lifting as he watched a purple flower bloom beside Esme's boot.

"I'm…not sure what's going on," Tearlach admitted through clenched teeth.

Sully came up beside Esme. "If it's not her magic," he said, resting his hand on her shoulder—a simple gesture that made her feel less like an aberration, "then it must be the magic of the land."

"What do you mean?" Tearlach demanded, crossing his arms over his chest.

"She's not a high-priestess. She can't summon it," Hazel argued.

"That, she is not," Sully agreed softly as he peered down at Esme's feet. "Then perhaps it…recognizes her." He met Esme's eyes and cocked his head slightly to the side. She waited for him to elaborate. He didn't.

"You think the raw magic"—she furrowed her brow—"*knows* I'm the Princess of Tremaene?" What a ridiculous notion. How could magic sense such a thing as a royal title? Why would it even care?

But Sully's statement didn't seem to be in jest. The smile that spread across his face reminded her of the way he'd explain things to her as a child, like he had endless patience to help her grasp a new concept.

"Not that," he corrected gently. "Your signature. I believe it recognizes *you*, Esme. Your being, what you're made of."

"I don't…I don't understand." Esme shook her head. "This has never happened before." She gestured to the path behind her. Though she realized that wasn't entirely true. As she'd reasoned with Tearlach, rains and storms had responded to her long before her magic had manifested. Perhaps that hadn't been *her* magic either.

Sully merely shrugged. "I suspect your magic grew considerably more powerful when you restored life to Killian. And now that it's started to return—after being depleted—it's far more concentrated."

What Sully proposed was...possible. But it still didn't explain why the magic that dwelled inside their world would recognize *her*. Would be drawn to her.

Esme's mind flashed to the vision she'd had in the cave—of what she could only assume was the place where all magic was created. It had called to her that night, purring up through the bedrock, through her skin, into her bones.

She remembered the other feeling it evoked. Being trapped.

Esme glanced down at her feet, at the life rising up around her. It was almost as if—in the absence of high-priestesses—she was being used as a bridge, pulling raw magic to the surface.

The usual sensations of summoning magic were still absent, so she couldn't very well stop it from happening. Though why would she want to? Orianna had stripped their lands. If Esme's presence could restore a bit of life, she'd deem it a small victory against the treasonous high-priestess.

Chapter Forty

HAZEL STARED DOWN at the stacked branches. Her hands flexed like she was fighting the urge to set the wood aflame with her magic. Only when Armel returned with water did Hazel seem to pull out of its thrall, kneeling down to attempt a spark with her stone.

Esme kept her distance. The bare-branched forest was slowly returning to life with her presence and she didn't want to give Hazel more trouble by accidentally sprouting green leaves from the dry tinder.

The path of green that had followed Esme all day was mostly concealed inside the wooded area. They'd been forced to veer east, away from the lowlands where her trail could easily be found, passing a few patches of cultivated land where rows of crops were watered through an elaborate system of hanging buckets and carved spouts strung above the thirsty stalks.

The tinder finally caught and Hazel stepped back—her clear frustration ebbing at the sight of the flames.

At the sound of a branch snapping, weapons were drawn, and Killian and Tearlach flanked her in an instant.

There was a slight rustling, and Esme stretched to peer around Killian's shoulder.

She inhaled sharply, pushing past him.

A wolf paced between the cover of two giant oaks—his snout angled down as he set his yellow eyes upon their group. It was the first of his kind she'd seen since returning to Tremaene.

Tearlach grabbed her arm before she could take another step. The others drew close, weapons at the ready.

Killian took her other hand. "Esme," he said softly, "there's little food out here."

She turned wide eyes toward him. They were going to kill the wolf?

"No." She fought not to shout the word. "He means us no harm."

The animal turned his sights on her. Esme could feel the tension rippling off the others, could practically hear their muscles and tendons pulling taut with the instinct to protect, to kill.

The wolf's yellow gaze never left hers as he settled down onto the ground and lowered his head to his paws.

But his posture did little to convince the others. "Lower your weapons," Esme commanded, pivoting to face them. It was a voice she hadn't used since the meeting in the war room.

Hazel and Armel looked to Tearlach, awaiting his order, but Esme fixed him with a stare that warned him not to. She'd already given one.

He shrugged his shoulders, returning to the fire.

Weapons were reluctantly lowered.

Later that evening, when the fire had burned down to embers, Esme told them of the wolf back in Debarrow—the one she'd brought back to life, who'd later warned her of the assassins stalking her home.

"I managed to escape, but one of them gave chase." She flattened her shaking hands against her legs. "By the time I reached the village, she was almost upon me. I didn't know where to run, where to go. But then Tearlach"—she glanced over at him—"he found me and…"

"I took care of it," he said easily.

The others looked between her and Tearlach, hearing the story for the first time. Esme hadn't confessed much about her time in Periwen, trusting only Cadwyn. But the people sitting beside her had sworn their lives to protect her. To see her safely to Meallán. To see her take her rightful place.

She owed them her story. All of it.

So she told them everything.

———————

"Taking out Briac is our first priority," Sully instructed once again the following evening.

Briac was Orianna's personal guard. It was perhaps the twelfth time Sully had gone over each stage of the plan. And every time, he made sure they all knew that Briac was the one they'd need to worry about.

"He leaves Orianna's side only during the early morning hours, when he retreats to his private quarters. The three of you will take him out." Sully gestured to Killian, Hazel, and Armel—who nodded their understanding. With Briac out of the way, and the guards stationed outside the royal apartments that night expecting them, Tearlach would be clear to slip into the queen's suite.

Everyone had a role to play in overthrowing Orianna. Esme's role? Remain close to Tearlach or stay out of the way. Even during the final stage of their plan, when Tearlach would strike down Orianna with his iron sword, Esme's protection would simply transfer to Sully. She'd play no part in claiming the throne that had been stolen from her family. No part in avenging her parents' deaths. It felt...cowardly. She'd spoken with such audacity with the generals back in Altan, but truth be told, she didn't know the first thing about war. The attacks she'd survived thus far had been nothing more than a few enemies tasked with taking her alive. Esme wasn't under any illusions that what awaited them in Meallán would be so easily thwarted.

Sully left later that evening. He'd travel through the night, not risking his magic until he reached the nearest village. There, he'd shift and fly west to the waiting army, then south to meet one final time with his informants in the capital city.

Killian dropped his bedroll beside hers. The dry creek bed didn't offer much in way of comfort, but traveling along it ensured they wouldn't leave a trail—that *she* wouldn't leave a trail.

He handed her a cup of tea and inclined his head to where Hazel and Armel sat across the dwindling fire. There was no more than a handsbreadth between the two of them.

"They seem to have gotten...closer," Esme observed.

"Mm-hmm," Killian agreed with a smirk.

"They almost lost you." She kept her voice low so only Killian could hear. "Maybe they realized how short immortal lives can actually be." She looked up at him. "That they could lose each other at any moment."

"It certainly puts things in perspective," he said softly.

Chapter Forty-One

NEITHER WOLF NOR *fog greeted her, and Esme knew the gravel beneath her boots was pale pink, flecked with white and black quartz, even before the darkness began to recede.*

Smoke stung her eyes and burned her throat, sending ash into the wind, choking out the sun and sky. She wasn't an observer. She knew that.

She was there, somehow. Again.

In Meallán.

Turning away from the billowing smoke, Esme stalked up to the palace, the hem of her bloodred cloak scraping over rubble.

"I'm afraid our last encounter was cut short, my dear. Do come in, I have something you'll want to see." Orianna's voice was sharp and practiced. Her long, flowing robes floated over the marble floors as she turned with a perfected grace toward the throne room in the center of the palace.

Esme followed, her eyes fixed on the spot where her lifeless body had lain in the previous dream. The glossy floor cast only her reflection. With her crimson cloak, the image looked horrifyingly similar.

Afraid of what might await her in the throne room, Esme cast a searching look at the adjacent halls she'd once called home. But there was only darkness beyond.

She paused at the open doors of the rotunda. Across the room was a lavishly ornate throne—not two, tastefully carved ceremonial chairs, with a smaller, more understated one to the side. Just the one.

Orianna stood in the center, waiting. But something to Esme's left caught her eye.

She clenched her jaw to keep from crying out. On the floor were five captives, kneeling in a perfect row, hands bound, faces hooded, with twenty or more of Orianna's men standing guard.

She couldn't see their faces, but she knew who they were.

Swallowing past the knot in her throat, Esme tore her eyes away from the sight to meet Orianna's. "What do you want?" she forced out.

"I know you intend to overthrow me." Esme struggled to keep every emotion off her face as Orianna continued. "Let me assure you, my dear, that will never happen. It's quite silly, really, that you thought five brutish warriors and a child could come close to matching my power."

With a flick of her wrist the guards removed their hoods and brought knives to each of her companions' throats.

Esme pitched forward, her hand reaching out to stop them. But she was stopped by an unseen force, her foot hovering inches above the ground.

Orianna walked to her side slowly. All Esme could do was glare at the woman.

"There is another option," she offered, her violet eyes shimmering in delight at the sight of her bound captives.

Even if Esme wanted to respond, she couldn't. Her body was locked in place.

"Surrender, and they live."

Esme strained her eyes to look at each of them.

Orianna stepped closer, and the grip she had on Esme loosened.

She yielded a step as the high-priestess advanced, seemingly amused by Esme's retreat.

"What did you think would happen, my dear? Did you really believe you'd stand a chance? Against me?" Orianna laughed, the sound sending chills down Esme's spine.

Darkness spilled into the room, creeping along the floor. Before the dream could slip away, Esme stole one last glance at her captured friends.

"This is the only way."

Orianna's words echoed in Esme's mind as the quiet of night returned. But the stillness of the lifeless forest no longer made Esme nervous. Instead, it served as a reminder of everything that'd been lost— what Orianna had done. What she'd taken.

What she planned to take.

Unless Esme changed the outcome of the dream.

Slowly, she sat up, her eyes scanning the perimeter. Armel was on watch until morning. She followed his movements, noting the pattern, counting the seconds he took for each pass.

He didn't look over to where she and the others slept, his eyes tracking the woods beyond.

Esme didn't hesitate. The moment he turned north, she quickly laced her boots and rolled into a crouch. She listened for any indication that Armel had heard, and when he didn't immediately return, she slipped away.

Traveling swiftly proved difficult with the crunch of dead leaves underfoot, so she crept carefully away from camp, Orianna's words her only company. *This is the only way.*

To save her companions, Esme needed to leave them. That was all she knew for certain. As for a plan, she could only hope that some brilliant scheme would form in her mind before she reached Meallán.

The river curved east, so she angled away from it, staying as true to a southern course as she could with only a trickle of light from the waning moons. The sun's path would give her a better sense of direction when it rose.

Dried leaves crunched nearby and Esme froze. Every muscle in her body tightened as she waited. Had Armel found her so quickly?

"And where might you be going?"

Shit.

For a moment she was back in Debarrow, up on a ladder, trapped. Tearlach moved to block her path.

"Just clearing my head. I couldn't sleep." She wasn't sure why she bothered to lie.

"You wouldn't be thinking of doing something stupid, would you?"

"I don't know what you mean." How was he always one step ahead of her?

One corner of Tearlach's mouth curved up into a smirk. Almost like he admired her tenacity. "You knew you wouldn't get far. Or have you forgotten about our little connection?" He tapped a finger to his chest.

She hadn't. She'd simply hoped that if he was asleep, he wouldn't be able to feel as she pulled away.

"How could I forget?" she muttered.

"Now turn around and go back to camp."

She couldn't go back. Her heart thudded like a hammer against her ribs.

"No." Her voice was small, but she didn't look away.

"I'll give you a choice." Tearlach's voice was deep and controlled, but she could sense the tension beneath the words. "Either you turn around and walk back on your own..."

"Or?" She took a step, bringing her closer to him.

"Or, I'll carry you back." The fury in his eyes told her she shouldn't test him.

There was no way he'd willingly let her leave. But perhaps...if she ran...

"Don't even think about it," Tearlach growled, moving to tower over her.

She closed her eyes and pressed her palms against them. She could... maybe she could tell him what she'd seen. Maybe he'd let her go.

When she looked up again, Tearlach's entire body was taut, restrained, and Esme realized she likely had only seconds before he swung her over his shoulder.

"I've seen it, Tearlach. I know what will happen." She bit her lower lip hard enough that she couldn't feel the prick of tears in the corners of her eyes. "It won't end well."

His expression remained the same—determined, unyielding—but his shoulders released some of their tension. Would he allow her to leave? She searched his eyes for any indication.

"I have to do this myself. It's the only way."

"It is *not* the only way, and you know that."

"No other deaths need come of this. I can put an end to it. Just please, let me go. Please, Tearlach." She wasn't above begging, or tears—whatever it took to make him realize.

"*We* will put an end to it. You need to trust us. Trust *me*."

She stared up at him. Flecks of amber sparked in the depths of his dark eyes, like the embers of a growing inferno. His magic might have been air, but there was fire in him too. Esme wondered if her eyes looked the same in that moment, as she recalled the dream.

Tearlach's eyes darkened, his fists clenching hard enough for his knuckles to crack. Could he see what she saw, through their connection?

"It won't come to that." He moved closer, his voice dropping even lower.

"You don't know," she whispered.

"Nothing is written, Esme. It doesn't have to end that way, and it most certainly *will not* end with you sacrificing yourself."

"But what if everything I saw *does* come to pass? What if we fall into a trap? What if everything we've planned goes up in flames?" She couldn't keep her voice from climbing higher, flooded with desperation.

"Everything will be fine." His words turned gentle, like he intended them to be a comfort. But they only served to remind her of the lies she'd been told since the night her parents had died—before that even. Words that were meant to keep her in the dark, to protect her.

"Don't lie to me. I'm not a child anymore. You and I both know what we risk simply by setting foot in that city—the dangers, the unknowns. And you know better than most that we might not walk out again."

The slightest dip of his chin told her she was right. Her breaths shallowed out, quickening as fear settled around her like a cloak.

"No matter what happens, I *will* protect you. Nothing and no one will harm you. This, I swear."

"It's not me I'm worried about." She looked up at him.

He exhaled slowly—the only evidence that her words had any effect on him. His response lacked the conviction he'd had moments before. "We'll be fine, all of us."

"Don't lie." She repeated the words quietly.

Tearlach lifted his chin and stared up at the night sky, like he might find the words to convince her scrawled through the Loinnir Lights.

"This is what we plan for—contingencies. It's why we prepare, why the Northern Rebels have built up their army for nearly a decade, and why we'll have those forces at our back, ready should anything go wrong. It's why we have enough weapons between the six of us to bring down every guard that stands in our way, in *your* way." He took a breath, his chest rising and falling more rapidly as he went on. "It's why I let that poisonous metal blacken my blood for years, so that one day I could wield a weapon deadly enough to match the evil that shattered our kingdom— that killed your parents, *my* king and queen. So I could protect you and everything you are. So *you* could save our people and our kingdom. That,

Esme, is why you are here." He paused, but didn't waver. "There is no lie in that."

He took another step, closing the distance between them. Esme angled her head up to meet his penetrating gaze. There was a time when his nearness would have made her uneasy, triggering her internal alarm that cautioned her to stay away. But she was no longer afraid. He'd pushed her to be strong, to not cower from him or anyone.

She wasn't afraid because she couldn't be. There was no room for it inside her. He'd taught her that too, whether intending to or not.

"But even all that may not be enough," he added softly.

There was a strange sort of comfort in his admission. His hands rested on her shoulders, then gently coaxed her to turn back. It didn't feel like an order, but rather like he was doing it to assure her that she wasn't alone. No matter what happened, she wouldn't have to face it alone.

"And if it all goes up in flames..."

Esme glanced back.

"Then we'll burn together," he promised.

Chapter Forty-Two

SULLY FOUND THEM the following afternoon. The trail Esme left behind after they'd been forced to leave the rocky riverbed and head west toward Meallán, had led him straight to them. Thankfully, the land continued to show more life the closer they got to the capital city, thus concealing their whereabouts.

The army was in position, and Sully had confirmed plans with his contacts inside the city.

By the time the sun dropped below the horizon, the citadel came into view. Settling within a copse of elms and oaks, with enough sparsely leafed undergrowth to offer cover, they set up camp one final time. Unwilling to risk a fire, the remaining food stores were silently passed around as the sky, for a one, single night, grew dark.

Tearlach and Killian took the first watch, allowing the others to sleep. But Esme was determined not to. She stared through the thick trunks and spindly branches, keeping her eyes trained on the dark gray wall in the distance—barely visible against the inky black sky.

When her eyelids grew heavy, she rose, pacing the small campsite until she'd worn a path as she repeated Orianna's warning. *This is the only way.*

Esme sifted through the details of the dream again, searching for a clue, a weakness...an escape from its fate. *The red cloak.* It had been wrapped around her shoulders, same as it had in the previous dream in which Orianna had appeared. For some reason, the anomaly confused her. When she'd worn the unfamiliar cloak, the dreams had felt strange...unsettling. Both times, as she'd walked through the destroyed city of Meallán and through the palace, she'd had a vague sense of being watched.

Esme paused in front of a tree, leaning against it. The darkness tried to lull her into an unwanted state. Still, she couldn't help sliding her back against the rough bark to settle onto the ground.

Tearlach noticed and stalked soundlessly over to her. "You need to sleep."

She shook her head, fighting off a yawn that she wouldn't dare let him see. "I'm fine."

"Esme," he warned, his voice reverberating through her tired body. Before she could protest further, she felt her body go limp, slumping against the tree. Her teeth clamped together and her throat worked, but she couldn't manage to growl at Tearlach before his sleep magic pulled her under.

When the dark ring of trees came into view, Esme was relieved to find herself wearing the same clothes she'd fallen asleep in. Her eyes lifted, and when nothing appeared on the ground, she looked to the trees.

The owl waited, as if sensing her trepidation. But she knew that clearing and felt safe in the benevolence of the message she'd receive. A warning, yes. But not a certainty.

Esme tipped her head toward her winged guardian, and it leapt silently from the branch, soaring into the mist.

A wooden door with silver hinges came into view. The stone surrounding the frame had been worn smooth. It looked gray in the darkness, but Esme could tell it had been kept in immaculate condition. Swaying gently on a hook beside it was a cold lantern. A hand reached out and rapped lightly on the heavy door—a woman's hand. Shrouded by a dark hooded cloak and impenetrable shadows, Esme wasn't able to make out her face as she stepped into view.

A guard, wearing a familiar gold and copper chest plate with fine silver chainmail beneath, appeared at the threshold. He handed over a lantern with a low flame, then returned to his position beside the door. The woman slipped silently through the dark halls of the palace—though Esme wasn't sure where in the palace, precisely. The wall sconces had all been extinguished and the lantern barely lit the corridors. It could have been a precaution the guard had taken, to keep the uninvited guest hidden, but Esme was fairly certain that she was witnessing an event that would come to pass that very night—the darkest night, when lights throughout the kingdom were snuffed out at sundown.

But even if she could surmise the when, she wasn't sure as to the whom. Was it possible she was watching herself?

The passage seemed to open into a large space, though Esme couldn't see anything beyond the shadowy vignette that framed the cloaked woman. When a door appeared, the woman ducked inside and started up a narrow staircase that curved along the wall. At the top of the steps, the woman blew out the flame.

"No," Esme breathed, thinking the vision had ended, then heard a slight scrape of metal as the lantern was placed on the floor. A sliver of light sliced through the darkness, and with a flurry of movement, Esme was staring at the thin gray veins of a marble column.

When the woman risked a glance at the room beyond, Esme's eyes widened in horror.

The woman was most definitely not her.

Because Orianna stood in the center of the throne room, with a long-lost princess kneeling before her.

Esme felt the roughness of bark at her back, only she wasn't sitting. She was resting against something warm and hard...yet soft.

Her eyes fluttered open to find her cheek pressed against a very muscular leg. A small smile teased at her lips, and she couldn't resist running her finger along the smooth, protective fabric of the formfitting pants.

"That tickles," a voice groaned.

She rolled to face Killian. His head was tilted to the side and his eyes were still closed, but he slowly opened them to look down at her. "I'm glad you got some sleep." His voice was sleep rough and warm.

"Me too. How did I..." Her eyes roved over him and the tree behind.

He chuckled. "You must have been quite exhausted. One minute you were sitting against the tree, staring up at the sky, and the next..." He chuckled again. "Well, I couldn't let you sleep in such an uncomfortable position."

Her cheeks flushed. She hadn't realized anyone else had seen her crumple to the ground. She fought the urge to shoot Tearlach an irate look for putting her to sleep against her will. But she supposed he'd done it for her benefit. She'd desperately needed sleep and was refusing to give in to it.

"Thank you."

Killian nodded, then slid his broad hands beneath her, easing her to a seated position—though the look in his eyes said he would've enjoyed letting her stay in their sleeping arrangement for a while. But they weren't alone.

Esme glanced around. Only Tearlach was awake. She wondered if he'd seen her dream. His face, as always, revealed nothing.

Around midnight—or what everyone agreed was midnight—they set off toward the city, leaving all but weapons behind. The others were armed to the hilt. Weapons she hadn't seen since the day Hazel had them laid out in the dining hall in Altan appeared from concealed compartments within their packs. Esme pulled on her deep green jacket, clasping each of the dozen silver clips while praying to the gods that she wasn't dressing for the last time. Sully wordlessly assisted in securing the gray gauntlets around her forearms—their opalescent shimmer gone in the dark of night. She wondered if the others felt the same foreboding weight pressing down on them as she sheathed her sword and slipped her dagger into her belt. They'd seen war...endless battles. But this was her first.

With Cadwyn's cloak around her shoulders, she blended into the night. It was the same way she'd started her journey nine years earlier, wrapped in that cloak. And again when she'd left her home in Debarrow. Perhaps it would protect her again...if a piece of cloth could do such a thing.

Her magic thrummed fervently inside. The pressure had been building steadily since she'd woken from her deep sleep after bringing back Killian. But as she stood there, gazing at the city wall, Esme felt it grow stronger, as if sensing that she had returned to her place of birth—where the magic had first chosen her.

———————————

Soft grass muffled their boots as the wall rose before them. In her mind, Esme could see the pure white stones joined so perfectly that it looked like a solid curved block of marble encompassing the city. But in the darkness the wall blended with the night, thrusting out of the earth to block the pinprick stars.

Avoiding the two main gatehouses, they crept silently toward one of the many bastions lining the parapets. The small tower appeared to be unguarded. Sully's doing, no doubt.

Esme had felt safe in Meallán as a child, but she'd never considered the reason for the presence of guards in every corner of the palace, along the gates that circled the grounds, throughout the city, atop the wall. Their uniforms, formations, statures—they'd all seemed ceremonial, ritualistic. A way of displaying the loyalty and strength of Tremaene. Never had any of it seemed precautionary. Or necessary.

But the wall and the sentries had stood guard against threats her young mind knew nothing of.

And now I'm standing on the wrong side, she thought, staring up at it. It stood to keep her out. To keep a murderous traitor safe and untouched.

Her hand grazed the thinly jointed stones as they moved into a single line, keeping close to the wall while keeping their eyes trained on the parapet above. Even though Sully had guards on the inside, they couldn't risk drawing attention from others.

The ground dipped down toward a grate that was scarcely tall or wide enough for a grown man to fit through. Rocks trailed down a tapered gully, leading away from the wall. Careful not to make a sound, Hazel, Sully, and Armel rolled the larger rocks aside. Without fire magic to cut through the metal bars, Killian and Tearlach knelt down on either side, and with a screech that made Esme cringe, the grate pulled free.

Inside, the storm drain was tall enough for Esme to stand upright. Her larger companions weren't so lucky. A single torch was lit, showing centuries-old lines of previous water levels. She expected the damp smell of the caves, but the air was earthier, without so much as a rivulet running down the tunnel's lowest point. It was disheartening, but Esme was nonetheless glad not to slosh through rainwater and muck.

More torches were lit and passed back as they navigated the web of tunnels. Esme tried to imagine the roads and alleyways mirrored above— anything to keep her mind off the fact that every step brought her closer to Orianna.

Sully halted them beside an alcove. Esme didn't think they'd traveled far enough to already be at the palace, but the others seemed to concur as Armel stepped forward to test a ladder that angled up into the darkness. It scarcely looked strong enough to hold her own weight, let alone those who were two and three times her size.

Sully handed his torch to Armel, which illuminated the ledge and a recessed section covered by planks of wood in the ceiling.

They climbed up one by one, then Killian boosted her into the dark room above.

Her suspicions were immediately confirmed. They most assuredly were *not* in the palace. Wooden casks were stacked three-high along one wall. Shelves with dark bottles lined the others. *A tavern.*

Hinges squealed and Esme spun around to see guards crowding into the room.

There were so many. Too many. She stumbled back. Killian steadied her, giving her an amused look.

Right. They're with us, she realized, smiling sheepishly at him, her cheeks heating with embarrassment.

Still, she was surprised that the sight of her own city's guards had caused her such panic. Her mind felt like nothing more than a tangle of fear and uncertainty. Things once safe and familiar no longer felt so.

But if Sully trusted the men and women who'd come to help them breach the palace gates, then she too would trust them.

The half dozen armored guards bowed their heads when Esme finally stepped away from Killian's side. Acknowledging them with a dip of her chin, she noticed that not only were they in full armor—something she'd only seen during cavalcades and formal occasions—they also wore two swords each and an array of smaller blades tucked neatly into their belts.

How safe was the city if its guards were armed for battle? She caught Tearlach's eye and saw that he was considering the same thing.

Armel, Hazel, and Killian donned matching armor and weapons, then each offered her promises before Killian swept her up into a tight embrace.

To everyone else it looked like nothing more than gratitude toward a friend who'd given him a second chance at life. To Esme, it felt like much more.

The metal strips on his armor were cold against her fingers as she tentatively pressed her hands against his back. He squeezed tighter, then tucked his head next to hers. His breath caressed her neck, and she could feel the heat of his lips near her ear as he whispered, "Don't worry, love. I'll be right back." Then quickly, before anyone could notice, Killian pressed a kiss right below her ear. Esme sucked in a breath, trying to suppress a shiver as Killian stepped back with a grin. He winked, then turned to leave with a majority of the guards.

Neither of them knew where the following hours would lead, or who would be left standing in the end. Fear, she realized, wasn't something a warrior—or even a man that had seen the other side of death—could ever, truly conquer.

Esme followed Sully, Tearlach, and the two remaining city guards out into the night. The streets were deserted and dark. Not one light flickered in the windows. Back alleys were unrecognizable. But if she were being honest, the main streets weren't familiar either. Her family hadn't made a habit of venturing outside the palace gates all that often.

One of the guards halted them where three roads converged. They waited silently in the darkness as a city guard at the opposite end completed his route, continuing on via one of the adjacent streets.

It took another half dozen turns before they stopped outside an unmarked door. Esme searched the alleyway.

Where are we? Perhaps there was another secret passage that would at last lead them to the palace?

Three quick knocks on the small mullioned window had a large man opening the door. Large was perhaps an understatement. The man filled the doorframe and then some.

One guard remained at the back door as the other made his way through the lower level of the building.

As Esme stepped into a cramped space with a desk and a single oil lamp, Sully introduced her to Beglan. His grip was gentle as he smiled warmly at her.

Beglan owned the shop—a bookshop, she gathered as soon as Tearlach lit another lamp and set about checking the front room that was crowded with rows of bookshelves.

Esme's confusion grew. Why bother checking the premises if they were just going to leave?

"Keep your post until I return," Tearlach addressed one of the guards, who nodded in response.

"Wait…What?" Esme approached him. "What's going on? Why do they need to guard a bookshop?"

Tearlach moved past her, shielding the light he carried as he peered behind the heavy curtains covering the front window.

"You're staying here." He brushed past her in the narrow space between the shelves.

"I most certainly am not." Esme followed as Tearlach inspected the windows in a small nook that held a stone hearth and a dwindling fire. When he turned back, Esme was furious, her hands propped on her hips.

"Yes. You are." When Tearlach tried to pass, Esme blocked his path. She could hear a growl deep in his throat as he lowered his head to meet her eyes. "I'm not letting you anywhere near that woman."

Esme jabbed a finger into his chest, but Tearlach only glared at her attempt to fight him. "You lied to me." Her voice was lower than she'd ever heard it, and lethally calm.

Tearlach merely arched a brow, challenging her.

Her face fell and she stumbled back. With everything they'd discussed, he'd never once mentioned what would happen when they reached the queen's suite. It had been assumed, but never voiced.

He hadn't lied.

But he also hadn't told her the truth. Esme turned to where Sully and Beglan were watching their interaction. "Sully?" she pleaded. "Did you know about this?"

He nodded once. "I did."

She took in a shuddering breath. "And you didn't tell me?"

Sully didn't answer, and Tearlach had resumed checking every door and window.

"What about everything you told the generals?" Esme practically yelled as she followed him through the shop.

She huffed out a breath when Tearlach ascended the stairs in the corner.

"Well?" she demanded when he returned.

Tearlach crossed his arms over his chest and finally addressed her. "Everything I told those war-hungry generals was to keep them from destroying not only the palace, but this very city, and every citizen in it. I knew they wouldn't risk an all-out war with the kingdom's sole heir here in Meallán."

Oh. *Oh.* Some of her anger subsided. She took a slow breath, then quietly asked, "Did the others know about this?" Had Killian kept it from her?

Tearlach dipped his chin once.

Everyone had known? She could feel her hands begin to tremble and clenched them into fists. Everyone knew and no one had told her?

"Fine." The word felt rough in her throat, but what choice did she have? Even if she thought of leaving after Tearlach and Sully were gone, there was no way she'd make it past the guards blocking the doors. Or Beglan. The shopkeeper seemed harmless, but his size alone was reason not to cross him. He likely had orders to keep her there as well.

Besides, Esme admitted to herself, participating in a ruse was better than sending in the entire army of Northern Rebels to sack the city. So, she'd wait, hidden amid the maze of city streets, while the others dispatched Orianna.

Tearlach checked every window, door, and closet—apparently the supply closet beneath the stairs could house a threat—once more, then addressed each of the guards. When he seemed satisfied with the location and her protection, he shared a look with Sully.

Esme could feel the captain approaching from behind. "Esme?" His firm, yet comforting voice reminded her so much of her father's. "My Queen."

At that, she turned and met his deep blue eyes. "Captain Sullivan."

He allowed himself a tight smile, then pulled her into a fierce embrace. He'd already lost his king and queen. He couldn't lose her too. So she hugged him back, and when her body began to shake from tears she couldn't hold back, he sighed. "I'm sorry. For everything."

"I know," she choked.

"It will all be over soon, my dear. I promise."

She nodded into his chest.

When he finally pulled away, Sully held her at arm's length, looking down at her once more. She wondered if he saw her mother in her eyes. Then he nodded once and turned away, striding toward the back door.

"Esme," Tearlach said from behind. Not a question, a command.

She turned, not bothering to wipe the wetness from her cheeks.

"You are *not* to leave this place with anyone but me."

"I know," she ground out.

"You will wait for me," he enunciated each word. "Understand?"

"Yes," she snapped.

"Say it."

She exhaled harshly. "I'll wait."

His eyebrow arched in that way it always did.

"For you," she said through gritted teeth.

He narrowed his eyes, searching for the lie. But she wasn't lying. What would be the point? Tearlach had won.

A muscle feathered in his jaw, though he seemed satisfied.

Then he left.

Without any sort of touch or embrace. Not even a goodbye. Not even to tell her he'd return. *Nothing.*

Why did that bother her more than his deception?

Chapter Forty-Three

ESME ACCEPTED A cup of rose tea from Beglan, then wandered through the shelves. She knew the wait would stretch on for some time and needed a distraction. Copper nameplates identified the genres in each aisle. Walking to the farthest one, she glanced back to where Beglan was watching her. After the way Tearlach had nearly torn the place apart to make sure of its safety, she assumed the bookshop owner had no qualms with her harmless perusal.

Some of the oldest books she'd ever seen lined the cases, rivaling even those in the royal library. She leaned her head around the corner. "How long have you had this shop?"

Beglan lumbered over. "Oh, a long time. I've been here since the early years of your mother's reign."

Her mother had been a great ruler. The people had loved her ardently.

What would the people think of Esme?

Not wanting the comparison she assumed was coming, Esme blindly pulled a book from the shelf. Opening the black cover to the title page, she read, "Ordained: The complete history of the Order of Tremaene's high-priestesses." Scowling at the words, she quickly turned the page and feigned interest as she heard Beglan approach.

He reached over her head and pulled down a book from one of the shelves above.

"She's from the north, you know? Like me."

Esme met his eyes, which were brimming with pride. She slipped the book back onto the shelf and gave Beglan her full attention.

"She wasn't of noble birth, you know. She was just like the rest of us. Suppose it was something inside her, something she was destined for—to be queen."

He paged through the heavy tome, then held it open for her. Esme's eyes went wide at the sight of the beautifully illustrated map.

Beglan inclined his head toward a table at the end of the row. He gently set down the volume and pointed to a small town. Beglan's home, she gathered. It wasn't far from where her mother and Sully had grown up. Esme's mind filled with questions, finding herself suddenly interested in conversation, but a bang at the back of the store halted her.

She turned to find Sully striding purposefully through the shop.

How much time had passed? They couldn't have been gone more than an hour.

Fear quickly replaced her surprise. "Sully?" her voice quavered, expecting the worst.

"Princess." He nodded in greeting.

Princess? He hadn't called her that since—Esme shook her head. "Why are you...where's Tearlach?" The promise she'd made to wait for him rang in her ears. Sully wasn't supposed to retrieve her. That wasn't the plan.

"He's been held up."

"Held up?" Her brows pressed together.

"He sent me."

Esme nodded skeptically.

"It's time to go," he told her, holding out a hand.

She glanced at the guard stationed at the front, trying to reconcile the turn of events. But before she could ask more, Sully spoke again, his voice void of emotion. "Everything has been taken care of. You're needed at the palace."

She'd expected a bit more...reassurance. The stony man standing before her was not the same Sully who'd embraced her earlier. Then again...she didn't know what had transpired since he'd left with Tearlach. Perhaps it was his way of shutting out the unwelcome emotions that came with battle—with ending life.

Forcing her doubts aside, she agreed. "Yes, of course." Turning to Beglan, Esme smiled and thanked him.

"It was a pleasure to meet you, My Queen."

She ducked her head, feeling a blush spread across her cheeks. But before she could respond to the kind man, Sully took her by the elbow and guided her to the back of the store. Both of the guards met them at the door, and shared a glance that didn't go unnoticed by Esme.

The taller guard addressed Sully. "Sir, we weren't expecting Tearlach... or *anyone*," he corrected, "for at least another hour. The guard shift hasn't happened yet and your escorts may not be ready."

Sully waved a dismissive hand. "Not necessary." He pulled Esme out the door and into the night before either guard could protest further.

She glanced back to see both men standing in the alley, bewildered.

Well, *that* had certainly not gone according to plan.

"Wait! My coat. I forgot my coat." She pulled out of Sully's grip and spun on her heel. She'd left it draped over the arm of a chair near the hearth, along with Cadwyn's cloak, and her sword.

"There's no time. We need to go." He yanked her forcibly, turning her away from the shop.

"What do you mean there's no time? Sully, what happened at the palace?"

"It's secure."

"Okay, then. What happened with Orianna?" Her breath suddenly felt trapped in her lungs. She *needed* to hear the words.

"She's been detained."

"What?" The word came choking out of her throat.

He stopped, giving Esme an irritated look. "Detained. No longer a threat."

"I know what the word means. What I don't understand is why you didn't—why Tearlach didn't—kill her."

"It was not necessary."

"Not necessary?" Was she actually hearing those words?

Then they were moving swiftly again. Esme had barely noticed when Sully urged her on—his words echoing in her head. *Not necessary.*

Something wasn't right.

She could hardly keep up, but Sully kept hold of her arm, as though he was worried she might try to escape.

That was *exactly* what he was worried about, Esme realized.

"Sully!" She pulled her arm from his ever-tightening grip.

He spun to face her.

"What's going on?"

"I told you, Princess." *Again with the 'Princess?'* "I'm bringing you to the palace."

The way the muscles in his shoulders tensed—like he might lunge at her if she moved out of his reach—set her instincts on fire.

Suddenly she was back in Periwen, trying to outrun assassins.

Out of the corner of her eye, she saw movement—a flutter of feathers. An owl was perched on the eave of a building. Silent on the wind, she swooped down, flying parallel to the ground behind Sully. Where only Esme could see.

A warning.

Sully grew visibly agitated at their prolonged standstill, but Esme dared one more question. "Where are the others? Are they okay?"

There was a hint of a smirk—one she wouldn't have noticed had she not been watching for it. "The others await your arrival," he told her easily.

His response sent a chill down her spine. He took her arm again, all but dragging her through the empty streets.

Esme was certain something wasn't right. The man beside her wasn't *her* Sully. Was it possible...Had Orianna somehow managed to gain control of the captain's mind? Or perhaps the high-priestess had threatened him.

No. Sully would have warned her somehow, gotten her out. He would die for her.

But something was off. His return to the bookshop a mere hour after he'd left with Tearlach...it was all too easy.

And nothing about overthrowing an all-powerful enemy could have been easy.

She risked one more look at Sully. Then ran.

The streets might have been unfamiliar, but after three turns, Esme was able to put some distance between them. Back to the bookshop? Would the guards still be waiting?

Rounding another corner, Esme put her back against a wall that led into a courtyard. Vines covered the stones, thick in the darkness, shielding her briefly from sight. But she had to keep moving. Toward the palace. There was no way she'd leave without the others.

The dream with Orianna flashed through her mind.

No, she told herself vehemently. It wouldn't come to that.

Then she recalled what Tearlach had once told her—that hiding instead of fighting was often the best course. There was no way she could fight off Sully, so until she found her bearings in the city, she'd hide within it.

Sidling toward the end of the vine-covered wall, she peered carefully around the corner, her heart rioting in her chest. A spoked wheel from a handcart was visible beneath a dark canvas sheet. With one last glance over her shoulder, Esme ran for it, ducking under the cloth and tucking herself into its shadow—her white linen shirt no longer a beacon in the moonless night.

She was hidden. And safe. At least for a time. *Think, Esme, think.* Perhaps getting out of the city was the wisest option. If she could find her way back through the storm drains and head west, she might be able to reach the Northern Rebels.

Nodding at the idea, Esme let the plan take shape. With an army, she'd have a better chance of rescuing her companions, wherever they were.

She knew that with the Lifeblood Oath, Tearlach couldn't be killed while she was alive. A small comfort. And if he was still alive, then Killian, Hazel, and Armel were too. At least...that was what Esme convinced herself of as her breathing slowed to a steadier rhythm.

First, she decided, she needed to—

A hand closed around Esme's neck.

She was yanked up as she gasped for air. Her feet scrambled to make purchase, kicking as shadowy curtains closed around her vision.

She wanted to shout for help, but knew it was more important to conserve her energy for the upcoming fight.

So she let Sully take her.

When he set her down, Esme sucked in a breath only to growl at him. He tied her hands roughly behind her back as she spat, "Did you betray my parents too?" She needed to know if the man who'd vowed to keep her safe since the day she was born was still in there somewhere.

The man remained silent as he bound her legs together.

"Was this your plan all along? Put that *murderer* on the throne and send me away? Why not just kill me when you had the chance nine years ago?"

"What would be the fun in that?" His taunting voice slithered up her neck, making her stomach churn with revulsion.

A black strip of cloth was tied around her head, cutting into her mouth and keeping the abhorring words she had for the captain trapped inside.

"That's better," he sneered, then hoisted Esme over his shoulder and strode through the vacant streets. He hadn't covered her eyes, so Esme hoped she'd see a guard—one that might recognize her.

But he kept mostly to the alleys before marching through the open palace gates.

The palace. Exactly where she needed to be. Someone was waiting for her inside, and Esme intended to greet her with every bit of vengeance she had.

She stretched to see the guards lining the front steps. They were expecting her. Some had enough shame not to meet her eyes.

Sully stalked through the main doors and into the throne room, then dropped her unceremoniously on the floor.

Her knees slammed into the cold marble before she toppled to the side, unable to catch herself.

Then the cloying smell of jasmine assaulted her senses, and Esme knew exactly whose face she would see when she craned her neck toward the center of the room.

She struggled to get her feet under her, refusing to die on her knees.

"Unbind her," Orianna instructed with a flick of her wrist. "She is our guest, after all."

Once the ties were broken, and her mouth once again hers, Esme clambered to her feet, ready to tell the high-priestess exactly what her *guest* was going to do to her. But as she stood, she realized they weren't alone.

Her heart stopped in her chest as she slowly peered over her shoulder. Four warriors knelt on the floor, bound by invisible restraints. A wall of guards stood behind, weapons at the ready.

Chapter Forty-Four

DREAD POOLED IN Esme's stomach. Her mind reeled, but Orianna interrupted her cacophony of thoughts before any ideas materialized.

"Impressive, is it not?" Orianna grinned down at the warriors kneeling on the cold marble, leashed like her own personal pets. She extended her hand in front of her, admiring her many bejeweled rings and silver bracelets that wrapped around her slender wrist, as though she had all the time in the world.

She did, Esme realized. Orianna had every advantage. And Esme had no doubt she'd take her time.

The high-priestess looked almost ethereal with her silver hair and white diaphanous gown, with sleeves that pooled at her elbows, draping down to the floor to swirl with her skirts. Silver studs sparkled all the way up to the tips of her ears. Thin strands of clear crystals swept down from her crown, resting against her hair. She was the portrait of innocence and purity, save for the crown itself, and its razor-sharp, silver spikes.

It seemed she wasn't able to completely conceal her true nature.

"I sometimes surprise myself with the power I can wield." A smile crept over Orianna's face. The deep red that colored her lips pulled back to reveal teeth that were perfectly white and blunt, though Esme wouldn't have been the least bit surprised to see fangs.

"Orianna." She regarded the woman, finally meeting the violet eyes that had haunted her dreams. Esme struggled not to react as visions of the smoking city returned to her mind. She was alone in a battle that would likely end with her on the floor beside her companions.

"You will address me as *Queen.*"

"I shall do no such thing," Esme replied with equal calm, willing her voice to possess a confidence she didn't feel.

"Ah, but you will. As you can see," Orianna said as she gestured around the room, the jingle of her bracelets lilting through the rotunda, "there is no Fae stronger or more powerful."

Though hesitant to look again, Esme turned her head. Whatever power Orianna held over her friends had left them immobilized and unable to speak. They were vulnerable, powerless.

Not even Tearlach had been able to siphon her magic. Or if he'd tried, it hadn't been enough. Perhaps Orianna possessed a similar ability. With all the magic she'd stolen, it was entirely possible.

Esme met Killian's eyes—scorching blue and ready to rain down fire the moment he was freed.

The guards stationed behind them stared straight ahead, and Esme wondered if Orianna had them in her thrall as well, or if they willingly accepted her command.

Tearing her gaze away, Esme quickly scanned the rest of the room, tallying the guards, the exits—

A flicker of a shadow on the floor drew her attention up to the glass dome. She immediately looked away, hoping Orianna hadn't noticed.

There was a hawk perched on one of the narrow cornices high above.

Esme made a show of looking around the room again, turning last to the man standing beside Orianna. Did she dare wonder if it was possible? The man gave her a maniacal grin—one Sully had never once bestowed upon her...or anyone, for that matter. He cocked his head and shifted his gaze to Orianna.

A moment passed as the two of them shared a knowing look. Then Orianna turned her smile on Esme before lifting her eyes to the glass dome.

The hawk plummeted toward the ground, driven by an unseen force.

Its pained cries echoed through the chamber. Esme covered her ears at the sound, her eyes fixed on the feathery form. With a glimmer of light he shifted, then collided violently with the floor, fracturing the tiles beneath his knees. Esme's eyes filled with tears at the sight of Sully sprawled before her, grimacing in pain. Injured, but not dead.

She whipped her head back to the other man in time to witness a similar shimmering light shift him back into his true form. Not Sully, but a shapeshifter nonetheless.

His vicious smile told her he could be none other than Briac, Orianna's personal guard. The one they'd been warned about. Yet it seemed no one had been aware of his most cunning talent.

Sully was already being dragged away. Esme pressed her lips together, holding back a whimper as his spine straightened and he was forced into a kneeling position, rigid beside the others.

"I was wondering when we would meet again, my dear Sullivan." Orianna sauntered over to her row of captives, her train slinking along the floor. "You've been visiting my city for years now. I wonder why you never bothered to stop by and see me."

Shit. What else did she know?

"But it does seem you've been busy. I was beginning to wonder when your little band of rebels would arrive. You know you could have remained captain if you'd placed your loyalty with the one who had power. Instead, you waited for a useless child to lead you."

"I'm not a child," Esme spoke up.

Orianna laughed, gliding back to the center of the room. She stopped directly between Esme and the garish throne at the far end. "Of course not, my dear. But still young. I've done you a favor, really. Being queen is so much work, more than you know. I've saved you from a life of service. Although"—Orianna stepped closer, seeming to note Esme's clenched jaw and wild eyes—"it seems you're more stubborn than I thought. It's a pity it's come to this, and a shame that you brought an army with you. You might have spared them from the traitorous deaths they'll now receive."

If Orianna knew about the Northern Rebels too, then no one was going to save them. Esme's shoulders dropped, her jaw slackening in shock. But with a deep breath, she managed to pull a look of civility over her features as Orianna turned to the guards lining the wall.

"Though I do wonder who of my men has been feeding information to dear old Sullivan. I think I'll enjoy finding out after this small matter is dealt with."

Esme took in the sight of her companions again. Only it wasn't anger she saw in their eyes, it was fear. They were afraid...for her. Horrified at what Orianna would do to her—what they'd fail to stop.

She couldn't cower. Esme had to fight. As futile as it would certainly be, she was their only hope.

The kingdom's only hope.

Her stomach churned at the thought as she dropped her hands to her sides. They hovered inches from the one weapon she still had. The one Tearlach had made her swear to keep on her at all times.

With a tug, she could free her dagger, send it sailing into Orianna's throat. Whether or not she'd perfected that skill during her training with Armel didn't matter. It was the only defense she had.

But the singular moment it took for her to swipe it from her belt, the dagger was ripped from her hand, clattering across the floor.

"Oh, don't be silly, my dear." Orianna gave the dagger a dismissive look.

Esme dropped her gaze, trying to conceal the shock at witnessing another of Orianna's many abilities. Her panic surged.

Esme.

The rough whisper of Tearlach's voice stole her breath. She wasn't alone.

His voice—always deep and potent—sounded weak, far away, like he was calling to her from beneath layers of earth and stone. Still, he'd managed to breach Orianna's hold. The high-priestess's magic was nearly unparalleled, but the connection that bound Tearlach and Esme was something different, something stronger. Made of magic, but also of blood.

Magic. Of course. In her frightened state, she'd completely forgotten that her strongest weapon wasn't made of sharpened silver. After so many days of letting her power lie dormant, she'd all but forgotten about it.

Her shield is strong. Tearlach's voice reached her again. *But she's expending considerable power to keep us bound this way. You need to deplete her magic.*

Esme desperately wanted to know how the woman had managed to capture and bind all of them—especially Tearlach—but she focused instead on the information she could actually use. Orianna had a shield. It made sense she'd have that sort of ability, given the amount of magic she'd stolen. But how could Esme weaken it? How could she draw Orianna out while protecting herself at the same time?

She dropped her chin to her chest, knowing her every movement and expression were being watched. She stared at the tiles, considering her next move. Four of the tiles had been cracked when Sully crashed to the ground, disrupting the intricately painted vines and flowers.

Start with a storm. Tearlach interrupted her fledgling plan. *It could strip away her shield layer by layer.*

Esme resisted looking up toward the glass dome. What kind of damage would it cause? Could she actually manage to draw out Orianna's magic while keeping herself and her companions safe from the inevitable destruction? Esme wasn't convinced she could control it that well. Though a storm had its advantages. It would likely be effective against Orianna's shield, and storms were large, powerful. Most of all, a storm would offer the perfect distraction.

Esme became aware of Orianna's voice as the woman began pacing slowly before her. How long had she been speaking? From the cadence of her voice, one thing was apparent—Orianna had been waiting nine years to address Esme, and was going to savor the opportunity.

Esme was only too happy to oblige. Given enough time, she could weaken Orianna's shield, and perhaps even the restraints on the others. Not having to face Orianna alone in a full-out battle was infinitely appealing.

"The treaty may have seemed to you *royals*," Orianna continued, saying the word with disgust as if she herself was not wearing a crown, "like the noble thing to do. But when I joined the Order, I saw the treaty for what it really was—a way for your father to control us, to keep us from realizing our true power. How could those that summon the majesty of the gods be seen as anything less than godly themselves? There are none higher." She raised her arms to accentuate her point.

"So you killed your sisters?"

Orianna tilted her head in a look of pity, like Esme was nothing more than an ignorant child in need of a lesson. "They did not see the truth as I did—that your parents sought to control us, to leash our power. But we cannot—*must not*—be bound. What I did was the will of the gods."

"It doesn't seem that our benevolent gods would condone the killing of innocent people," Esme countered.

"Innocent?" Orianna's laughter rang out. Esme cringed at the shrill sound. "Those who speak against a high-priestess threaten the gods themselves."

The woman was delusional, that was certain. But combined with the power she possessed—the power she'd stolen—Orianna was deadly.

Draw your magic up. Slowly. Keep her talking. And Esme? Breathe. You can do this.

She repeated his words in her mind, counting her breaths one by one, letting them steady her. Then she chanted her own words. *Not alone. Not alone.*

Her magic was already vibrating beneath her skin, prickling her fingertips. She felt vines grow at her feet, crawling soundlessly—*invisibly*—across the floor. At first, every ounce of her awareness was channeled into those vines, but as she eased off a bit, they continued, knowing what she needed from them. As easy as breathing. She almost smiled at the thought.

Hearing something about the Tamslo Mountains, Esme's focus returned to Orianna. Though she only picked up the end of the woman's speech, it was enough to realize that Orianna knew about the camp in the north.

Esme's shoulders tightened as she awaited Orianna's threat to the people of Altan. But what came wasn't that at all. Instead, Orianna offered to free them, assuring her that the people in the mountains could even be allowed to keep their land, to live peacefully.

Esme's eyes narrowed. It was some kind of trick. Surely Orianna wouldn't make an offer unless it benefitted her in some way. Though her pure white gown and ordained position said otherwise, the woman was in no way pious.

"Spare them from the death and destruction you know is coming. You've seen it, you know I speak the truth." Orianna paused, letting her words sink in. "You know this is the only way."

Esme's heart caught on those last, carefully chosen words. *The only way.*

Orianna knew about her dreams? Had she been a part of them the way Esme had?

Had she known Esme's companions would sneak into the palace because she'd already seen them bound on the throne room floor?

*Although...*Esme thought carefully. It wasn't happening precisely the same. The city *wasn't* burning. And Esme's clothes—She glanced down. The bloodred cloak that had only appeared in those dreams wasn't around her shoulders. Her clothes were her own.

She met Orianna's piercing violet eyes—so focused as they attempted to conceal the truth. But there was a tiny flicker. There and gone. But it was enough to confirm what Esme suspected.

The dreams weren't real.

Orianna had somehow cast the illusions, infiltrated her sleeping mind. Another twisted ability to hold sway over her enemies. Effective...Almost.

As the vines continued their trails along the floor, Esme focused on the sensation of her magic, spinning out in tiny threads, letting it ground her as she held Orianna's gaze—keeping her from revealing that she knew the woman's secret.

Instead, Esme pressed her lips together, doing her best to look conflicted. She glanced between her friends and the woman before her, then forced her hands to tremble.

"If I..." Esme began, then took another breath as though she couldn't bear to say it. "If I let you...kill me"—her voice broke—"they go free?" She sucked in a ragged breath and brushed tears from her cheek. "All of them?"

Tearlach raged inside her mind as a devious, bloodred smile spread across Orianna's face.

Chapter Forty-Five

DON'T! TEARLACH GROWLED. Do not bargain with her.

You will NOT give up! Do you hear me? You will fight! That's an order!

Esme stood firm, letting Tearlach's words sink in.

Orianna cocked her head to the side in a haughty way that made Esme want to rip it off.

"Now, my dear, why would I want to kill you?"

Esme had no intention of surrendering to Orianna, but the woman's response surprised her. If she wanted her alive, it couldn't be good.

"Then what do you want with me?" Esme let her voice catch on the last word.

"You're far more use to me alive. The power we can wield together will be a force greater than any have ever seen."

Esme's jaw tightened. She was no puppet.

Don't listen to her! Tearlach shouted.

Orianna looked down at her like she was nothing more than a bug under a glass, analyzing, probing, as if she could see through Esme's skin to what pumped inside her veins.

"If you have even a drop of the magic your mother had…" Orianna frowned—though Esme knew better than to believe the woman capable of sympathy. "But I have yet to see this formidable power you're said to have." She paced in front of her again, back and forth. It was clearly a strategy to make Esme impatient.

And it was working.

When Orianna turned to face her again, Esme could tell her next verbal attack would strike deeper.

"It's too bad your mother didn't see things my way, it might not have ended so badly for her." Orianna had the audacity to shake her head, as if Queen Erena had chosen her fate. "And what a pity that I didn't discover that taking a life with my own hands would allow me to absorb one's magic." She admired her hands, turning them over. "I might have had a little more fun with your parents instead of sending them into that ravine." Her sympathetic facade dropped away as her crimson lips turned up into a wicked grin.

Orianna's admission fueled Esme's rage. A storm gathered in her mind, threatening to get out, to show the woman who'd murdered her parents exactly how much power she possessed.

But Tearlach's words quelled her swelling magic before it could break free. *Don't listen to her, Esme. You're strong. Your heart makes you strong. Strength, Esme, not power. Strength is what will win this.*

He was right. Reckless magic would land Esme quickly on the ground, crushed beneath Orianna's heel. The woman ruled the people of Tremaene by making them afraid. She was no leader. Orianna was nothing like her parents.

Nothing like her, Esme realized. It was the first time she'd truly let herself believe that she was worthy of the crown. *She* was the queen Tremaene needed.

Orianna moved closer, gliding soundlessly across the floor. She paused, then, in the blink of an eye, moved from her position six paces away to stand directly in front of Esme, as though she'd somehow…*leapt* through time and space faster than any could witness.

Shit, Tearlach growled. Esme muttered the same sentiment as she stumbled back.

Orianna seemed pleased at the reaction her little trick had caused.

Fearing the other facets of Orianna's magic, Esme knew she couldn't wait any longer. The problem was, she'd never wielded a storm within the confines of a building...let alone one with a glass ceiling directly above her head. Would her magic even work if there was nothing to pull in from her environment?

It will work, Tearlach assured. *It's no different. You know how to do this. Now quit stalling.*

Breathing in deeply, Esme let the smell of petrichor fill her senses. The sound of rain beating down matched the wild rhythm of her heart. She could *feel* the storm.

That's right, you're almost there. Draw it up slowly.

"And if I refuse to surrender?" she dared to ask.

Before Orianna could respond, Esme raised her hand, then slashed it down toward the ground. Bringing a storm with it.

The sky fell, shattering the glass above.

Sheets of chilled rain pelted through the empty silver arches of the dome. The room darkened as thunderheads gathered and proliferated, charging the space. Magic lanced through Esme's veins, pulsing with the storm that swirled around her.

Orianna backed away, shielded from the howling winds and lightning that spread out in a web of purple light when it struck the invisible edges.

Lightning. It was the first time Esme had been able to intentionally summon it.

She held the surging storm close, rising and twisting it up around her and Orianna, keeping her companions safe on the other side of the dark winds.

Easy, Tearlach warned. *Don't let it drain you.*

Backing off, Esme lessened the rain to a steady rhythm. Water pooled at her feet, running in rivers toward the outer walls of the chamber. Her magic was far from exhausted, but Tearlach was right, she shouldn't throw everything at Orianna at once. And the longer she could drag their encounter out, the better.

"Ah, a storm wielder," Orianna spoke as a final roll of thunder rumbled through the floor.

Esme looked the woman over. She hadn't been touched by the elements at all, standing amid the aftermath without a hair out of place. The last of the rain trickled along the invisible armor surrounding Orianna.

"What an impressive show. But really, is that all, my dear? I was hoping for a bit more." Orianna stepped closer. "You know your mother could—"

She was cut off with a blast of wind capable of knocking even a warrior off his feet. But the high-priestess's shield stood strong as the forceful storm buffeted against it.

Esme blinked the water from her lashes and shoved her sodden hair off her face as the onslaught of rain assaulted her. Dense clouds spun between her and Orianna—blurring the sight of her.

But through it all, Esme could feel every inch of her hidden vines. Shoots multiplied, weaving through the path she'd laid. Layer upon layer they formed a thick, invisible mass, slithering along the floor, seeking the defensive wall that protected Orianna. Ready to choke the life out of it.

For all the power Orianna possessed, she seemed unaware, too focused on the spectacle Esme carefully created in front of her eyes.

"Don't ever! Mention my mother! Again!" Esme yelled through the cyclone. She inhaled, filling her lungs, letting the storm expand with her breath, ripping chunks of stone from the walls and columns. She lifted her hand and the garish throne across the room was ripped from its dais and swept away. Thunder cracked and lightning hissed inside the rising, twisting wall of rain and wind. It was a tempest the magnitude of which Esme had never been able to control before, crowding every inch of the room.

The beautifully painted tiles fractured under the pressure of the storm.

Esme widened her stance. If she wasn't careful, her own magic might crush her too.

As the storm kept building, Esme expected the dizzying feeling of exhaustion to claim her. But as she flung more and more power into it, her magic never felt close to shallowing. Instead, it seemed to be gaining strength. It was almost like she was pulling it up, through her, from the earth beneath the palace.

Her power felt infinite. There was no beginning, no end.

A jagged bolt of lightning struck between her and Orianna, blinding Esme momentarily. She almost expected to see the palace split in two when her sight returned. Instead, she caught a glimpse of the guards as she let the storm wane for just a moment. They braced themselves against the wall as thunder shook everything around them.

Good, Esme thought. *Be afraid.* If they thought her more powerful than their treasonous leader, maybe they'd flee, leaving the fight to her and Orianna alone.

But Orianna remained untouched, even as Esme ratcheted up the winds swirling around them, assailed the woman's invisible barrier with hail and lightning. Still, Esme knew Orianna was expelling magic to keep her defenses impenetrable.

Her hold on us is weakening, Tearlach shouted into her mind through the howling winds.

She struck without hesitation, watching as a flicker of lightning crackled along the invisible wall separating her from Orianna.

Esme sucked in a breath. Orianna's shield was failing.

She's not invincible, Tearlach reminded. *Didn't I tell you that?*

His certitude actually made her grin for half a second. Until Orianna's expression shifted.

She was no longer impassive to Esme's assault. And there was clear anger in her violet eyes.

Esme braced herself an instant before an immense wave crashed in from the open roof.

She raised her hands, hoping to gather her thunderclouds to block the deluge. But it was too late. Water swallowed her.

She twisted around, unable to orient herself, struggling to hold her breath.

Tearlach's voice was distant. Far away.

She tried reaching for the water, to redirect it, but darkness crowded her vision.

Then all she could hear was ringing. High pitched, deafening.

Her lungs burned and she couldn't help but open her mouth, letting the water fill her throat.

She slammed into the ground, choking.

The water streamed away, leaving a perfect ring of splintered glass encircling Orianna.

Coughing to clear her lungs, Esme struggled against her strangling, sodden clothes. When she finally managed a full breath, she glanced up.

"I think that was quite enough, my dear." Orianna's disinterest was gone, her bloodred lips pressed into a stern line. "I wouldn't want you to deplete all of your magic just for a little show."

Esme glared up at her, panting. She felt like curling up, closing her eyes. She could barely keep her head raised. Her body was beyond exhausted, even as she felt the strong pulse of her magic.

Tearlach growled inside her head, ordering her to get up, to fight.

Esme had other plans.

It wasn't hard to keep her breathing rough and labored as she pressed her shaking hands against the crumbled tiles for support.

She's losing her grip. Just a little more, Esme. Now, get up! Keep fighting!

Just a little more. She repeated Tearlach's words as she rose to her knees.

Spreading her senses out, she felt along the trails of vines toward the tapered ends. She almost had what she needed. One more bolt of lightning. That was all it would take.

Esme swallowed. She was near the end. But could she do it? Could she take a life?

Before, it had all seemed so clear. It had been the only path, the only logical option. But in that moment...the reality of it was too much.

How could she kill? Even if the victim was the woman who'd taken her parents' lives and countless others?

You can do this. You must.

Esme took in the wreckage of the room, like she might find an alternative hiding in the shadows. Only a few pillars remained standing, but seeing them summoned the dream she'd had earlier in the night.

Perhaps there was another way.

Chapter Forty-Six

STILL ON HER knees, Esme plucked a shard of glass from the debris on the floor. The edge sliced into her palm as she struggled to her feet. Blood ran down her arm as she clenched it tighter, dripping to the ground and blooming bright across the wet floor.

She embraced the pain, focused on it, as she lifted her eyes to meet Orianna's.

Tearlach had gone quiet in her mind, but she didn't need his words. She was ready. Her body trembled with exhaustion, but not with fear. Esme could defeat Orianna. She *would*.

She stepped forward.

Her eyes slammed shut and she cried out in pain. The weapon dropped, shattering on the ground as she pressed her hands against her temples.

Talons clawed at her mind, trying to cleave it open. Esme dropped to her knees, covering her head like it might protect her from Orianna's invasion.

Images of the false dreams flooded her mind, dominating her senses until all Esme knew was blood and smoke and the suffocation of death that littered the streets of her city.

She couldn't breathe. Her hand shook violently as she reached out to connect with the floor beneath her.

It's not real, she told herself as her hand sifted through broken glass and the grit of crumbled marble. *Not real.*

She tried to open her eyes, fighting the thrall of Orianna's power as the images from the dreams twisted through her skull, warping the world around her.

The hooks dug deeper into her mind, and Esme screamed out, clawing at her scalp, trying to tear them away. But Orianna's magic was strong. And she wasn't letting go.

Her temples throbbed with almost unbearable pressure. Her jaw locked up, clenching so hard her teeth felt like they might crack. Then the muscles around her ribs started constricting. She tried to fight against it, redirecting some of her vines like they might fight off Orianna's attack. Her legs shook violently in a futile attempt to deflect the paralysis traveling down her body. She held her breath, pressing it out against her ribs even as she heard the first one snap.

"P-please. Please, stop," she whimpered through her clenched teeth, letting go of her last breath as she fell limp.

Esme! Tearlach bellowed as air rushed back into her lungs.

Orianna had released her hold.

Tears streamed down Esme's face. She curled onto her side, pressing her cheek against the wet tile, feeling her ribs knit back together painfully.

Esme. Tearlach breathed her name like a prayer, caressing her ravaged mind. She clung to it, keeping her eyes closed as she reached out to feel her magic.

Almost, she thought, trailing her senses along the thick mess of vines.

Slowly, she opened her eyes.

Orianna peered down at her with a satisfied grin. "Now have we finished or do you plan to throw about your juvenile magic once again?

We know how well that turned out for you." She tilted her head and Esme felt the scrape of talons inside her temples.

"No." Esme exhaled sharply, pressing her fingernails into her thighs—needing to feel anything else.

"Then we have an agreement?" Orianna smirked. "You for them." She glanced lazily over at her captives.

"Aren't you afraid I'll find a way to stab you in the back?" Esme gave a slight nod at the last word, slow and deliberate. *Aim for her back.* She prayed the directive was received—unwilling to let her eyes stray from Orianna as the woman flung her head back and laughed, joyless and arrogant.

"You forget so quickly, my dear." Orianna shook her head, her bloodred lips tipping up into a grin. "I know all. See. All."

Esme shuddered as the hooks grazed her mind again.

"Have I not proven my prescience? I would see you coming. I'd see it before you could so much as lift a weapon. Before the thought even formed in your simple, puny mind."

Not every thought, Esme nearly refuted aloud, silencing the words instantly as she strived to keep her eyes on Orianna and her mind vacant of her aims. With each breath, she counted, occupying her thoughts as completely as she could—visualizing the perfectly scribed numerals, feeling the rise and fall of her chest—while keeping the sensation of her magic buried deep in the recesses of her mind, hidden from Orianna's prodding.

"I see all." Orianna came to stand directly in front of her.

The woman might have seen what was transpiring right behind her if she hadn't been so fixated on breaking her rival.

Esme lifted her chin, but didn't respond, only needing to hold on a moment longer. Because while she didn't contain the multitude of stolen powers Orianna did, she knew everything that was going on around her. Tearlach, Killian, Armel, and Hazel had each taught her to be keenly aware of her surroundings at all times. To mark every exit, every potential opponent, every obstacle. And every available weapon.

Esme only needed to trust that the moment was upon her. That everything had transpired just as the owl had shown her. That *everything* was in place.

She released her magic, feeling the invisible vines slither back along the broken tiles.

"This is the only way." Orianna's eyes went hard, darkening as her pupils expanded. "I've little patience left. Make your choice. *Now.*"

"Now," Esme agreed, jolting as the dagger struck.

Her heart stopped mid-beat.

Orianna's lips parted. Blood trickled from the corner. Her perfectly arched brows lowered slightly, as if she couldn't quite believe what the young, inexperienced woman before her was capable of.

Stumbling forward, Orianna sunk to her knees, landing eye level with Esme.

A commotion rumbled behind her as Orianna's magic palpably deteriorated. She knew Briac was still a threat, and the many, many guards. But Esme couldn't look away.

Get up! Turn and fight! she urged herself, but her eyes stayed locked with Orianna's, her heart thumping slowly, powerfully in her chest. She needed to watch the life fade from the woman's eyes.

With a final exhale, Orianna slumped to the ground in a pool of white silk steeped in blood.

The woman had been so blinded by power, she hadn't noticed the hole in her shield. Esme's vines had eaten away at it bit by bit until they'd broken clean through. A hole just large enough for Cadwyn's dagger— planted precisely between Orianna's ribs, piercing her heart before her body could heal the damage.

She startled when Tearlach's iron sword was thrust into Orianna's neck. The sudden nearness of the iron sent a wave of nausea rolling through her, but Tearlach left it embedded.

Esme peered up at him. Tearlach lifted a shoulder stiffly and let it drop, as if to say, *Just in case.* His jaw worked, like he wanted to say something. But in her mind, he was silent.

After a moment passed between them, he sighed. The simple act seemed to loosen every taut muscle in his body. Like knowing that she was finally safe had released him from the weight he'd carried for nine long years.

A weight they'd all carried.

She looked down at the small blade buried in Orianna's back, then lifted her eyes to Cadwyn as she stepped out from the shadow of a pillar.

Chapter Forty-Seven

A FEW CLOUDS gathered in the gray, predawn sky. Though none looked threatening. Esme breathed more easily, knowing her magic hadn't spilled out into the streets. The city beyond the palace gates lay quiet, peaceful, unaware of what had transpired in the night.

Esme gazed out at the brightening horizon, willing the sun to rise, to wash away the longest, darkest night. The city would rise with the sun to celebrate the Dawning of the Light and the goddess Aeveen. But for her, the day would hold new meaning. As it soon would for all citizens of Tremaene.

Her tired legs carried her into the gardens—green and lush, vanquishing the images of charred ruins from her mind. The city had not burned. Her people were safe.

She dropped to her knees as tears blurred her vision. A soft, warm rain misted the air around her, coating her skin with tiny droplets and comforting her weary soul.

Many had been lost—a pain that would always grip her heart—but she was *home*. Finally home.

The fine misting drops became warmer, heavier. Grounding her to the land from which she came. Lifting her face to the sky, she let it wash over her.

———————

Esme woke once in the night to find Cadwyn curled around her on a small bed in what looked to be a servant's quarters. When her eyes opened again hours later, she was alone. A single sconce was lit, flickering soft golden light against the far wall. Tearlach was waiting outside the door when she emerged, and Esme knew he hadn't slept at all.

He looked her over, then opened his mouth to speak, but Cadwyn interrupted, breezing down the corridor to inform Esme that her room was finally ready.

"My room?"

"Your old room."

She wasn't sure how she felt about staying in the royal apartments, though her own, smaller room was better than taking the queen's suite.

She followed Cadwyn tentatively up the servant stairwell, her eyes shifting to each room as they made their way down the corridor on the second floor, as if Orianna might be lurking in the shadows.

Maids scurried out of her former suite before Esme could thank them or ask for their names. Her room looked the same, and it didn't appear as if it had been lived in. In fact, it looked as though it had been locked up for nearly a decade. Dust motes glittered in the late afternoon light.

Cadwyn left her alone to bathe, then returned with an early dinner.

Esme settled into a seat at the round table near the balcony, which overlooked the western grounds. Her muscles felt considerably better after the hot soak, though she still felt bone-tired.

Perhaps it was because her mind refused to forget—even for a second—the events that had happened in the throne room.

"Knife throwing is only a hobby?" Esme glanced at Cadwyn, thinking of her friend's claim that it had been nothing more than a diversion.

Cadwyn shrugged as she took a sip of wine.

"And don't think I've forgotten how you put yourself in danger when you promised you wouldn't."

"Did I promise?" she asked as she swirled her spoon through the creamy mushroom soup, her melodic voice tinged with a tone of trickery.

"Cadwyn," Esme pressed.

Cadwyn lifted one of her auburn brows, but didn't reply.

"I never should have told you our plans," Esme grumbled, shoving an entire buttered scone into her mouth—she hadn't realized how hungry she actually was.

Cadwyn chuckled as if withholding information would have somehow stopped her, reminding Esme how her lady-in-waiting had carried her unconscious body past numerous guards and through the streets of Donellis completely undetected. To protect her. Cadwyn would do anything—had done everything—to protect her.

Esme sipped her tea, blinking back the tears that gathered along her lashes.

"You needn't shoulder the burden alone," Cadwyn said softly. She'd always had a way of sensing Esme's thoughts. "You're not the only one who lost family...friends. These are my people too."

Esme pressed her lips together and nodded.

"How did you know of Orianna's shield? Could you sense it in some way?"

"What shield?" Cadwyn canted her head.

Esme covered her face with her hands and started laughing. Or crying. She wasn't sure anymore. So many things could have gone wrong. If Cadwyn hadn't been there, ready to throw her dagger, if Esme hadn't broken through Orianna's defenses...If Cadwyn hadn't aimed exactly where she had...

She felt Cadwyn's hand on her shoulder and let her hands fall away.

"Seems the gods were on our side."

"Indeed." Cadwyn smiled.

"I don't think…" Esme whispered, staring down at her lap, "I don't think I could've done it…Strike the final blow." She looked up, meeting the green eyes she'd seen in her dreams every night in Periwen. "Thank you for being there when I couldn't do it myself."

———————

In the days that followed, Esme kept herself secluded in her room. Tearlach had insisted she stay there unless escorted. But truthfully, she wasn't ready to reacquaint herself with the palace or the people she'd left behind. Her childhood suite seemed to be one of the only places untouched by Orianna's occupation. The only place that still felt like home.

Word of Esme's return spread like wildfire. Not only did the kingdom rejoice that their cruel and oppressive ruler had been dethroned, but that the heir of the late king and queen was very much alive and had returned to claim what was rightfully hers.

People had traveled from every province in Tremaene to see the long-lost princess with their own eyes. Carriages lined the gravel roads leading into the capital city. Crowds gathered in the streets of Meallán. And every inn was filled to capacity.

The palace was also brimming with new arrivals. There was a constant thrum of shouted orders and servants dashing about to ready rooms as members of the royal council who'd gone into hiding returned—with their own staff and families—to occupy much of the west wing.

Thankfully, the staff that had remained through Orianna's rule didn't seem loyal to the woman. Even the guards had surrendered immediately upon Orianna's death. They'd gazed at the wreckage of the throne room as if waking from a trance, then dropped to their knees and pledged their loyalty to Esme—their true queen.

Chapter Forty-Eight

LEANING OVER THE edge of the balustrade, Esme gazed down at the grove of trees. Their leaves were a deep, mossy green from the dimly lit night sky. She could still taste the sweetness of the myriad of succulent fruit the trees provided, yet in that moment, all she wanted was a simple apple. Perfectly ripe, covered in swirls of golds and greens, and smelling of autumn.

Autumn. Another thing she'd miss.

An ache bloomed in her chest, longing making her arms and legs heavy. It wasn't only her home in Debarrow she'd miss. Tearlach, Killian, Armel, and Hazel would be returning to the mountains with the army. They'd fulfilled their duty, after all.

Esme didn't want them to leave. Wished they'd choose to stay. They'd come to feel like her family, the way Cadwyn and Captain Sullivan did. But she couldn't ask them to give up their lives in the north. Palace life was far different from that of a warrior.

The soft click of her chamber doors had her blinking back to the balcony and the night. She glanced down at her hands, clutching the railing tight, and loosened her grip as footfalls approached. They were heavy on the wood floors. Steady instead of quick and urgent. Not Cadwyn, then.

Killian.

She wondered when he'd seek out her company, in private.

Her heart began to beat wildly in her chest, before he even reached her. She didn't turn toward him; rather, she lifted her eyes to the Loinnir Lights above, sifting through the whirling colors until she found Neve. The smaller of the two moons had chosen that night to appear again, shining brilliantly as she waxed into a fat crescent.

"She must like you better. I can never seem to coax her out into the night sky." Killian's deep voice slid along her skin, leaving goose bumps in its wake.

He rested his forearms on the balustrade beside her, and Esme forced a grin at his joke, knowing it was an attempt to ease her overactive nerves. But as the stillness of the night settled around them, she managed to relax. Her gaze remained fixed on the sky, and even though they were separated by several inches, Killian's warmth seemed to wrap around her, his scent threatening to overwhelm her senses—warm spices and woodsmoke, like hot apple cider on a cool autumn night.

"You must not be looking very hard. She shows herself every third night."

"Is that it?" Killian cocked his head and narrowed his eyes at the moon, then he turned to Esme and winked.

Her skin vibrated with awareness, her nervousness transforming into something more heated. She held on to the railing, the coiling vines of wisteria pressing into her palms.

"Your gift from Tahra still amazes me."

Esme glanced down at the bright green shoots and pale purple buds that were forming. New life sprouting at her fingertips. She glanced over at Killian's chest—the sight of the iron-tipped arrow protruding from his blood-soaked shirt forever burned into her memory.

The goddess of land and fertility had granted Esme her earth magic, but had she also bestowed the remarkable life-giving ability?

"If you can learn to wield fire like me," he said, nudging her gently with his elbow to draw her back to the present, "you'll be able to channel all the gods."

"Now that would be far too much power for a queen to possess," she whispered, thinking again—and not for the last time—about Orianna's terrifyingly vast arsenal of magic.

"Power is not inherently bad." His flirtatious tone deepened to something more serious. "It depends who wields it."

Esme met his eyes then—deep blue, almost indigo. He watched her; his smile gone. What did he see when he looked at her? Could he see the weight of responsibility in her eyes? Overwhelming her mind and body? Did he sense how unprepared she felt? How the thought of the expectations left her feeling panicked almost every second of every day?

She shied away, unable to withstand the intensity of his gaze.

Killian rested his hand gently atop hers. His skin was warm, comforting. He didn't say anything, didn't press her to speak. He simply stood at her side, offering what she needed. Anything she needed.

After a moment, Esme turned her head slightly, taking in his linen tunic. Her eyes traveled slowly to where it tied loosely at his neck. A smattering of dark blond hair was visible between the laces. She could still remember the feeling of the silky hair beneath her palms when she'd laid her hands on his chest—when his heart had been silent. And when it had finally beat again.

She clenched her teeth together, fighting back another swell of emotion, and forced her gaze to travel higher. Up the thick tendons of his neck. The dusting of stubble along his jaw. His lips. Esme stared at them for a breath before meeting his eyes once more.

He didn't give her the same perusal. Though, knowing Killian, he'd probably taken in every inch of her the moment she'd come into view. All the way down to her bare feet.

Instead, he kept his eyes locked with hers.

Then something shifted, and his eyes darkened.

Esme stood perfectly still, waiting for him to speak. Or move closer.

Killian glanced away, looking out across the city, unseeing. When he spoke, his voice was a rough whisper. "I know you still need time." He turned back to her. "Just know...I'm here." He reached up, then hesitated, as if seeking permission.

Esme's eyes fluttered closed in what she hoped would be taken as a yes. Killian's hand grazed her cheek—a barely there touch that left her leaning into it. His fingers slipped into her hair, combing through the loose waves hanging about her shoulders. Her scalp tingled at the sensation, setting her body ablaze.

When his touch vanished and she felt him stepping away, Esme opened her eyes. Killian held her gaze for a moment that stretched on so long she thought she might burst. Then she watched as he slowly wet his lower lip, like he might say something.

But he pressed his mouth into a firm line and turned to leave.

Her heart raced as her body thrummed frantically. She called out to him without thinking, unsure of what she even wanted. Killian halted and glanced over his shoulder.

"You will be?" she asked, her voice pitched embarrassingly high. "Here, I mean? You're...not going back to Altan?"

He took his time striding back to the balustrade. Esme planted her bare feet firmly to the stone floor of the balcony, willing herself not to run to him, to fling herself into his arms.

When he finally came to stand before her, he was even closer than he'd been before. He dipped his head, bringing his eyes level with hers, his lips close enough to—

"I'm not going anywhere, love."

That word, that *name*, rolled through her body, making her toes curl.

"Killian, I..." She searched his eyes, wondering if she could communicate her thoughts without speaking the words aloud. Her gaze dropped away. "This is all very...new to me. I don't know what I'm doing." Her cheeks flamed at the confession. Killian was more than a century older than her. By the gods, he could make a woman swoon with little more than a smile. His experience was so much greater than her lonely twenty-four years.

"You'll learn, just as every ruler before you."

Her head snapped up. "That's not what—"

Killian grinned, knowing exactly what she'd meant. Her cheeks flamed anew, and she shied away.

"Esme." He lifted her chin. "My life will forever belong to you."

And then his eyes weren't just peering into hers, they were touching something deep inside. He looked at her the way he had when she'd breathed new life into him.

He moved even closer, one of his boots stepping carefully between her bare feet. His palm slid a maddeningly slow path down her arm as the other came to rest carefully on her hip.

Then he waited.

The air sparked between them. The warmth of Killian's fire seeped into her skin, her bones, turning her core molten, even as her every muscle tightened with anticipation. Her eyes were drawn to his mouth again. The desire to have his lips pressed against hers was so severe it was nearly painful.

Her body was vibrating, humming with need when she finally exhaled, sighing Killian's name like a plea.

His lips met hers. Soft, yet firm. There was nothing tentative in the kiss—the brief press of flesh against hot flesh. But he pulled away, leaning back as if to gauge her reaction. She stroked her lower lip with her fingertip—his heat lingering there.

"I've wanted to do that for a very long time," Killian whispered as his tongue grazed his own lips. She wondered if he could still taste her.

"As did I," she breathed.

When Killian didn't immediately claim her mouth again, she rose up on her toes and kissed him back. Longer. Slower. So lost in sensation, she didn't realize her hands had drifted to his chest—the texture of his shirt almost rough compared to the softness of his lips.

Killian's teeth pressed gently into her lip and Esme gasped. He pulled back a fraction, his eyes dark, flicking between her eyes and her lips that were surely pink and swollen. Moving her hands up his chest, she finally reached bare skin. Killian closed his eyes at the feel of her, shuddering as her fingers brushed along his throat, curving around the back of his neck. She gripped his hair, causing him to inhale sharply.

When his eyes opened, they searched hers. Asking, waiting. Wanting.

He was motionless against her—as though every muscle in his body was straining to hold him back. To be patient? To give her a chance to change her mind?

She pulled him to her, and his mouth crashed into hers. No longer careful or sweet. She opened instantly to him—his tongue invading her mouth, tangling with hers. Spreading heat across her cheeks, her throat, up to the tips of her ears. Killian was wild and passionate—exactly as she'd imagined—but his hold on her was still gentle, tender, almost protective. His arms held her close, though she didn't feel trapped or possessed by him. It was as though he was holding her up, holding her together. Making her feel safe enough to let go, to stop worrying, to stop thinking through each movement. And just be.

She let her hands rove along the hard muscles of his back, dragging her nails down his spine. Killian groaned into her mouth, tightening his grip on her.

When at last they broke apart, breathless, Killian took a shuddering breath and looked away. "Esme..." He spoke her name as if it were life itself...or perhaps a curse—his hands clenching into fists against her back.

"Why did you stop?" She peered up at him, her vision hazy.

He stared down at her—his mind clearly warring with a decision.

She offered a coy smile. And with that, the tether on Killian's restraint broke. His lips claimed hers again. Searing hot. Then trailed hot kisses along her jaw.

Esme struggled to draw breath as he moved down her neck, every thought narrowing to his touch. His lips found the sensitive spot just below her ear, his teeth grazing her skin before he gently bit down.

She yelped.

Killian chuckled, the sound vibrating against her skin, sending a shiver down her spine and weakening her knees. He held her tight as his lips worked their way down her neck. Then lower. His touch made her skin tingle, and she wanted nothing more than to feel his mouth everywhere.

With a single finger, he traced the neckline of her tunic, easing it down an inch, revealing more skin that needed to be kissed. Esme tipped her head back, arching into his touch. Killian moved lower, his lips leaving featherlight kisses along the tops of her breasts. Her blood heated to near boiling, coursing through her veins, and suddenly her clothes felt too tight, too restricting. She braced her hands against his chest as his lips found her neck once again. Her hands dipped lower, slipping under his shirt to touch his hot skin. Killian hissed as she slid her hands up the firm muscles of his stomach, then higher, until her fingers spread out across his chest.

His lips paused just beneath her ear, his warm breath sending shivers all the way down to her toes. She felt the nip of his teeth before his tongue grazed up the shell of her ear to the delicate point. Esme gasped at the sensation. She'd had no idea how sensitive that spot could be.

Her response only made Killian more frantic. His mouth was on hers in an instant. He gathered the hair at the nape of her neck, tilting her head gently back so he could deepen the kiss. Then his hands were running down the length of her body. His mouth never left hers as he gripped her waist for a second, then slid his hands lower toward the backs of her legs. When he lifted her up, a thrill shot through her and she instinctively wrapped herself around him.

Killian's mouth continued to scatter her thoughts, but Esme could feel his long strides carrying them into the privacy of her bedchamber. Expecting to be perched on the edge of the bed, or lowered onto one of the sofas, she sucked in a breath when her back was pressed against a wall.

With one of Killian's strong hands holding her firmly in place, the other splayed out at her waist. She could feel the heat of his touch through the fabric of her tunic as his hand moved higher. Then higher. Her stomach quivered with anticipation and she tightened her legs around him. His fingertips grazed the underside of her—

"Ahem."

Esme's eyes sprang open.

Killian stared back at her with a mixture of shock and frustration.

Cadwyn.

"Her Highness has a very important day tomorrow and—"

"Ca-Cadwyn...Can you just give us...a minute?" Esme's voice sounded more flustered than she intended.

"I most certainly will not, milady."

Esme rolled her eyes. Of course Cadwyn would pick that moment to refuse her orders.

Killian rested his forehead against hers, then gently lowered her to the ground.

Esme looked up at him, offering an apologetic half smile. His jaw was clenched tight, but he gave her a regretful, yet understanding grin before closing his eyes and steadying himself with a long, ragged breath.

"Goodnight, milady," he tendered with a strained voice.

"Milady?" Esme couldn't help but tease.

Killian shook his head down at her, then leaned in to kiss her cheek.

He offered Cadwyn a nod as he strode across the room, tossing Esme a wink just before he slipped out.

Chapter Forty-Nine

ESME STOOD ALONE on her balcony, trying to focus on the feel of the silky fabric against her skin instead of the twisting in her stomach. Her moss-colored gown clung tightly to her hips and chest, but the long, flowing skirts caressed her legs as her body swayed gently with each breath. She toyed with the silver filigree bands that anchored the sheer sleeves just above her elbow. They matched the intricate design of the belt—which not only cinched the many layers of fabric at her waist, but managed to constrict her internal organs as well.

She curled and flexed her toes, wishing she could feel soft grass beneath her feet. Wishing she could avoid the crowd gathered in the streets below.

Her breaths quickened at the thought, and Esme reminded herself— as she had repeatedly throughout the morning—that she merely needed to show herself, to offer a wave, a smile. The people needed to see, with their own eyes, that the rightful heir of Tremaene was alive and well. And that Orianna was no longer their queen.

Esme closed her eyes. That wasn't the true reason she dreaded the day.

The city had been deemed safe enough for a public appearance, therefore the army would soon retreat. And that meant saying goodbye.

It hadn't been discussed—due to Esme avoiding the topic like it was poison—but she knew that Tearlach, Armel, and Hazel would return to Altan. Sully, Cadwyn, and Killian would stay, but she couldn't bear the thought of the others leaving, of never seeing them again.

She slipped back inside to let Cadwyn finish her hair, only to find Tearlach waiting instead.

Esme glanced toward the dressing room.

"I asked her to wait outside."

"I see." She narrowed her eyes suspiciously.

"There's a matter that needs to be discussed."

A lecture? Truly? She wasn't sure she could handle another, though she felt a pang of longing that it might be their last.

But when Tearlach exhaled and dropped his head forward, Esme suddenly felt worried.

"I'm sorry I couldn't protect you." His voice, deep as ever, came out rough.

"What do you mean?" She stepped toward him. "Of course you—"

He held up a hand. "I swore I would protect you and I failed. I failed you."

"What are you talking about?" Esme shook her head. "You didn't fail me. You kept me strong. You gave me everything you possibly could when I stood before Orianna. I'm so, so grateful for everything you've done for me. More than I can ever hope to express."

She took a tentative step closer. His eyes were darker than she'd seen before, shadowed by something she feared she'd never be able to vanquish. At least not with words. Yet she tried anyway.

"Tearlach, accept my gratitude. Please."

He nodded his head slightly, though he didn't reply.

"You've done more than was asked of you. I've been thinking of ways I can repay you for your service. And I decided...I want to free you from the Lifeblood Oath." It wasn't fair to keep him bound to her. She averted her gaze, unwilling to see the reaction in his face. "I'll find a way. You've more than fulfilled your obligation. You didn't fail me, and you most certainly don't owe me a thing, least of all an apology."

His broad hands wrapped around her shoulders, and she stilled. A tense silence hung between them until Esme slowly met his gaze.

"You really think you can get rid of me that easily?"

She blinked. "But...I...I thought...Don't you *want* to go back to Altan?"

"I belong here. And I believe you're in need of a personal guard."

She was in need of...*a personal guard?*

He arched one of his dark eyebrows, as though that were explanation enough. Nevertheless, Esme understood. She wasn't just an assignment to him, an oath to be honored. She wasn't a burden. At some point along the way, he'd come to care for her. *Her.* Not the crown she'd soon carry.

He's going to stay.

Something flashed in Tearlach's eyes and she wondered if he'd heard the thoughts running through her mind. Although, she hadn't heard his voice since the night in the throne room. Perhaps that particular aspect of their connection was only possible when she was in danger. She canted her head to the side, considering him a moment, then decided she could live with that.

"I would be honored to have you—"

Tearlach dropped to one knee before Esme could finish, crossing his sword over his chest.

Understanding struck her. The oath she'd witnessed so many times as a child. Different from the one he'd already sworn to her, and yet...it felt far more significant. An oath sworn to the woman he knew, not the girl he'd only heard of.

Her hands trembled as she began, trying to recall the vow. "Tearlach, do you swear your loyalty to the crown of Tremaene, to protect and to serve your queen, and thereby the kingdom, with your life?"

"To the end of my days, I will protect *you*, Esme."

She blinked back tears as Tearlach rose, taking her swiftly into his arms. She buried her face in his chest.

"Tearlach?" Her voice was quiet as she pulled away to look up at him. "I don't know if I can do this. I froze out there. I panicked. That moment, when I needed to end it? When I needed to kill Orianna?" Esme shook her head, feeling tears threaten again. "I couldn't do it."

"Everything worked out in the end. That's all that matters. Things might not have gone according to plan, but they rarely do. And things won't go as planned when you step into this new role. There's much you'll need to learn, so mistakes will be made. You'll make choices that make people unhappy. But you'll always do what you think is best for the people of Tremaene. I know this of you." He rested his hands on her shoulders again—his weight grounding her, steadying the frantic beat of her heart. "And you aren't alone, Esme. Not in this, not in anything. You never were."

"Okay. Enough is enough; we don't have much time," Cadwyn chirped as she swooped in, pulling Esme into the dressing room.

Tearlach simply shook his head and left them alone.

Watching Cadwyn in the mirror, Esme couldn't help but smile. It was as if the fate of the kingdom rested in the perfect shape of each curl. But when Cadwyn placed a wooden box on the bench beside her, Esme's smile faltered.

Erena's crown.

Esme stared at the circlet her mother had worn, astonished that Sully had found a way to keep it hidden from Orianna. It was simple, yet elegant, with thin, twisted strands of silver, and intricately detailed leaflets. A single, round emerald rested within the interwoven silver vines at the apex.

As Cadwyn lifted it into place, their eyes met in the mirror, and Esme wondered if her lady-in-waiting had always been able to see the queen in the reflection.

Esme felt tears prick the corners of her eyes, but before she could tell Cadwyn what it meant to share such an important day with her, a page was ushered into the main room.

He seemed new to the palace—his livery hanging loose in some places. Esme found herself relieved at that, hoping it meant he hadn't suffered Orianna's reign.

"Well?" Cadwyn eyed the page.

"Your Highness, a woman has arrived at the palace who requests an audience with you."

"She can make an appointment like everyone else." Cadwyn waved him off.

"Yes, of course. It's just that..."

"Speak."

"She claims to be Orianna's sister."

"Sister? As in high-priestess?" Esme questioned.

"No, Your Highness. Sister by blood. She says she has information about an urgent matter."

Esme shared a look with Cadwyn, whose impatience had turned to concern.

"Tell her to come back tomorrow morning," Cadwyn instructed the page. "I'll speak with her then."

"Certainly." He bowed and quickly took his leave, scurrying past Tearlach.

It was only then that Esme took in her personal guard's attire—the page's message all but forgotten at seeing Tearlach dressed in the finest armor.

Noting her reaction, he allowed a half smile, then gestured toward the door. "It's time."

Cadwyn moved to Esme's side, giving her hand a reassuring squeeze.

Outside her room, Armel, Hazel, Killian, and Sully stood waiting for her—their armor similar to Tearlach's. Then, as one, they knelt.

"We have decided," Hazel addressed her, "to pledge our lives to our queen, and humbly ask that we have the honor of beginning a new royal guard in your name." She held Esme's gaze for a moment, then inclined her head toward Sully. "With Commander Sullivan as our captain."

Before tears could blur her vision yet again, Esme pressed her lips together firmly and nodded her acceptance. Adamantly.

Cadwyn urged them to stand, scolding the lot of them for nearly making Esme cry after she'd just finished lining her eyes delicately with kohl.

Tension broken, they rose and escorted Esme down the grand staircase and through the palace, passing rows of guards who lined the main corridor.

Esme could hear the crowd beyond the tall, formidable doors as Cadwyn adjusted her crown and arranged a few errant curls.

The massive doors groaned as they were pulled open. The midday sun was blinding, the roar of the crowd near deafening. But all she could feel was the weight of the crown.

Her mother had stood in that very place. A queen whom the people of Tremaene had loved dearly.

Esme exhaled slowly and told herself that the people would love her too.

She cast a glance over to Tearlach, then to Cadwyn. The others stood behind—their presence a solid reminder of the journey that had delivered her to that very spot.

She was not alone.

A familiar voice drifted into her mind. *Your people are waiting, Majesty.*

She raised her chin and stepped forward.

Epilogue

ATHDARA STOOD BEHIND the metal gate, watching as the people of Tremaene welcomed their rightful queen to the throne.

The forgotten princess had returned, just as she'd seen. The man with dark eyes stood beside her—more than once, the young queen's life had rested in his hands. One such vision had revealed the man drawing a blade across the throat of an enemy. One of many.

She turned her attention to the light-haired warrior in the queen's retinue. The one who had seen the other side. His death had been written—she could feel the burn of poison from the iron-tipped arrow. It had been the only way. The young queen required a forceful awakening, and bringing him back from death had summoned a great power. A power capable of defeating the false queen.

Athdara had seen her death as well, many times—each vision diverging slightly, but all ending the same way. In a pool of blood.

But her death had not been the end. The dark one would return. And with the heir standing atop the palace steps—wearing a crown that had belonged to another with great magic—he would not be long.

She scanned the mass of people gathered to see their long-lost princess, then turned her gaze again to the young woman draped in green with a silver-leafed crown encircling her golden hair. The bringer of life had returned to Tremaene, and magic would soon follow. If she chose the right path.

For the paths were many and not all were good.

And each came with a price.

She pivoted on her heel, exiting through the throng of people. The young queen would find her soon enough.

PRONUNCIATION GUIDE

People

Aeveen: Aa-vEEn

Ainsley: AYNZ-lee

Armel: AR-mell

Beglan: BEG-lahn

Briac: BREE-ah-kuh

Cadwyn: KAD-wayn

Carrick: CEH-ruhk

Eimhir: AE-veer

Erena: EHR-ae-nah

Esme: EZ-may

Ffion: FEE-on

Fulton: FUL-tn

Gittan: GIH-tahn

Hazel: HAY-zl

Killian: KIL-ee-an

Muirín: MWIR-in

Neala: NEE-lah

Orianna: Aw-ree-ON-AH

Sullivan: SUL-uh-vuhn

Tahra: TAE-rah

Tearlach: TCHAR-lakh

Torin: TAOR-ahN

Tuireann: TEER-ee-auhn

Places

Altan: AWL-tin

Belfay: BEHL-faye

Briganport: BRI-guhn-pORt

Clavlin: CLAh-v-lihn

Debarrow: DEH-bah-row

Donellis: DOH-nel-lis

Eoin: OH-ih-n

Isloran: EES-loh-rehn

Loinnir: LUN-neer

Meallán: MEL-awn

Periwen: Peh-ri-when

Rhoswen: RAAS-wahn

Tamslo: TAHM-sloh

Tremaene: TReh-meyn

Valdis: VAL-dees

Winslow: WIN-sloh

WILD HEART OF THE CROWN

Wild Heart of the Storm, Book Two

With Orianna defeated, Esme has taken her rightful place on the throne. But unraveling dark secrets and ancient deceptions may be the only way to save her kingdom.

As Esme navigates the expectations of her new role amid scheming court members, the land beyond the city walls is dying. Barrenness spreads; rivers run dry. With no high-priestesses left to summon raw magic, Esme must uncover the true origins of the Order and all its secrets.

Ancient texts and an infamous seer reveal long-concealed truths about the nature of magic—truths that will crumble the faith of an entire kingdom. So when members from a secret sect claim to possess the gods-blessed gifts of the late priestesses, Esme must decide if they can be trusted. Do they know the dark history of the Order? Will their fledgling magic be enough to restore the land?

Desperate for answers, Esme discovers that certain knowledge comes at great cost, and that inconvenient desires of the heart can only be denied for so long. Will she make the necessary sacrifices to save her kingdom...and to save herself from heartache?

Available Now!

ACKNOWLEDGMENTS

Thank You

To the wondrous humans I've met through a shared love of fantasy and science fiction:

You've introduced me to incredible authors and worlds I never thought possible. Our discussions of magic systems and physics, unlikable MCs, and unexpected villains have not only brought a whimsical sort of joy to my life, they've enriched my world-building skills and character development. Without all of you and your beautifully brilliant brains this story wouldn't be what it is today. But really, I'm most grateful for the friendships we've forged along the way.

To the fellow members of the local romance book club:

Every month, I deliver overly animated depictions of the latest bonkers book I'm reading (which all too frequently involves blue aliens or gay hockey players). Despite my theatrics, you still trust my recommendations. And you open my eyes and my heart to characters and stories I might otherwise miss.

To my animals:

You are my everything. My calm and my joy. My constant companions. My heart. Your sacrifices do not go unnoticed. When your dinner is minutes late because I have "one more sentence to write," your patience is truly inspiring—in that it inspires me to close my laptop and feed you immediately because patience is not a word any of you ascribe to.

To my friends and family:

I cannot thank you enough for reading the (much longer) first draft, chapter by chapter. You embrace the magic and the characters when the genre itself is mostly unfamiliar, and puzzle out magical logistics with me when a fight scene isn't quite working.

To those who made this book look professional:

Chris (Hidden Gems) and Stefanie (Seventhstar), your editing and design talents elevate this story in an incredible way. Chris, thank you for catching the typos that survived over a dozen rounds of edits. I promise to learn the difference between further and farther before the next book. Stefanie, thank you for taking my rambling notes and and turning them into fantastic art.

And finally, to the thousands of fellow members of fan pages and reader groups:

You unknowingly encourage me each and every day. With your endless enthusiasm for favorite authors and genres, you give me hope that readers just like you will one day stumble upon my books and fall in love with the characters. Your supportive posts, book recommendations or requests, and general excitement over wildly specific subgenres help me stay the course with my own writing—especially when I doubt myself. You prove that the world can never have too many stories, and I'm incredibly grateful to be adding mine to the great, never-ending TBR list.

ABOUT THE AUTHOR

Erica Sebree lives in Austin, Texas, where she works in public service as a graphic designer. She reads too much romance and drinks too much tea—usually at the same time. She makes frequent attempts at gardening, and will happily talk to any animal who crosses her path. She believes lists should be written in colorful ink, and dreams of one day having a farm sanctuary with many adorable cows. When she escapes into fantasy worlds, it's to places where magic is vital, animals are guardians, and a stubborn bodyguard's only weakness is the fierce, reluctant heroine he's sworn to protect.

Find her online:

ericasebree.com

facebook.com/ericasebreewrites

twitter.com/erica_sebree

instagram.com/ericasebreewrites/

goodreads.com/erica-sebree

bookbub.com/authors/erica-sebree

Newsletter:

bit.ly/WildHeartMail

ericasebree.com

www.ingramcontent.com/pod-product-compliance
Lightning Source LLC
Chambersburg PA
CBHW060604300726